W9-AXW-821

UNQUENCHABLE
FIRE

BY THE SAME AUTHOR

Salvador Dali's Tarot
A Practical Guide to Fortune Telling
78 Degrees of Wisdom

UNQUENCHABLE
FIRE
RACHEL POLLACK

The Overlook Press
Woodstock, New York

Copyright © 1988 by Rachel Pollack

All Rights Reserved. No part of this publication may be reproduced or transmitted in any form or by any means, electronic or mechanical, including photocopy, recording, or any information storage and retrieval system now known or to be invented without permission in writing from the publisher, except by a reviewer who wishes to quote brief passsages in connection with a review for inclusion in a magazine, newspaper, or broadcast.

ISBN 0-87951-447-7

Printed in the United States of America

Dedication

For belief and help and everything else, this book is dedicated to Edith Katz.

Acknowledgements

There are many people who assisted in the writing of this book, most without even knowing it. I am indebted to them all, but especially to Ingrid Toth, for listening and for believing.

Disclaimer

Poughkeepsie, and New York City, and Wappingers Falls, etc. are real places, and some of the buildings or streets described in this book have their counterparts in the outside world. However, this book is a work of fiction, and nothing said about any of the locales implies anything whatsoever about the actual place. The characters have no counterparts at all in the outside world. Any resemblance to actual people or events would be entirely coincidental.

And on the way I told a tale of such power that all who heard it had thoughts of repentance.

Rabbi Nachman of Bratslav

God's works are great. The greatest, however, is not his writing in the sky . . . God gave Far-li-mas the gift of telling tales in such a way that has never been equalled.

Joseph Campbell quoting Leo Frobenius quoting a Sudanese camel driver.

WE REMEMBER THE FOUNDERS

1

On the afternoon of the Day of Truth, eighty seven years after the Revolution, Jennifer Mazdan, a server for the Mid-Hudson Energy Board, fell asleep and underwent a strange dream, one not found anywhere in the catalogues. Jennifer hadn't meant to sleep that afternoon. A respectable single woman who lived in a surburban hive development south of Poughkeepsie, some seventy miles north of New York City, she had planned to go to the recital and take her place among her neighbours. There she would listen to Allan Lightstorm, the great Picture Teller, recite one of the prime Pictures.

Like everyone else, Jennifer had passed the entire week in a state of high anticipation. It wasn't every year that an Allan Lightstorm came to a town like Poughkeepsie. Usually the Living Masters stayed in the huge Picture Halls of the big cities, or travelled to the national parks for the major recitals. Lightstorm himself had been expected to speak that year in the massive stone and stained glass hall on Fifth Avenue in New York City.

Usually Poughkeepsie had to make do on the Day of Truth with its own three or four more prominent Tellers. There was Dennis Lily, who could speak with great passion, yet often gave so much stress to the Inner Meaning that he raced right through the story itself. And then there was Alice Windfall, 'poor Alice' as people called her. Alice had shown great promise in her early years, 'flying on wings of story' as the saying goes, so that all who heard her on the day she came

1

back from college found themselves drifting into the air, like so many bright-coloured balloons, to look down upon their bodies sitting on the hillsides with the stooped shoulders and pained expressions of their daily lives. But Alice never repeated that glorious moment. Maybe it was because of the scandal when Martin Magundo, the Town Comptroller, got his soul tangled up in the blades of a helicoper hired by German tourists to look down on the recital. Though an official inquiry cleared Alice completely, and Martin Magundo's family lost their lawsuit against Alice and the New York College Of Tellers, poor Alice never did fulfil the early promise of her career. Now, years later, she had hardly kept her voice up. She still spoke on the important days; people went to hear her in the hope that the Living World might take pity on her and restore her powers. In fact, her voice often came out slurred and the rumour had spread that Alice got drunk before she had to appear in public.

Occasionally the mayor or the city manager would appeal to the New York College Of Tellers for a new Teller of somewhat more magnitude. The answer always came back that the College had to look after the whole state, had to weigh all the factors, and so on and so on. If a mayor decided to ask what factors sent the most talented Tellers to New York or Albany, he or she always received the same answer. A non-Teller, who judged things only by their rational surface, who never travelled into the heart of the Sun, or sat beside Chained Mother at the bottom of the sea, could hardly question the basis of the College's judgement.

Once, Bob Gobi, fresh from his victory as the first non-Revolutionary Republic city manager in thirty years, asked the current Public Secretary, 'And when's the last time any Tellers did all those things?' adding,

'The real Tellers died off years ago and you know it as well as I do.'

The Secretary stood up from his desk. 'If we refrain from exposing the spirit in its raw state,' he told city manager Gobi, 'we do so for our listeners' well being, in respect of their weaknesses and fears.'

'Sure,' Gobi said, angry beyond all sense. 'Don't give me that shit. Everyone knows you "refrain" because you can't. You don't know how any more. The last true Teller died forty years ago.'

Unfortunately for Bob Gobi, whatever the current Tellers' limitations, they could still work a simple curse. The next night, when Gobi got up to speak to the Town Council about plans to change the zoning laws, he opened his mouth and a frog came out to hop onto Joan Lafer's left breast, and from there to the floor. Everyone laughed, but when Gobi again tried to speak and again a frog leaped out, people realised it was no prank. They began to back off, then to push for the door. When Gobi tried to shout at them to stop, a winged lizard flew out of his mouth to fly right into the shrieking face of the town secretary.

Five days later Gobi returned to the College Of Tellers on Madison Avenue. He had walked all the way from his ranch house on Poughkeepsie's south side. He wore nothing but a black shirt with the sleeves ripped off, and a dirty towel from the Young Men's Truth Association wrapped around his genitals and ass. When he came to the door he crawled through the entranceway beneath the pictures of the Founders until he came to the desk of the Secretary he'd seen the week before. The man smiled. 'What can I do for you?' he asked. Gobi looked at him. 'Come on,' the Secretary said. 'Don't be afraid. Tell me what you want.'

Gobi wondered if the man had lifted the curse. He opened his mouth and out came a dragonfly. 'Very

3

amusing,' the Secretary said. 'Now will you tell me your problem?' Crying, Gobi signalled for paper and pencil. 'No, no,' the Secretary said. 'No forms. We're not that bureaucratic, whatever people say about us. Just tell me. Go ahead.' Gobi's thumb jerked at his closed mouth. The secretary made a show of going back to his work. 'I have no time for charades,' he said. 'If you won't say what's on your mind, I'm very busy.'

Gobi crawled away, having forgotten to get back on his feet. He took a train (no ticket required for a pilgrim) to the edge of the Oceanfront Spirit Reserve, and according to the forest rangers was seen heading for the row of skulls on wooden poles that lined the Forbidden Beach. Many years later, during her own pilgrimage to the Beach to talk to the skulls, Valerie Mazdan met a bent old man who sat hugging himself amid a congress of frogs. She walked over to him and parted the carpet of hair that covered his face. He blinked in amazement, not so much at the sight of another human as at the sun, hidden by his hair for so long he vaguely thought of it as a story he'd heard as a child. 'Who are you?' Valerie said, kneeling down. The man shook his head. 'You can tell me,' coaxed Courageous Wisdom. 'I won't hurt you.'

A flash of anger made the man open his mouth. A butterfly flew out, circled once around his head, then vanished in the sunlight. Valerie nodded, somewhat like a doctor acknowledging symptoms. She touched his lips. 'Now,' she said, 'who are you?' The man thought to turn away from his tormentor but something held him. He opened his mouth wide, as if to expel a great bullfrog at her, but instead a croak came out, not unlike the sound a frog makes as it digests its dinner of flies. 'G ... G ... Go ...'

Valerie touched his shoulder. 'You just need practice,' she said. 'It's been a long time.'

4

'Ye . . . yes,' the former city manager said. He ran off, terrified the woman would change her mind and bring back the curse. But Courageous Wisdom had already set off again to find the skulls of her predecessors. Bob Gobi walked out of the reserve and was picked up by the Suffolk County Sheriff's office, who took him to the local Hospital of the Inner Spirit. He stayed there for the rest of his life, working in the clinic for autistic children. The night he died a wave of frogs washed over the hospital, engulfing it in a storm of croaks. They vanished the next morning.

With Bob Gobi as an example subsequent officials never made much protest at the lack of a first class Picture Teller to 'serve the greater Poughkeepsie community' as the *Poughkeepsie Journal* editorials put it. Nevertheless, the people's souls shrivelled listening to such weak voices as those of Alice Windfall or Dennis Lily or the many Tellers who spoke on minor Recital Days in the neighbourhood Picture Halls around the city. So when the Mid-Hudson College of Tellers (a branch of the New York authority) announced that Allan Lightstorm would come to speak at the recital, headlines filled front pages, and the local television station did specials on his life, his calling, his interpretation of the lesser Pictures, his private audiences with the President and foreign dignitaries.

The current mayor and town manager, fantasizing that some truly appreciative response would make Lightstorm see the advantages of permanent settlement in a smaller community, arranged for a devotional parade of children bearing three yard high banners to greet Lightstorm as he walked up the long path to the peak of Recital Mount. The banners were held up by 'artbirds', half genetic manipulation, half plastic, and one of Poughkeepsie's two major products (the other was a thick yellow syrup that promised to revive freshly

5

dead persons for a period of five to ten minutes). In electric colours the banners depicted the True History of the city of Poughkeepsie and the life story (exaggerated even beyond the exaggerations of official biography) of Allan Lightstorm.

As the Teller passed each banner a voice sounded from a speaker set on the ground beneath it. Explaining the Pictures, the voices told how Poughkeepsie's original inhabitants – twelve foot giants whose skin changed colour according to the season – had carved the city out of huge cedar trees uprooted in a storm from Mexico and dropped beside the Hudson River. The city prospered until a thirty year drought, during which the people shrank to two foot seven, and the river cried every night in maudlin memory of its former might. One morning all the inhabitants went out to perform a rain enactment in the high school football stadium. With little confidence the townspeople chanted along the yard lines and sprinkled blood on the goalposts. At the same time Poughkeepsie's wonderful cedars, fed up with constant thirst, all marched to the Traprock Quarry and Blasting Corporation on the edge of town and jumped into a gravelly pit. In this moment of despair, with the people's homes destroyed and their ears battered by the river's incessant self-pity, a multi-tiered UFO landed in the field of dandelions that would one day become Dutchess County Airport. The space beings, whom the banners depicted as shining foetuses with overlong fingers and toes, not only showed the people how to make rain seeds out of common flowers, but also demonstrated how to build modern houses, and even how to set up a government, complete with school systems, police force, and Spiritual Development Agency. When the True Revolution came, and the Army of the Saints sailed up the Hudson from New

6

York they found Poughkeepsie more highly evolved than any of its neighbours.

The last part was actually a deliberate lie. In fact, Poughkeepsie, once the home of an old-style corporation called something like International Bureaucratic Mechanisms, resisted the revolution longer than any other part of New York State. Technophiles from as far away as Cincinatti and Santa Barbara came to Poughkeepsie to bolster the resistance to the 'black tide of mud', as one of their spokesmen put it. From Poughkeepsie they issued proclamations and spies, until at last they announced they had arranged with 'loyalists' (as they called the rejectionists in the old secular government) to smuggle several missiles with fusion warheads into their stronghold. Doomsday, they promised, would follow unless the Army of the Saints and all their followers renounced what the technophiles called 'pseudomystical insanity.'

Now, the banners actually related this incident, perhaps out of embarrassment at the city's tainted history. But they transferred the place to Newburgh on the other side of the river. And they then related how Allan Lightstorm, travelling in a one man boat, glided up the river to the woods just south of that city. From there, the banners declared, Lightstorm changed himself into a golden Great Dane and penetrated the rejectionist fortress. Around his neck, disguised as a dog licence, hung a metal plate inscribed with the Names of the Founders.

In full sight of a group of technophiles Lightstorm (so the speakers said) changed back into his human form. Holding the metal plate to his forehead he told the Secret Picture, a story of such power that no Teller has ever dared to repeat it. The techs fell to the ground and covered their heads with dirt. 'Forgive us, Master,' they said. 'We didn't know.' Lightstorm raised them

7

up and gave them each a broom. Chanting Lightstorm's name, they swept the evil out of the missiles, and Newburgh (Poughkeepsie) belonged to the Revolution. Now, for many historians, the disarming marked the turning point of the war. But Allan Lightstorm, born fifty three years later, had nothing to do with it. Everyone knew that Mohandas Quark had done the disarming, just as everyone knew that he'd become a Fox Terrier, much less conspicuous than a Great Dane. What's more, Lightstorm knew that everyone knew. Nevertheless, by attaching the incident to Lightstorm, the townspeople demonstrated what they called 'proper respect' for their eminent guest. Lightstorm himself expected nothing less. Some years later, Valerie Mazdan would denounce what she called 'flattering an empty present with an exaggerated past.' On that day of Jennifer Mazdan's dream, however, people took it as normal that the major Tellers of their time should inherit the marvels of their predecessors.

The particular marvel chosen did make sense, for Lightstorm had copied his recital skin directly from that of Mohandas Quark. In great folds of multicoloured satin Allan Lightstorm made his way up the hill towards the seat where he would fold his Mohandas Quark wings about his body and tell one of the prime Pictures proper for the Day of Truth.

If nothing else, Lightstorm was a master of gesture; as he climbed the hill, he swept his blue and gold skin first one way and then another, howling pain and joy, his voice so perfectly tuned that everyone who listened (and that included all of Poughkeepsie except for sad Jennifer Mazdan, asleep at the foot of an energy guardian) everyone felt the Earth must open up to release a flood of light that would wash them clean of fear and sorrow. Later – that night, the next day – a sense of frustration would set in as they discovered that the expected purge had never come, that in some way nothing lay beneath Lightstorm's wondrous voice and gestures, so that the recital became a pie with a delicious crust and no filling. But in that moment of approach they listened with such anticipation that many thought their skins would evaporate into the sun. He *must* stay, they told themselves. Why would he come if he didn't plan to stay?

Actually, the impulse to go to Poughkeepsie wasn't Allan Lightstorm's at all, but came to him as a command from the Living World. One morning in June he left his residence, the building known as 'the Palace', across the street from the back of the Fifth Avenue Hall. He walked up 51st Street to Fifth, where he went into Valentino's and ordered two white shirts with pearl buttons. From there he strolled up to Nat Sherman's for a case of his favourite cigars. He was about to head back when he noticed a small crowd of people across the street in front of a spiritual aids bookshop. He crossed the road for a closer look.

A man in a purple tracksuit had spread a sheet of black plastic on the pavement. Around him stood men watching him move three metal shells about the cloth. One of the shells was painted gold, for the Sun, a second silver, for the Moon, and the last speckled blue, for the Stars. One of them, Lightstorm knew, would contain a steel ball, symbol of the Earth. As he moved the shells the man hopped them back and forth, shielding them with his waving hands so that it became harder and harder to know which one contained the ball. While Lightstorm watched, a man in a green shirt handed a coin to the man on the ground. Bending forward, greenshirt pointed at the Moon. The shellman lifted the silver dome. Empty. With an embarrassed grin greenshirt straightened up. The shellman showed

9

the crowd the Earth – it lay under the Stars – and then he began again to shift the heavenly bodies.

Idiots, Lightstorm thought. He knew that even if someone guessed correctly he wouldn't keep his winnings very long. A block or two away a so-called 'heavenly rectifier' would get a signal to follow the hero to some quiet corner and relieve him of his victory and anything else worthwhile in his pockets.

Lightstorm thought of going back. It was getting chilly out despite the bright sun. But he only stood there, watching the hands break up the sky. Odd that the man wasn't talking. Nobody said anything. Lightstorm realised that no one on the street, no one passing or crossing the road, or selling pretzels or hot dogs or earrings, no one looking at shop windows or waiting in their cars for the light to change, no one made any noise at all. And then he realised he couldn't hear the cars and buses. No engines, no horns, no squeals of brakes or tyres. He looked up and down the street. The traffic moved – silently. The crowds of people still flowed up and down the block, New Yorkers with that purposeful stride, tourists unsure of their steps. None of them made a sound, not their feet, not their bodies bumping into each other.

I've gone deaf Lightstorm thought, *I've gone deaf.* But he knew the emptiness was not in his drums or neurons. It lay in the street, in the cars and the people. They looked frail, almost transparent. Even the huge buildings so beloved of tourists, you could put a hand, a finger, right through them. His sight slid up the garish front of Trump Tower. Something had emptied out the Sun. No heat remained in it, though it shone bright enough to hurt his eyes. He squinted. It wasn't the heat that had left.

The stories are gone, thought Allan Lightstorm. Something had emptied all the stories, cleaned out the people, the city, even the sky and the Earth. He could stamp his foot and it would go right through the crust.

On the plastic the three shells stood in a row. Behind them the man in the track suit looked up at Lightstorm. When he smiled, his mouth opened so wide Lightstorm thought he could fall inside. A Malignant One. A Malignant One. *Help me*, Lightstorm prayed. He knew he should speak the 'standard formula of recognition' on encountering a Bright Being. 'Ferocious One. I beg you to release me. I know that nothing I have done deserves your evil intervention.' But his mouth wouldn't work. He didn't know if he could move his tongue.

The Malignant One waved a hand over the shells. Choose, he was saying. Choose the correct one and I will release you. Lightstorm bent forward. How could he know which one? He hadn't even been watching. His hand moved to the Sun, then he pulled it back again. A wrong choice and he would never get it back. His hand shook as it moved closer. The Ferocious One grinned and nodded his head.

At that moment a woman tripped and fell on her hands and knees on the plastic. The shells scattered and the steel ball rolled free. 'Oh shit,' the woman said. 'Excuse me. I'm sorry.' Lightstorm grabbed the steel ball and held it up in front of the shell man. For a moment the Being bared his teeth – yellow, as if stained with tobacco or smog – but before he could do anything the woman tripped again as she tried to get up. She fell against the Malignant One, knocking him back against the store window. He shoved her out of the way but it was too late. Lightstorm tossed the ball back at him and the noises, returned to the street. People were shouting, horns announced a traffic jam, a man selling jelly beans ridiculed someone who wanted to pay with a fifty dollar bill. As Lightstorm helped the woman to her feet the shell man gathered his plastic and his heavenly bodies and walked quickly down the block, away from a couple of cops in short sleeved shirts and baseball caps.

Lightstorm looked at his rescuer. A tall woman with wide shoulders, she stood an inch or two above Lightstorm in her high-heeled sandals. She wore pink sunglasses with blue lenses, a white skirt and a pink jacket, the kind worn by hairdressers or women demonstrating cosmetics. In one hand she carried a red plastic purse, in the other a small gold shopping bag with some Japanese name written in black brush strokes across the front. 'Hey,' she said in a thick New York accent, 'I'm sorry if I messed up your game.'

Lightstorm laughed. He was about to thank her, maybe even offer to buy her a drink at Rebirth of the Spirit Plaza, when a light flared about her hair. It lasted only a moment and might have come from the sun catching the coating of henna. Lightstorm knew it wasn't the sun. She wanted him to know who had come for him. Stepping backwards he said, 'Devoted One, I thank you for your devotion. I know that nothing I have done deserves your precious intervention.'

The Bright Being nodded her head. In the same accent as before she said, 'Gratitude is not enough.'

Lightstorm glanced quickly at the crowds, the syrupy flow of traffic. He wondered for an instant if he could jump into a taxi and make it to the safety of his residence. He said, 'Do you want me to do a penance?'

'We need your help,' she said.

'My help? What do you mean? Do you want me to make a contribution somewhere?'

The Benign One laughed. She laughed so loudly Lightstorm discovered he wanted to slap her and tell her to shut up. He stepped backwards. 'Go to an Oracle,' she told him. 'Have the Speaker do an incubation. You'll find out what it is you have to contribute.' Still laughing, she turned and walked away.

Three days later Allan Lightstorm stepped onto the rooftop of the World Trade Center. A few hundred feet away the tower's twin sister hosted a network of radar, television antennae, weather monitors, and government tracking devices. Here there were only rocks, earth, a few gnarled trees with blackened fruit, and a constant whispering.

Traditionally, Tellers disliked Speakers. Lightstorm made a face at the sight of the gangly woman sitting on her stone bench in the middle of a small circle of ugly trees. Beside the bench lay her guardian, a large lump of black stone, its surface dotted with pasted on bits of coloured glass. She sat with her legs apart, her elbows on her knees, her head bent forward as if she'd been drinking. She wore a baggy old smock and men's torn shoes. She probably hadn't washed or cut her hair since her appointment. He could see pebbles in her hair, even twigs. When he approached her, and the woman lifted her head he grunted at the deep lines cut into her cheeks. 'Journey lines,' the Speakers called them, one scar for each of her initiations.

The incubation lasted over an hour, extremely long for the Great Speaker, who sometimes saw thirty clients in a day. By the time it was halfway, Alan Lightstorm thought how he never knew he could hate someone with such a passion. He was sure that many of the things she made him do, the rolling around, the eating of filth, had nothing to do with gaining access, but only with humiliating him. If only he could have asked for a simple reading – sticks, fingernail cuttings, cards – instead of an incubation.

When the Speaker finally settled into it – rocking back and forth with her hands around her knees, the

13

sound of her high-pitched singing made Lightstorm want to strangle her. Finally it stopped. Finally she looked up at him with her eyes clear, and Lightstorm knew she was ready to give her declaration. He expected some cryptic fragment, like 'The dead geese fly backward' or 'Your mother's tongue is broken.' He would then take it down to the computer experts at the Spiritual Development Agency, and if he didn't like the interpretation he could apply for a revision. Instead the woman grinned at him and said, 'They want you to go to Poughkeepsie.'

Lightstorm said, 'What?'

'Poughkeepsie. They want you to recite there on the Day of Truth.'

'Like hell I will. I'm telling the main Picture at the Fifth Avenue Hall that day, RTV is broadcasting it. Live.'

The woman started to laugh. 'All right,' Lightstorm said. 'Fine. Poughkeepsie it is.' He turned.

'Something else,' the woman said.

'Great. What's that?'

'They want you to tell a certain Picture.'

All the way back to the hall he plotted his revenge against the Great Speaker, against the whole Association of Oracles and Speakers. Who did she think she was, ordering him to give up a satellite broadcast on the most important day of the year? If there was ever a faked declaration . . . More to the point, who did she think *he* was, some country amateur who would scurry off to do whatever some maniac Oracle told him? He was already plotting his moves – the people he would call, the line he would take – when he arrived at the Palace courtyard, and there, in the centre of the four marble circles, stood the woman in the pink jacket and the high-heeled sandals, still holding her plastic purse and her Japanese shopping bag.

Lightstorm took a step towards his benefactor. 'Please,' he said, 'you can't ask me to do this. I'm doing the main Picture.' The woman said nothing. 'Another recital. Choose another one. Founder's Day. I'll do Founder's Day.'

She shook her head. 'Please,' Lightstorm said. 'It's not fair.'

She unbuttoned her jacket and light flowed from her body to warm Lightstorm's face and chest. She stepped towards him and opened her arms. Lightstorm bent down so he could lay his head between her breasts. They were smooth and warm, and her arms around his shoulders lifted him from the growl of the city into a world of softness and love.

The next morning Lightstorm handed in his official withdrawal from the Fifth Avenue celebration of the Recital of Truth. That same afternoon he sent a letter to the Mid-Hudson College of Tellers requesting an invitation to appear as guest Teller for the city and the town of Poughkeepsie.

A part of a version of the Story of THE PLACE INSIDE, first found by Li Ku Unquenchable Fire (in beauty and truth lives her name forever).
(*Hands covered in ash, the Teller reaches into the sack of winds and lifts out the Face Blackened By Fire, a charred wooden mask with the eyes and mouth rimmed in silver.*)

I am the one who has taken a face
My fingers are birds, my fingers are beasts
My fingers are rocks and the water which lies on the rocks
My fingers are children
The dead, the living, and the never born
My fingers are sticks to beat away time

I am the one who has taken a face
I am the one who speaks

15

I speak in all the voices
I am the wife of the sun
The sister of the night
I speak from the beginning to the end
I leave nothing out

There once lived a boy, and his mother named him He Who Runs Away. He lived in a far country, a dry land open to the sun. This land lay beyond the Sea of Sorrows, where confused souls hang over the water. They are the souls of those who took a wrong turn, who did not pay attention when their guides were leading them to the land of the dead.

His ancestors came across the sea. Propelled by boredom, they set sail in boats covered with tar to prevent the stranded dead from eating the wood. They covered their bodies in nets to keep off the clouds of souls who flew at them like mosquitoes. They set sail, assuring each other that the Sea of Sorrows guarded the entrance to some lost paradise, a place where food of all cuisines fell into your mouth the moment you tilted back your head, where every few years you could clean, sparkle, and even reshape your body, like bringing your clothes to the laundry. Carrying their seeds and saplings and cows and pigs and dogs and cats and caged birds and baskets of snakes, and followed by rats and flies and cockroaches, they crossed the great water, their eyes painted over with images of palaces and winged children, their noses stuffed with flowers.

They made it over the sea and smashed their boats. For they thought they had found it – paradise. They were grinning and slapping each other on the back, when suddenly they remembered to wash the paint from their eyes. At their first sight of the brown rock many thought they must have left a residue of turpentine on their retinas. They scraped and scraped until the eyes fell out of their heads. Even now, if you pass the Sea of Sorrows to the Bitter Beach you will see masses of eyes staring up at you, to be appeased only with photographs and picture postcards of the lost world.

He Who Runs Away came out of his mother with his eyes

16

open, all of them, even the ones behind the head, which most people leave safely closed until after death. He saw the world. He saw the cracked flatlands of his birth, he saw the hidden bridge back across the Sea of Sorrows, he saw the unspeakable green of the hill country, the grey teeth of the mountains, the holes covered by clouds. And having seen, he forgot.

He called himself Son Of A God.
He promised them his Father's anger.

The children pinched and kicked him, they shrieked at him to call down Daddy God and destroy them. Three times He-Who-Runs-Away tried to fulfil the prophecy of his name. The children hunted him down, they dragged him back to his mother with his wrists and ankles tied together like a fox or a cat.

In his fifteenth year an earthquake ripped open the ground. Houses leaped into the air like enraged grasshoppers, whole caravans tumbled into cracks (some emerged years later to discover highways paved with glass, towers for collecting moonlight to use on cloudy nights, and tax agents disguised as rocks on the sides of the roads). In the middle of the quake Son Of A God climbed on his mother's roof. He shouted above the roar of the Earth, the screams of the people. His father had come, had come at last. His father would punish them for their monstrous sins and unspeakable rudeness. The people crowded through the storm of rock to bow down and beg the boy's forgiveness, asking him please, please, would he send his father home again. The earthquake stopped. The people looked around, laughing and vomiting at the same time. Then they all picked up rocks and began to throw them at the boy. They would have killed him except for a fear that maybe, just, maybe, his father was teasing them and would return. So they drove him into the desert, where dust swirled in more shades of yellow, red, brown, black, and purple than any Eastern hill dweller, drenched in green, could ever imagine.

Blinded and sick from the sun, his skin a mountain range

17

of insect bites, the boy wandered for days until he came to a rock tower pitted with holes. Hundreds of coloured pebbles filled the pockmarks, stories left there by the birds and desert rats. Shivering with fever, half crying, half moaning with nausea, chills, and a rage as massive as the Moon, He Who Runs Away lay down in the shadow of the stone. He closed his eyes and shouted for death.

But when he looked up, instead of Our Winged Mother Of Night, he saw before him a Visitor, an agent of the Living World. The being wore a mask half as high as the boy. Splinters of bone and strips of skin hung from the mask's sides. The forehead was pasted with photographs of burning bodies. Flies filled the mouth.

He Who Runs Away tried to crawl. A finger touched him at the back of his neck and his soul flew out his eyes. The next morning, when he returned to his body, he found the mask beside him.

On most Recital Days the people of Poughkeepsie attended their various halls. They went to the row of glass and brick 'moderns' on Park Avenue. They went to converted Old World monuments, like the grey stone towers on Cannon Street, a block from the Blessed Path parking lot south of Main Street. They went to the garishly painted storefronts of the New Purity movement. For outdoor enactments, such as Earth Day, they went to parade grounds or the park by the YMTA or baseball fields. But on the Day of Truth, the summer solstice, the community gathered together in large groups. For on that day, according to doctrine, each person's experience drew from all the others (in contrast to the Day of Isolation, the autumnal equinox, when each listener's universe emptied of everyone but himself and the Teller). On the Day of Truth, when the city paraded its best Tellers, the majority of Poughkeepsie's citizens attempted to squeeze together on the sides of Recital Mount, an artificial hill built after the

18

Revolution by the Holy Recovery Agency, Rebecca Rainbow's emergency response to the unemployment that grew with the collapse of the Old World economy. And this year, when Allan Lightstorm would speak and *everyone* wanted to attend (except, perhaps, some New Purity purists), the city had set up gates and guards to keep out anyone who could not show proof of local residence.

Though some began lining up, with sleeping bags and tents, five days ahead, most people came early in the morning or the night before, hoping to get a good spot in clear sight of the platform. For two or three days before, throughout the city and the surrounding town of Poughkeepsie, in wood or fieldstone houses, in brick apartment buildings, in trailer parks and welfare hotels, people marched in private processions, their bare feet burnt by the wax of candles held in front of them, their heads adorned with baseball caps covered in little metal tokens of the Founders. Alone or in small groups they prayed and did penance in the hope that some Devoted One would arrange a good seat for themselves and their families.

The candles and the caps were not a local custom. Sold all over the country in spiritual aid stores they were a regular feature of the Day of Truth, said to bring blessings for the coming year. Most of the people in Jennie Mazdan's hive had bought theirs at the special display counter Sears had set up in the South Hills mall. As an extra benefit, the caps sold locally all displayed portraits of Allan Lightstorm, with his signature in glittery letters.

Not everybody came early or gave offerings for a good seat. Some, such as city officials, officers of the Spiritual Development Agency, executive officers of the Bird of Light Factory, and the Directors of the Chamber of Commerce and Poughkeepsie's three

19

hospitals, had their seats guaranteed. Various groups could count on an automatic place as well, including the various hive housing developments outside the city. In Glowwood Hive, where Jennifer Mazdan had lived for over three years, people slept late and awoke with the smile that came from knowing that for at least one day the lower middle class families in their cheap identical houses shared a privilege denied to the doctors and lawyers in their expensive homes on Wilbur Boulevard and the south side of the city. By mid-morning, however, these people too had made their way through the traffic jams and the miles of official and impromptu parking to find their allotted places and wait, wait for the procession up the tiled path, wait for the glimpse of a voluminous costume, wait for the legendary voice to fill their hungry bodies.

The citizens of Poughkeepsie sat on wooden benches, on cushioned seats under citybuilt canopies, on lawn chairs and blankets, and all through the branches of trees. Those who came later ended up standing as the crowds piled in tighter and tighter. The Mount occupied an area south of the city. North of it stood the mayor's Mansion, a glass-walled pavilion where every year the city manager mimed the beheading of the mayor as an appeasement to any Malignant Ones hovering about the town. To the south of the hill, along the riverbank, stood a row of concrete shelters set up for pilgrims on their way north to the national parks in the Adirondack Mountains near the Canadian border. For the past weeks, ever since the announcement of Lightstorm's coming, the city had kept the shelters closed for fear that out of town pilgrims would try to take spots reserved for residents. Today, both the shelter area and the mansion grounds would fill up with the overflow of the crowd. East of the shelter, but still south of the Mount, began the strip of malls and

20

shopping centres that dotted the Highway of the Nine Wonders between Poughkeepsie and Wappinger's Falls.

To the east of Recital Mount, just the other side of the highway, lay a town recreation centre, with a swimming pool ringed by concrete water guardians. Past the pool began a golf course whose location near the Mount produced low scores, thereby attracting players from as far away as New York City and Connecticut. Several years before Lightstorm's day in Poughkeepsie a golfer playing out of bounds next to the highway sliced his ball over the road to hit an out-of-work gardener looking through the fence surrounding Recital Mount. The gardener decided that God had chosen him for a Speaker, and for the next few weeks he predicted various developments for the local area, including the discovery of mineral deposits under the civic centre on Market Street. For a time he maintained a certain fame, with investors coming up from New York, until the city hired an earth sensitive from Denver to tell them the best place to dig up the foundation and begin drilling. Her report found nothing but granite and one or two captured spirits from before the Revolution. The gardener/prophet tried to insist that Ferocious Ones had taken away the deposits as a punishment for Poughkeepsie's sins and would restore them if everyone followed him in a month of prayer, fasting, and sexual excess. Only a few people, mostly teenagers, paid any attention. The investors returned to New York, the sensitive had to sue to get her fee, and the gardener, evicted from his house by an angry city council, moved to Wappinger's Falls where he set up a small temple of penitence in a former movie theatre around the corner from the bridge over the falls.

On the north side of the Mount, southwest of the

21

mayor's mansion, stood a walled complex of residences maintained by the Poughkeepsie Teller's Committee in an official 'poverty' so splendid the Chamber of Commerce used to feature sketches of it on the cover of its investment brochures until a court order forced them to stop. From here Lightstorm would begin his march up the Mount to the platform.

To the hill's west, like a green and silver cat forever stretching in the sun, flowed the Hudson River, 'our ancient mother' as Maryanna Split Sky once called it, bounded by cliffs and forests and homes and railroad tracks. On that day the water churned with fish who'd gathered to hear the master whose fame had spread to the birds of the sky and the beasts of the sea. Many years ago the Army of the Saints, released by the victory in Poughkeepsie from its headquarters in New York, had sailed up the river in barges covered with white and yellow flowers (a journey enacted weekly in Spring and Summer and sold to the public as the Boat Ride to Poughkeepsie). The Malignant Ones who had fled the technophile bombs had hidden in the river. Now they floated in the water, ready to devour the boat. To protect the Founders the Living World sent a group of children into the river, their mouths filled with stones to throw at the enemy. A Ferocious One in the form of a beautiful woman rose up before them. To each child she appeared as the child's mother, purified of weakness or jealousy or rage, shining with love. The children dropped their stones and swam to the woman, whose kiss sucked the souls from their bodies. Her own greed defeated her. She swelled up so large that the Army saw the bloated body and discovered the trap. Sadly, they could not help the children. Though they punctured the Malignant One the children's souls fled into the water before the Founders could restore them.

22

In Jennifer Mazdan's time you could still hear children crying every night after eleven o'clock, a wailing that made it impossible to build housing along the riverside. Sailboats, barges, and tourist boats would sometimes get bits of souls tangled up in their rudders, causing the boats to spin in circles until the children came loose again.

Some time around one in the afternoon Lightstorm emerged from the residence. He travelled up the hill in the grand manner, sweeping the path with the folds of his recital skin. Bills and coins lay all over the tiles, offerings of the people who'd managed to make their way through the crowd. The gesture of 'cleaning the road' with his sleeve demonstrated the Teller's non-interest in personal gain. (After the Recital the faceless Workers from the residence would come and pick up the money in baskets the shape of squatting pigs.) As he climbed the hill Lightstorm thought of the satellite hook-up that should have been carrying his voice across the continent. He wondered whom his chairperson had found to replace him. He glanced over at the privileged hicks (presumably the mayor and the City Council if that's what they had here) sitting under parasols on velvet-covered benches right along the pathside. Right along side. He'd be lucky if they didn't try to touch him. Their mouths hung open as if they expected him to feed them their dinner. The hicks might decide they'd got a little richer food than they wanted when they discovered just what picture their imported star was planning for this feast of theirs.

The fact was, the Tellers didn't like doing 'The Place Inside' any more than their listeners liked hearing it. Telling it could leave you depressed for weeks. According to Judy Whitelight, Gail Morningsun over in Brooklyn had once needed a bleeder to drain off the scum of guilt left over in her from the end of the Picture.

23

When he'd heard that about Gail, he remembered, he'd said 'What could you expect from someone who went around saying "our people" need us to give them back the "beauty" in their lives?' Now – now he wished he could leave the hicks gaping down each other's mouths and go home to New York for a long soak in the pool in the courtyard.

'The Place Inside'. He needed that as much as he needed this exile up the Hudson in the first place. Misery. That was the Inner Meaning of the Picture. He thought *Great work, Li Ku. Just what I need. A Picture that teaches misery.* Dedication to insanity was more like it.

Somehow the story contained – something – you couldn't really say what, except that it had nothing to do with the official meaning. But who could understand Li Ku? No one liked her. Even in the Revolution they called her the Insane Founder. They almost killed her that time she dragged in those tattooed followers of hers to spit at Rebecca Rainbow's feet.

Finally Lightstorm got free of the rows of 'distinguished' hicks. At the top of the Mount he sat down in a highbacked chair made of polished mahogany with nicely cushioned seats and snakes inlaid in gold along the arms. Hopelessly garish, but at least they'd given him something decent to sit on. If only they'd thought of some shelter from the sun.

He stroked the chairarms, thinking of the time John Thundervoice had accepted an invitation to go out to Utah (Utah! Lightstorm could hardly believe such places existed) for the Day of Truth. He'd returned in shock with tales of frozen food and a Teller's chair that was little more than a stone bench. 'They think it's still the Time of Fanatics out there,' he'd told Allan. 'I mean, what could I do? Jaleen Heart-of-the-World used to kneel on stone with bare knees. So I couldn't say

24

anything. But that was the Revolution, for God's sake. I mean, we fucking won these battles. Someone should tell those people that the goddamn Revolution is over.' He'd gone on like that for months.

Lightstorm looked out at his listeners. There were so many he could only see the tops of their heads. Even the ones nearby, even the local Tellers sitting on the tier below him, appeared to have lost their bodies, become abstractions of faces. Suddenly he decided to give the Picture everything he had, to let it all out like he hadn't done in years. He took a deep breath, then slowly turned his head from side to side. The hicks would remember this Day of Truth for the rest of their squealing little lives.

He laid his hands on his belly like someone who's eaten a big meal. And then he began the story of 'Too Pretty For Her Own Good' and her lion lover.

2

That morning Jennifer Mazdan had woken to a loud clamour outside her house. It was the Day of Truth and the Spiritual Development Agency had sent out its crews of 'sweepers' to clear the area of destructive spiritual configurations. She lay in bed and listened to the noise – the detection machines with their bells and sirens, the sweepers' whistles, their hoarse voices (they tended to hit the hives last, since everybody else left before sunup to get a good place) shouting back and forth and up and down the street. She groaned and got to her feet, scratching her right breast and then her side. She couldn't tell if she was just dirty or the mosquitoes had found a hole in the screen door.

She half smiled, her mouth too groggy to grin. Maybe the itch was just the first signs of possession. Wasn't that how it started with Mike's aunt, what was her name, Margaret? Itching all over, then the next thing she knew she was eating rocks and spitting out gold. Jennie laughed. Mike said his uncle had refused to turn Margaret in, hoping to sell the nuggets. Only, when he brought them in they burned right through the jeweller's tray or whatever it was he put them in. Poor Uncle Jack. The jeweller turned out to be an amateur meta-psychologist and knew right away how Jack had come by the gold. When the SDA came to defuse Margaret – apparently lights were going out all over Poughkeepsie, and some brass band down by the civic centre had started spraying the audience with oil from the bells of their horns – they found Margaret bouncing around the walls like a ping-pong ball. Mike said she nearly bit off some woman's nose before they could net her and drive out the Ferocious One.

Jennie sighed. She was thinking about Mike again. Almost three years and she was still . . . One of these days she'd have to go down to that place by Ellenville and get scourged for all the guilt she was piling up violating the annulment. As the noise in the street came closer Jennie looked at the clock. She winced. Ten past six. She still couldn't understand what had made her volunteer to work on the morning of the Day of Truth. It wasn't the money, at least she didn't think it was. Not that she couldn't use the bonus.

She got herself up and waddled over to the window. About to yank open the dark brown curtains she realised she had better put something on. Marjorie Kowski was probably staring out of her window across the street, hoping the sweepers would find some cobwebs in someone along the block. The last thing Jennie needed was to parade nude for Marjorie Kowski. Ever since the annulment Jennie was sure Marjorie was making up stories of frustrated Ms Mazdan seducing everyone in sight, from the retired cop down the street to the Holy Sister who rode through the hive on her bicycle, blessing the neighbourhood.

She grabbed her yellow bathrobe from the dream stick at the end of the bed. For a moment she squinted at the wooden guardian. She'd never liked that grinning face and bulging eyes. There were two guardians for the bed. The stick supposedly scared away evil dreams hiding in the sheets. Above the headboard a doll with a blank face lay under a tiny blanket in a wooden box. By setting a good example the guardian would bring Jennie a restful sleep. She rubbed her neck, stiff every morning this week. Some rest.

Holding the robe closed with one hand she pushed aside the curtain over the bedroom windows. Outside, the sweepers, in their nylon jumpsuits and plastic helmets, were coming up to her corner. Some checked their instruments while others slashed the air with long poles wrapped in copper strips. Jennie remembered how Mike's niece Glissie (short for Glissander of all things – idiot parents) used to love this ceremony almost as much as the Recital itself. She'd stayed with Mike and Jennie once the night before the holiday and the next morning had stood up on the couch and shrieked every time the sweepers blew their whistles.

The thought of the Recital relaxed Jennie a little. She wondered how Allan Lightstorm had ever decided to come to Poughkeepsie. At work people talked of nothing else, coming up with the craziest ideas and rumours and justifying them with every authority they could imagine, from cousins in the mayor's office to dream visions of Lightstorm receiving commands from the Founders to go to Poughkeepsie. Jennie herself couldn't imagine why someone who'd appeared on the cover of *Time* would even think of coming to a place like this. 'Ours not to reason why,' her supervisor had said. 'Ours just to jump for joy.'

Then why wasn't she jumping? All week, since the announcement, Jennie had slumped through work, tired, aching, then dragged herself home at night to sit and stare at the TV or even go to sleep right after dinner. She couldn't figure what was wrong with her. She'd even gone down to the company infirmary, wondering if she was anaemic or something. Nothing. Blood bright and sparkly. The nurse had spent the whole time chattering about Allan Lightstorm moving to Poughkeepsie and setting up a blessing centre for the Mid-Hudson Valley Mystery Society.

The sweeper team advanced to the stretch of road in front of her and Ron Miller's bits of lawn. Jennie was glad she didn't work for the SDA. It was already so hot she'd begun to sweat in her bathrobe, and they were stuck in those protective suits. Mid-Hudson Energy didn't pay much, but at least you could wear shorts.

Jennie took a step back from her window as the crew hesitated in front of her house. Why were they stopping? Was there something wrong? For some reason she thought of her father's death, and her grandmother explaining how 'Daddy' (she'd never called him that, it was always 'Jimmy') had gone to the Living World.

The sweepers moved their arms in wide loops, swinging their detectors like swords, first at the sky, then down at the ground. And then they went on walking. Not even a step onto her property. Jennie sat down on the bed, then let herself fall so that the top of her head extended over the edge of the mattress. She was all right. No destructive configurations. No possession by 'Being or Beings unknown' as the courts described it. Whatever else was wrong with her Jennie was clean.

She got up and closed the curtains again, then took off the robe to stand in front of the narrow mirror on the closet door opposite the bed. She looked so tired, her breasts starting to sag, her face all drawn and thick looking.

Old. She was getting old and she wasn't even thirty. It wasn't fair. She stepped closer. She was getting a double chin, just what she needed. Tilting her head back, she stressed the neck muscles. Maybe she should sleep with a strap. Did anyone actually do that? Did such things really exist? Maybe Lightstorm could peel the years off her. Like Ingrid Burning Snake did to those people in the old age home. She tried fluffing her hair, but it didn't help. She should have left it long. It was supposed to be bouncy, that's what the girl at the beauty parlour had called it, but the sides just hung there and the top stuck up like an ornament.

Maybe she should go somewhere. Vacation. That's what people did in the Summer, wasn't it? Get restored by the Day of Truth, and then take off somewhere. But where? And who with? She didn't want to go alone and she couldn't think of anyone to ask.

She put on a pair of faded tiger-striped panties (special for Allan Lightstorm, who'd once claimed the tiger as a personal totem), pleated Bermuda shorts rolled up a couple of times to look sexier, and a V-neck T-shirt with small cap sleeves, blue to match the shorts. She glanced at the clock. If she didn't get going soon she'd have trouble making her rounds and still getting to the Mount in time for the recital, reserved place or not. Maybe Lightstorm *would* fix her up. Every year after the Day of Truth the TV was full of stories about cripples dancing, blind people painting portraits of the Tellers, impotent men fathering triplets.

She wondered what picture Allan Lightstorm had chosen to tell. Maybe the river story, or the origin of fire, or maybe First Teller creating the world out of her own body. Jennie had always loved that one as a kid. She would hold on to her father's hand and Jimmy would promise her that they'd fly together through the roof.

Feeling a little more excited she went into the small bathroom. As she sat on the toilet seat she remembered how Mike used to complain if she came in to talk to him while he was shaving. 'Wait'll we get a bigger house' he used to say.

In the kitchen Jennie made a face at the dishes piled up in the sink. She plucked a bowl and soupspoon from the sink, ran hot water on them, then wiped them dry with a dish towel spotted with chicken grease. Got to do a wash, she thought as she filled the bowl with Spirit

30

Bits, roasted oats shaped into faces. Supposedly they represented divine Beings and would give you a sacred infusion as you ate them. Grinding God with your teeth. The back of the box contained a crude portrait of Francesca Heaven's Pride, part of a series on the major living Tellers. Jennie glanced at it then left the box on the counter to open the refrigerator for the skim milk. When she'd wet the cereal she stared at the coffee pot, wondering if she had time, or energy, to make a fresh pot. With a twist of her mouth she plugged it in, remembering just in time to take out last night's grounds so the coffee wouldn't recyle itself. She should get a drip pot, she knew. Everybody had them. But there was something Jennie liked about the old-fashioned electric percolators. She liked the sighs and whispers it made as it bubbled the coffee. They reminded her of a Teller her father had once taken her to hear. Still standing she mumbled a thank you to the food and began to spoon the Spirit Bits into her mouth.

Now that the sweepers were gone noises came from the houses and lawns around her. Someone – Gloria Rich, she thought – was shouting at her kids. Ron was saying some prayer or other, probably an apology for cutting his lawn. That reminded her, she should get the Kowski kid (she could never remember his name) to cut the grass. This time she'd make sure to pray the night before. Last week she'd forgotten entirely and half the lawn had withered while the other half got choked with weeds so that she'd had to give it a blood offering, not to mention five hours of yanking out crab-grass and laying down fertilizers.

Maybe she should move back to the city. It was Mike who'd wanted to move to Poughkeepsie in the first place. His home town. But what kind of work would she find in the city? She couldn't imagine being a Server there. Probably get raped or mugged twice a

31

day. Anyway, her mother would take a return to the city as proof that Jennie had finally decided not to run from her true calling in the arts. Like the time Jennie had dropped out of college and Beverley had filled the house with artists, hoping they would 'shatter that bourgeois cocoon you've spun around yourself', as Beverley put it.

She poured herself coffee while it was still lukewarm, then walked with it back to the bedroom for her sandals. A few gulps more and she grabbed her fake leather bag and was out of the door. In the driveway she made a face at the sticker on the back bumper. 'Lightstorm must stay' it read. She felt so stupid having that thing on her car. It was just . . . everybody at work was doing it and she didn't want to look like a snob. Anyway, Lightstorm would leave in a day or two and she could take it off.

As Jennie got in the car a voice said, 'Good morning.' Jennie jumped before she recognised it as the computer that reminded her to fasten her seat belt or warned her when some Malignant One had lowered the oil pressure. But when did it ever wish her good morning? 'Fair weather,' the voice piped. 'Temperature and barometric pressure both within acceptable limits. A lovely day for a journey.' And when did it ever give weather reports?

'Personification,' she muttered. Some power or other had entered her car's computer. Her goddamn car. To celebrate the Day of Truth.

'Excuse me?' the car said.

God, Jennie thought. *I don't need this. Pick on someone else.* She remembered her college course in spiritual anthropology, 'spanthro' as everybody called it. Personification, the textbooks claimed, indicated an ongoing or immanent crisis. Jennie thought, *I've already gone through a crisis. My husband annulled our marriage. Isn't that enough?*

The car said, 'I'm pleased to report high levels of harmony between Earth and Sky. Fine indications for long trips or expeditions.'

Expedition. Was that a code word or something? She said, 'Blessed powers, protect me. I swear a penance for all my sins.'

The car quoted, 'A journey of a thousand miles begins with a single prayer.'

'You idiot,' Jennie said. 'I'm not taking any journey. I just have to go around town.' She started the engine. If they wanted to personify a crummy old car like hers . . .

'I'm sorry,' the dashboard said. 'I just thought you should know.'

'Shut up!' Jennie shouted, then immediately added, 'I'm sorry, I'm sorry. I just want to get to the recital.'

The car didn't answer. If the Visitor remained inside, it had decided to sulk. Jennie turned left onto Blessed Spirit Drive, then left again onto Heavenpath Road. It's nothing, she tried to assure herself as the car wobbled down the street. Just a random charge ahead of the recital. Probably everyone in Poughkeepsie was suffering spontaneous eruptions, even complete occurrences. Because of Lightstorm. Someone with that much power coming to a place like Poughkeepsie. The valley couldn't handle it. All the dormant patterns were rising up. Perfectly normal.

At the exit she pulled over for a moment. Beside the car stood the hive's 'celestial guardian', supposedly a meteorite, but in fact a plain grey boulder. At the moment it lay under a blanket of sanctified aluminum foil, a shield to reflect evil away from the hive on this most important day of the year. Jennie wondered if she should get out and touch it, ask it to protect her. She was afraid to leave the car.

And something else. A few feet from the guardian a disc of green metal lay in the ground. A soul-map they called it, with a diagram of the streets etched into its raised surface. A promise of spiritual unity with all your neighbours. Just step on it and feel yourself joined to the hive. Jennie and Mike had stepped on it once. On their way to the Supermarket. And then Mike had left her.

After what seemed a long time Jennie put the car in gear and drove forward to the edge of the highway. The dashboard stayed silent. A moment later she was driving north on Route 9.

A couple of minutes later she turned off onto Spackenkill Road, empty of people yet alive with the spirit of celebration. On the left, silver faces decorated the high thorn bushes marking the entrance to the public labyrinth. On the right silk ropes bound together the guardians standing at the entrance to the private school where movie stars and New York Tellers sent their children. Further along, banners floated from the houses, and the trees displayed seven foot strips of paper with Allan Lightstorm's name written thousands of times. Papier mâché dolls made in school art classes hung on screen doors, their arms straight out to welcome Lightstorm and his picture into their homes. Up the road the tombstones in the Dutchess County Tellers' cemetery shone with blue and yellow paint.

Seeing all this preparation Jennie found herself half excited, half guilty that she herself had done so little. She hadn't even decorated her house or put out any signs. She hadn't even *cleaned* her house. Maybe the Visitor had come to remind her of her duties. But it was too late now. She'd have to go straight from work to the Mount. 'I'm sorry,' Jennie said.

34

A car passed her – there was almost no traffic, everyone was queuing up for a place – and the driver honked and waved at her. Jennie waved back. Turning up Cedar Avenue she tried to remember more of what she'd learned in spanthro about personification, about breakthroughs in general. There was so little, it was all so long ago. In fact, Jennie knew, she'd never learned much in the first place.

I would have made a good scholar, she told herself. *If I'd just had the chance.* She'd hoped to study True History, especially the Founders. That goal had held her for years, since childhood really, when her father had given her a copy of *The Lives Of The Founders* shortly before his death. A month after he'd died, when Jennie'd been walking with her head drooped forward, Janet Artwing's face had appeared in the sidewalk on Hudson Street, in front of the Post Office, telling her not to cry for her father, saying Jimmy loved her and sent his blessing from the land of the dead. 'Read the book,' Janet Artwing told her. All through school, and high school, Jennie had assumed the Living World had chosen her for a scholar. She would dedicate her books to her father's memory. And then, somehow, when she entered college, it had all fallen apart. She couldn't concentrate, she kept sleeping late and missing classes, she even failed a basic course in her main subject. *I just didn't get any support*, she told herself. *If I'd had a little help, or encouragement, from my mother, or Mike . . .* What was she thinking? She didn't even meet Mike until she'd dropped out of school. She was working that temp. job at Bloomingdale's the day she and Mike had met.

And as for her mother . . . Jennie knew very well what Beverley thought of Jennie's hopes of scholarship. Mommy had expected (still expected, against all the evidence and Jennie's insistence) that Jennifer would

35

follow in her Mommy's footsteps and become a
musician. Or at least an artist or a writer. Never mind
that Jennifer had gone to college. Never mind that
she dropped out only to betray all sanity by getting a
suburban husband, a surburban house, and a suburban
job, and then, when she lost the first, keeping the other
two. In Beverley's eyes, it was all just 'sleepwalking.'

Jennie drove along Cedar Avenue up to 376 where
she turned right to the end of Raymond Avenue. She
drove up Raymond Avenue, past Vassar College and
the primary Tellers' residence, then past empty shops
hung with banners and posters. Clothes boutiques lined
the blocks near the college. Like many native Pough-
keepsieites Jennie never shopped there. Today, all the
window dressers' models, male and female, bore Lightstorm's face.

With no traffic to stop her Jennie drove straight up
to Main Street and then right to the interchange that
brought her onto Route 44 going east out of town. Even
on the multi-lane road she saw almost no cars. When
44 changed back to a normal country highway she
passed a group of teenagers on bicycles. They all wore
sleeveless jackets with the number three on the back,
a proclamation that they were eternal pilgrims on their
third incarnation as a unified group. Jennie wondered
why they weren't at the Mount fighting for seats in
that obnoxious way group pilgrims had of linking arms
and trampling anyone who got in their way. Maybe
they were going later. As a government registered unit
they might have got the county SDA to order them
reserved places. Like the hives.

Finally Jennie pulled her car into the gravelly
parking lot of Mid-Hudson Energy's administrative
offices. She didn't notice any cars from any of the other
Servers. The few who were working besides herself had
probably got their assignments and gone. Which meant

36

that Maria had to wait for Jennie before she herself could go and queue up for a seat.

A large cardboard cut-out of Allan Lightstorm greeted her with a wave of its hinged arm as the glass door slid open into the building. Jennie punched her time card, then realised she wouldn't be coming back at the end of the day and would have to write in her hours. She hurried down the corridor, past the mural of the Benign Ones who lived inside the Sun pouring their streams of burning elements onto a grinning Earth. In the servers' staff room a couple of white plastic cups and some scattered sheets of paper were all that remained of the meeting.

Maria Canterbury, Jennie's dispatcher, raised her eyebrows as she played with her single braid of hair. 'You look awful,' she said. 'You look like you've just washed up from the underworld.'

'I'm late,' Jennie said stupidly.

'Late?' Maria raised her hands in a show of surprise. 'How could you possibly be late? My star Server. The others must have all gotten lost. Seduced by incubi and succubi lurking on the roads.'

'Please,' Jennie said. She could hear how close her voice sounded to tears. 'Can I just get my list and go?'

Maria slid off her desk to come stand next to Jennie, who winced at the huge woman's approach. A former weightlifter and wrestler, twice champion of Dutchess County sacred bench press, Maria moved like the great boulder that had rolled down Storm King Mountain to come and hear Jonathan Mask Of Wisdom. 'What's wrong?' she said.

'It's nothing.'

'You sure about that?'

Jennie wished she had the nerve to tell her boss about her personified car. She said, 'It's nothing, Maria. You've got to get to the Recital.'

37

'Bullshit. I'll put on my tough face and everyone'll get out of my way. Watch, put on the news tonight, you'll see me sitting next to the mayor.'

Jennie smiled. 'In your fluorescent sweatshirt?'

'Yeah, that's it. Now what's wrong?' Jennie shrugged. 'Come on. I'm an old-fashioned boss. I'm in charge of my workers' spiritual welfare.'

'I don't know,' Jennie said. 'Really. It's just . . . I just feel so low lately.'

'Have you been for a scan?'

'A scan? No–no, I don't need–I don't need anything like that.'

'Okay, then, how about a shrink?'

'It's nothing that serious. It's just – I don't know, I just can't seem to get excited about anything. . .'

'How about Lightstorm? Are you excited about that?'

'I guess. I don't know . . .'

There was silence for a moment, then Maria said, 'Well, maybe Lightstorm's not all they say he is. Not all *he* says he is.' She laughed.

Softly Jennie said, 'None of them are.' Maria didn't answer. Looking at the floor Jennie said, 'I wouldn't feel this way if the Tellers did what they're supposed to do. People in the Days of Awe didn't feel like this.'

'I guess not. Maybe you need a holiday. You've got some time coming, haven't you? You could go tomorrow, pack tonight after the Recital. I'll get the others to cover for you.'

'I've got no place to go.'

'Go to the beach or something.'

'I haven't any money. Anyway, beach places get booked up for Truth week months in advance.'

'Well, go and visit your mother or something.'

Jennie made a noise. 'That's just what I need.'

'Well, you can just stay home and watch television. You need a rest.'

'Can't I just have my assignment?'

'Forget your assignment. They'll keep until tomorrow. You can get out to the Mount and wait for the Recital to start up.'

'Please, Maria.'

Maria sighed, her breasts rising on her muscular chest. She reached into the pocket of her jeans for a sheet of yellow paper. 'Here,' she said, 'there's only a few but you'll have to move fast. Don't forget to log them.'

Jennie grabbed the list and rushed outside before Maria could show any more concern for her. In the parking lot she hesitated before touching the car. The Visitor had left apparently; she slid into the seat without any comments from the dashboard. She checked the card. Four services, none of them anywhere near each other. The price she paid for coming late.

'Service' meant tending to the guardians watching over Dutchess County's energy system. There were hundreds of these protectors, the same as the many thousands scattered over the rest of the country, one for every neighbourhood, housing development, hospital, factory or shopping mall. The guardians lived in 'husks,' rectangular steel or bronze monoliths with the corners and edges rounded off. Ranging in height from five to eight feet the husks all bore a face on one side – horizontal diamonds with lines across them for the eyes, three vertical lines for the nose, a row of short vertical lines for the mouth. Jennie liked this face, liked the fact that no one had elaborated or decorated Arthur Sweetwind's original design.

The back displayed a trio of etched drawings. The first showed the chaos after the Revolution, when the liberated electricity ran wild, blacking out, over charging, starting up factories and can-openers without permission. The second depicted Sweetwind (in beauty and truth lives his name forever) summoning the guardians from the invisible world. The last showed a city gleaming with light and humming with obedient energy.

The sides of the husks held double rows of small hooks for people to leave things for the guardians. Usually wrapped in silk and placed in small mesh bags these offerings might include newspaper clippings, vacation souvenirs, photos of friends and relatives (especially dead ones, for if it pleased them the guardians might pass along messages), chips of wood from a new house, or odd items that only the owner might understand – a broken shoelace, a singed dish towel, the cap from a shampoo bottle. Jennie and the other servers had also found sexual mementos, ranging from torn panties to ornate nipple clips. For the past week almost all the hooks contained signifiers of Allan Lightstorm. There were signed photos, newspaper articles, small beanbags with his face painted on them, copies of his official biography, and drawings and paintings of Lightstorm done on paper, wood, and stone. Those few hooks not given to the Teller held bags with requests. People asked the guardians (or maybe Lightstorm) for healing, for love, for the return of husbands and wives, for work or promotion, for passing grades in summer school.

When Jennie first started work she'd been shocked to discover that the Servers would sometimes take out such requests and read them. They would sit in the staff room and pass on the wilder things people had written. After a while Jennie thought she should try it. She didn't want to sit there like an idiot while everyone traded stories. She'd chosen a long message only to discover that the overlarge writing alternated between explicit descriptions of sexual torture and wild pleas to 'drive the Malignant Ones out of my head.' For a week

40

Jennie had stayed at home, terrified to watch TV for fear of news bulletins about mass graves. Nothing had happened.

Jennie's job required her first to wash down the husk with sanctified cleaning fluid. Then she adjusted the alignment. Buttons allowed the statue to turn on its base. Using instruments and a table of dates with alignment numbers Jennie made sure that the face looked in the direction of the rising sun. Finally she recited a company prayer of appreciation and burned a fake stock certificate made out to Arthur Sweetwind. Then she logged the place and the time and moved on to the next one.

It wasn't a difficult job, certainly not an intellectual one. Jennie sometimes thought it beneath her – Mike had thought so. Yet whenever she told herself she should look for something else she never got beyond glancing at the want ads in the *Poughkeepsie Journal*.

Her first service brought her to Founders' Street, despite its name a small road in the north of the city, near the Hospital of the Inner Spirit. It was a pretty area, with old two and three storey houses, and a lot of trees. Though the company had chosen the street because of the slight elevation compared to the surrounding area, they still had had to mount the husk on a metal frame tower to get it above the trees.

Jennie always liked this stop, especially in Summer. She liked climbing up and looking down at the branches, at the rooftops, the rich lawns with their precisely cut bushes. You could even see a glimpse of the river, a patch of silver among the green. She parked the car at the foot of the tower and grabbed her small bag of equipment from the seat next to her. She was about to get out when she decided she'd better take along her Allan Lightstorm cap to protect her head against the sun. She wasn't sure she liked the cap. She'd got it the week before, when she and a couple of the other Servers had gone shopping one evening after work. It seemed, well, indecent almost, the way they'd superimposed Lightstorm's face over the emblems of the Founders. 'Old-fashioned,' she accused herself and stuck the thing on her head.

Jennie climbed the ladder and stepped out onto the platform. Even with goggles she had to squint against the roar of sun coming off the steel face. As she hurried through her routine she thought how she'd soon be travelling with Allan Lightstorm, nice and safe inside the Picture, packed in with all her neighbours. She shook her head. The idea didn't seem real.

Jennie's next service took her all the way to Well-of-Hope Junction, a small collection of houses, offices, some garden apartments, and a small shopping mall southeast of Poughkeepsie. In the centre of the village stood the well, a deep pool of yellow oil. Once a year people gathered at dawn in Poughkeepsie and marched behind a group of Tellers to this pool, where a black metal fence prevented people from falling or jumping in. Along the way they drenched their clothes – special head-to-toe outfits of absorbent paper – in a pink liquid meant to contain all the past year's guilt, fear, and despair. When the exhausted crowd reached the well they all ripped off their paper suits and threw them in the oil which digested the paper but left the miseries bubbling on the surface.

It didn't work. Not any more. Some people managed to drop a few obsessions or annoyances, but most left their basic catalogue of unhappiness intact. In the Time of Fanatics people had stripped off not only their fears but even their memories, and sometimes their entire personalities. They had to pay people to drive them back to town and teach them who they were supposed to be.

The people who lived in Hope in those days after the Revolution would sometimes, on windy days, find themselves coated in other people's emotions, causing them to run up and down the street acting out long-gone crises. Even today, it took a certain kind of person to live in Hope, despite the money made from tourists who came to photograph or take part in the ceremony. They enjoyed suddenly getting enraged at someone they'd never met, or mourning the end of a love affair they'd never experienced.

Jennie finished her service and left Well-of-Hope as quickly as possible. The next service took her back to Poughkeepsie, to the guardian living on the roof of the county offices building on Market Street. Though the building was closed for the Recital (Jennie had her own key) a large crowd had gathered in the small plaza in front of the lobby. Mostly out-of-towners who would later go on to recitals at Wappinger's Falls and Beacon, they had come to visit Poughkeepsie's holiest site, the Founder's Urinal.

Originally a fountain decorating the old lifeless building, the Urinal marked the spot where the Army of the Saints had gathered after their boat ride to Poughkeepsie. Ecstatic at the victory, the water in the fountain had leaped into the air, drenching a flock of geese, a pair of crows, and a pilotless helicopter, all of which had come to witness the liberation. Either to celebrate, or because their bladders had pressured all at the same time, the Founders, men and women alike, had pissed together on the dry concrete, filling the basin with a bright light and a wonderful smell, noticeable on the other side of the river. You could also see, if you put on dark glasses and looked closely, a few drops of blood from one of the Founders whose prostate had sold out to the enemy. Over the years, instead of drying up or even subsiding, the liquid continued to bubble and hiss and give off its fragrance (the light had sadly dimmed from dilution with the inferior urine of the local Tellers.)

Poets and artists, especially those with creative blocks, came from all over the country to sip from the sacred water. The night before, in a televised ceremony, Allan Lightstorm had added his own stream to the pool, and now so many pilgrims were lined up with their tiny cups (on sale at a kiosk beside the building) that Jennie had to shove to get to the door. She smiled, thinking of Maria booming through the crowds on the Mount. On the way out she saw the police carrying off some man who'd attempted to add his own profane urine to the holy liquid. According to the crowd the police had slapped his penis away just in time, causing it to bathe some scrawny dog who was now trying to shake himself dry. Laughing, Jennie made her way back to the car.

She sat a moment, watching the crowds from across the street. She still loved such things – relics, shrines. She'd studied True History because of them, thinking of the subject as a sort of grown-up *Lives of The Founders*. She leaned back in her seat. Maybe today would lift her out of her depression after all. Maybe Lightstorm would dissolve all the layers in a spray of story more powerful than the Founders' piss. Anyway, if she didn't get the damn car going she'd boil away. She started up the engine and drove up the empty street, heading towards her last stop.

As she reached the highway and swung north towards Hide Park Jennie thought about the changes she could make in her life if Allan Lightstorm reconnected her to existence. She could go back to school. She could go and see her mother, throw so much love at Beverley she'd have to love Jennie in return. She could even try to start things up with Mike, arrange to meet him all over again. *God*, she thought, *all I can think of is the past.* No plans, no ideas, not even any hopes. Just an idiotic desire to revive a dead life.

The last husk on her list stood on top of a hill instead of a tower or a rooftop. One of Jennie's favourites, the guardian watched over the complex of buildings that formed the Poughkeepsie Bird of Light factory. She parked the car in the small space reserved for Servers and stepped onto the grass to stare up at the husk, one of the largest in the area. Sometimes she could feel the power buzzing all around her. She made a face. Not today apparently. Today she just felt – tired. She squeezed shut her eyes, then opened them wide. Just a few minutes more and then she could go to the Recital.

From the top of the hill she looked down at the factory. Officially started by Rebecca Rainbow, the Founder who'd restored the economy after the Revolution, the Poughkeepsie Bird of Light Corporation displayed in all its centres a lifesize statue of the great Teller. Staring down at it Jennie could see, at the bottom, one of Rainbow's quotations, something about financial life based on spiritual truth.

God, she was tired. She just wanted to lie on the grass. She leaned against the husk a moment, then took out her cleaning equipment and tables of alignments. When she'd done the service she had to sit down and catch her breath.

How could she drive like this? It was crazy, unfair. She'd done her work, she was free, there was even a spot waiting for her, and now she was so exhausted . . .

Jennie could see the dream coming even before she actually fell asleep. Like some huge creature it lumbered up the hill towards her, blotting out the factory, the trees, the river. 'Get away,' Jennie said. She ran to her car. 'Leave me alone. I'm going to the Recital.'

45

The car door stayed shut. 'You see,' the dashboard crowed. 'I told you you were taking a journey.'

'Please,' Jennie whined, 'Open up.' She slid down against the door. There she lay, in a thick lump, her head a smaller lump propped against one of the wheels. Her eyes closed and the dream leaped on her.

She was crying – walking along the riverside down by Lower Main Street, and she was crying because she knew she was dreaming, and even though the ceremony didn't start for another two hours, she knew, with dream certainty, that she wouldn't get there, she wouldn't get to hear Allan Lightstorm after all.

As she walked she began to notice things lying on the ground, first money, peculiar coins embossed with masked faces instead of queens and presidents, then little statues of animals, or sticks of wood with feathers attached to them, or dog whistles. Whatever she found she picked up and stuck in voluminous pockets that soon bulged out in front of her.

On the yellowed grass along the water's edge people lined up to stare at her. She could hear them talking, telling jokes by the tone and the looks. But she couldn't make out the words, just bits of words, broken syllables. They began to laugh. The sound puckered Jennie's skin and made her itch, like insect bites.

The water leaped up at the grass. The lines of people moved closer, their jokes and gulping laughter getting louder and louder. They began to clap and snap their fingers, and then to stamp their feet and whistle, until Jennie screamed at them to leave her alone. 'It's not me you want,' she shouted, her hands cupped before her mouth because that was the way they did it in the mystery plays when they announced the birth of the Great Stories. 'It's not me, it's my daughter. My daughter.' No one heard, and childless Jennie wondered, even in the dream, why she should have said that.

She pushed aside two laughing women, each with a breast cut off, like the Living Mothers in their underground refuges outside Cincinatti. She wanted to run and jump in the river.

46

But when she reached the little metal railing that kept sleeping pilgrims from sliding into the water she stopped and stared. A huge gathering of fish swam before her, all sizes and shapes, from a great flatbellied thing with fanged teeth and hard bumps all along its back, to a tiny finback with pointed teeth, to a short stubby creature with a triple chin and layers and layers of scales sharp enough to slice bread. At first she thought the fish all roaring with colour, but when she squatted down to get closer to the water, she saw that they had all turned a dreary grey. Something had sucked the colour from them, had drained it away over years and years until nothing was left. They knew it. They swam aimlessly, avoiding each other's touch, many of them ramming the rocks that stuck out from the surface of the water. Jennie began to cry and looked around for a handkerchief, as if the Parks Commission would set them out in case someone needed to blow her nose.

Just then a new fish swam among the others. Long and thin, almost eel-like except for its small tail and flippers, it glistened black. Its tiny mouth, human-shaped, opened and closed. Jennie realized it was speaking to the other fish, who swam around it in concentric circles. They reminded Jennie of the mandala ballets held on Enactment Days. And then, as the black fish told her stories, the colour returned or came awake in all the others.

They gave off so many greens and golds and purples and yellows and magentas, some with every scale in three different tones, so many colours that the excess of light changed into sound, music getting louder and louder, great chimes and gongs and whistles and thundering booms, flying out of the water and into the air where they bounced off the trees and buildings and turned back into colour to fall on Jennie like a sudden flood. Dripping with orange and red and gold and auburn, Jennie turned around, just in time to see the crowd of people rising into the air, some with their eyes rolling around, others flapping their arms, as if they refused to admit that the rain of colour had released them from the Earth, and pretended instead that they flew under their own power. Jennie too tried to fly, giving little hops

47

along the riverside. She only twisted her ankle. She sat down to rub it, moaning through the pain, 'It's not fair, it's not fair. She's my daughter, isn't she?'

She was walking through her mother's house, plodding in her tattered green bathrobe past rows of locked doors. She entered a room and found herself in ancient Persia. Someone was running a street organ, a girl in a black turban was slitting open a snake, someone else was announcing a free fuck, any position you liked, with the hidden Imam. Somewhere behind the carnival stalls, the Persian baseball team was getting set for the All-star game. Jennie thought they looked pretty bad, even for foreigners. She'd heard that the royal team of Kush could beat them easily.

Jennie was hungry, she hadn't eaten in fifty years. 'You're too picky,' Mike used to tell her, and she had to agree, every stall she passed here in the Persian carnival looked great from a distance but when she came close – to the baklava and whipped cream, or the yakmeat hamburgers, or the kosher hotdogs coated in candied sesame – they all looked overdone, or melted, or much too peppery. 'You always want something perfect,' Mike said, deepfrying what looked like a long cucumber. 'But only the Living World is perfect. As long as you've got a body you've got to stick things in it.'

She began to walk faster, hoping to reach the end of the stalls and hide in the forest she could see beyond the street. Above and behind the stalls, on rickety wooden balconies, people in hooded nightgowns shouted at her. 'I don't understand Persian,' she shouted back. No one listened. She had almost reached the end when an old legless woman came rolling up on a motorised carpet to block Jennie's way. The people on the balconies laughed and applauded as Jennie tried to dodge past her.

Jennie could see the animals running through the forest. The small ones, the rabbits and the monkeys, rode on the backs of the jaguars, the zebras, the elephants. Overhead the birds flew, directed by the beetles and the cockroaches pinching and tugging on their wingtips. Jennie wanted to run with them. She wanted to rip away her clothes and let

48

the wind dry the sweat on her breasts and thighs. But every time she tried to reach them the old lady cut her off. 'What do you want?' Jennie pleaded.

The woman said something in Persian and held out a tube-shaped silver box about ten inches long. Jennie shook her head and backed off; the woman rushed forward, shrieking at her, nearly jabbing her in the belly. Jennie looked at the animals, saw the rows thinning out, and in the sky only a couple of hawks and sparrows.

'We're hungry,' the woman said. 'Eat.' Behind her someone jumped up and down on a trampoline. Jennie grabbed the box and opened it to find another box, all of gold so soft she could stretch it out to twice its original length just by rubbing it. Inside she found a third box, of white satin, and on and on, until she held a perfectly shaped pine-wood coffin about three quarters of an inch long. She pried it open with her fingernail. A seed of some sort lay inside. It looked like a fur-covered lima bean. She picked it up between her thumb and second finger.

There was something disgusting about it, the way the fur waved or maybe a sliminess at the tips. But Jennie was hungry, and she wanted to get out of Persia and join the animals. She popped the seed in her mouth, then spun around, afraid everyone would laugh at her.

Instead, they all sighed, a sound like a monstrous organ, and lay down on top of the stalls to go to sleep. 'How am I supposed to go home?' Jennie said. 'It's not fair. It wasn't me you wanted anyway.' She tried to run back and wake them but the ground had turned to ooze, thick and hot, with black steam coming off it. With every step she sank almost to her ankles and had to pull herself loose with a loud plop that made her blush. In her belly she could feel the seed taking root, growing, sending out its tendrils like telephone wires.

In one of the stalls a sleepy snake charmer kicked over his rubber box – 'Macy's' the cover said. All the snakes tumbled out, right in front of Jennie; she tried to jump sideways and fell in the mud. Instantly it slurped her up, despite all her frantic flailing.

But when she finally got herself turned over she was lying in a desert of baked mud. Everything about her had got larger, thicker, clumsier, her feet like tree stumps, her thighs like standing stones, her breasts like the concrete lumps gangsters tie to their partners when they throw them in the river. A long time she lay there, tired and sad, while the Sun got hotter and hotter. The Sun didn't want to hurt her, she knew. It just couldn't help itself. Her skin dried and dried until suddenly she cracked open, ten, twenty places up and down her body. Great rivers of milk flowed out of her breasts to soften the brown earth.

Joy lifted her head. She saw all the animals, and the Persian baseball team, and the legless lady and the people from the river, all of them with their faces deep in the milk, making great slurping noises. From her groin the fish swam forth, all their colours releasing rainbows of light into the thirsty sky.

Jennie laughed and lay down again. There wasn't much left of her now. She tried to close her eyes but the half-eroded lids only cut the sky in half. She opened them again. She saw a flock of artbirds from the Poughkeepsie factory. They were circling down, coming to lift away that small unbreakable thing, hard and bright, that lay forever hidden in the base of the heart. The dream Jennie smiled and went to sleep.

She woke up wet. Her shorts and T-shirt, her tiger panties, even her plastic sandals, hung heavy with sweat. She groaned and lay down again, dizzy. Above her the setting Sun gave an orange glow to the hood of her car. She sat up slowly and rubbed her eyes and forehead, wondering if she had time to go home and change her clothes before the Recital. Suddenly she turned her head so fast towards the west she heard a sharp crack and winced in pain. The Sun was setting. She could see it settling itself among the mountains across the river. 'Goddamn it,' she said. 'Oh shit.' She'd missed Allan Lightstorm.

A Version of the Tale of First Teller, Found in the Ancient Empire and brought to the New World by Ha'Ari Lionmouth, hero of the One True Revolution.

It was the time before time before time.

It was the time before day. It was the time before night. This was the time before light and dark, before colour and sound, form and shape. It was the time before memory, before the losing and the finding.

First Teller.

First Teller.

First Teller awoke.

No man. No woman. Man and woman. More than man and woman, First Teller began to touch her body. He touched himself. He touched the arms, he touched the thighs, she bent the fingernails and pressed the eyes. First Teller pulled and rubbed the nest of genitals. He separated the parts and she brought them together. Light and darkness escaped from First Teller's groin to begin their endless somersault.

First Teller said, 'This is not enough.'

She said, 'This is not enough.'

He said, 'This is not enough.'

She said, 'I will imagine something. Something hard. And huge.' A mountain appeared. First Teller began to climb.

He said, 'I will imagine something soft. And strong. And vast, vast as the inside of my body.' A sea appeared round the base of the mountain. Waves beat at the rock, the sea shouted at the mountain. First Teller called the mountain Vision and the sea Chaos.

The Teller climbed. The stone tore pieces of his skin. He said, 'I will make something from these pieces of myself.' A piece of skin dropped between his legs. A snake slithered over the rocks. It showed First Teller the best places for her hands and feet. Pieces of skin fell to either side. On the right ran a dog, on the left a cat. The dog barked and light leaped from his mouth to show the Teller the way. But when First Teller stopped, and closed her eyes, the cat breathed darkness over her body and First Teller slept.

Blood dripped from First Teller's wounds. Three drops

51

rolled down the rock to the sea. The first became a dolphin, the second a shark, the third a crab with the secret of First Teller's birth inscribed on its back. The crab dived. It dived to the bottom. First Teller never saw it again.

First Teller said, 'The air needs creatures, too.' She breathed in all directions. The winds sprang out from their hiding places behind his teeth. He spat. A crow flew above his head.

Finally he reached the summit. She stood on top of the mountain.

First Teller closed his eyes. She closed her eyes. She pressed her hands against her eyes. She sat down. With the dog and cat on either side, with the snake around her feet, with the crow on his shoulder, he sat down and closed his eyes.

He stayed inside. For longer than ten breaths of the universe he stayed behind his eyes. She travelled. She crossed the boundaries. She set down the landmarks, the names and the faces, he broke the fire and scattered the pieces. At the end, when all the places had crumbled, First Teller stood in a tunnel. The walls curved black overhead, and at the end shone a white door.

In two steps the Teller reached the door. Both hands pulled it open. She stood at the bottom of Chaos. He breathed the water of the sea. One leap took him to the base of Vision. A second carried him to the peak.

The dream Teller sat before the silent body. They examined each other's faces, they touched the arms and the legs. When they made love they joined together.

With a sweep of her arm First Teller spun out the sky. A stamp of his foot created the Earth. His right eye sprang from his face to become the Sun. Her left eye became the Moon. His thousand teeth became mountains, her million hairs the trees. Milk from her breasts formed the seas, saliva from his mouth the rivers and lakes. First Teller shouted. The skin opened and the bones lifted into the sky. They became the stars and planets. They copied the Sun and the Moon, they were small but they became large when they escaped the Earth.

Finally the Teller gave his penis to the dog, her vulva to the cat. The cat set the female organ like a gate. The dog pried open the door. He opened it and creatures came through. They crawled or flew or swam. At the end a woman and a man fell through the gate. Someone had pushed them and they fell through the gate. The gate closed behind them.

The world frightened them. The Sun burned them, the night froze them, the creatures around them shrieked and growled and hissed. The woman and the man held each other and tried to hide behind a rock. First Teller appeared to them. They saw his face in the sun, they heard her speak in the rain. 'You are my children,' she said. 'I have made this world of dreams and you to celebrate it.'

In this way First Teller created existence from her imagination. He created it from his body. It will not last. The creatures will die, our children will die. The light will grow tired, dust will cover it. The mountains will lie down, the rivers and seas will forget their places. They will drift apart into the grey air.

From this weariness a new First Teller will awake. He will awake. She will touch herself. A new world will begin.

3

Jennifer Mazdan sat on a pink plastic folding chair in Gloria Rich's living room. By her side, on a narrow metal stand, stood an empty coffee cup and a plate with a half eaten piece of Founder's Cake. Jennie poked at the cake with her plastic fork. If only Gloria would buy the Sara Lee version instead of trying to bake her own. She examined the size of the remains, hoping she'd eaten enough so that Gloria wouldn't ask if she was ill. Shifting in her chair Jennie made sure not to moan, or cry, or shout, or do any of the other things she wanted to do (such as going home), but instead look eager and attentive. Or at least not so depressed.

Excerpt from THE LIVES OF THE FOUNDERS:
Miguel Miracle Of The Green Earth

After the liberation of Vera Cruz, Miracle Of The Green Earth (in beauty and truth lives his name forever) saw that the people needed to break with the past. He sent each one a dream in which a yellow dog whispered, 'Break down the storehouses, burn the food, the world begins today.' When the people woke up they piled all their food in the streets and burned it. Then they ran to destroy groceries, silos, even the crops waiting in the fields. When they had finished they stood swaying in the morning rain, listening to the wind blowing through their empty stomachs.

At that moment a tribe of Malignant Ones, on the run from the Battle of Dallas, infected the people with a terrible hunger. The people shouted against the Founders. 'We were better off as slaves,' they cried. 'At least then we had food. How can we sing without bread?'

Sadly, the Founder shook his head at the weakness of the people. He stamped his foot and a chasm opened in the town's main shopping street. When people climbed down to investigate they found pieces of cake neatly wrapped in green and white striped paper. The first bite took away their hunger, the second satisfied them completely, and the third sent joy flooding through their bodies.

Months later, when the last cake was finally eaten, the Revolutionary Council of Vera Cruz wrote to Miracle Of The Green Earth, politely asking if he would please restock the chasm for them. They considered themselves entitled to this request because of the sincere efforts they had made to find every piece. The Founder answered only with a letter about the 'honour of commercial realization' and the nutritional value of stoneground bread. The people tore their clothes and lay on the ground, but they knew there was nothing they could do. They planted crops and imported food from nearby cities.

Meanwhile, other communities, jealous of Vera Cruz, burned all their food supplies as well. They then sat down and waited for Miracle Of The Green Earth to rescue them. So many people died as a result of this and other attempts to repeat some saving event that the government issued Proclamation 29, banning the practice of 'forcing the Founders.'

Months later, when food once again filled the shelves of Vera Cruz's kitchen, someone remembered the Founder's instruction about 'commercial realization.' The city organized a contest for the closest replica to the wonderful cake that had saved them. A carpenter won the contest with a mixture of honey, nuts, and cocoa wrapped in green and white paper and boxed in a miniature coffin painted with a picture of Miguel Miracle Of The Green Earth, who had died the week before the competition.

'Founder's Cake' they named it. We still eat it today.

It wasn't enough she'd missed the Recital, now she had to sit in Gloria's living room (central air conditioning turned up too high as usual) and listen to everyone talk about it. All over the hive meetings like this were going on, each one representing a totem block. Jennie and the Riches lived in the Raccoon block, a designation originally revealed to the hive's builder, Jack Abramowitz of the Abramowitz Construction Company, when he was praying for guidance for his bulldozers. According to Mr Abramowitz he'd laid out a plan of the hive and the different animals had all come up to leave their droppings on the appropriate spots on the map. Jennie was never sure what to make of this story, but whether it was true or not, her house belonged to the Raccoons.

The kids all loved their totem. Every Hive Day, and at school Enactments, they would dress up in coonskin hats and long striped tails. For the adults, being a Raccoon meant serving mock coon pie (which Jennie detested) on official days, drinking spring water (which Jennie loved) one day a week, and rigging up the official Raccoon poster whenever the block association came to your house for a meeting. The poster, faded now from its original electric colours, showed a line drawing of a fat-bellied raccoon with exaggerated eyerings, a too-long tail that curled into a question mark, and roller skates strapped to his oversize hind paws. He stood upright with his armlike forelegs bent like a runner's. In flowing pink script the name 'Racy Raccoon' appeared at the bottom.

Originally the poster had come from the publicity department of a television show, but when the first families moved into the hive, Joanna Weston (now dead five years) had found the thing folded up among her daughter's pile of comic books. 'It's an omen,' Joanna told her husband. 'We were meant to use it.' The Riches now lived in the Weston house. Whenever the rota system brought the meeting to Gloria's place she would say that the poster had 'come home.' 'Don't you think his smile gets bigger whenever he comes

56

here?' she'd said to someone just as Jennie was entering the house.

The living room was crowded, filled with neighbours in folding chairs. Gloria and Al and Jim Browning sat on a grey velvet couch. In front of them a glass coffee table held the small silver tea service with which Gloria always served Al, as if he was a visiting dignitary. Endless knick-knacks and souvenir totems from family pilgrimages clogged the bookshelves above the television.

Gloria leaned forward. 'Jennifer,' she said, 'did you say something?'

'No,' Jennie said. 'Nothing. It's okay.' She jabbed a piece of cake and stuck it in her mouth.

'You've hardly said a word,' Gloria went on. 'You know everyone should contribute at a block meeting. Or don't you feel that?'

'I'll say – what I experienced. Later.' Jennie wondered, as she did so often, why she was so weak. Her mother would have put Gloria Rich in her place long ago. Her mother would have shrivelled Gloria into a tulip bulb and planted her in the sacred grove on top of the hill.

Jim Browning said, 'Leave her alone.' He'd been speaking when Gloria interrupted. 'She'll speak when she wants.'

Gloria said, 'A block can't work unless everyone contributes. Especially after a Recital. *Especially* after such an important one. Though of course they're all important.' She frowned, worried she might have said something improper. 'The point is, we're a spiritual family, not just a collection of houses. A spiritual being.'

Next to Jennie, Karen D'arcy rolled her eyes. 'Oh, for God's sake,' she said. Jennie glanced at her. She was never sure what to make of Karen. Like Jennie, Karen lived alone, had done so since her divorce a couple of years before Jennie and Mike had entered the hive. Karen dressed up more than most women Jennie knew; even now, with everybody else in shorts and tank tops, Karen wore a fake-silk sleeveless blouse, a loose skirt of a soft blue and white cloud pattern, and high-heeled sandals. Jennie used to think Karen came round to make passes at Mike, but even with Mike gone Karen would sometimes drop in for coffee. Coffee and complaints about the men who were mistreating her. Jennie suspected that Karen saw her as a compatriot among all the happy families. Her disastrous love life sometimes seemed to Jennie a warning of what could happen to single women.

'No, really – ' Gloria said, 'Jennifer chose not to sit with her fellow Raccoons – '

'She had to work,' Karen said. 'She couldn't get there till late.'

'I'm not condemning her. Not at all. It's certainly not my place to condemn another Raccoon. I'm sure she can add to our experience.'

Jennie's voice came out louder than she planned. 'I told you, I'll speak later.' She blushed at her own anger.

Gloria sat back. 'I didn't mean anything,' she said.

'Can we go on?' Jim asked.

Karen whispered to Jennie, 'Good shot.' Jennie tried not to smile as she watched Karen pretend to sip her cold coffee. There was something very attractive about the way Karen's black hair threatened to come loose from the sloppy twist she'd fastened with a wooden slide.

Jim was saying, 'Nobody's claiming it wasn't a powerful experience. If you ask me, it was a little too powerful. More like terrifying.'

'Even terror has a place,' Carol Blinker said. 'Didn't Joybirth say, "We swim in terror like a freezing sea"?' Carol thought of herself as a scholar, though she mostly read popular histories from *Reader's Digest* or *Time-Life*. Jennie had tried to talk to her a few times but had never got past Carol's distrust of Jennie's two and a half years of college.

'Well maybe the Tellers swim in terror,' Jim said, 'but they don't have to drown us in it.'

Al Rich said, 'Are you saying we should dictate to the Tellers what Pictures they choose and don't choose for the Recitals? Is it our place to "tell the Tellers"?' He smiled at the quotation, then puffed on his pipe. The bowl was carved into a likeness of Allan Lightstorm's face; as the tobacco flared into life the Teller glowed with health and happiness. According to the manufacturer, each time you smoked the pipe you extended the Teller's life span by ten seconds, twenty if you used sanctified tobacco from the SDA plantations in Virginia. Jennie was sure Al used sanctified tobacco.

'Oh, come on,' Karen said, 'I'll bet his telling "The Place" upset you as much as the rest of us.' While Karen may or may not have made passes at Mike Al definitely made passes at Karen.

'Speak for yourself,' he said, then smiled to show no hard feelings. 'I'll always receive with joy, and, I hope, genuine humility, whatever Picture the Tellers choose to give us. And not just Allan Lightstorm either. Who are we to criticise or rank the Tellers, let alone the Pictures?'

Karen said, 'Al, you wouldn't know genuine humility if it ran up and spanked you.'

Gloria reared up. 'Karen!'

'It's all right,' Al said, laughing with everyone else, as if his day reading had said 'disarm by rueful acknowledgement.' He puffed on his pipe while his other hand boyishly pushed his wavy hair from his forehead.

I've got to get out of here, Jennie thought. She considered

59

locking herself in the bathroom, but she'd done that less than half an hour ago. Gloria watched that sort of thing. Once, at another meeting, she'd come knocking at the bathroom door to ask if Jennie was all right, and Jennie had rushed out, almost forgetting to flush the toilet.

Marcy Carpenter, wearing shorts so tight her thighs ballooned out from them, leaned forward. 'Getting back to what Al said, I think we do have a right. To criticise, I mean. Everyone knows we've asked for years for someone like Lightstorm. And we showed our appreciation, didn't we? With all those parades and everything? He didn't have to tell . . . that one. He could have told, I don't know, "The Woman Who Walked On The Sun." Everyone would have liked that.'

'I'm sure they would have,' Gloria said, 'but that's hardly our choice.'

'Of course not. But – ' She stared down at her lap. 'You know how you all felt. From the Picture, I mean. Sort of scared and a little sick? Well, I had my period – '

'Marcy – ' Her husband Sam tried to take her hand, but she pushed it away.

'Let me finish,' she said. Everyone was looking at the floor, or their empty coffee cups, all but Jennie, who found herself staring at Marcy's half crumpled face. 'I had my period, and when – the end, you know – '

Again Sam tried to break in. 'Please, honey – '

'Let me finish!' she shouted. 'When the lion – when she's cut open, and, you know, the blood – I just – it was like – oh, shit.' Unable to finish after all, she let Sam take her in his arms. They got up and walked to the door, not saying goodbye. Marcy tripped on Ron Wilson's foot. 'Goddamnit,' she said. Someone snickered. As they were leaving, Sam turned, as if about to say something, then just gestured with his head. He was about to close the door when his wife slammed it. Jennie thought how she could have got away like that if only she'd thought of it first.

'You see?' Jim Browning said. 'That's what I mean.'

Karen said, 'You sure don't let a little sensitivity stop you, do you?'

'There must have been other women, uh, like Marcy. And what about women who were actually pregnant? Wasn't there something on the news a couple of years ago about some woman in Cleveland? She was expecting twins and went to the Recital where the Teller did "The Place." She got such a shock the twins came out monsters and had to be put in that zoo or whatever it is they've got up in Boston.'

Jennie missed the reactions to this information. Certain thoughts were nesting in her head. The Picture – some of the things it involved, a desert, a woman giving birth to monsters, her blood disfiguring the Earth – In some funny way they resembled pieces of Jennie's dream. Wasn't there a desert at the end of the dream somewhere? And didn't her body crack open, with milk pouring out of her? The opposite. Her dream was the opposite of Li Ku's Picture. In the story the woman's blood kills the land, and in the dream Jennie's milk – and her body falling apart – brought life. She remembered the coloured fish and the birds flying out of her womb. In some way, her dream answered the story. *That's why no one ever understood it*, she thought. *I hadn't had my dream yet.*

Jennie whimpered. It was bad enough to think of her dream as somehow caused by Lightstorm's telling, but an answer . . . 'The Place Inside' was one of the Prime Pictures, not some little training story, but a Prime Picture. Found in the Days of Awe. By Li Ku Unquenchable Fire. Even the Living Masters, people

61

like Allan Lightstorm and Greta Airsong, even they didn't dare to change one single word. Or gesture. Or noise. Nothing. So how could Jennifer Mazdan, college failure, annulled marriage, shame of her mother, think that *her* dream could in any way –

Jim Browning said, 'You all know I've got a cousin who works in the main New Orleans hall.'

'Really?' Diane's husband Mark said. 'How come you never told us before?'

'Very funny,' Jim said. 'I just bring him up because it gives me a little special insight none of the rest of you have.'

'Sure,' Karen said. 'And a little special status too.'

Jim said loudly, 'According to Tommy, the Tellers themselves sometimes argue over 'The Place.' And not just because no one likes to tell it. Some of them don't really understand it.' There was a silence; everyone seemed to look at the floor or around the room. 'I mean, that Meaning. You know. Everyone knows it doesn't make any sense.' Again no one spoke. 'Oh hell.' Jim sat back. 'You all know I'm right. You just don't want to admit it.'

Marjorie Kowski leaned forward. 'What Jim said,' she started timidly. 'About the Meaning. And the Tellers.'

'Maybe we should drop it,' Ray put in.

'Well, no,' Marjorie went on, with a forcefulness unusual for her. She tended to prefer rumours to meetings. 'This is our block. Shouldn't we say whatever we think? We're all Raccoons, aren't we?' No one argued. 'Then shouldn't we say whatever we think?'

'It's not a matter of suppression,' Al said.

'No?' Karen asked.

'No, it's not. It's just that as Raccoons together we should all help each other to follow the correct ways.'

Marjorie persisted. 'But if Jim says even the Tellers talk about it – '

Diane said, 'That's just what his cousin says.'

Marjorie's husband Arthur threw a few threatening glances around the room. 'What's the matter with you people, anyway? Is this a Raccoon meeting or not? If Marge wants to say something, let her. She's not going to poison anyone.'

Everyone looked at Marjorie, who looked at her hands gripping her paper coffee cup. 'Well,' she said, 'this is actually something I've thought about before. Actually, I've thought about it for years.'

Jennie felt embarrassed. Marjorie went on, 'The first time I heard "The Place Inside" I was – twelve, I think. That's right, because it was the Summer before my last Summer in camp. Anyway, I got very sick. My mother had to call in the healer. There wasn't much he could do, because he couldn't drive out what was hurting me since it was a Prime Picture. Well, I got better of course. You know how they say the Picture leaks out of your body and that's why there's got to be regular Recitals. But the thing was – Oh, I'm sorry . . .' She'd gestured with her hand and some of the cold coffee had spilled on the rug. Now she put the cup down on the plastic stand between her and Mike, and began to dab at the spot with her napkin.

'It's all right,' Gloria said, annoyed. She went to the kitchen for a rag.

'Go on,' Ray told Marjorie.

Marjorie picked up the cup, quickly put it down again. Her hands seemed confused without the prop. She said, 'Well, when my mother tried to comfort me, she thought it was the story that had upset me. The healer too. He said it had got trapped in my head and couldn't travel down my nervous system and that's why it hurt. But it wasn't the story. It was the Meaning.

63

I couldn't – I couldn't accept that it justified such, such horrible things.'

Al said, 'They shouldn't need justification.'

'Then why have a Meaning at all? I could have accepted that. If the Teller just said, okay, here it is, it's horrible, but it doesn't – But they don't say that. They give us this, this Meaning, this lesson, that's supposed to, to uplift us or something – And it doesn't. It just doesn't.' She started to cry. Her husband put his arm around her.

'God,' Mark mumbled. 'First Marcy, now her. Some Recital.' His wife hissed at him to shut up.

Anne Hatter, who with her girlfriend Jackie Schoenmaker was new on the block, said, 'Didn't the Meanings come later? I mean, after the Founders had already told all the Pictures?'

Carrie Perkins said, 'Yes, of course, but that doesn't make them any less true. Remember, the Council of Guadeloupe made that its first pronouncement, that the Meanings constituted a revelation as true as the Pictures themselves. "Inseparable and indivisible" they called it.'

Carrie's statements often conveyed a schoolteacher quality. Older than most of the others, Carrie and her husband Marty had raised two kids, and when both boys had left home they'd taken in foster children captured from the kid gangs roaming the cities. People resented Carrie, and sometimes joked (when she wasn't there) of expelling her from the hive on a charge of sanctimoniousness.

As if Anne's contribution had given her courage Jackie spoke up. A small round-faced woman, she was wearing a man's long shirt as a dress belted with a plastic snake. 'The Teller who first found the "The Place", she was that really strange one.'

'Well,' Al said, and tried to blow a smoke ring, 'you

could use that expression. But I don't think it's really up to us to make judgements on the Founders.'

Jackie sighed. 'I'm sorry I said anything.'

'Now, Jackie,' Gloria said, 'Al didn't mean anything nasty. When you've been in the Raccoon block a little longer you'll realize that.'

Jackie flashed her girlfriend a look, as if to say, 'This hive stuff was your idea. I wanted to join the Women's World collective outside Wappinger's Falls.' She went on, 'All I meant was it helps us accept how strange the story is when we think of the Teller. Li Ku Unquenchable Fire.' She shuddered slightly. 'She tied herself to that ferris wheel.'

To herself Jennie quoted, ' "And screamed in such a piercing voice that all the trees split in two and all the windows melted for five miles around the amusement park." '

'I still think,' Al said, 'and I don't mean this personally, Jackie, that it's not our job to judge the Founders.' Jackie shrugged and sat back.

It was funny, Jennie thought. They all hated it, but none of them wanted to say so right out, not even Marjorie or Jim.

Mark Chek said, 'Look, we're not really getting anywhere. I don't know about the rest of you loafers but I've got to get to work tomorrow.'

A couple of people mumbled agreement. Anne Hatter gulped down her coffee. Jennie didn't want to get up until someone else did. But just as Karen was getting to her feet Gloria said, 'Now wait a moment.' She smiled. 'We're all Raccoons here together, and I don't think we should be so careless about each other's needs.'

'What?' Karen said. 'Get to the point, Gloria. We're tired.'

Gloria sipped her coffee. 'Well, it's just that we

65

haven't given Jennifer a chance to speak. We've all been talking so much she hasn't got a word in.'

Jim Browning made a noise.

Al's face formed some expression or other. He said, 'I don't know about anyone else, but I think we owe Gloria a vote of thanks. I know I'd feel pretty low if I suddenly remembered we hadn't given Jennifer a chance to say anything.'

Karen said, 'Jennie, you better tell them something or we'll never get out of here.'

All the lines Jennie had been rehearsing dropped from her mind. Looking straight at Gloria's smirk she said, 'I didn't go to the Recital.'

Gloria's face twisted. Jim Browning said, 'What the hell?' and Karen made a low whistling noise.

Mark Chek said, 'Great. Now that's settled we can all go home.'

Carrie Perkins said, 'This is not a time for jokes, Mark.'

'I don't understand,' Gloria said. She looked about to cry.

'It's not all that difficult,' Jennie told her. She was shaking, but exhilarated. 'I didn't go to the Recital. I fell asleep and missed the whole thing.'

'You fell asleep?' Al demanded. 'Who gave you the right to sleep during a Day of Truth?'

'Al,' Gloria said. 'Please.'

Al must have thought his wife had grabbed him, because he shook his arm. Pointing his pipe hand at Jennie he said, 'Do you mean to say you stayed in bed on Recital Day?'

'I didn't say that. As a matter of fact, I fell asleep by my car. In the Artbird parking lot.'

'And what about your duty to your block? Did you think of that before you decided you could use a nap?'

'Come on, Al,' Mark Chek said.

Jennie crossed her arms. 'No, I didn't think of my duty. To the hive or anyone else. I was tired.' Deeper and deeper, she thought. What would they do to her?

'So you just snuggled up and took a nap?'

'Actually I fell down in a big lump.'

'No wonder we all got so – such little spirit. We were incomplete. We had a big chunk missing from our block consciousness. We finally get a Living Master here and you decided you'd rather catch up on your goddamn sleep. No wonder Marcy got so upset.'

Jennie said, 'Don't you blame me for everything. You know damn well what's bothering you. It's that story. You're furious at Allan Lightstorm. You wish he'd stayed down on Fifth Avenue. But you're too chicken to say so. And you're just angry at me because I managed to escape the whole thing.' She stood up, trying to be graceful, but knocking over her coffee cup. 'Shit,' she muttered, and headed for the door.

Gloria cut her off. For a moment they danced back and forth, Jennie trying to get around her hostess, Gloria sidestepping to block her. Finally Jennie stood still. 'Gloria, what do you want?'

'You can't leave like this.'

'I'm only going home, Gloria.'

'You're a Raccoon.'

'Do you want me to wear my hat to bed? As a penance?'

'The hive loves you.' Jennie pushed her aside and stepped out the door. As she walked along the flagstone path to the driveway she heard Gloria calling after her, 'We're not just a bunch of houses. We're an organism. We love you, Jennifer.'

And then Al's voice booming over her. 'You're not going to shit on us and get away with it. We'll strip you from the hive. You bitch.'

4

SOME THINGS THAT HAPPENED AT THAT TIME...

In the town of Rhinebeck, New York that summer, at the Dutchess County Fair, a group of stunt pilots went up in their Old World bi-planes for the annual antique air show. But instead of twenty minutes of mock dog fights the planes flew for seven hours in the pattern of a figure eight tilted on its side. People on the ground saw faces in the two circles, a man on the right, a woman on the left. The woman told the man stories, and the man laughed.

In Brooklyn a mugger waited inside the hallway of a building for an old woman he'd robbed and beaten twice before. But when he grabbed her shoulders to throw her against the mailboxes he couldn't move her, he couldn't even turn her round. And when he tried to let go his hands stuck to her body. She turned her head, and fire filled her face. 'Aren't you ashamed of yourself?' she said. The mugger's hands came loose and he knelt down to beg forgiveness.

Outside Central Park one evening two women from Cleveland, Ohio stepped into a hansom cab for a romantic ride under the Moon. When the driver jerked the reins the horse turned his head and began to speak to them. He told them of the Old World, when people were as empty as forgotten dresses hanging in the closet. He told them how the buildings wept with joy at the coming of the Revolution, and he described how the slaves of the mounted police threw off their owners and pounded down Broadway to greet Ingrid Burningsnake at the Public Theatre.

68

'Soon,' he said, 'we will march again, in the name of Courageous Wisdom.'

After the horse had finished his recital the women rushed from the cab, no longer interested in a ride through the park. They paid the driver (who demanded triple the normal cost of a journey) and then gathered up a lump of the horse's manure. They took it home to Cleveland, where they kept it for the rest of their lives at the foot of their bed in a goldplated box.

At the 14th Street subway in New York City a group of people were waiting for a delayed train when they saw smoke coming out of the tunnel. They'd been waiting for almost twenty minutes and were getting very angry – angry at the missed appointments, angry at the smell of hot uncirculated air, angry at their own decisions not to walk or take taxis – when they saw the smoke and cried out in disgust at yet another tunnel fire, the fifth one that month. A moment later, before they had even turned to go they saw that the smoke did not come from the tunnel walls but from a train that slid into the station with flames spitting out its windows and clouds rolling up its sides.

There was no time to run. They pressed back but the smoke rolled down their throats. Instead of burning they felt only a gentle warmth, like late Spring, and instead of choking they discovered they could breathe more deeply than ever before, as if the smoke had dissolved plugs that had stopped them up all their lives.

They looked and saw that the fire had vanished, leaving the train gleaming brightly. When they stepped inside, the fans – overhead fans with mahogany blades – hummed a song of welcome. When they sat down, the red leather seats sighed with happiness. The train took them wherever they wanted to go, and when they arrived they found they were just on time, even those who thought they were late. People smiled at them, and shook their hands, and said how much they loved them. And everything they ate tasted delicious.

For two weeks after the recital Jennie avoided her neighbours. She was sure they hated her. She was sure they blamed her for everything. They probably blamed her for Allan Lightstorm driving back to New York as soon as he'd done his purification. For two weeks Jennie ate in a diner after her services, then went to the movies or out drinking with some of the women from work. On the Wednesday after the Recital she went with Marilyn Birdan, another Server, to a male strip show, a weekly event held in a bar in Red Oaks Mill. The main attraction – the programme leaflet described him as a doctrinal student from the hermitage outside Wappinger's Falls – wore a mask with Arthur Sweetwind's picture painted on it. While Mar and the other women stuffed five dollar bills into the band of Sweetwind's jock strap Jennie had to struggle not to avert her eyes. She hated being a prude, but somehow it didn't seem right.

The weekend was the hardest. She had to force herself to go out or she wouldn't have had any food in the house. She knew she mustn't keep doing this. If she continued to hide she'd end up scared to look out of the window. 'If you don't face them,' she wrote carefully in her Mid-Hudson Energy assignment pad, 'they'll blame you for everything.'

She remembered the awful months after her annulment, when she never went out except to work or shop. At first, she would watch TV at night, then she found herself afraid to turn it on, in case somebody would hear it and come and knock at the door. And then, after a while, she didn't even read, because someone might see the light and realize she was home. At the worst point, the night that made her realize she had to force herself out, Karen D'arcy had come to see her, and Jennie found herself lying on the floor holding her breath, even after Karen had left, just in case Karen had only pretended to leave but was really waiting for Jennie to expose herself.

She knew she couldn't let that happen again. What would her mother do, she wondered, but she couldn't imagine Beverley living in a hive in the first place. Or sleeping through the Day of Truth. Confrontation, she decided. She needed to confront them.

The second Saturday after the block meeting Jennie was sitting in the dinette in a green and pink house dress, staring at her coffee, when she looked out of the side window at Gloria's place and saw Gloria talking with Karen D'arcy and Joan Bergin, one of the Squirrels from Sacred Mystery Drive. *This is it*, she told herself, and before she could change her mind she threw on a sleeveless yellow sunsuit and rushed outside.

'Hi,' she said a little too soon.

There was a moment's silence, then Gloria said, a little too rapidly, 'Good morning, Jennifer. You're up early, aren't you?'

'You're up, why shouldn't I be?' Karen grinned at her.

'I didn't mean – I just mean – I thought you didn't – I thought you slept late on Saturdays.

'I don't sleep through everything,' Jennie said. Good, she thought. Good. Her panic was starting to subside.

Karen unfolded her arms from across the bib of her overalls to push a lock of hair back from her forehead. 'We were talking about the universal subject. Lawns.'

Jennie wished her laugh sounded more natural. 'I'm afraid I'm not exactly an expert on that,' she said. 'Look at that mess.' She gestured with her hand. 'I think I've surrendered. I'm settling for a nice crop of weeds.' She felt ashamed for a moment, imagining her mother overhearing this conversation.

Gloria said, 'It's not your fault, Jennifer. We know what a rough time you've had the last few years. Still,

71

it would be nice if you could mix some grass in with the rest. For the hive, I mean. It can be a little depressing, you know, to spend all those hours on your hands and knees, digging at roots, and then to look up – '

Karen broke in, 'I'm sure it's the weather. All this mugginess is just right for crabgrass.'

Gloria said, 'You act like it's not possible to grow a decent lawn. Look at that.' She waved a hand at her green rise of neatly clipped grass. 'It's really just a matter of work and prayer, you know.'

Jennie thought, *You bitch. You saw me the other week breaking my back with those weeds. You even stood there and listened to me chanting during the fertiliser offering.*

Karen said, 'Maybe your house is just blessed.'

Gloria tried to appear thoughtful. 'That is possible. Our block's totem originally came from here, you know.'

'If your place is blessed,' Joan said, 'I don't know what mine must be. I can hardly get a crop of weeds. All I ever get is patches of brown earth. When the Squirrels meet at my place in Summer I tell them to come late so they won't see my lawn. It's so embarrassing.'

'What kind of fertiliser do you use?' Jennie asked.

Joan laughed. 'Everything.'

Karen said, 'What kind of Enactments have you done?'

'Every kind I could think of. I drove poor Earl and Jimmy nuts one week waking them up at dawn every day for a Candle Parade round the house. And then – ' She looked around, as if someone might be eavesdropping, then leaned forward slightly. She whispered, 'Then I made Earl go out one night – it was real late, so nobody would see – and, you know, do it on the grass. As an offering to the Mother.' She giggled. 'It

72

took him ages. He said he couldn't get it up for clover and Kentucky blue grass.' She and Karen laughed while Jennie made a nervous noise and Gloria frowned. Joan added, 'It didn't work.'

Gloria said, 'What about guardians?'

'Of course,' Joan said. 'Guardians, fertility mothers, everything. I got one of those sets at the garden shop. You know, wood from each of the national parks, little boxes filled with seeds? Cost a fortune. We planted them all over. Nothing.'

'I just asked,' Gloria said. 'There are some people who think they can flaunt the spirit and the grass will grow anyway.' Her eyes darted at Jennie who pretended not to notice.

'Listen,' Joan said. 'I've got so many little statues around my house Jimmy came in crying one day because he said there was no place he could play without violating a territory. And Earl's mother actually tripped over a Dancer guardian I'd put at the bottom of the back steps. I was terrified she'd broken her leg and would end up staying for weeks.'

Gloria said, 'I don't think you should call them statues.'

'Come on, Gloria,' Karen said, 'what do you want her to call them?'

'Their proper names. Guardians. Or Living Beings. That *is* what they are.'

'And what's going to happen if she calls them statues? Will they blast her kids at the bus stop?'

'Karen!' Gloria said.

'I'm sorry,' Karen told her, 'but sometimes, Gloria . . .'

Jennie said, imitating Gloria's sugary tones, 'The inner feeling is more important than the words, you know.' Karen laughed. Joan looked embarrassed. Jennie thought that her mother would be proud of her.

73

Gloria said, 'But really, she did say her lawn refused to grow. Maybe if she didn't speak that way – '

'I don't know,' Joan said. 'I think it's something in the lawn. After the Recital last week I wondered if the real being I should pray to was He Who Runs Away. Or maybe Li Ku herself. That's what my lawn's like. It reminds me of the desert at the end of the Picture.'

There was a silence and Jennie found herself wanting to run back in the house. Instead she said, 'What did you think of the Recital?'

'What did I think? It was very good. I guess.' She looked down. 'Well, it was – I don't know, maybe – we discussed it in the block, the Squirrels . . .' Her voice trailed off, and then she said, 'What did you think of it?'

'Me?' Jennie said. She glanced at Karen, who was looking at the ground.

'Yeah,' Joan said. 'I mean, you know, Allan Lightstorm coming and everything, and then doing – that story. Some of the people in our block felt sort of, not really angry, I mean, that would be a transgression, but sort of, like it wasn't really fair. But what did you think of it?'

She doesn't know, Jennie realised. She looked at Karen who still stared at the grass, and Gloria, whose eyes moved back and forth from Joan to Jennie. They hadn't told anyone. They didn't want anyone to know. She said, 'What can I say? It is one of the prime Pictures.'

'Of course,' Joan said. 'Of course. But you've got to admit – '

'I'd say the Recital had a powerful effect on me. It sort of took me into another world. A dream world.'

Joan said, 'I didn't really find that. That's what I expected. I figured, oh, Allan Lightstorm, he'll really do it. But somehow . . . Anyway, to tell you the truth,

74

I'm glad he didn't do it to me. Like that, I mean. Weren't you scared or anything?'

'Actually, I didn't get a chance to be scared. In fact – '

Gloria broke in loudly, 'I don't think we should talk about the Recital. Outside our own blocks. Isn't that what the blocks are for? You are a Squirrel, Joan, and we are Raccoons.'

Jennie said, 'Isn't inter-block communication supposed to be good for the hive?'

'Of course, Jennifer, of course. But there are some things that are meant just for the block. That's the mystery of block unification. That we all join together into one experience.'

'Well,' Jennie said, 'that's something you probably know more about than me.'

Joan said, 'If you really think we shouldn't talk about it – '

Karen said 'Anyway, we were talking about lawns. I once read that how a person's lawn grows doesn't depend on them. It has to do with the spirits of the people who occupied the land in earlier times. They come back in the grass or something.'

Joan made a face. 'Come back in the grass?'

'You know,' Karen pushed on, and Jennie was sure she was improvising. 'Whether they did good things in their life. Whether they enjoyed it. Or maybe how they treated the land. Things like that.'

'You mean dead spirits?'

Jennie said, 'Of course. You can't ask living spirits to stay in the grass. They could always just move to another lawn.'

Gloria said, 'The people who left the Raccoon totem in my house are dead, but I'm sure the totem was meant for me. For me and Al.'

'But Gloria,' Jennie said, 'That's because Racy

Raccoon is a being all by himself. Those people were just vehicles. To allow Racy Raccoon to reach you. Obviously you and Racy were intended to meet. That must be the reason those people lived there before you. So they could leave the totem for you. The blessed spirit was using them.'

Gloria seemed to find this idea so appealing she didn't want to believe Jennie was faking. 'It is true,' she said, 'that people sometimes think they do something for their own reasons but actually the Living World is using them to manifest itself.'

Karen said, 'You sound like you're reciting something.'

'Well, it is true, isn't it?'

'Imagine,' Jennie said. 'Those people living here all that time, paying their mortgage, voting on taxes and school bonds, maybe arguing with each other or thinking when their kids grew up it was time to leave or something, and the whole time, even their getting married and having kids in the first place, even growing up and going to school or work or a baseball game or wherever they met each other, even their *parents* meeting each other, all that, just so they could leave that poster there, and Gloria and Al could move in with it.'

Gloria's face tightened, but before she could say anything Joan said, 'I once left my Name beads on a plane. I always get scared on planes and like to count the Names, and anyway, when I left, I knew I'd left them but something stopped me from going back to get them, and I had the strangest feeling. Like someone, a cleaner or someone, was meant to find them. That maybe those beads had some special purpose for that person and I was meant to leave them there.

'I'm sure you were,' Gloria said. 'Some people might

think such things are silly, but if you respect the spirit world – '

'The spirit world respects you?' Jennie said.

'Exactly.'

Joan laughed. 'Then why doesn't my lawn come up? Maybe the last person to live there was an axe murderer.'

Karen said, 'Or a hypocrite.' She glanced at Gloria. 'Remember what Adrienne Birth-of-Beauty said, "Hypocrisy is the lock that bolts shut the door." '

'I've always loved that one,' Joan said. 'The Shout, I mean.' Jennie thought, *me too*. As a child she must have read the chapter on 'The Shout From The Skyscraper' thirty times. It still gave her shivers to think of the Founder clinging to the giant radio antenna, and her voice so strong everyone could see their bones under their skin.

'Sometimes,' Joan said, 'I think about just that part of it too. The thing about hypocrisy. I mean, we're all sort of hypocrites now, aren't we.'

'What do you mean?' Karen said.

'Well, even the Tellers. They're not – you know, they're not like they used to be. Not like the Founders, anyway.'

There was a silence, then Karen said, 'I wonder what it was like to live then. With all the miracles.'

Joan laughed. 'I think it must have been very scary.'

Karen sighed. 'Maybe that's why the miracles stopped.'

Gloria said, 'Maybe they stopped because of the transgressions of the worshippers.'

'No,' Jennie said. 'It's got nothing to do with that. Transgression.'

Joan asked, 'What do you mean?'

'I don't know. It's just – I don't know.'

77

For a moment they all stood there, then Joan said, 'I guess I better get back to my transgressed lawn.'

When Joan was safely around the corner Gloria turned on Jennie. 'You're really determined, aren't you? You just want to ruin the whole block.'

Karen said, 'Gloria, stop exaggerating.'

'You heard her. She was positively flaunting herself.'

Jennie smiled. 'I thought you loved me, Gloria.'

'What?'

'At the meeting. I wanted to go home and go to bed, but you wouldn't let me. You told me how much you loved me.'

'The hive. I said the hive loves you.'

'Aren't you part of the hive?'

'Of course, of course. But – you're the one who's not part of the hive. Who just goes off and does what she wants. You're just trying to twist the hive's love. If you loved your block you would have gone to the Recital.' She looked around to make sure no outsiders had been hiding when she'd said the forbidden words.

'By the way,' Jennie said. 'I'd thank you for not telling the others, but I'm pretty sure you didn't do it for my sake.'

'It was a group decision,' Gloria said.

'Actually,' Karen said. 'Most of them just didn't want anyone to know.'

Gloria said, 'Why should outsiders know? It's bad enough you letting us down like that. Why should we broadcast it to everybody?'

Jennie waved a hand. 'I've got to go, ladies. Saturday's my errand day.'

'Sure,' Gloria said. 'Just traipse off like that. Just like you did at the Recital. And the meeting.'

Karen said, 'See you, Jennie.'

Back in the house Jennie thought about the look on Gloria's face when she'd said that about being trans-

78

ported to a 'dream world', or the part about Gloria loving her. She sat down on the couch in front of the picture window. Leaning back she remembered how she used to scold Mike for resting his head on the cushions. Without any conviction she reminded herself yet again to stop thinking about him. She laughed. Mike should have been there. He never could stand Gloria.

She stretched out her legs and kicked off her sandals. She should turn on the air conditioner. And close the door. Bar the mugginess from the house. She smiled, remembering Gloria's face when she'd realised Jennie was making fun of her.

Why had she said that? About transgressions not mattering. What *did* she mean by that? It had something to do with the dream. In the dream the fish came and saved them and it didn't matter whether they'd sinned or not. The fish didn't care. And the end, when she – when the milk and all the creatures came out of her – it wouldn't have mattered what sins she'd done – if she'd killed people, or burned all the guardians on the Main Mall, or maybe become a saint, stopping bombs in mid-air by the power of her holiness. The creatures didn't care. They just wanted the milk.

It's like 'The Place Inside', she thought. *At the end, the woman doesn't deserve what happens to her. That's the reason everyone gets so upset, it's not just because it's horrible, it's because they think* – she strained to catch hold of the idea before it slid away from her – *it's because she's like them, an ordinary person, and then this thing happens to her. Something she doesn't deserve.*

But none of us deserve it. None of us deserve anything that happens to us. Good things too.

This was crazy. Soon she'd set up a box by the Founders' Urinal and start preaching sermons.

The Founders' Urinal. The county offices building.

Jennie put her sandals back on and went to the dinette for her bag. She checked to make sure she had her keys and then went outside and got in the car. As she started the engine she thought how she should have done this days ago. What else do you do when you get a strange dream, but check it in the catalogue?

5

She parked the car in her usual spot by the county offices building. With most of the agencies closed for the weekend the building was almost deserted. A couple of tourists were taking pictures of the Urinal, but there were no pilgrims. Outside the door a dog slept, his tongue hanging out before him.

Inside the glass doors Jennie turned left to the stairs, too impatient to wait for the elevator. The ground floor belonged to the Motor Vehicle Bureau, the second to the computers and file systems and giant bound books of the Records Office. On the third Jennie walked down a corridor with closed doors on either side until she came to a green metal door marked, 'National Oneiric Registration Agency.' Inside, a woman sat behind a wooden counter, reading a newspaper. 'Good morning,' Jennie said.

The woman continued to read. Feeling silly, Jennie sat down on one of the two wooden chairs set against the wall. The woman's stool must have been quite high because Jennie found herself looking up at her. After a while she said, 'Excuse me, I'd like to do a dream search.'

The woman sighed. 'Obviously,' she said, and tossed the paper on the counter. A thin woman, about twenty or a little older, with a slightly curved spine, she made a face and grunted softly as she tried to reach to the side for something. 'Damn,' she said finally, and got off the stool. She bent down, then came up with a long sheet of paper. 'Fill this out,' she said, and jumped back on her seat to pick up her newspaper.

Jennie thought that that was why she hadn't done a check before. Paperwork. Paperwork and the legendary courtesy of NORA officials. The questions, in green type, began with the usual, name, age, occupation, and went on to things like 'date of last search' (as if anyone could remember) and 'spiritual training; give details.' Certain she was getting everything wrong, Jennie filled it out by the counter and held it out to the clerk.

'Relax,' the woman said. 'I'm sure your dream's very important. But you've already had it, huh? It won't go away.'

'I might forget it.'

'You didn't write it down? Well, that's your problem. Only, I hope you don't fudge the details or you won't get an accurate reading.' She heaved herself off the stool like someone twice her age and size. Taking the form and her newspaper she walked through a door behind the counter. About five minutes passed, and Jennie wondered if the woman had gone for lunch. Finally she came back; she had a paperback novel in her hand.

'Nothing much in the news?' Jennie asked.

'Nope,' the woman said. 'Same garbage as usual. The mayor claims Allan Lightstorm's gonna come back next Recital. Claims he liked Poughkeepsie so much. That's just what we need, to have some big New York name come tell us "The Place" once a year. Thanks a lot.'

'I don't think he tells the same Picture every recital.'

'Once is enough.' She waved a hand. 'Go down to Room 5'

Room 5, a couple of doors down, was a cubicle even smaller than the NORA office. The single chair filled almost the whole space before a light green wall containing a roughly nine-inch white square. Above the square was a pink light bulb. A sign next to it read,

82

'Do not speak until the light goes on and you hear the buzzer. Recite your dream in clear even tones. Try to make the details precise and simple.' Startled, Jennie realised she still expected to have to type it out onto a terminal. She knew they'd changed the system. She remembered all the stuff on TV about NORA's new 'voice registration software.' Actually facing it, however, was something else.

She wished she'd rehearsed at home, in front of a mirror or something. The light flashed on and a loud buzz made Jennie jump. She began speaking, too loud and too fast, about the river and the people shouting at her. She realised that that wasn't the beginning and stopped. She took a breath. Hoping she hadn't messed it up completely she said, 'I'm starting again. Don't count that other part.' She added, 'Sorry,' then felt even more stupid, apologising to a computer. Sitting up straight she began the dream again, very slowly, trying to get everything right. Finally she said, 'That's it,' and stood up, wondering if the light would flash again or something. After a moment she grabbed her bag and returned to the office, where the woman sat curved over the counter, reading her book. Jennie asked, 'How long will it take? Before I get a reading, I mean.'

'The usual. Haven't you ever done a search before?'

'Sure,' Jennie said. 'But not in a while.' She added, 'I've never done it that way before. I mean, by voice.'

'Makes no difference,' the woman said. 'Come back in about twenty minutes.' Jennie nodded and went out. She crossed the street and walked half a block to the diner next to the old turreted armoury with its red brick walls and heavy arched door. The diner was long and narrow, a stuffy place with greasy food and good coffee. Sitting on a stool near the back she wished she'd brought a book or borrowed the clerk's newspaper. All she could think of was the dream and the way it connected to Li Ku's Picture.

She heard a noise outside and walked with her coffee to a front booth where she could look. A marching band was coming up Market Street, drummers and brass in front followed by a whole line of high-stepping girls in fluorescent red boots. The girls looked beautiful, Jennie thought, with their bare breasts painted in Sun bursts and Moon phases, with stripes running down their arms to their fingertips, like rippling rivers ending in five bright tributaries. The oil on their arms (to prevent Malignant Ones fastening on to them) made the muscles flash.

Jennie wished she could join them, with no worries other than remembering the 'constellations.' She knew that that was what the girls called the patterns made by the striped stick with the (plastic) skull of a small bird mounted on either end. You had to get the twirls just right or else the blessing on the street would go wrong and there'd be car crashes the following weeks. The girls didn't seem to worry. As more and more people came to watch they stepped higher, grinning as the sweat and oil ran off them.

Jennie stepped outside the door of the diner to get a better view and to hear the chant more clearly. They were doing 'Sight', the one based on Adrienne Birth-of-Beauty and her 5th Proposition. It was what they called a progressive chant, with each repetition getting faster and louder.

See what there is to see
Hear what there is to hear
Touch whatever you touch
Speak the thing you must speak
For your teeth are mountains
Your fingers forests
Your eyes are the oceans of life.

84

I'd love to do that, Jennie thought, then felt silly. She must be regressing, wanting to do the things she was too shy to do in high school. She laughed, then blushed in case anyone might think she was laughing at the Enactment. Anyway, if she'd tried to join a marching band in school her mother probably would have stopped her. She probably wouldn't have passed the test.

The band made its way down the street and Jennie went back inside. After the tenth check of the clock above the shelf of stale cake, she decided it was time to go back.

The woman was waiting for her. Not reading a book or paper, just sitting there with the printout in her hands and squinting at Jennie as soon as she walked in. 'You made that up, huh?'

'Made what up?' Jennie said. She put out a hand to take the sheet, then pretended she was flicking her hair off her face when the woman held it away from her.

'The dream,' the woman said. 'The so-called dream. You didn't really dream that. You made it up.'

'No.' Jennie wondered what the woman was talking about. 'Of course I dreamt it.' She was sure now that something horrible had come up. 'Let me see that,' she said, and grabbed the printout.

Jennie glanced quickly at it, then read more slowly. She said, 'This isn't possible.'

'Oh really?' the woman said.

'But I did dream it. I did.' She stared again at the sheet. The computer had broken the dream into 'elements' as it always did, but instead of the usual listing of 'concurrences', that is, how many people in the past three months had reported something similar, followed by several paragraphs of 'reference, significance, and analysis' the only words beside any of Jennie's elements were 'no reference.' About the fish –

no reference. About the Persian carnival and the food stalls – no reference. Even the desert at the end – no reference. *This is crazy*, Jenny thought. Even I can see the reference to the Picture, why can't the stupid computer? She said, 'There's got to be some mistake.'

The woman said, 'Sure. You dreamed something and the NORA computer can't find anything about it in any of its banks? Come on, huh?'

'But I did dream it.'

'Sure, that's right,' the woman said. 'Listen, that computer's got every kind of dream anyone's ever dreamt. No one can dream something they can't find and reference. You can't even make something up like that.'

Jennie stared at the sheet again. Even the part about her walking by the Hudson River full of fish. How could that come up no reference? There had to be something in her dream – something deep inside – that made it so strange even the most ordinary parts were – were different somehow. She couldn't see it, but the computer could.

'When did you dream this wonderful dream?'

'Recital Day,' Jennie said, and wished she'd lied.

'Yeah? Maybe you'll tell me next it was a special present from Allan Lightstorm. Look,' she said, and Jennie stepped back slightly. 'This is a holy office. Do you understand? Next time you want to play some trick, you go and take it down to the Tellers' residence. They're used to bullshit around there.'

Outside, Jennie stood squinting at the Sun coming off the concrete entranceway. The dog had crawled under a wooden slatted bench and lay on his side with his tongue out. A skinny teenager with cropped blonde hair and tight jeans and a black muscle T-shirt sat on the opposite bench smoking a cigarette. Jennie looked at the printout as she fumbled on her sunglasses. 'It's not possible,' she said.

'Sure it is,' the teenager said. 'Anything's possible. That's the whole fucking point.' He laughed as Jennie rushed away.

She got in her car and drove out of the parking lot heading south. At the corner of Teller Street and Market Street she stopped for a light. To the right lay the wide road leading to the Mid-Hudson Bridge and beyond that the Catskill Mountains, grey in the haze of the Sun. On the other side of the road some boys were playing basketball on the YMTA outdoor court.

Jennie looked at the printout sheet lying beside her. 'Shit,' she said. She crumpled the paper up and threw it at the windscreen.

That night, Jennie was scrubbing grease off the broiler pan when a strange thought came to her. It wasn't Mike's idea to annul; something had made him do it, something that wanted him out of the way. The same something that gave her that dream. She dropped the tray and pad in the sink, splattering filthy water on herself. Instead of dabbing cold water on the spots she sat down on a dinette chair. *This is crazy*, she told herself, while behind her the water ran in the sink.

What had Gloria said? That people think they do things for their own purpose, but really some agency is using them for some deeper purpose. Not everybody and not all the time. Just people in particular situations at particular moments, when they can do something useful without even knowing it. Like Joan leaving her Name beads on the plane.

Gloria was a pompous idiot, but that didn't change the principle. And it wasn't an unknown, or even such a radical idea. Jennie had studied it in college, in Correct

87

Doctrine, when they'd had to read *The Dialectic of Ignorance and Certitude*.

Something had grabbed hold of Jennie. And that same something had got rid of Mike. However much he himself believed his conscious reasons for annulling their marriage, however real they seemed to be, they were manufactured, no, manipulated, no, she couldn't find the right word. The point was, Mike had been in the way. That's all there was to it. With Mike around she couldn't have the dream. Why, she didn't know, but she was sure of it.

She discovered the dish cloth in her hand, and without thinking dabbed at the front of her blouse. How could they – it – do something like that. Push her around, get rid of her husband. No. The idea was ridiculous, absurd.

With a groan she got up to turn off the tap. A moment later she realised she hadn't finished the dishes and turned it on again. As she got back to work on the broiler pan she thought, *It's true. I'm sure it is.* An image came into her mind. She saw again the coloured fish from the dream as they swam out of her, and she saw the people rise into the sky, and as she saw these things the anger and fear lifted out of her, almost against her will, and her body seemed so light she became scared she'd float up and bang her head on the ceiling.

But when the strange sensations passed she discovered she was angry again. 'Keep out of my body,' she wanted to shout, and even though she wasn't sure what she meant she knew that this thought was hers, not anything put there by any outside force. She scrubbed the pan harder.

Two days later Jennie had just finished a service at the Hospital of the Inner Spirit north of the city and was standing by her car when an ambulance pulled up to the emergency entrance. Two para-healers jumped out of the back to open the door to the hospital. The Sun sparkled on the white make-up covering their faces and arms. Jennie watched as they reached in for the stretcher. The woman lying there stared at the sky, her eyes so wide one of the paras had to shield them with his hand to keep the Sun from burning the retinas. Despite the restraining sheet her body jerked every now and then against the blanket. One of the other paras kept her hands on the woman's ribs to cushion the internal organs. Through the doorway of the hospital Jennie could see a healer and his assistant, waiting for their patient to pass the gate. The healer was breathing deeply, to build up a current for the battle with the Ferocious One who had invaded the woman. On his left arm he wore a puppet of Jaleen Heart Of The World, patron of healers. The purple recital skin reached to the healer's elbow, while the lacquered wooden head bobbed back and forth, ready to begin the work. Behind the healer, Jennie could see the gleam of a sanctified operating table as well as banks of instruments for scanning the woman's configurations.

'Poor woman,' Jennie said, and got in the car. She put the key in the ignition, then let her hand drop. For a moment she sat with her eyes closed, then with a small shake of the head opened them again. She shouldn't have looked. She was too impressionable. As she started the car she remembered her mother telling her, 'You've got a soul like a sponge.' She drove down the highway, past lawns and trees and the edge of a private golf course for the staff. There were no patients visible anywhere, and no healers. Behind her no sound came from the complex of buildings.

6

Odd things were happening to Jennie's body. She missed a period and then another. She woke up nauseous. A pressure on her bladder required her to urinate more often. Her breasts started to tingle and then hurt. When she examined them she noticed that the veins stood out slightly, and that the nipples and aureoles had darkened. Jennie did her best to ignore these things. When her stomach or her breasts forced their attention on her, she worried that a Malignant One might have invaded her body. Though she tried to tell herself that she didn't take the idea seriously she sprayed the whole house with demon-breaker, the perfume made from flowers hateful to Ferocious Ones.

She knew she should go see a doctor. She couldn't seem to make herself phone for an appointment. She was always too tired or too hot to think of such things. The truth is, though it worried her, she didn't really mind not 'flowing' (as Gloria called it in the Raccoons' women's meetings). The heat had continued all through the Summer, the humidity too, despite occasional storms around sunset. Slight nausea and sensitive breasts seemed a fair exchange for cramps and headaches and having to worry about Tampax.

No periods also meant she could skip visiting the women's house at the edge of the hive. From the first Jennie had hated the squat round building with its pink dressing booths, its coffee bar, and its Enactment chamber, an overheated room where the women sat on wooden benches with towels around them while they gossiped about TV, family problems, and whoever wasn't there. In the middle of the floor a hollowed-out circle held a mound of wet mud. Each woman who came in squatted down at the edge of the circle with her legs apart (and Tampax or sponge safely in place), and pretended to 'offer her water to the Earth.' Then she would dab a bit of clay on her arms or legs, or maybe (giggling) her breasts, mumble a prayer of acknowledgement for the mystery, then hurry over to her friends on the benches. The only thing anyone took seriously was the fertility/infertility blessing on the way out. If you wanted a child you said a prayer and rubbed the guardian to the left of the door – a three-foot-high husk with mountainous breasts and hips, and pudgy fingers holding open the vaginal lips. If you wanted to avoid pregnancy you rubbed the sister on the right – the same statue except that the fingers covered the opening.

Jennie didn't know why the women's house annoyed her so much. She didn't think of herself as a prude, and certainly not a purificationist. But it was all so casual, so quick. As a girl she'd learned about the original 'female Enactment', with Ingrid Burningsnake in San Francisco, and the 'winter flowers' that bloomed in Golden Gate park. What would Burningsnake say if she could see these chatty suburbanites hardly going through the motions? Not that it was any different anywhere else. In high school the girls had all talked about boys or practised dance steps, in Beverley's neighbourhood the women discussed relationships and restaurants. But somehow the hive . . . maybe she was just a snob, infected by her mother's contempt for hive dwellers.

So Jennie's periods vanished and she did nothing. One month, two, she tried to ignore the changes in her body. On the day she found out she was pregnant her mother called.

The call came at mid-morning, an odd time, for Jennie should have been at work. She'd woken up that day more nauseous than usual. Sitting on the edge of the bath, wondering if she could throw up, she'd thought of the scolding Maria had given her the day before for sloppy work. When she finally dared to leave the bathroom she'd phoned up and in a voice she hoped sounded as awful as she felt she'd reported herself sick. And so was at home when the phone rang.

'Hello sweetheart,' her mother said. 'How are you?'

'Mom,' Jennie said. 'Why are you calling now?'

'Are you doing something? Shall I hang up and call back a few hours later? Just say yes if you can't talk.'

'No, of course not. It's nothing like that.' Jennie often felt embarrassed at the lack of wondrous tales to excite her mother. 'It's just the time. I mean, usually I'm at work.'

'You know I can never follow such things. People who work the same time every day – ' She let the sentence drop.

'But you never call so early.'

'How do you know if you're always at work?'

Her mother's high laugh made Jennie hold the phone away from her ears. She wished she'd accepted Beverley's offer to call back later. She could have made up some story to placate her mother's sensationalism.

'How are you, Mom?' she said.

'Wonderful. I'm working on a new piece. It explores the sound possibilities in traditional women's work. It's called "Improvisation for Alto Saxophone, Clothes-pegs, and Amplified Washing Machine." How are you?'

'I'm all right.'

'Do you ever think of returning to the city?'

'What a rare question.'

'Don't be sarcastic.'

'I'm very happy in Poughkeepsie.'

'And don't be silly, either.'

'I'm not being silly. I wish you would let go of this ridiculous crusade of yours.'

'What have you been doing?'

'Not much. I went to see a play last week.'

'Oh God, in that place you told me about? With the red satin curtains?'

'People like it.' She remembered sitting in the Bardavon Theatre watching *Murder In The Coven* and whispering to Marilyn Birdan what an awful production it was.

'Alice's new play opens next week. She's very excited about it. She says she can feel a presence in the theatre the last few rehearsals. Benign Ones eating the excess energy created on stage.'

'Maybe she can get them to possess the critics.'

Beverley laughed. 'Or at least their typewriters.'

'Mom, I've got some errands to do.'

'Jen, are you all right?'

'What?'

'I asked if you were all right. Do you find that such a strange question for a mother to ask her daughter?'

'No,' Jennie said, 'I'm fine.'

'Are you sure?'

'Of course I'm sure.'

'Jen, do you miss me?'

'I haven't gone that far, you know. I do come down and visit you.'

'Do you miss me?'

'Yes, as a matter of fact, I often do.'

'I miss you a lot.' Jennie didn't answer. After a pause, Beverley said, 'A vision came at me last week. About you. I wasn't sure I should tell you, but I think you should know about it. That's why I called.'

There was a silence, during which Jennie had to fight

the desire to slam the phone down. She said, 'You'd better tell it to me.'

'It happened across the street. In front of the deli, actually. I was walking to the bead shop and I glanced in the deli. window. To see if they had any of that cheesecake. You know, with the chocolate flakes.'

'Please tell me what happened.'

'I am. Anyway, there was nothing in the deli. All the shelves were empty. Except they gave off light, it was so strong my eyes hurt. At first I thought there were no people either, but then I saw someone. I had to shield my eyes against the light for a closer look, and then I realised it was you.'

'What was I doing?'

'You were kneeling down. On your hands and knees. I think you were scrubbing the floor.'

'Wonderful. Maybe the vision wanted to tell you what would happen if I came back to New York.'

'Please don't joke. This was a genuine vision, it penetrated my whole body. I was black and blue afterwards and I could hardly eat. I still feel sore inside.'

'Was that all you saw? Me scrubbing the floor?'

'No. I heard a growl. I thought you were crying or something, but then I realised it came from the back, the stockroom. Then – an animal came out and leaped on you.'

'What kind of animal was it?'

'A cat. A night cat. Completely black.'

'What did it do?' Beverley hesitated. 'Tell me,' Jennie said.

'It attacked you. It . . . it cut you open. It cut you in pieces.'

'Oh shit.'

'I tried to get inside and help you, but I couldn't find the door. I tried screaming for help, but I don't think anyone heard me. A vision separates you, you know.'

'And that was it? It just cut me up and that was the end?'

'No. There was more. The cat ran off and then the shop filled up with people. And the shelves were full of food. Everyone started eating. I even found myself incredibly hungry. I had to fight not to rush inside. The food was you. It looked like ordinary deli. stuff. Like the vision had ended. But I knew it hadn't. I knew that all those cakes and macaroni salads and turkey rolls were *you*. Everybody was grabbing it and stuffing it in their mouths so fast they hardly had time to swallow.'

'Did they fly into the air?'

'No. Not at all.'

'Go on.'

'There's not much more. I just kept watching them. Except – well, I felt so good. I mean, part of me did. A part I couldn't control. Mostly I couldn't stand to look at it, all those people eating my daughter. There was even that cheesecake with the chocolate flakes. But a part of me – I can't describe it. Just – like everything poured out of me. It was like I'd kept . . . kept all this pain and anger bottled up inside and now it had all drained away.'

'How long did this glorious feeling last?'

'Please don't get angry. It was a vision. How could I control what I felt? As soon as it ended and I realised how horrible it was I started screaming. All these people crowded around, including Alice, who has that dress shop, you know, and I didn't even recognise her. A couple of cops from the precinct house came and helped me back home. Then someone from the SDA came and gave me a check-up. He said they'd never seen anyone with such a low level. Almost no placement

95

at all. He gave me a prescription for sanctified meat, fresh killed from the mountains, and I had to send Mark to pick it up for me. I could hardly move, let alone eat.' Jennie said nothing. Her mother went on, 'I lay in bed for two days, just thinking about it. I couldn't even practise or do my drawing or anything.'

'I'm honoured.'

'Please don't hide behind sarcasm. What do you think it means?'

'How should I know? It was your vision. I'm sorry. I'm just upset.'

'Do you know what I think? I think it means you've got tremendous potential and if you don't use it it will tear you apart. You can't run from yourself, Jen.'

'For God's sake, will you knock off the propaganda?'

'Can you think of a better explanation? Why do you think the vision came to me? And not you? Because I could give it the proper interpretation.' Jennie didn't answer. 'Jen?' Beverley said. 'Are you there?'

'Look, Mom, I can't tell you what I think it means. I don't know. I'll have to think about it.'

'All right. And think about coming home. And think about your potential.'

'Anything else?'

'No. Just be careful.'

'Sure. I'll watch out for black cats in delis.'

'I love you, Jen.'

'I love you too. I'd like to hang up now, okay?'

'Call me when you've thought about these things.'

'I'll call you when I've got something to say. I'm sorry. I didn't mean that the way it sounded. I'll call in a few days.'

'Goodbye, Jen.'

'Goodbye, Mom.' Jen placed the phone gently on the box.

She sat down in a dinette chair. Why didn't her

mother just keep it to herself? From the bedroom a game show blared on the television. Jennie had been watching a soap opera when the phone had rung. She thought, *What do they want from me?* and couldn't think of who 'they' might be. She said out loud, 'I just want a normal life.'

Maybe she should go see a Speaker. Throw some stones or mix up some cards or something and have it all explained to her.

She got up and walked into the bedroom to shut off the television. Her back hurt and she moved heavily. It wouldn't work. The speaker wouldn't see anything. It was just like NORA. No one could tell her anything. She was cut off.

She went into the living room, where she stood looking out of the picture window. Everything looked so normal. Kids playing on the street, a couple of girls on bikes. Alice Kowski was shifting the rocks that bordered the flower patch beside her front door. Down the block Jim Browning was taping a rag doll to his front door. Probably meant to symbolize some gratitude Enactment. She remembered Karen D'arcy saying something about Jim getting promoted.

Jennie gestured at the air with her hand. It all looked so normal. Jim Browning didn't get calls from his mother about people eating him in a deli. Alice Kowski didn't fall asleep on the Day of Truth. 'I just want to be normal,' Jennie said.

The mail van rolled up. The postman shoved something in Jennie's box and drove on. She walked out of the house to the road. Junk mail. Advertisements, bills, requests for money from charities she'd never heard of. The *Holy Digest* informed her she may have already won $25,000 and all expenses paid on a pilgrimage to Hawaii. At least her mail was normal. She grabbed the

Poughkeepsie Journal from the tubular paper box and headed back to the house.

Jennie glanced.at the headlines as she walked up the driveway. With one foot on the step she stopped. An article on the bottom of the page announced that a hook Enactment would take place at the Plaza of the Saints on the Main Mall. By tradition the newspaper didn't give the name of the hooker or describe what favour the Devoted Ones had done for him that he should want to hang himself in payment. The way the article was worded Jennie got the impression she was supposed to know. Poughkeepsie politics, she thought. Maybe it was Jim Browning, giving thanks for his promotion. She laughed.

Jennie knew it didn't matter who was doing it. What counted was the access state. Suspended in the air by wires attached to fishhooks in his back and legs the hooker answered questions with the metaphoric assurance of someone siphoning off information from the Living World. A hooker meant problems solved, advice to the lovelorn, hope for the sick and jobless. All around general help and information. And if anyone needed help – and information – it was Jennie Mazdan.

12:45, the article said. There'd be a mob, Jennie knew. Even if the hooker could tell her anything she probably wouldn't get close enough to ask. She went back in the house and told herself she should forget it, make some lunch. Instead, she went to the dinette for her pocketbook and sunglasses.

In her car, driving up Academy Street and then Blessed Path Road towards the parking lot, Jennie wondered why she was going to see a hooker when she didn't think a professional Oracle could tell her anything. Maybe because of the professional part, she thought. Or maybe she wanted to go to someone who'd been in trouble and got through it.

There were no places left in the parking lot. Jennie thought she'd have to give up and go home but she found a space – illegal, but people were even parking on lawns – in a school parking lot by White Street. She hurried back to the mall. By the time Jennie got there a large crowd had gathered. In Poughkeepsie, most hangings took place, not on the aptly named Hooker Avenue, but here in the 'Plaza of the Saints', where brass statues of five of the Founders (you couldn't tell which ones without looking at the name plates) surrounded a sputtering fountain. Concrete benches for weary shoppers formed a circle around the statues. In fact, most shoppers, and most shops, had deserted Main Street for the highway malls and mini-malls. The few people who came into town – for the camera store, or the sacred costume shop, or the Joybirth Pizza Parlour (a copy of the Washington restaurant where Alexander Joybirth ate twelve pepperoni pizzas and announced he'd consumed the zodiac), usually avoided the benches, leaving them to drunks and addicts. Now and then, for political campaigns, or parades, or hangings, the city cleaned the statues, chased away the vagrants, and hung a few coloured streamers on poles around the fountain.

Today a large crowd had spread up and down the mall from the ring of Founders. People stood on wooden benches, others shouted at them to get down, children climbed on their parents' shoulders. Here and there Jennie saw adults or teenagers wearing masks representing Ferocious Ones, with bulging eyes and fanged teeth. It was the custom to taunt a hooker, at least until the trance took hold. Jennie stood on tiptoe and tried to look towards the centre. She could see the gallows they would use for the hanging, a pre-fabricated metal L. If she squinted she could make out some of the pictures and quotations decorating the side.

Wires ran from the gallows arm down to a few feet above the ground, where the hooks moved slightly in the breeze.

Jennie turned to an elderly man in a linen suit. 'Who is it?' she asked, but the man only rolled his eyes and turned away.

'Don't you know?' a woman said. 'It's Mary Landis.' She added, 'Sticky Landis.' A few people laughed.

Someone mock-scolded, 'Now, now, she was acquitted, you know.' The laughter got louder.

A man said, 'Obviously a miracle.'

'Of course,' the first woman said. 'Why else do you think she's offering herself?'

As Jennie attempted to sidle a bit closer she wondered if it mattered whether or not the hooker sincerely wanted to atone for something. Maybe the power came impersonally. From the action and not the goal.

When the FBI arrested Mary Landis, vice-president of the Poughkeepsie Bird of Light Company, no one expected her to avoid a long prison term. Embezzlement, extortion, bribery of public officials, industrial espionage, even illegal advertising seemed to guarantee a forced penance that would keep her on her knees lighting candles the shape of the Founders for years to come. The *Poughkeepsie Journal* even ran a report that Landis had kept a harem of teenage boys in a trailer off Camelot Road, south of the city. No one took this last charge seriously, though it brought some TV people up from New York; the State stuck to what it considered a sure case.

The very magnitude of Landis's crimes gave her her defence. Describing her actions as 'obscene beyond the point of greed' the defence argued for Malignant possession. A jealous colleague, a competitor, or an ex-lover must have called down a Being to infect her soul. Besides creating a plausible line of argument the approach allowed the Defence to usurp the Prosecution's privilege of luridly describing all of Mary Landis's crimes. The jurors began to lean forward like pets waiting for dinner. So did the Judge.

When the verdict came in 'Not guilty' Mary Landis appeared on a local breakfast radio show to announce she would give an offering, her 'fee' as she put it, to the Benign One who had guided the jurors to the truth. Most people expected a donation, or a decorous pilgrimage (the *Poughkeepsie Journal* suggested a trip to the thieves' sanctuary in Nevada). Some thought she might do a 'shame Enactment' dressed as the Being who supposedly had possessed her (various non-accredited Speakers and card and coin Workers offered to track down the demon). Instead, Mary Landis had decided, as she later told *Newsweek*, 'to hang myself before the people my possessed soul victimised.'

Jennie had pushed and slid nearly to the front when a noise from the back excited the crowd. Barefoot, dressed in a torn tunic of purple suede, her hair knitted into braids with a miniature totem at the end of each one, Mary Landis came stumbling along a path cleared through the mob. People jeered at her or poked her with sticks. Some threw crumpled papers listing her crimes.

'I think she's overdoing it,' said a woman near Jennie. A man said, 'Reminds me of Allan Lightstorm.'

A shout signalled the end of the procession. Now Landis stood still while the attendants ripped off her clothes and then began slapping her with globs of mud flecked with yellow glitter. Despite Jennie's worries a sharp thrill pricked her at the sight of this remnant from the Days Of Awe. In the Revolution's early days a contingent of Barefoot Workers, the zealots who first recognised and followed the Tellers, found themselves

101

chased by the secular government to the shores of a swamp in Tennessee. Panic began to spread among the Workers, especially those who had just 'broken the blood' – given up their families for the truth. Refusing to move, the Founder, Marion Firetongue, stood at the swamp's edge with her eyes half closed as a sign she'd gone 'travelling.' Only when the Workers could hear the yelps of the hounds did Firetongue 'return to her face' as the saying goes. She smiled at the frantic crowd. 'Listen,' she said, 'I will tell you a story.' The veterans sat down, ignoring the approaching dogs as well as the complaints of the newer members. Soon the new ones too slipped into the rapture that marked the Time of Fanatics.

When they emerged the landscape had changed. Behind them, instead of scraggly woods, loomed a wall of rock, from the top of which barked a pack of outraged dogs and confused police. In front of them, instead of the swamp, stretched a field of mud. Still talking, Firetongue stood up and began to stroll across it. The Workers followed as the police emptied their guns into the ooze. Years later, when the government built the Marion Firetongue University Complex, they discovered that the mud could dull the pain of a hanging or one of the other 'hard' enactments.

Unfortunately for Mary Landis the original mud was mostly gone by now; what was left was so diluted that Jennie doubted it would help much against the hooks. She hoped Sticky Landis was doing this at least partly from devotion. Cynicism didn't seem like much of an anaesthetic.

When the attendants finished with Mary she looked like a child's clay sculpture of a woman. A moment later they scraped bare the spots for the hooks. A cold feeling settled in Jennie's groin as the silver fishhooks drifted down and then out of sight. Soon a cheer spread out from the centre of the crowd as the body tilted horizontal, then lifted into the air. There were four hooks, two along the spine, one in each thigh. Jennie could see little triangles of skin pulled up through the mud. Though no wires raised the arms Mary Landis held them stiffly out to the sides. With her head up she looked a little like a comicbook superhero on the way to a rescue.

The questions began while they were still hoisting her up the gallows. Questions about marriage, jobs, children's futures or health, which house to buy, where to go on vacation. There were so many, all of them shouted, with everyone crowding forward, that Jennie just stood there, not even sure what she wanted to ask. Has some power possessed me? Is some agent using me? Did someone make my husband leave me? Most of the hooker's 'clients' waved scarves or flags decorated with pictures of Tellers or public shrines or maybe their personal totems. Supposedly, bright colours could penetrate the trance and make sure the hooker heard your particular question. Jennie had forgotten to bring anything. Stupidly she let the crowd push her backward as they shoved to shout their questions and listen for the hooker's sing-song voice.

'From the spring in your legs to the knife in your heart.' (This to a teenage girl who asked if her friend really loved her.) 'Low, low the water flows, the Sun sings from beneath the bed.' (Advice on buying a house.) 'Seven rows of snakes crawl on the tabletop. Show them your face, they will bite out your eyes.' (A man had asked if someone was after his job.)

Through the crowd people passed out cards or leaflets advertising guaranteed accurate explanations. Some of these touts wore costumes, others had attached flags or pennants to their painted bodies. People used to set up stalls at hook hangings until the competition

103

had become so aggressive the government had banned on-site interpretations.

Only once did someone not accept the cryptic answer. 'Will my son get well?' a woman asked, and the mud face squeaked at her, 'The softest bones snap in the cold. A warm tongue licks off the dirt.'

'I don't understand,' the woman said. 'Will he be all right? Am I supposed to do something? Is that what you mean?'

The hooker said, 'A warm tongue – ' and stopped, as if she realised she was repeating herself.

The woman's husband tried to lead her away, but she waved him off. 'I don't understand,' she pleaded. 'Can't you just explain?' But people were shouting her down or pushing her aside. Finally a policeman threatened to arrest her and she left.

An hour passed, with Jennie still buried in the press of people, and enough questions in front of her to keep the hooker going for a week. She knew she would hate herself if she didn't at least try. But everybody else sounded so certain, with such simple questions. The noise broke only once. A woman, a girl really, had called 'Should I become a Teller?' and the hooker answered, 'Dead mouths cannot talk to a living tongue.' For a moment shock moved through the crowd. Jennie thought, *It's true. Everyone knows it. They're all dead mouths.* But then a man asked 'Will my wife come back to me?' and the carnival continued.

When the attendants got up from the benches to begin lowering the hooker, Jennie still hadn't moved. People pushed each other, even trying to climb on each other's shoulders as they babbled their questions in the last seconds of the enactment. Disgusted with herself, Jennie wished she'd stayed home. The stiff body, its arms and legs still extended, began its slow descent. Jennie thought, *she couldn't have helped me anyway, I don't*

104

even know what to ask. She decided to leave and try to get to her car before the crush.

And instead startled herself as much as anyone when her voice boomed over the cries of the petitioners. 'What's wrong with me?' Everyone turned and stared at her – or so it seemed to Jennie. Why did she have to do that? Why didn't she just stay home? The hooker wasn't even answering.

But she did answer. In a voice suddenly deep and cavernous the mudwoman chanted, 'A fish is swimming in your womb. Your uterus is boiling with colour. A fish is swimming in your womb. The dawn is boiling with colour. A fish is swimming – '

'Stop it!' Jennie screamed, then turned and pushed people wildly out of the way, even some who had already stepped aside. A man tried to give her a card; she slapped his arm. And behind her the voice droned on. 'A fish is swimming in your mud. The Earth is boiling with colour. A fish is swimming in your waters, the sky is boiling with colour. A fish is swimming in your womb – '

7

A Part of a version of THE TALE OF HE WHO RUNS AWAY

He named the mask 'the head of his father' and placed it on his shoulders. He began to run, moving like a hot wind across the pebbles and soil. He came to a village and scooped up rocks to announce his coming. Every stone split a skull or caved in a chest, and when he reached the houses he began to use his hands, so that even after everyone lay dead he clutched at the air for victims, while his feet shuffled like an infant dancing in the slippery street.

Finally he tripped and the mask dropped off him into the torn belly of an old man. The boy stared around him. Who were these strange faces? What were all these strange buildings? Where was his house? All around him a harsh whistling sounded, the arguments of the dead as they tried to establish some rule of place on their way to the new world.

When the boy realised he'd slaughtered the wrong village he thought how tired he was, how he'd have to do it all over again. He went into a mud house to find some food. He was eating a blackened cheese when he heard a thumping noise outside in the street. He peeped outside, frightened the dead had returned to life. Instead, he saw a sight as terrible as the bodies piled in the road. A group of women danced up and down in the street, waving their left fists in the air and pounding their bellies with their right. Dressed in lion skins with lion skulls on top of their shaven heads, and phalluses made of cast iron strapped to their groins, the women only displayed their original gender through an occasional breast visible underneath a sloppily hung skin. The 'lion-men' they called themselves, creatures who lived in the hills north of the Bitter Beach, and they announced in shouts and stamps their allegiance to the Great One who had liberated so many souls in such a short time. From that day they served him, as a force, as a priesthood, until the night he decided to become a wise ruler, beloved as well as feared, and knew he must rid himself of his loyal band of monsters.

They called themselves the Death Squad, and it took them a week to find his village. In that week of murders something strange happened to He Who Runs Away. As he lay at night with the lion-men asleep and the mask behind him an odd purpose awoke in him. He wanted to create the world.

He looked at the stone and dust and he saw paved roads with buses and trucks propelled by blue sails that filled the sky. He thought of the shack where he'd lived with his mother and he saw apartment buildings miles long, with rooms lit by lights plucked out of the sky and hung from the ceilings. He licked his dry lips and tasted water from underground lakes, carried thousands of miles through pipes so wide whole cities could live inside them. By the time he reached his home town he only wanted to fulfil the punishment and begin his true work.

The lion-men herded everyone together and He Who Runs Away shouted, 'I have come on my father's business.' His voice stripped the layers of dust from his victims' eyes so that the sun burned through their closed lids and they saw the world as it really is, a place of such misery they only waited for this strange being to relieve them of life. The Death Squad took up their double-headed axes. Led by He Who Runs Away, they split the villagers' skulls, outdoing each other with the swiftness and elegance of their strokes.

When it was finished, and the lion-men were celebrating, He Who Runs Away sat down to listen to the black birds with white necks who fluttered down to peck at the bodies. In the beat of their wings the killer heard a voice, a teacher who told him about laws and government, administration and bureaucracy. And when it ended its instructions the voice told him how to find the hidden bridge that would take him and his followers across the Sea of Sorrows to the bulk of the world.

The Death Squad rolled across the continents. In each land He Who Runs Away left behind him – along with

107

mountains of dismembered bodies – repaved roads, and district courts, and laws and licences, and progressive and regressive taxes. When he had killed the kings and presidents he turned their palaces into distribution centres for free food, clean clothing, and explanations of the new code of equality and opportunity. Besides supplies and weapons he began to carry paint. When he conquered a city he would wait until night and then send the young women to paint the streets and trees and buildings, so that when the sun rose the people saw a new world brighter than the sky. In a country pockmarked with caves he found a large black rock. He took it with him and called it the Seat of Heaven. Wherever he went he would sit on the rock, draped in black, to hear petitions. When the time came for judgement he would throw off the black cloth and stand up dressed in gold and purple.

The lion-men understood none of this – not why their leader moved so slowly, not why he kept so many people alive, not why he spent so many hours talking, not why he sat on that stone listening to people's complaints. Most of all, they did not understand why he was building an army from all those weaklings. For in each place Son Of A God ordered a tax of young men, stripping them bare and ordering them to flay themselves until their blood washed away their past lives. Then he would kiss each one on the lips and tell him, 'This is your birth, and I am the breath of your life.'

Late one night, while the army camped beside a waterfall, the leader woke the lion-men and whispered to them that he'd discovered a plot to kill him. Silently they followed him into a cave behind the foam of water. It was only when the young men rolled the Seat of Heaven against the cave's mouth that the lion-men realised their god had tricked them. In the darkness they could hear the buzz of the flies as he raised the mask onto his shoulders. Later, when the young men opened the cave, He Who Runs Away handed each of his generals a cast iron phallus wrapped in human flesh.

Jennie Mazdan went to a clinic on Smith Street on the north side of town, to find out what she already knew, that she was two and a half months pregnant.

When the doctor had done the test Jennie sat in the bare waiting room for the results to come through. The clinic was a poor one, with hard benches, torn magazines on a chipped table, and old posters giving advice on spiritual hygiene. Graffiti made the posters half illegible. Through the closed door Jennie could hear a rheumatic patient complain that neither the doctor's pills nor the chants of the healers down the hall had driven the Malignant Ones out of her knees. A few minutes Later Dr Karim called Jennie back for the results.

'The Spirit has breathed its life into your womb,' he told Jennie formally. Jennie closed her eyes and sagged deeper in the narrow chair.

'Do you want a copy of the report?' the doctor asked. Jennie shook her head. 'Do you want me to send a copy to the father?' He was a bald man with a slight potbelly. He wore a stained shirt and no jacket.

Jennie opened her eyes again.

Under his metal desk the doctor tapped his foot on the floor. 'Do you know the father?'

'No. Not exactly.' A moment later she smiled slightly. 'Yes. Yes, I know him.'

'Is this your first pregnancy?'

'Yes. I'm a virgin.'

The doctor half spun round in his seat to stare dramatically at the ceiling. 'I don't think that's very likely.'

'I was married once,' Jennie said. 'But my husband got an annulment.'

The doctor didn't bother to hide his grin. It occurred to Jennie that the doctor assumed her husband had made her pregnant and then pressurised a judge to annul the marriage. 'So you're a virgin,' the doctor said.

'Yes.' She was about to leave when the doctor said,

'There's an Enactment, you know. You're supposed to perform it on the discovery of – '

'No.'

'It's very simple. We can do it right now if you like. Usually the father does it with you, but since you, since you're a virgin – '

'No.'

'Ms. Mazdan, the law requires we do the Enactment within a week of positive lab. results.'

'I don't want any Enactments.'

He sighed, tapping his foot again. 'Enactments join us to the Living World. The Founders gave them to us as actions we can perform to help recognise the Spirit in our lives.'

'I know what Enactments are. You don't have to explain them to me.'

'It doesn't signify a wanted pregnancy, if that's the problem. I mean, you won't be a hypocrite. In fact, even if you get an abortion right afterwards, the Enactment will still apply. More so, actually.'

'No.'

'The Chained Mother will help your abortion. But you have to join with her first.'

'I know. And then join with her in the abortion clinic. That way the abortion signifies the breaking of her chains rather than the denial of life.'

He sat back, unprepared for this sudden eloquence. 'Well,' he said, 'if you know all that, you'll also know you should do it.'

'No!' She got up. 'What do – do I pay something?'

'No, you don't pay something. This happens to be a free clinic. For people who can't afford to pay.'

'I'm sorry.'

'Next time maybe you'll take your problems to someone who has time to waste. I've got patients who need me.'

'I won't bother you again.'

'Please don't,' Doctor Karim said.

On the way out Jennie passed a partly open door. Inside, a healer had begun work on some teenage girl who looked as though she couldn't have weighed more than eighty pounds. Not a 'pure' (the kind who worked without props or systems), the healer had drawn a series of concentric circles with coloured chalks on the wood floor. The sick girl sat in the centre, the 'heart of life', Jennie knew. She'd studied the system in college, and remembered now that the circles represented the different worlds: the Earth, the Sky, the Land of the Dead, she forgot the others. As he travelled through the circles the healer acquired power and knowledge from each one so that when he reached the centre he could clean the girl's soul by pressing his charged hands to her forehead and the base of her spine. Anyway, that was the idea. Jennie caught only a glimpse of him hopping from one circle to the next before an assistant slammed the door.

Outside in her car, Jennie looked at the shabby six storey brick buildings, the people sitting in the folding chairs by the small patches of yellowish grass. Children dashed past the car, shouting in code. Double doors of peeling red paint stood open to let some air into the buildings. Jennie glanced at the totems that squatted above the doors. She wondered if the tenants chose their own building totems, or if the city housing bureau made the choice for them.

'Why did I do that?' she said softly. Would the doctor report her? Probably not. Too busy. She'd never refused an Enactment before. Never.

She looked at her watch. She'd better get back to work, or else she wouldn't reach her last service, a factory, before they closed for the night. As she drove slowly down the street in the direction of the housing

111

project guardian (her excuse to herself for coming to the clinic) she noticed a group of children playing some game which required them to roll around on the grass. She stopped across the road to watch them. A picture game, she saw, for one of the children stood over the others and gestured with her short arms, like a Teller declaiming a story. She wore a necklace of artificial flowers, like the kind kids get in Woolworth's to wear on Founder's Day. A wool blanket was tied around her shoulders – her 'recital skin.' A couple of mothers hovered nearby. They looked worried, as if they feared the game might go too far in some way. Jennie wondered what Picture they were doing.

She drove round a corner. Had she made a mistake refusing the Enactment? She remembered that weird idea she'd had, of some sort of *agency* making her do things. She was pretty sure the refusal had been her own decision.

At the building that housed the guardian she pulled over, then got her equipment from the trunk. No one paid much attention as she walked past the children and old people gathered outside. On the roof the husk looked a little shabby, not quite as gleaming as some of the others. Jennie set to work, spraying it with cleaning fluid and rubbing it down with her cloths.

Outside, she hurried back to her car. She just wanted to finish her rounds and go home. She wished she didn't live in a hive. She didn't belong there, with all those people bound together, going to Recitals together, doing Enactments together. Hell, she thought, if she started refusing Enactments she didn't belong anywhere.

As she approached her next stop, a research lab., she had a sudden pang of missing her father. Jimmy. The Jimmy and Jennie show. She remembered snuggling onto his lap while he read to her from *The Lives*

112

Of The Founders. So long ago. Maybe that was the last time she belonged somewhere. And now she was pregnant. Her very own baby. Hers and – She didn't want to think about that.

That night, after dinner – she'd made herself an egg salad and hardly eaten it – Jennie sat in the dinette with the phone book in her lap, determined to find an abortion clinic and end this nonsense once and for all. But what should she look up? She tried 'abortion', 'pregnancy', 'birth control', even 'marital advice'. Ridiculous. She must know the name, everyone knew it. Named after one of the Founders. Why couldn't she remember? *It's the agency,* she thought. *Bastards.*

'Keep your secrets,' she said, and threw the phone book on the floor. Karen. Last year Karen D'arcy had got pregnant by that guy from the record company, the one who turned out to have a wife in North Carolina. Jennie remembered her surprise that Karen had confided in her. She grabbed her light zipper jacket from the couch and marched outside.

With each step a little of her militancy leaked away. What she was planning was crazy. She should be giving thanks or something. Going on a pilgrimage or something. When she reached Karen's house she nearly walked on, as if she'd just gone out for a stroll. But then her anger returned. They didn't ask her. That was the point. Nobody had asked her. She had to keep herself from pounding on Karen's door like some Hollywood Viking demanding entrance to a castle.

Karen came to the door almost immediately. 'Oh,' she said when she saw Jennie, 'Hi.'

'Are you expecting someone?'

'No, not at all. Come in.' When Jennie had stepped into the little alcove that led to the living room Karen laughed and said, 'Well, to tell you the truth, I wasn't

113

expecting anyone, but I sure was hoping it might be this guy I know.'

'Oh, I'm sorry,' Jennie said. 'Should I go?'

'No, of course not. If I didn't see anyone until Jack came I could apply for hermit status from the government. Come on, sit down. Want some coffee?'

'Yeah, Okay,' Jennie said, and sat down on the short grey couch. Karen's house always looked a little like an illustration from a furniture catalogue. The couch and the two gold chairs and the pale gold tables with their bulbous porcelain lamps all went together, but none of it reflected Karen. Furniture didn't interest Karen any more than it did Jennie. She just made more of an effort.

She came back with a couple of speckled mugs. 'I made a whole pot,' she said, and added, 'Milk, no sugar, right?' Jennie nodded and took the mug.

Karen sat down on one of the chairs. In a narrow skirt and pink blouse she looked as if she'd been hired to grace the furniture. She said, 'Sorry I got so silly at the door.'

'That's okay. Who's Jack?'

'No one.'

'I'm sorry.'

'No, I didn't mean you shouldn't ask. It's just – ' She pushed her hair back with her hands. 'I met him through work. He's a buyer. And I thought he might become – someone. I guess I still hope so. Never give up D'arcy.'

'Married.'

'Yeah.' She laughed. 'At least he told me.'

Jennie knew she should ask what happened but she couldn't make herself speak. Karen went on, 'You know what I thought? You know what I told myself? That it was a good sign. I mean, that he was married and he told me. Showed he was honest. Isn't that incredible?'

114

Jennie didn't answer. 'Oh hell,' said Karen, 'I'm sorry. I'm sure you didn't come here to listen to me complain about life.'

'It's okay.'

'No, really. I'll tell you, though, sometimes I wonder why I do it. Go for these bastards. Is it just because the choice is so narrow? Have you started dating yet?'

'What?'

Karen laughed. 'Sorry, didn't mean to catch you like that. I'm a little – disconnected, I guess. But it's been a long time now, hasn't it? Since – ' She waved her fingers, 'You know.'

'I haven't really thought about it,' Jennie said.

'You should. Not that I make a very good case for the singles lifestyle. Sometimes I think I'm on a pilgrimage that never gets anywhere.'

'You do all right.'

'You think so? You must not be paying attention. God, I'm sorry. Still, at least it would give you something to worry about besides Gloria Rich.'

Jennie did her best to smile. 'I can manage Gloria. And I can certainly find things to worry about.'

'Can't we all.' The two women sipped their coffee. Hesitantly Karen touched Jennie's hand. 'Jennie,' she said, 'is something wrong?'

'Wrong?'

'Yeah, you don't look too great.'

'No, of course – it's – ' She stopped.

'Why don't you tell me what it is?'

'Karen, I've got a problem.'

'I'm listening.'

'Umm – I need – do you remember that guy you went with a year or so ago? Bruce, I think.'

'Sure. Good old Brucie. What about him? Don't tell me he's grabbed you now.'

Jennie said seriously, 'No, I don't even know him.

115

But, you remember when you got – pregnant?' Karen nodded. 'Where did you go? For the abortion, I mean.'

'You're pregnant?'

Jennie looked down. If only she could have found the name and avoided all this. 'In a way,' she said, and felt like an idiot.

'In a way. Jennie, you said you're not even dating.'

'Well – '

'Oh shit, you weren't, you weren't attacked?'

'No, no, it . . .' She stopped. 'Yeah, I guess that's what it was. A kind of attack.'

'Oh, Jennie.' Karen jumped up to hug her, then let go when Jennie stayed stiff in her arms. She sat down next to Jennie on the couch. 'Where did it happen? When did it happen?'

'Recital Day,' Jennie said. If only she could get the information and get out.

'The Day of Truth?' Karen asked. Jennie nodded. 'Great Mother,' Karen said, 'that's horrible. How could someone – Wait a minute. That's why you didn't go to the Recital?' Jennie nodded again. 'Oh, Jennie, sweetheart. God, that makes me want to go over and pound Gloria Rich's tiny head against a fucking wall.' She saw Jennie's alarm and added, 'Don't worry. I won't tell anyone. Especially not our local saint.' She thought a moment. 'Did you call the police?'

'No.'

'Maybe you should. Look, I don't want to tell you what to do, and I know how awful the police can be, but this guy could go after someone else.' Jennie said nothing. 'Just think about it, okay? I'll go with you if you want.' A moment later, she added, 'Do you want to talk about it? Where did it happen?'

'At one of my services. One of the guardians.' Worse and worse.

'The bastard. The goddam bastard. At a sacred site.'

'Look, Karen can we not – '

'Oh, I'm sorry. Really.' She jumped up. 'You want more coffee?' Karen took the mugs into the kitchen. When she returned, Jennie had bent even further forward with her hands clasped between her knees. She took the mug and murmured her thanks without looking up.

Karen said, 'There's one thing. Whether or not you go to the cops. Have you done a banishment?'

Jennie shook her head.

'Yeah, I thought maybe . . . Look, Jennie, I know you don't want to even think about it. But a banishment will help. That's what the Enactment is for. To clear the rape out of you. A rape – a rape upsets everything. It invades – Someone like that, he just leaks garbage. You've got to clean it all out of you.' Jennie said nothing. 'The women's centre can do the enactment with you.' *Shit*, Jennie thought, *I could have called the women's centre for the name of the clinic.* Karen went on, 'It won't hurt, and they won't ask you any questions.'

Jennie said, 'I'm pregnant.'

'It doesn't matter. The banishment works only on the rape. Not the foetus. You've got to do it, Jennie. It'll help the abortion.'

That's what that idiot doctor said, Jennie thought. *Different enactment, same stupid idea.*

'In fact,' Karen said, 'even if you wanted to keep the child the banishment would help that too. Purify it.'

'I'm not keeping it. I don't want it.'

'Of course, of course. I didn't mean you should keep it. I sure as hell wouldn't. I just meant – I just think you should do the Enactment.'

'I'll think about it.'

'Don't think about it. Do it. Do you want me to go with you?'

'No. No, I'll – look, can't you just tell me where to go for the abortion?'

'Yeah, sure. Will you promise me you'll go to the women's centre?'

'All right.'

'It's on Teller Street. It's called the Centre of the Unquenchable Fire. You know, after Li Ku.'

Jennie made a face. 'That's right,' she said. Why couldn't she remember it? For a moment they were both silent, thinking of the Great Abortion, in the last days of the Old World. A thousand women had gathered on an island to pray for the Army of the Saints. When they arrived, they burned all their clothes, refusing to wear anything made in Old World factories. The secular government decided to take revenge on these women, using their nakedness as an excuse for sending in an army of police. When the women became pregnant from the mass rape they prayed for guidance. One of them fell over with a vision that a great flame had burned up a tree, releasing a wave of perfume from a rock hidden in the trunk. Because of this vision they went all together to see Li Ku Unquenchable Fire (in beauty and truth lives her name forever). The Founder told them a picture – it was not recorded which one – and then she touched the women's bellies and released the foetuses from their imprisonment.

After the women had returned to their island Li Ku stayed in the place she called the Home of the Non-born. When she returned she reported that the foetuses lived in their own stories, considering their existence far superior to the world they called 'the land of decay'.

As so often the thought of a Founder (even Li Ku) lifted the women out of their personal swamps. They sighed – simultaneously – then laughed. Karen looked at Jennie, then took her hand. 'Funny,' Karen said after a moment, 'that Li Ku should have been the one to do the abortion.'

'Why is that funny?'

'She found "The Place Inside". And if anyone ever needed an abortion it was She-Who-Runs-Away.'

Jennie slid loose her hand. She anchored it on the mug of tepid coffee.

'I'm sorry,' Karen said.

'It's okay.'

'I said something wrong, I guess. Mentioning the Picture. That was really stupid. I'm sorry.'

'It's okay,' Jennie said. 'Look, um, thanks. For helping.'

'I didn't do very much.'

'You gave me the name. For some reason I couldn't think of it.'

'Maybe because you haven't done the banishment.'

'Please, Karen.'

'Remember, you promised me.' Looking at Jennie a sadness filled Karen. She wished Li Ku would come back. The Tellers just didn't burn like they used to. There was nobody left. Nobody who could make you melt.

Jennie said, 'I hope things work out. With that guy Jack.'

Karen shrugged. 'It's no big deal. Either he'll call or he won't. I'd probably be better off if he didn't.'

They stood for a moment, then Jennie said, 'Well, I better be going.' At the door she turned and hugged Karen, a kind of payment.

'I'll come round,' Karen said. 'And if Gloria or any of the others bother you, you tell me. I can handle those creeps.' Jennie nodded and left.

The next day Jennie took a vacation day, then called the Centre of the Unquenchable Fire whose receptionist informed her they did not give consultative appoint-

119

ments by telephone. Women who made appointments on the phone, she said, often 'forgot' when the time came. She managed to imply that Jennie belonged to this weak-willed community. 'I'll come in this afternoon,' Jennie said, trying to inject some of her mother's absolute conviction into her voice.

'Whenever you like,' the receptionist said.

Teller Avenue ran across the city, from the Mid-Hudson Bridge to the triangle of highways leading into the hills and toward Connecticut. Without thinking, Jennie expected to find the clinic near the river end, among the slightly shabby homes, the ageing apartment houses and small office buildings. Instead, she found herself driving through the midday traffic into the realm of one and two storey houses with small but neat lawns and bright porches. The clinic itself occupied a modernist rectangle of wood and frosted glass. A long narrow lawn, free of weeds, set the clinic somewhat behind the woodframe houses on either side of it. Above the dark red door Jennie could see a small painting, but she couldn't make out the details. Probably the Great Abortion, or some other marvel of the clinic's patron.

She parked the car across the street and got out to stare at the building. Was she doing the right thing? Maybe Karen and the doctor were right, maybe she should do some Enactment or other before taking any definite steps. What would she think about the whole thing years from now? Would she regret denying the dream – the Agency? Not finding out its plans for her? And yet, the thought of that . . . that fish swimming around inside her . . . The thought that they could just commandeer her body, like – like some truck carrying soldiers to the front . . .

Hesitantly she crossed the street, only to stop again on the far sidewalk. A young woman in jeans and a

120

flowery blouse stepped quietly from the red door. As she passed Jennie she smiled and said, 'Go on. They're really very nice.'

Jennie nodded and took a step onto the flagstone pathway that cut through the lawn to the house.

A bush blocked her way. About three feet high, its tangled branches and sharp thorns sprawled across the stones. She frowned at it, then stepped onto the grass to walk around it. Two steps to the side, and she turned forward again. Another bush filled the space in front of her. Sweat erupted on Jennie's face. For several seconds she looked from one bush to the other. Then she fixed her eyes on the open space to the right of the bush. She sidestepped until she could see a bare lawn and beyond it the building, where a couple of people now stood in the open doorway. Jennie held her breath and stepped forward.

A tree blocked her. Fat and low, its thick old branches stretched more horizontally than vertically. Around the hump of its roots grew yellow flowers and spiked grass. A squirrel glanced at Jennie then ran down the trunk in front of her feet. She screamed, out of frustrated rage as much as fear, and sprinted to the left.

She cut around so fast she couldn't stop when she saw the trellis hung with a prickly vine. The tiny thorns raised little welts on her face and up and down her arms. She began to cry. A blur of noise answered her from the house. Through the trellis Jennie could see a group of people in the doorway, all women, some in lab. coats, one or two in hospital gowns. Someone called, 'Come on.' But no one came to get her.

She got up and walked all the way to the edge of the lawn where a low picket fence marked the border with the house next door. When she looked at the clinic she could make out the painting above the door: Li Ku on her ferris wheel. Jennie stared at the painting as if she expected it to glow or move. She only saw faded wood, here and there chipped by bad weather over many years. She took a deep breath and stepped forward. The saggy old willow that blocked her looked as if it had stood there for years. At the base lay a battered doll in a polka dot dress.

Jennie got down on the ground to lay both hands on the grass. 'Please,' she told the Earth. 'Let me go by. Please. They shouldn't have picked me. I'm no good for this sort of thing.'

'Miss,' said a voice behind her. 'Could you tell us what's happening here?' Jennie looked over her shoulder to see a woman in a pink blouse and yellow skirt bending over her with a microphone attached to a bag at her waist. A few feet away stood another woman, in jeans and a sweat shirt, with a small video camera mounted on her shoulder. By the kerb a man lounged against a truck marked 'WPKP Action Now News.'

The woman with the microphone said, 'What is your name, please? Are you trying to go inside?' Jennie looked from her to the people in the doorways. 'Did you come for an abortion? Can you give us a statement?' The woman with the camera was panning the house and the bushes.

Jennie got to her feet and the camera swung back to her. She looked at the woman with the microphone. 'Walk ahead of me,' she ordered, and gestured at the open space next to the willow tree.

The newswoman stared into the camera. 'I've just been asked to precede the anonymous visitor into the Centre of the Unquenchable Fire. Will more trees spring up? I don't know.' Gingerly she took a step, then another. The camerawoman hovered behind her. The woman said, 'I seem to have passed the barrier.'

Jennie stepped after her. A large bush stood between her and the reporter. Small red berries gleamed among its shiny leaves. Behind Jennie the camerawoman whispered, 'Beautiful. Come on, lady, do another one.' The reporter stood on tiptoe to make sure her face and shoulders would appear above the bush. 'There you see it,' she said. 'The Great Mother herself in a militant action against one woman's abortion.' She cut around the bush to stick the mike in Jennie's face again. 'Did you expect this to happen?' she said. 'Can you give us a statement?'

Jennie turned and walked back to her car, followed by the reporter who tried to get between Jennie and the car door. While Jennie pushed the woman aside and fumbled with her key, an old skinny dog shook itself awake from its post under the car. It growled at the camerawoman who scowled at Jennie, as if to accuse her of playing unfairly. When Jennie had climbed inside the car the dog pissed once against the front wheel, then shuffled a few feet away to crouch down on the sidewalk.

Jennie didn't hear the Action News woman's final questions. As she drove away, a car with a couple of men, one of them with two cameras around his neck, nearly slammed into her as it spun sideways to block the road. She kept going, driving over someone's lawn while the car and the television van ended up blocking each other. *They have no right,* Jennie thought. She hoped Karen wouldn't see her on television. Or Gloria. Or Maria. *No right.*

Late that night, when Jennie finally fell asleep, she dreamed she lay on an operating table with a group of women holding open her legs. One of them spread Jennie's vaginal lips and a tree sprang into the air. Its branches broke open the roof of her house and stretched into a blue sky. Higher and higher the tree grew until the dreamer found herself climbing the trunk, looking down on the curve of the Earth. Villages sprang up in the branches, cities, whole planets. Jennie kept climbing until all around her she could see the stars. Creatures climbed alongside her. She couldn't see them, but she could hear them moving up the trunk. But when she looked down, at the base of the tree, she saw a dead woman, her skin as grey as stone.

THE THREE SISTERS: A training Picture, told, with some unauthorised revisions, by Valerie Mazdan shortly before her expulsion from the New York College of Tellers:

Long before the world became so crowded there lived three sisters, Lily, Asti, and a third. One day when they were young their mother left them, setting sail in a small boat out past the waves that washed their green island. For many years they lay in the sun, or watched the coral grow, or called down storms to excite the sea. One afternoon Lily ran with Asti to a high hill in the centre of the island. They dove down into a pool where they stayed for hours. When they surfaced they were lovers. Centuries long they rolled across the sky, locked in each other's arms and legs. Their sweat mingled and flowed into the sea as warm currents. Caressing the continents the currents ended the ice age that had claimed the world since the sisters' mother had sailed away in her black boat.

All this time the third sister sat on a stone bench behind their house and watched the lovers. The wilder Lily and Asti got the more she stared at them, her eyes unblinking, her lips slightly narrowed.

One morning Lily woke up to find the bed empty beside her. When she went outside she discovered her two sisters side by side on the porch of their house. The third sister said, 'We have to choose.'

Lily yawned. 'Choose what?'

'Our domains. Our territory.' And she quoted an old song

124

their mother had taught them. 'One for the Earth, one for the Sky, and one for the Land of the Dead.'

Lily rubbed her eyes. Then she laughed and took Asti's hand. 'Come on,' she said. To her amazement Asti pulled away.

'She's right,' Asti said. 'They need us.'

'Who needs us?'

'Our children. The world. We've got to become the mothers now.'

The three sisters went to a restaurant on a pine-scattered cliff overlooking a lake. There they played a game with nine copper coins thrown at the wall. The game went on for a week – you can still see the marks all over the restaurant – and when it ended the third sister had won.

Lily ran outside. Asti sat on a kitchen stool and stared at her knees. While Asti wondered what their mother would think of them, the third sister leaned back in the restaurant owner's captain's chair and considered the possibilities. The Sky would give her a lot of room and a good deal of power; but it was all so empty. The Earth was crowded enough but nothing ever stayed in one place. The third sister knew, or at least believed, that she would love all her creatures in whatever domain she chose for herself. If she ruled the Earth she would have to watch her children snapped away into the warehouses of death before they even learned to recognize her. She knew that Lily and Asti considered her hard, but she believed herself secretly weak, and she feared that if she ran the Earth she wouldn't schedule enough disease and war.

But the dead – the dead never leave. She thought of room after room of frozen bodies, the walls and floors covered with layer on layer of bodies, so thick that even if you could reach all the way to the bottom it would still take the lifetime of a star to touch your fingertips to the earliest residents. She imagined their mother arriving some day; the thought made her smile.

Therefore, when Asti asked her, please, would she choose something, the third sister stared out the window a moment, then said, 'I choose the Underworld.' Asti's mouth fell open. She knocked over a table as she ran outside to tell Lily.

125

Lily laughed and kissed her sister. The two girls nearly brought down the restaurant with their shouts of joy as they ran up the path. When they got inside, the third sister had already gone.

The other two choices went very easily. Lily considered the Earth too much work and was glad to take the Sky, while Asti secretly calculated that as Lady of Earth she could take time off to walk along the seabed and search for an ancient woman who had left her daughters.

So at last the three sisters separated. At first Asti did search the sea. She even mounted grand expeditions, officially to look for lost continents. She never found a thing. After a while she managed to bog herself down with enough bureaucratic mechanisms – tides, climates, volcanic scheduling, radioactive decay – that she could tell herself it wasn't really her fault that she'd given up looking.

Lily played. She stretched herself thin enough to roll in the dust between the galaxies, she squeezed herself so tight she jerked gravity out of its compulsions. Now and then, when she would admit to boredom at the same games over and over, she would visit Earth and try to persuade Asti to take a holiday. More and more, however, Asti refused to leave her desk, even for an evening. 'I'm their mother now,' she told Lily. 'They depend on me.'

And the third sister – Lady of a Thousand Names, as one of her assistants called her – she took to walking endlessly along the cold corridors of her house. Now and then she stopped and stared into the faces embedded in the walls, or pressed her fingers to the mouths or eyes. Never did she get back the slightest recognition.

She wasn't alone. She could always find her assistants lounging in the staff rooms. They sat around card tables and made up lists, or they traded stories about 'appointments in Las Vegas' and other tricks they played on their 'clients.' But the third sister could never stand their tone of voice, or the way they leaned back with their hands behind their heads, or the gaudy costumes most of them affected (strings of skulls, belts made out of teeth and fingernails, leather dresses dripping blood). Most of all she couldn't stand the

126

way they all fell silent the moment she entered the room, the way they stared at her. She knew very well that they could run the place without her.

Sometimes she walked down to the ferry dock and watched the new arrivals as they stumbled off the boats. The assistants would let them look around for a moment, then they would shout in their faces. Meekly the dead would allow the assistants to lead them to the walls. Once frozen, they never saw or heard anything again. A couple of times the third sister thought of taking a consignment to herself, before the workers could fix them in their places. She didn't dare.

Finally Our Blessed Mother of Night (as another assistant called her) decided that only her beloved sister Asti could blot away her loneliness. By this time she had convinced herself that Asti had loved her and not Lily. She convinced herself that Asti missed her, that Asti longed for her and would rush to give up the noisy Earth for the cool beauties of the Underworld. If only she could go herself, the lady thought. But she was always the responsible one. She didn't want Asti to think she'd become flighty.

She sent two assistants, a male and a female, in a Silver Phantom Rolls Royce. The lady stood on the shore of her land and watched them drive across the grey river. She watched them wave and shout at the bent humans, the silent mice, the still mosquitoes coming across in the latest shipment. When the messengers were gone the third sister walked back to her magnificent bedroom, where she sat on the corner of her white sheets.

The assistants found Asti at her desk, mapping out new routes for the high winds that sealed off the planet. They smiled at the smell of blood in the air; someone must have run a sacrifice to get the Mother Of Earth's attention. Asti jumped as a hand curled round her shoulder. 'Blessed One,' said a sarcastic voice, 'we would very much like it if you would take a ride with us.'

'This is my territory,' Asti said. 'Get out.'

One of them fingered a necklace. Asti saw, among the teeth and snapped bones, nine copper coins. 'I'll tell you what,' the messenger said. 'If you can prove your . . . dominance, we'll get in our car and go tell our lady you were busy.'

Asti's heart jumped. She'd always hated Death's ultimate claim on all her children. She asked, 'What do you mean by proof?'

The two of them smiled. 'We'll choose a group of targets. Nothing very difficult. A child, a beetle, an orchid, that sort of thing. If you can save one of them, just one, we'll go home.'

Asti stared at them. The tips of their teeth showed over their white painted lips. 'Make your list,' Asti said.

The contest lasted ninety-nine days. At first Asti tried to counter their every move. She would protect her creatures with her body, or snatch them in her arms and leap from one wind to another. She would hide them in caves, in crowded subways, in the centre of blizzards. When she saw the enemy penetrate to every one of her children she knew she must change her tactics. Only one, they'd said. She just had to win one time, and they would leave her alone.

She chose one of the last targets on the list, a young girl who worked in a sweatshop in Taipei. Asti met the child one morning on the way to work. A touch on the eyes caused the girl to forget her job, her family, her name. First, her Mother armoured the child's body. She bathed the girl in a river that flowed from Asti's own mouth, she rubbed her in the leaves of a tree that grew behind her office. Then she began the disguises. She wiped away the girl's personality, then substituted layer upon layer of fake identities: an actress in Italy, a shoemaker in Beirut, a striped cat living in the back of a grocery in Utrecht. For the final layer, the outer coat, Asti dressed the girl in her own face and dress and set her down at the great desk. With absolute conviction in her personal history as Asti, Mother of Life, the child set about ordering the latest growth rates for orange trees in Portugal, for rainstorms in Ohio.

Asti herself returned to that morning in Taipei. In the shape of a young girl she sewed 'made in Taiwan' labels on the insides of black and yellow jeans.

Days went by, weeks, months. One afternoon she was

returning from her work when a Rolls Royce pulled up alongside her. She kept walking. Two figures stepped in front of
her. They took her hands and a shock of cold went through
her. In the car she sat without a word. She didn't look at
them or speak until they came to the riverside, where the
ferryman stood looking at his watch. Only when the two
waved her onto the ramp did she fold her arms and quietly
shake her head.

'I don't think so,' she said. 'I'm not the one you think I
am. I am her Mother, and I've beaten you.'

'Which one do you mean?' the female asked.

'You know which one. The one who looks like this.' She
pointed to herself. 'If you want her you can go to my office.
You'll find her sitting at my desk. She thinks she's me. You
can have her now because the contest is over. I've beaten
you.'

'Oh, that one,' the male said. 'We took her long ago. And
the others. You, Blessed Mother – you're the one we want.'

Asti stared at the boat. There, among the passengers, stood
a tall woman in a silver dress. When Asti stepped onto the
ramp she herself was dressed in moonlight, and the tall
woman became a ragged girl with filthy hair.

Even as the boat pulled away Asti saw the blight float
down like smog over all her lands and people.

Lily did not hear of the kidnapping for some time. She was
on a run, trying to outdistance the gigantic gas creatures
who kept rolling back the end of the universe. Bored with
her vast playground she wanted purity, escape. She wanted
to get out beyond even the incessant gossip of the quasars.
She was almost at the edge, almost in sight of the border
when the message came. *Lily, I need you.* The Lady of Heaven
hesitated, then picked up speed again. The hell with Asti.
All the times Lily had begged her to go into the dark, just
for a holiday, and now she just summons me? *Lily, help me.*
Help yourself, Lily thought. She could feel the universe slide
away from her like drops of water off a racer's back. A great
field of white opened in front of her. One step and she would
break apart into the splendour of endless nothing. One step.

129

She turned and headed for Earth.

It was in fact only desperation that made Asti pray to her reckless sister. From the moment the Queen of the Under-world had installed her in a room in the centre of the Great House In The Valley Asti had thought obsessively about their mother. *It's my fault*, she berated herself. *I should have kept up the search. I didn't love her enough.* And yet, whenever she tried to make herself pray to her mother nothing came. She told herself it was because their mother couldn't help, or because she, Asti, resented all the times she'd called and had never got an answer. The real stop to her prayers was something else entirely. She had become the Mother now. All the festering children of the world prayed to her. Why whould she give that up, even imprisoned in hell?

Her sister had placed her in a long narrow room with a large bed against the far wall. The posts of that bed were black diamond, the walls a constant waterfall of colours. Asti only sat on a thin-legged ivory chair beside the stone door that held her prisoner. Naked, with her shoulders curved forward, she pressed her fists against her cheeks, and when her sister came to talk to her, to stroke her, or threaten her, Asti only stared ahead as she willed her tears into ice. She looked at her sister only once, when the Lady of Night tried to remind Asti of the supposed love they had once shared in that spectacular time before they took up their duties. For a moment Asti turned to stare at her sister with a look half horror, half pity. She looked away again almost immediately, but the third sister got up and left the room. The next day two of the Lady's assistants came to take Asti to a crowded room where the corpses of women who had died in war hung on hooks along the wall. They jammed Asti onto the same hook as a young priestess who had prayed, thousands of years before, to Asti to save her from her murderers. When the assistants left, laughing at some whispered joke, Asti at last sent out a call to her sister Lily.

By the time Lily arrived on Earth that call had dissipated. Fragments of it hung in the air, soaked the ground. Wherever Lily walked she felt like she'd stepped on a wet sponge. The rocks, the grass, they all oozed Asti's voice, but no words, only pieces of syllables.

In one step Lily stood on the hilltop that held Asti's office. Insects crawled over the huge desk. For a while Lily stood there and listened to them weep for their vanished mistress, 'she who loves the beetle with the elephant, the cockroach with the eagle.' Honey and other offerings drifted down the table legs.

Lily stepped outside and cast her eyes across Asti's world. All the things that had worked so neatly under Asti's tight schedule now had flown to pieces. In one place no woman or animal could conceive despite constant intercourse, in another, streams of babies fought each other to get out of their mothers' wombs. In yet another, Lily saw a woman in labour for twenty-three days bring out a miniature doll, a wind-up toy with a metal face painted in a huge grin.

In one city ice formed on people's hands as they tried to eat, while in a certain village in France the sun set the people's blood bubbling in their ears so that they had to shout to hear their own prayers.

Great waves of prayer washed over Lily. Everywhere people beat the Earth and themselves, they sacrificed animals and each other until in some towns Lily had to wade through blood and bits of meat. Others burned whole forests in their hope to catch the mother's attention.

Lily was standing in a town hall somewhere in Belgium watching one man cut out another's tongue for some blasphemy or other, when a tall woman stepped up to her. The woman wore a red velour suit, red high-heeled pumps, a white ruffled blouse – and around her waist a belt strung with human eyes. Lily said to her, 'Tell my sister she's got some real class working for her.'

'You can tell both your sisters,' the woman said. 'Though I don't think the little one will have much to say about it.'

A great fear shook Lily, but she forced it back down her spine. With her mouth open wide she called down a storm on the messenger. The wind blew down skyscrapers to reveal the temples and pyramids underneath their basements, it blew the skin off stockbrokers and their secretaries, it ripped

131

open all the books so that they dumped their black ink into the rivers and lakes. But when it ended, the woman in the velour suit and the vulgar belt still stood, her back against the remnant of a wall. She smiled. 'This isn't your territory, Sky Woman. It's too hot here. You get confused. Would you like to come with me now? We can go in my private plane.'

Lily smiled back. 'Tell your lady I will visit her after I have properly cleaned myself. I've just come off the road.'

'But how will you find the door? You're not used to these small worlds.'

'I grew up here.'

'Of course, but even then you never did go down to the ferries, did you?'

Lily didn't answer, but instead stepped out upon the sea, heading for the island where she and her sisters had grown up together. When she reached it she found all the trees gone, the rock hot under her feet and the sand beach fused into glass. A sniff of the irradiated air told her that some government or other had used the place as a test site. As she climbed the hill to the house she passed a delegation of army officers under a red and white flag with a Lunar crescent, supposed symbol of the vanished Asti. In a show of ostentatious humility the generals were crawling on their bellies; Lily had to step over them to get to the door.

Inside, everything was the same, the chairs by the windows, the skylight, Asti's paints and dreadful portraits, the third sister's pebble collection perfectly arranged on a square of volcanic glass. Without any conscious plan Lily began to smash it all. Her legs kicked out, her hands slashed the walls. When she stopped, everything lay in dusty heaps. Beyond the mess the generals continued their oblivious crawl.

Now Lily dressed herself for battle. She reached into the sun for a long tunic of white light. Her hand swiped at the moon and came away with a mask of silver to cover her face, all but the teeth, which she cased in steel. She gloved her hands in mountains and shod her feet with the bottom of the Arctic Ocean.

One step took her to the ferry docks, another carried her across the river. For a moment she stood there and stared

132

at the huge house, with its thousand cold chimneys, its ten thousand corridors, its hundred thousand blacked out windows. Softly she said, 'Lady of Death, this is Lily of the Stars. I want my sister back.'

Room after room she marched through Death's house, until she came to a black door twice as tall as herself. Over and over she tugged at it or kicked it, but it wouldn't budge. A stoop-shouldered man in overalls came up behind her. 'That door is the Night,' he said. 'You cannot break it. But I have a fancy for your shoes. If you give them to me I will open the lock.' Lily kicked her salt ice slippers at his face. He caught them in his teeth, and then with a small key opened the door.

Through a thousand more rooms Lily ran, finding nothing but the frozen faces of the dead, until she came to a pale door half as tall as herself. 'That door is Sorrow,' said a woman when Lily couldn't break it. 'Give me your gloves and I will open it for you.'

Again she marched through the house, until she came to a wide gate, thick spokes of glass with empty air between them. Lily tried to break the lock or crash the glass. She tried to squeeze between the bars. Nothing worked. A woman in a glittery G-string appeared on the other side. 'You won't open this,' she said. 'It's made of fear. Pass me your dress and I'll unlock it for you.' Lily took off her dress of light and threw it through the bars. Instantly the door swung open. Lily ran along the swampy corridor.

She came to a door of yellow mud. Three women and a man appeared behind her. The man wore her shoes, one of the women wore her dress, another her gloves. The third woman said, 'That door is Anger. Give me your silver face and I will open it for you.' Lily stripped off the moon mask and threw it as hard as she could. It struck the woman's face and clung to the skin.

The moment Lily squeezed through the door her third sister loomed over her like a mountain. Lily tried to shout but nothing came out of her mouth except the steel plating that had coated her teeth. She tried to kick but could no longer feel her feet. At a gesture from Our Lady of Pity the

133

four messengers lifted Lily and jabbed her body onto a huge rusty hook. Across from Lily Asti groaned. The Lady stood over them. 'Now we are all together,' she said, and walked out of the room.

Asti moaned. Her tongue stuck out like a stick held between her teeth. Looking at her, and the arms and legs of the dead priestess behind her, Lily thought to say, 'I'm sorry,' but the words stuck in a mire of anger. It was all Asti's fault, all her stupidity, her selfishness. How could Lily ever have loved her?

'You've got to get me out of here,' Asti managed to whisper. 'My children need me.'

Lily was about to say that Asti's children could join her on her hook when a thought came to her. 'Asti,' she said, 'call your children. Tell them to worship their mother.'

Asti slurred, 'They already worship – '

'Here.'

'Here?'

'Call them here.' But it was no use. Asti had slipped off again. Lily pitched her voice high like her sister's and sent out a call. All over Asti's world her children began to kill themselves. The simple ones smashed themselves against stone or drowned in poison, or cell-divided so rapidly their nuclei shattered. Others set up competitions or gave exhibitions of their suicides. Newspapers reviewed the latest trends, neighbourhoods became fashionable for avant-garde deaths.

When the first crowds began to arrive, when the first extra boats were laid on at the ferry stations the assistants held a party to celebrate. The Lady attended but left quickly. The toasts had seemed like jeers. She went instead to her sisters. The dark room soothed her eyes after the garish decorations of the party room. She went to Asti and touched her shoulders. They felt like mould, like dead leaves. At that moment the Blessed Lady of Deliverance understood, before any of her workers, what was happening.

The workers soon began to see the signs. The boats began to arrive faster than the assistants could find their proper places. Soon, they paid no attention, just gathered in the

134

halls or down by the docks. Worst of all, the dead were laughing. They arrived like car loads at a political convention, they came in bright clothes, with banners, they sang songs as they marched off the boats. The assistants tried to order them to the walls. They paid no attention. The assistants tried to outshout them or command their silence. The dead only sang louder. And more came, animals leading litters of young, human children with their arms filled with pets, whole parades of painted faces and banners and megaphones.

The Lady walked downstairs, stepping over the corpses of cats. The mix of colours made her wince. When she marched through her once silent halls, mobs cheered and the dead threw flowers at her. She realised she had become so used to loneliness she could not tolerate the touch of fingers or eyes. At last she reached the room where her sisters hung on hooks.

'Go,' she told Asti as she lifted her off the walls. 'Get out. Get back to your job.'

Asti looked from her to Lily. In this one room no sound had come of the invasion. Lily laughed, a raw gurgly noise because of the hook in her throat. The third sister cocked her head at Lily. 'You did this, didn't you?' she said. 'Asti's not smart enough.' Lily smiled at her. 'She can go, but you're staying. When they're all gone, when there's nothing left, you and I will still be here.'

'Still hating each other,' Lily said.

'Exactly.'

Asti said, 'Let her go. Please. She doesn't know what she's doing. She's not like you and me. She doesn't understand.'

The third sister searched Asti's face. There was no trickery there, no calculations. Only love. 'If I let her go,' she told Asti, 'will you stay in place of her? Will you stop your children and stay here alone, with me?'

For a while there was silence. Then Asti said, 'I will come to you for six months of the year. I will rule beside you and show you how to control your workers. We will find a way to let your residents speak to you. But the other six months you must let me return to my children.'

135

The third sister lifted Lily off the hook, and set her down on the floor. Swaying slightly, Lily looked at her two sisters as they stood shoulder to shoulder. Their faces had begun to slide together. With a shrug Lily left the room to walk back through the strands of corridors. When the dead cheered her she couldn't tell if they thought she was Asti, or their new mother, or they simply didn't care.

She paused only once before she leaped across the river and back into the blessed cold of the sky. A group of three women and a man stood in the middle of a great crowd of dead souls. One of the women wore a yellow dress, another a silver mask. Lily couldn't see their hands or feet. She shrugged and jumped into the night.

136

8

Jennie sat in her living room, on the couch, bent forward with her elbows on her knees, and she thought about how God had taken the place of her mother. Why couldn't they let her alone in her mediocre suburban life? Why did they have to push her into something important? Her mother had tried to take over her eyes and hands for art. Now God had taken over her womb. For what? Not for art? It didn't matter. It was still someone – something – else's plan for her.

She went into the kitchen and filled the coffee pot. As soon as she'd plugged it in she decided she wanted something stronger and bent down to get the whisky from the cabinet under the sink. In front of the bottle stood the slightly grimy can of spirit-breaker. She remembered how she'd sprayed the house that time. Afraid a Malignant One had invaded her body. Maybe she could spray her womb, drive out the squatter.

With a shake of her head she put down the can and picked up the Scotch, Shouldn't drink while pregnant, she thought automatically. Alcohol coats the soul like shellac, makes it hard for the foetus to form around it. Makes the baby grow all stunted, or dull-witted or something. Not this foetus, she thought, and opened the freezer for some ice. This foetus came so charged up with holy fire it could burn half of Poughkeepsie if she did anything to offend it.

'To your good health,' she said, and raised her glass only to feel a stab of nausea and cramps that bent her double. The glass dropped out of her hand into the sink. 'Don't want any whisky?' she said through gritted teeth. 'Goddamn you, that was good Scotch.' She sat down and the nausea passed. 'Can't you find some other way to get your point across? I mean, you know, this goes with morning, remember?'

A pang of guilt touched her, as if she could see a tiny wrinkled face about to cry. 'It's not you,' she said, 'it's nothing personal. It's just the way you got there.' She shook her head. 'This is ridiculous.'

She poured a cup of half-brewed coffee, then gingerly lifted it to her mouth. No cramps. 'Thanks,' she said. Apparently, the creature's medical scruples stopped with alcohol. Creature. If she was stuck with it she better start thinking of it as her tender baby. Or something.

Drinking the coffee she allowed herself the fantasy that the pregnancy did indeed come from a Malignant One. She tried to remember any stories she'd read or heard about babies conceived by Bright Beings. There was that movie star, the one with all the divorces. She was doing some film about Danielle Book-of-the-People, and – the gossip magazines had implied – she'd run out of good looking men, so she'd bribed someone in the film crew to help her conjure an incubus into her dressing room. Vaguely, Jennie remembered some press conference the studio had tried to block, and all the reporters baiting the expectant mother. But how did the baby turn out? No arms or legs? How about all jumbled up with extra teeth everywhere? For all she knew, she was getting it confused with Jim Browning's horror stories of babies born after recitals where the Teller had told 'The Place Inside'. Actually, she recalled something about the child's great beauty, and how the movie star had gone insane when the SDA had confiscated it.

She shivered. The Spiritual Development Agency could take hers as soon as it popped out of its fortress.

138

What would they do to it? In high school there was that girl, Irene something. She'd dropped out for a while and people said a succubus had commandeered her body to seduce the principal. According to the stories the Ferocious One had left Irene's body pregnant and her parents had hushed it up instead of just aborting it. When the baby was born it flew out of the midwives' hands and all around the private clinic before anyone could catch it. Jennie laughed. According to the stories at school the SDA had trapped it in some kind of electrical field which made the baby dissolve like a sugar statue, leaving such an awful stench the clinic had to move and Irene's parents ended up with a huge lawsuit. Jennie laughed.

The laugh turned into a whimper and she slumped down in her seat. What was she going to do? She knew very well no incubus had done this to her. That stunt with the trees could only have come right from the top. 'A fish is swimming in your womb. The world is boiling with colour.' Why couldn't the world get back its colour without her? She got up and checked the calendar. The Recital was the 21st. She flipped the pages, then dropped them, realising what day the baby was due. March 21st, right smack on the equinox. How appropriate. Lamb's Birth Day. The Day of the Rising Fire. Anniversary of the Creation of the Universe. Shit. You could bet this toddler would toddle out right on the date. What time, dawn? Twelve noon?

Maybe she should start getting used to it. Go buy a stack of diapers and a crib. Disgusted, she left the kitchen, as if she could leave everything behind with the rag of wiped up Scotch. In the den she sat down on Mike's old recliner, only to jump up and turn on the television. Some soap was on; a woman with perfect make-up was trying to invoke a Devoted one to spy on her husband. Jennie stared at it hard enough for the

139

picture to turn back into dots. What did people do in the Old World? When abortion was forbidden and priests in black dresses burned women who tried to open clinics. She got up and went into the bedroom, leaving the television blaring behind her.

Somewhere – she opened drawers, leafed through underwear, tops, shorts, Name beads, old receipts – somewhere she'd stuck some . . . There. Two long blue knitting needles. From the days before she worked, when she kept trying to think of things to do. Knitting had been one of them. She'd bought the needles, some balls of wool, and a book. The book lay somewhere on the shelves, with all the cookbooks she'd never used, the wool had gone for solstice decorations, but there lay the needles, long and sharp.

Jennie held them in an open palm. Did women really do that? Really? Maybe they just told you that in school, scare stories of the Old World to make you appreciate the Revolution. Would it work? It would have to go into the uterus. She put the picture out of her mind, afraid she would get scared and not even try.

Jennie took the needles into the bathroom, where she got the bottle of alcohol from the medicine cabinet. She wet a tissue, then rubbed one of the needles. She took off her shorts and panties, then climbed into the bath and squatted down. With one hand she grabbed hold of the guardian above the taps. *Help me*, she thought, then wondered what kind of invocation you could say for a self-induced abortion. Maybe, 'Come, blessed spirits, and guide my hand.' She wondered if she should promise a penance. Or make an offering. She just wanted to get it done. Anyway, the abortion would be enough of a blood offering all by itself. Fighting off another bout of squeamishness, she said out loud, 'At the count of three. One . . . two . . .' Jennie yelped and

140

dropped the needle. In the white bathtub she could see it glow with heat. She sucked her fingers where the needle had burned them. Gingerly she touched it. It was cold again.

Jennie climbed out of the bathtub and dashed into the kitchen. She came back with a potholder mitten, asbestos or some other insulator covered in yellow cotton with red dots. She jerked it on her hand, then picked up the needle. 'Okay,' she said, 'here we go. *Damn!*' Her whole hand had started to burn. Quickly she yanked off the glove. With her other hand she reached out to turn on the cold water, as she realised the burn had vanished; the skin wasn't even warm. She picked up the needle and threw it at the wall.

Jennie got out of the bathtub and sat down on the lid of the toilet seat. So. No abortion. That much was clear. 'Goddamnit,' she said. What would happen if she tried to throw herself down a flight of stairs? Probably trip and slide gently down, step by step. And yet, she knew she was relieved. Would she actually have done it? She wondered how desperate those Old World women must have been. Was she desperate – or just angry?

She got up and put on her clothes. Back in the den, some man on television was promising some other man he'd never have to work again for the rest of his life. Jennie flipped the channel knob, settling finally on WPKP. At the moment 'Poughkeepsie's own' station was fulfilling its role as community servant with a report on some children's clinic in Pleasant Valley. Some of the children were acting out stories or something while the other kids drew pictures or talked about it. Or something. Jennie couldn't concentrate. *I should pay attention to stuff like this*, she thought. *Check out places to send my precious little dream baby once it's born.* But all she could think of was that mitten burning her hand.

As the TV droned on, however, another thought

141

pushed its way into her mind. In five minutes the news would come on. Full colour pictures of Jennifer Mazdan and her magic bushes. Karen and Maria and Gloria, oh God, Gloria Rich, watching her. Did Gloria watch the news? She never seemed to know very much. 'Just the eternal truths,' she'd once said when Karen caught her in some gross ignorance. Maybe nobody watched the Poughkeepsie news. Maybe it had a low rating.

Or would the networks pick it up? Beverley sat before the news every evening like an eager puppy. She claimed that the 'dance of the world' fed her music. What would Beverley do if she saw her daughter on television, starring in a local miracle?

For that matter, what would Beverley do when she discovered she had a grandchild? Especially one boiling with colour? 'Please,' Jennie whispered, to the foetus, or the Agency, or anything at all that might listen to her. 'Please keep my mother from finding out about this. At least for a while. At least tonight. Just my mother. And Gloria Rich.'

As the hourly round of commercials heralded the approach of the local news Jennie jumped up and grabbed the phone book from its wooden stand under the phone. She fluttered the pages until she found Gloria's number. It took her three tries before she could dial it right.

One of Gloria's kids – she had no idea which one – answered the phone with a whiney hello. 'Can I speak to Glo – to your mother?'

The kid shouted, 'Ma, it's for you.' An answering scream came back, and the kid said, 'Who is it?'

'Jennifer Mazdan.'

The kid let the phone clunk. Jennie waited, certain Gloria was watching the news and would come on with 'Jennifer dear, why didn't you tell us you were

142

expecting? And how silly of you to want an abortion.
I'm so pleased our Mother turned you back.' But when
Gloria did pick up the phone her syrupy voice only
said, 'Hello, Jennifer, what a pleasant surprise.'

'Hello, Gloria,' Jennie said, and her mind blanked
on anything further.

Gloria said, 'Did you want something, Jennifer?'

'Uh . . . No. I mean, I just thought it might be nice
to say hello. After all, we live right next door to each
other.' She tried to work out how long she needed to
keep Gloria talking. They'd probably show her right
away, tonight's big headline.

'What a lovely idea,' Gloria said. 'I am rather busy
but I do think we in the hive should stick together.'

'Especially Raccoons,' Jennie said. 'I mean, the
Spirit must have brought us together for a reason.
Especially you and me living right next door to each
other.'

There was a pause, then Gloria said, 'Yes. Yes, I
suppose we didn't become neighbours by accident.'

'No, of course not.' Jennie kept herself from saying
how their inner destinies had woven together on a
higher plane.

'Still, I didn't think you could spare the time for
such contacts. I know how busy you keep yourself.
How tired you get.'

'Well, I can't sleep through everything.'

'Only the important things? Forgive me, I didn't
mean to be nasty. Of course, when we think of the
other blocks, the Squirrels, or the Sparrows, all together
at the Recital. I know you did your best, we can't
always control such things as – as exhaustion, if that's
what it was – '

'How's Al?'

'What?'

'Al. Your husband. Tall, smokes a pipe – '

'I know who you mean, Jennifer. I just – we were talking about something.'

'Well, I was just wondering how he was. And the children. How are they?'

'We're all just fine, Jennifer. A little disappointed.' She let her voice fade.

Jennie knew she should ignore the bait, but she couldn't think of anything else to say. 'Disappointed?'

'Well, we did expect so much from Allan Lightstorm.'

'Everyone did. But it was a bit silly, don't you think? I mean, to expect we could get him to stay in Pough-keepsie just from one visit.'

'Perhaps if we had presented a united front.'

'It wasn't a battle.'

'A Teller can sense when people don't surrender fully. Even if everyone comes, a Teller knows when people listen with their souls or just their ears. Especially one of the Living Masters.' A crash sounded somewhere and Gloria shouted, 'Leave that alone. That's your father's.' To Jennie she said, 'I'm sorry, the children, you know. I have to watch them every moment.'

The children. The brats would see the news and tell their dear Mommy about it. She tried to remember any kiddie shows on the other channels that would keep Gloria's kids away from the news. And Al, suppose he'd come home early, suppose he was home sick?

Gloria said, 'When you get your own little ones you'll really learn what busy is.' She wafted a laugh. 'And tired.'

'No doubt,' Jennie mumbled. Silence again. Gloria said finally, 'It was lovely speaking to you, Jennifer, but I do have to run. Al will be coming home soon and I haven't even heated up the oven.'

'When's the next block meeting?'

144

'On the 15th, of course. Our usual date.'

'Whose house is it?'

She could just about hear Gloria's eyes roll. 'Carrie's house. Carrie Perkins. Don't you pay attention at all in Raccoon meetings?'

'I left early.'

'Oh. Oh yes. You didn't care for our company, I suppose.'

'It wasn't that.'

'Did you become tired? Need to sleep? Really, Jennifer, I do hope you can make it next time. And can stay the whole evening. If those of us with children can manage, then someone all alone, without responsibilities – '

'I'm sure I'll make it, Gloria. I'm really looking forward to it.'

'How nice. Then maybe our collective spirit can rise among us. Now I better – '

'Do you think the collective spirit rises in the other blocks?'

'The other blocks are not my responsibility. Or yours.'

'I was just wondering. I mean, before we start criticising ourselves.'

'Maybe you should wonder more about your own contribution. Or what you don't contribute.'

'But maybe none of the blocks really link together. Maybe no one does any more.' Jennie wondered how much time had passed. How long did the news last? Maybe they'd gone on to the weather. Or sports.

'We make the Revolution,' Gloria said in her quotation mode. 'If we lock up our souls in our bodies, then no wonder God can't paste us together.'

'You always put things so, so elegantly.' Jennie was sure Gloria had garbled something from one of her magazines, *Holy Digest*, or *Godsweek* or something.

145

'Thank you. The truth makes us all elegant. Perhaps you should think about that. Now I must make dinner.'

'Of course,' Jennie said. 'Give my love to Al.'

'Yes. Certainly.' A tone of confusion in Gloria's voice made Jennie wonder if Gloria would now suspect her of having an affair with Al. The thought horrified and delighted her. Gloria said, 'Goodbye, Jennifer.'

'Bye,' Jennie said brightly. She hung up, then ran in to the television. Ten after, the den clock said. It felt more like twenty minutes had passed. The reporter who'd hounded Jennie at the clinic was interviewing some forest ranger about wild animal attacks or something. Jennie didn't understand a word of it and didn't care. She wondered if this meant her own story had been killed for some reason. Would they run two features with the same reporter for the same evening? How many reporters did WPKP have anyway?

The weather began with a few jokes about the weatherman mowing his lawn, and God's plan for the mosquitoes. Jennie listened to all the talk of fronts and pressures and divine messages in the cloud patterns. Then it was over and a commercial came on for a carpet store on South Road.

Jennie wished she'd watched it all. So she'd know what they said. She thought of turning on one of the long news shows from the New York stations, but instead switched off the TV. They wouldn't run a Poughkeepsie story, not with pictures anyway. But what if the SDA had already certified it as a true event? They'd run that, certainly.

Did they show her? Did everyone know? She could call Karen, see if she said anything. They had to show it. If they could show that ranger . . .

The phone rang seven or eight times before Karen answered it. When she heard Jennie's voice she said,

'Did you go to the clinic? What happened? Are you okay?'

She doesn't know, Jennie thought. 'I haven't been yet,' she said, and before Karen could interrupt she asked, 'Listen, did you see the news just now? WPKP. The Poughkeepsie news.'

'I know our beloved station. Why? Was something special on?'

'Then you didn't see it?'

'No. What was on?'

'I don't know. I didn't see it, either.'

'Jennie, what's this about?' There was a silence as Jennie tried to think of an answer, then Karen said, 'Are you all right? Should I come over?'

'No, no, I'm fine. I just – I just thought maybe they'd run something about . . .' Her voice trailed away.

'About the guy?'

It took a moment before Jennie realised Karen meant the rapist who'd attacked Jennie on the Day of Truth. 'Yeah,' she said. 'Maybe someone else. Or something.'

'Do you have some reason – '

'No. No, I was just wondering.'

'Maybe you should go to the police. It's not too late. I'll go with you.'

'Come on, Karen, it's more than two months.'

'You know, Jennie, your real problem is that you just can't handle it. I'll bet you haven't done that Enactment yet.' Silence. 'Have you?'

'No.'

'Oh Jennie, you must. That's what's keeping you from going to the clinic.'

She knows, Jennie thought, then realised she'd already told Karen that she hadn't gone. 'I'll go,' she said. 'Really.'

'I wish you would just do the banishment. It's so important. It'll free you from all the garbage.'

'I've got to go,' Jennie said.

'You sure you're okay?'

'I'm fine,' Jennie said.

'If you need any help or anything, just call.'

'Thanks, Karen. Bye.'

'Bye, Jennie. And don't worry. It'll all be fine. Do the banishment.'

'Goodbye. Thanks.'

As soon as Jennie had hung up she wished she was still talking. How long could it be before people found out? What would happen when the TV made her a star? Would they track her down? Run her picture with the caption, 'Do you know this woman?' She imagined the mayor or the city manager (or whoever had arranged the Allan Lightstorm circus) using Jennie to 'put Poughkeepsie in the minds of the public' as the mayor had said about the Teller's visit. Maybe they'd arrange performances, with children or high school students acting out the roles of trees and bushes springing from the lawn to block someone whose shoulders proudly wore a papier mâché mask made from a model of Jennifer Mazdan's head. She had a brief vision of her mother offering to bring a band to play a suite self-composed in her daughter's honour.

Jennie counted that night as one of the worst she'd ever endured, on a level with Mike's leaving her, or the night before the annulment hearings, or even the night after her father died so many years before. Her thoughts became a slosh of helplessness, painless methods of suicide, rage against her mother, the baby, and God, terror at her blasphemous thoughts, memories of Recitals she'd attended, and anger at the Tellers' failure to 'clean it all out' as she put it to herself.

But as it always does, the night passed. Praise Our

Mother for her blessed gift, gravity, and all such institutions that keep our lives bound in safe monotony. Sometime towards the dawn Jennie thought she heard a soft voice, rather reedy, singing to her. Must be the birds, she thought, with their insensitive cheerfulness. But it sounded so – human, though with a strange, distant quality. The sound, very faint, calmed her and she felt her muscles slipping loose from the net of tension that held her awake. Consciousness washed off her and she fell asleep smiling.

Sometime in mid-morning a kid playing 'catch' threw the ball wide over his friend's head so that it banged against the front of Jennie's house, just below the bedroom window. Jennie woke with the thought that she was late for work and Maria would scream at her, the bitch. Then she remembered the television people. Could she just stay home without phoning? If she killed herself it wouldn't matter if she lost her job.

Jennie wobbled to the phone, staying as sleepy as possible so her voice would sound sick. Ridiculous. She could just make some reference to the failed abortion. By now the paper would have it. That would cover anyone who missed the TV report. But when she reached Maria the supervisor only said, 'Ms Mazdan. How nice to hear from you. Where are you? Puerto Rico?'

'I'm home,' Jennie said stupidly.

'Lovely,' Maria said. 'Maybe you could drop in on us sometime. When you're in the neighbourhood.'

'Can I have the day off?' Jennie said, instantly annoyed that she lacked the courage to report herself sick.

'Of course, of course. Funny, though, I seem to remember you took yesterday off as well. We've got a custom here at Mid-Hudson. Now and then we like to announce our vacation days before we actually take them. It helps a little in arranging schedules.'

149

'Uhh, Maria, could I have the rest of the week?'

'Of course. Painting your house?'

'No, I've, uh, got something to think about.'

'To think about.'

'Yeah.'

'Fine, Jennifer, fine. And here's something else to think about. You report for work, next Monday, 8 o'clock sharp, or I'll kick your tits halfway to Wappingers Falls. Got that?'

Jennie said 'Sure,' as if Maria had asked her to pick up a bottle of milk on the way to the office.

'Goodbye, Jennie,' Maria said, and hung up.

Jennie put the phone back on the hook. Scratching herself she went back to the bedroom and put on a sweatshirt and a pair of jeans before she pulled open the curtains to wince at the bright day.

The paper. The paper should be there. She ran outside without shoes and grabbed the *Poughkeepsie Journal* from the box. Instead of a bewildered Jennifer Mazdan standing outside the Centre of the Unquenchable Fire, the front page photo showed the President walking with the Chinese Premier alongside the pool fronting the Founders' Memorial. Jennie flipped through the pages. Nothing in the first section, nothing in the second . . .

No, there, page thirteen. 'Clinic Gets New Foliage.' With a picture of the willow tree, the article described the new 'beautification programme' at the abortion clinic. Jennie read the article twice. Was it a cover-up? Was the station keeping the story for itself? She read the piece a third time. It didn't actually say the city had provided the new trees. It just implied –

The Agency. The Agency had stopped the story. They didn't want her to become a star. How? What did they do? Threats? Send some Benign One – maybe they just wiped clean the tape and let the TV people draw their own conclusions. Jennie was almost as angry as she

150

was relieved. They had no right to manage her life. Arrange all the details. A twinge of nausea stirred her and she made a face, as if to scare it away. It went. If only they'd take someone else. Gloria. She'd give them Gloria. Let Gloria's womb boil with colour. She'd love it.

I'm not like that, she thought. *I'm not like Gloria. Or my mother. I want my own life.* If only she could call some number and complain. Back in the house she opened the front curtains. In the street Gloria's older boy, Al, Jr. was bending over a baseball bat with the Gotowski boy from down the block. A car waited for them to get out of the way. With a Boy Scout knife Al Jr. pricked his finger then dropped a little blood on the thick end of the bat. While the car honked at them the two boys covered their eyes and said a short prayer.

Jennie frowned. You didn't do that, make blood offerings in public like that. They could at least have waited for the car to pass. They were just flaunting themselves. God, what the hell difference did it make? 'Damn,' she said out loud as the wildness from the night before began to rise in her again. The nausea came up to join it, and Jennie thought how she wanted to scream, it was all so miserable. But then that faint singing came again, so cold and faraway, like a bird flying over a field of ice. Jennie moaned. Why couldn't they have taken Gloria? It would have been so much better. Somehow, though, she no longer cared as much, not right now. The singing continued, and Jennie smiled.

Outside, Al Jr. and Bobby Gotowski looked up, as if they thought someone had called them. They shrugged and walked to the side of the road. The driver, so impatient a moment ago, now hesitated slightly before he drove his shiny blue car around the corner, in the direction of the Sun.

151

THE NON EXISTENT MARRIAGE OF JENNIFER MAZDAN AND MICHAEL GOLD

1

Jennifer Mazdan dropped out of college in her junior year, after failing an exam in her major, True History. The exam paper had asked her to delineate 'the redemptive significance' of Jaleen Heart of the World's exorcism of the Pentagon. Alternatively, Jennie could have identified 'structural similarities and functional differences' between the creation of New Chicago after the northern war, and the Revolution's official starting point, the Parade of the Animals in Anaheim, California, when children in animal masks (mostly ducks and mice) ran through the streets burning the offices of the secular government.

Since Jennie couldn't see any connections at all between the two events she decided to answer the first question. For most of the two hours she stared at her paper or pretended to make notes in case the proctor was watching her. Finally she wrote down a clumsy retelling of the exorcism, describing how cracks appeared in the walls, and muddy coloured birds flew out of the computers which then issued proclamations of their loyalty to the Revolution. When Jennie got her paper back Dr Hadauer ('hate-hour' his students called him) had written, 'Very naive, shows no serious thought on subject. True History is a little bit more than *The Lives Of The Founders*. I question your aptitude for this study. F!'

For the next two days Jennie cut her exams and spent her time in her bed wrapped in a quilt (a present from her room-mate's mother) and reading *The Lives*. She loved this book, not just the text and pictures but this very copy, with all its bent and torn pages, its orange juice and coffee stains, the drops of blood she'd sprinkled from her fingertips when she was thirteen. Her father had given her this book on her sixth birthday, long before she could read all the words, let alone understand the stories. When he died, six months later, Jennie began sleeping with the book inside her nightgown against her chest. Later she decided a Benign One must have guided her father the day he bought the book for her while she was still so young.

Two days later, at her room-mate's insistence, Jennie went to see her faculty adviser. The interview didn't last long. An underweight art instructor who fidgeted with the locks of his attaché case, Dr Lindholm wanted to go home and scrub his skin with a hard brush and cold water. The penance would prepare him for an Enactment that night at the faculty club, one designed to provoke his chairman to offer him tenure for the following year.

They talked for several minutes, and then Jennie said, 'I don't know, maybe I don't belong here.'

'Well,' Dr Lindholm said, 'lots of students do drop out, take a leave of absence.' He asked how her parents would react.

'My mother. My father's dead.'

'Oh. I'm sorry.'

'It happened a long time ago. A Malignant One killed him during the Revolution Day parade. It leaped down his throat while he was singing and wrapped itself around his heart.'

154

Dr Lindholm pushed back from the desk. An awful omen, he thought, to have a student tell him a story like that just before his tenure Enactment. He squinted at her, as if she herself was a Ferocious One disguised as a student. He imagined her mouth opening in a wide grin to show huge teeth, sharp and blinding white. He squeezed shut his eyes for a moment. In control again he said, 'And how would your mother react?'

'Okay, I guess. She didn't want me to go to college anyway.'

'Why not?'

'She wanted me to be a musician. Or a painter.'

'What? Do you play something? Or paint?'

'I've tried. My mother plays the saxophone. A lot of her friends paint.'

'I see. I'll tell you what, Ms Mazdan. Why don't you go home, go to your dorm, and think it over. Then if you decide you can't, you need a leave, come back to me and I'll sign the papers.'

Jennie shrugged. 'Okay.'

'Fine then. Well, if that's all then – '

Jennie got up, clumsily holding her coat and canvas bag against her chest. 'Thank you,' she said. 'I'm sorry. I'll bring you those papers.' She shuffled to the door. But then instead of leaving she turned round. 'Sometimes – '

'Ms Mazdan, I do have my work.'

'Sometimes I get this really funny feeling. Like I can never do anything I really want, or even know what I want, because something's taken hold of me. And it makes me do things for its own reasons and not for anything to do with me. Do you know what I mean?'

'I'm sure it'll pass.'

Jennie stood there a moment. Finally she turned and left. As she walked down the hall she could hear behind her Dr Lindholm chanting. As if delivered from danger,

155

he was reciting the names of the Founders. 'Alexander Joybirth, Mohandas Quark, Danielle Book Of The People, Maryanna Split Sky, Jan Willem Singing Rock, Li Ku Unquenchable Fire . . .'

Excerpt from THE CONSECRATION OF A BOOK, Enactment performed on a child's thirteenth birthday, in honour of *The Lives Of The Founders:*

When lifting a glass to your mouth, or a fork to your mouth, or when finished dressing in the morning, or when throwing a ball at the opening of a game, or when beginning or ending the construction of a house, or when beginning or ending the writing of a book, or when leaving work at the end of the day, or when burning dead leaves, or when burying a parent or a sibling or a child, or a pet, or when swimming in the direction of the sunset, it is proper to say,

WE REMEMBER THE FOUNDERS.

For several weeks Jennie walked around the city or stayed in her room watching television. One day, during one of her walks, it began to snow. She took refuge in a temp. office, where she filled out a form. Two weeks later a phone call woke her up at 8:30 to send her off to the Sacred Rainbow Costume Distributors to help put together orders for the coming equinox parades. After several weeks Jennie moved on to consumer surveys in department stores, and after that a long stint processing personal ads for an intellectual newspaper.

The Summer passed. Jennie tried to think about returning to college. Autumn came and went and she stayed with her agency.

On March 9, twelve days before the officially designated Anniversary of Creation, Jennie reported to work at Bloomingdale's, her current assignment. For a week

156

she'd been dressing in a silver smock and mask, and offering female customers a free squirt of 'New Moon perfume – to release your Hidden Wonders.' The job tired her but she liked watching all the rich women from behind her mask – a little like one-way glass – and she liked standing in front of the famous 'endless road' escalator. But when she arrived, her supervisor told her that a group of purificationists had smashed the guardian husks along the escalator railing and the police had cordoned off that whole wing of the building.

'Well, what should I do?' Jennie said.

Her supervisor lifted her eyes to the images of paradise painted on the ceiling. 'How should I know? I've got enough troubles without doubling as an Oracle.'

Jennie took the IRT subway down to Astor Place where she transferred to the crosstown bus. When she reached her mother's street she stayed on until the last stop, then walked across the highway to the wooden pier sticking out into the river. Years ago, Jennie used to come here after school. She'd sit on the wooden benches, reading a book or just staring at the old black freighter docked on the side of the pier. She liked to imagine she could see the secular mayor and his gang in their pilgrim disguises trying to escape the Revolution, and the wall of water that kept their ship from moving. According to *The Lives Of The Founders*, when the world runs down, and the Unchained Mother breaks the curve of the night, then the Founders will return and board this boat to travel among the stories until a new First Teller creates the universe. According to the book they will come as 'bones without flesh' which is why the proper term for a skeleton is a 'refugee', in honour of the Founders and their final journey.

For a while Jennie stood at the edge of the pier, looking at the Freighter, or else across the river at the

157

eternal clouds covering the Broken City. When she turned to leave she bumped into a man standing with his hands in his pockets. 'Oh,' she said, 'I'm sorry.'

'Not much of a day for sightseeing' he said, casually moving to block her from getting past him.

Jennie made herself look up and smile at the plain face and thick brown hair of a man in his late twenties. 'Thank you,' he said, and smiled back at her.

'Thank you?'

He laughed at her confusion. 'You look cold,' he said. 'Can I buy you a cup of coffee?'

'I guess so,' she said, furious at her awkwardness. He was okaylooking. He had wide shoulders, though not too thick, not like those guys who worked out all the time. His nose was a bit large. But his mouth was nice.

'I don't know this area,' he said. 'You know a good place?'

'There's lots of coffee shops.'

'Just as long as it's not full of artists trying to show off.'

Jennie laughed louder than she had in months.

Sitting for hours in the Glowood Diner, in a red vinyl booth under a picture of Mirando Glowwood's 'Miracle of the Chocolates' (for two quarters in a slot a lump of chocolate would pop onto the table from a hole in the painted hand), Jennie found herself babbling about the last year. While Michael Gold told her about his crummy apartment, or his job as a messenger, or his ambitions, Jennie kept interrupting him, going on about temp work, about her mother, about school, about *The Lives*. Only once did she step out of the rush of laughter and history. She asked Mike if he often came to look at the black freighter.

He shook his head. 'I've never gone there before in my life.'

She stiffened. 'Are you just saying that?'

'Why would I say that? Look, I'm a messenger, right? Usually around this time of day I'm so busy running around town I wouldn't have time to look at the freighter if the Founders themselves came marching on board.'

'Then what happened?'

'I don't know, it was kind of crazy. I delivered an envelope to someone on Gate Street. Private delivery. Huge apartment. Real chandeliers. Well, this guy there told me my boss had called and I should call back. It seems everything was screwed up downtown. Some procession had come through with sweepers, pronouncers, the whole works. They were opening some grand jury investigation. Insider trading or something. Anyway, he told me not to bother coming back, just take the afternoon off.' He shrugged. 'And that's it.'

'But what made you go there? What made you stand right in that place?'

He raised his hands. 'I'll trace my movements for you, officer. From Gate Street I walked over to the river. Don't know why. Yes, I do. They were digging up the sewers and Gate Street stank, and I wanted some fresh air. As fresh as you can get in this city. As for my standing behind you, that, I'm afraid, was cold hard calculation.'

'But don't you see what a coincidence it all is?'

'What coincidence? I told you I did it deliberately.'

'Once you saw me, sure.' He laughed, and she blushed. She tossed her head, as if to fling off the distraction. 'I mean, before that. The procession, the sewers . . . And I should be working now too.'

'Well, so what?'

'I don't know.' She looked at her fingers playing with

159

a wrapped cube of sugar. Why did she have to meet someone and sound such an idiot? She said, 'Sometimes I get this feeling – like something wants to use me.'

'Use you for what?'

'I don't know. It's – it's like something gets hold of me and makes me do things. Nothing scary. Or even special. But as if it's manoeuvring me.'

'Manoeuvring you? For what?'

'I don't know. Into position. Or something.' She wondered if her weirdness or her dumbness would drive him away faster.

'Have you gone to a healer?'

She shook her head. How she wished she had never started this. 'No, it's not possession. I know it's not.'

'Do you get this feeling often?'

'No. No, I only really got it once before, in college. When I left. It just seemed like – like whatever reasons I had for going home, that wasn't why I left. I left because something wanted me out of there. Wanted me home.'

'And now it wanted you to meet me?'

She blushed again, then giggled. 'I guess it sounds pretty silly.'

'Silly? Look, if these clever manipulators lined me up to meet you maybe I should give them an offering. Here.' He placed an ash tray in the centre of the table. He waved his hand in the air. 'Got a consecrated knife? I could scrape some skin off my thumb and burn it right now. Pay my debts.'

She laughed. 'Stop it,' she said. 'People will see.'

'Well, what's wrong with that? It never hurts to show some visible respect for invisible forces.'

That was how Jennifer Mazdan met Michael Gold. She began to see him every week, then twice a week, then three or four times. The feeling of manipulation evaporated in the excitement of getting to know him.

160

She would not understand it until years later, in a hive kitchen in Mike's hometown of Poughkeepsie, New York. And by then, Mike was gone.

2

Despite their different childhoods Jennie and Mike shared a great deal. Like her, his father had died, though only a couple of years before. And his mother was strange, just like Beverley – well, hardly just, but she'd left her family when Mike was ten, joining a bus load of pilgrims to New Orleans. There she signed away her civil rights to become a 'Faceless Worker' serving the Tellers. 'You know about the New Orleans halls, don't you?' Mike asked, and Jennie looked away. Mike said, 'Yeah, I guess you do.' When Mike was fourteen a TV report about the 'body paths' showed, for just a moment, the former Ann Gold, naked except for a snakeskin belt hung with plants, miniature daggers, and carved animals. For the next two weeks Mr Gold's hardware store was full of customers, most of whom kept watching him from the side while pretending to look at hammers and saws. And Mike had dropped out of college, just like Jennie. Well, almost just, for while Jennie had blown away like a fallen leaf, Mike had left deliberately, even performing a severance Enactment at the school's main gate. For several years he'd worked in the store with his father and his uncle, but a year or so after his father's death he'd decided he wanted something more. He came to New York, and even if the only job he could get was as a messenger, at least he was on Wall Street.

The day Jennie told her mother about Mike Beverley was rehearsing for a solo performance of her 'Just A

Housewife Suite.' The whole time they talked, sitting on mats in the rehearsal room under a photo of Jaleen Heart-Of-The-World, Beverley either popped the keys of her saxophone, or else fiddled with silverware, frying pans, or huge clumps of steel wool held together with rubber bands.

The conversation seemed to slide around an impenetrable bubble. When Jennie described Mike's job as a Wall Street messenger Beverley laughed. When Jennie said that Mike hoped eventually to become a commodities trader, Beverley laughed louder. As Jennie got up to leave her mother asked if Mr Gold could get her a tickertape machine, if they still used that sort of thing. She wanted to try the essentially male sound as a counter against the female rattle of dishes and clothespegs.

A week after Jennie's declaration to her mother Jennie and Mike went to the Maryanna Split Sky Clinic north of 14th Street near Unity Square. They'd been lovers for a couple of months but Jennie had resisted the formal step of going for pills or a device. That had left them with the only form of birth control that didn't require a sacred Enactment – Mohandas Quark condoms. Jennie knew that Mike hated the things. He hated the sensation and he hated the idea. She didn't tell him that she secretly liked the thought that Quark was penetrating her along with her boyfriend. Mike became more and more irritable, finally shouting one night that he didn't like 'sharing my cock with another man.'

'It's not some other man,' she said. 'It's a Founder.'

His laugh made her wince. 'Well, I still don't like it. You ever read those stories of some man who puts on a quarkskin and it grafts itself onto his prick? I don't want anyone taking me over. Not even a Founder.'

'I'm sure that would never happen to you.'

162

'You sound like you'd like it.'

She was silent briefly, then she said, 'Well, who wouldn't?'

He kissed her, holding her face as if he expected her to dodge. 'I think you mean that. Sometimes, Jennie – sometimes you really scare me. You're weird. You know that? You're a lot weirder than your mother. Do you know that?'

At the clinic Mike surprised, and in a way, disappointed Jennie by taking a full and solemn part in the ceremony of fitting her diaphragm. Afterwards, sitting in the park, she accused him of putting on a show for the tattooed nurses.

'Sometimes you've got to put on a show,' he said.

'What? You're not admitting – '

He laughed. 'I don't mean because they were women.'

'And naked. No, of course not.'

'Naked? They were covered with pictures. They looked like subway trains. "Flowing muscles of truth." Isn't that the phrase?'

'Since when have you cared about truth?'

'I care as much as most people. Especially when someone's looking.' He put his arm round her.

'Mike,' she said, 'if you didn't feel anything in the mystery – why did you do it? The man doesn't have to take part.'

He shrugged. 'People expect it.'

'What people?'

'Everyone. Society. If you don't take part in things like that people look at you strange. And talk about you.'

'But is that all there is? It wasn't like that in the old days.'

Mike said, 'You mean the Time of Fanatics?'

'I guess so. The Days of Awe.'

He shook his head. 'I don't understand you. I don't

163

understand anyone who looks back on that and thinks it was great. When I was a kid just hearing about it scared me. I remember once – I must have been about nine – we had this teacher, Ms Bowen. She started telling us all this stuff one day, I don't even remember any details, but that night I was playing when suddenly I got really scared. Crying wildly, couldn't breathe – '

'How horrible. Oh, poor little Mike.'

'God knows how long it took my folks to figure out what I was screaming about. I just remember them telling me how the Time of Fanatics was over and was never coming back. They had to tell me about ten times before it sunk in.'

She kissed him. 'Poor little sweetie.'

'It's okay. I survived.' He moved his hands along her shoulders and down her back. 'Let's go home and try out your new transporter.' Jennie hugged him and they got up from the bench.

Jennie and Mike got married exactly a year and five months after they first met. From the moment the engagement was announced, three months ahead of the date, Mike and Beverley began to argue over the wedding. Beverley wanted a 'contemporary recreation' of 'Dustfather and Mothersnake', the Prime Picture Ingrid Burning Snake had told at the mass wedding held after the liberation of New York. She wanted to hold the event in her own house, planning to rope off the street and fill it with giant terra cotta dolls signifying the characters in the picture. She wanted Mike and Jennie to go up on the roof and throw down more dolls to smash them on the pavement, a 'direct incarnation' as she called it, of Dustfather's dismemberment. She wanted tapes played on loudspeakers all through the house and even in the street. Some of the tapes would recite the tale, but out of synch. with each other, producing an outward chaos, while subconsciously the Picture would 'drench' the participants. Other tapes (she never got around to specifying how many tape decks she would need) would blast each other with instruments, cars, trucks, thunder, recorded earthquakes, and wrecking machines (to represent Mothersnake's revenge on the city after her husband's death). The noises would slowly build 'to a density of sorrow' until the moment of Dustfather's song in the nursery. Then everything would stop until a single electronic voice emerged from the destruction.

Mike, on the other hand, wanted a traditional wedding, held in a hall, with Burning-snake's picture recited by a local Teller (he suggested importing his family's neighbourhood Teller from Poughkeepsie). He wanted himself and the bride painted in simple, literal images of the key moments. He wanted groups of children in giant gold-painted cardboard boxes equipped with horns and ratchets for the children to chase away the Hooded Man whenever his name was mentioned.

Beverley said, 'If you want literalness so much, if you really want a traditional wedding, maybe you and Jen should act out the Picture. Literally. We can hold a lottery to see which of the guests gets to help Jennie cut off your – '

'Mother!' Jennie shouted.

Mike said, 'Why bother with a lottery? I'm sure you'd rig it so you would win. Maybe you should go and sharpen the knife you used on all your husbands.'

'Mike,' Jennie said, 'please stop.'

The arguments went on for weeks, with Beverley and Mike each making their own arrangements in defiant ignorance of the other.

Jennie refused to discuss her wedding with either of them. 'Just let me know who wins,' she told Mike. 'Okay?'

'You've got to stand up to her sometime.'

'I don't want to stand up to her. She's my mother. And I don't want to stand up to you either.'

In the end, Mike's cousin Sophie had a meeting with Jim Pepper, Beverley's current lover, and the two negotiated a compromise. The wedding would take place in Beverley's house, but with a traditional Telling. Mike's family could provide the Teller but Beverley was to compose a march for the beginning and a fanfare for the end. Both compositions, however, would use only acoustic instruments and no tapes. The children would sit in traditional boxes and would be responsible for noise at the appropriate moments. Beverley, however, could supply their noisemakers, an opportunity which helped to deflate any anger or disappointment. They kept the idea of giant dolls, but only two of them, one for Dustfather and one for Mothersnake. Rather than smashing them, Mike and Jennie would crawl inside them for the last stage of the ceremony. 'How literal,' Beverley said. 'How completely literal. Mike must be thrilled.'

After the announcement of the truce Jennie went to her room where she sat on the floor facing a small copper statue on a wooden stand. The statue was of a faceless woman standing with her feet together and her arms crossed over her breasts. Jennie had received the statue on her thirteenth birthday in a 'joining' Enactment held in the local Picture Hall on Christopher Street. Now she crossed her own arms on her chest and bowed her head. 'I thank you, Devoted One, for your devotion. I thank you for rescuing me from my mother and my husband. I know that nothing I have done deserves your precious intervention.'

Six weeks before the wedding Mike entered the East Side Hospital of the Inner Spirit, where a healer in a black hood circumcised him. The hospital invited

Jennie to take part by laying gloved hands on her an-aesthetised fiancé. She refused, allowing Mike and the hospital administrators to think it was squeamishness. In fact, a strange longing had taken hold of her. She had found herself wishing for a genuine Enactment, the kind they used to hold in the Time of Fanatics, when the bride would actually circumcise her husband and throw the foreskin from the roof. She tried to banish the idea – it was unsafe and barbaric, not to mention ruining the wedding night – but it kept coming back, entering her thoughts at odd moments. She found her-self wondering if a gust of wind – 'Mothersnake's shout' they used to call it – would lift the foreskin into the sky.

The wedding went smoothly, at least as smoothly as Jennie could expect. They used Beverley's rehearsal studio, the largest, and emptiest, room in the house. Throughout the ceremony and the party Mike's family tended to huddle together at one side of the room. By unspoken agreement Beverley's guests surrendered one wall to them, and once they saw that no one would accost them, the Gold family and friends relaxed. After the ceremony a few even tried dancing to the bizarre music pounding them on all sides. Jennie did her best to divide her time equally between the two sides, propelled from one to the other by a seesaw of guilt.

Mike's uncle paid for their honeymoon. Mike had told Jennie he wanted to surprise her, and kept secret their destination until they checked in at the airport. Jennie guessed he just wanted to forestall another battle with her mother. She could have told him Beverley wouldn't care. They flew to Bermuda, and a beachfront hotel full of newlyweds drinking champagne, and dancing, and blushing or laughing at the clumsy innu-endos of the comics in the nightclub. When they got back they found postcards from Beverley, who'd gone on a pilgrimage to the messenger towers in the Arizona desert.

3

On their last afternoon in Bermuda, Mike and Jennie rented mopeds and puttered along the cliff road leading to St George. Halfway there, in the middle of the road, Jennie jerked to a stop. Mike shouted and ran his moped up the steep embankment. Then he shook himself loose and shouted at his wife, 'What's the matter with you? Are you nuts?' Jennie didn't answer. She stood in the road, her head slightly to the side, her hands up near her mouth. 'Darling?' Mike called. 'What are you doing?' He jumped down.

'Don't you hear it?' Jennie said.

Mike led Jennie to the side, then picked up her moped and leaned it against a tree. 'You can't just stand in the road' he said.

She waved a hand. 'Shh.'

Now Mike heard it too, a rumble, no, a moan, like someone chanting from deep in the belly. His skin prickled. 'C'mon,' he said. 'We're getting out of here.'

Jennie fluttered loose from his grip. 'Where's it coming from?' she said. She walked back in the road, where a car swerved around her. She paid no attention, but a moment later continued to the narrow shoulder between the road and the cliff edge. 'Mike!' she called. 'Honey, come here. Come here.'

He went and stood about a foot behind her. 'Don't stand so close,' he said. 'And don't bend over like that.'

'Look,' Jennie said.

Mike squatted down to lean forward on his hands and knees. About seventy feet below them the shoreline curled in to form a small inaccessible beach of sand

and stones and weeds. In between the cliff wall and the water stood a semi-circle of five upright stones, each about four feet tall. And in front of them, right at the water's edge, stood a man. He was wearing some sort of animal skin hung with bright coloured feathers, bones, pieces of metal, and large beads. Long, thin slivers of wood ran through his ears, his wrists, and his ankles. Paint and clumps of mud covered his exposed skin, while some sort of heavy black grease coated his long matted hair. He stood with his arms out, like a scarecrow. The wind rocked him back and forth, and the waves slapped his legs. His moan continued to fill the ground under Mike and Jennie.

'A precursor,' Jennie whispered. 'Oh, Michael, a precursor. How fabulous. I wonder when – he might be from thousands of years ago.' And *where* was it from? Local? Did Bermuda have precursors? She'd read the island's 'True History' at the hotel but she couldn't remember. Anyway, a displacement could come from anywhere. Siberia was supposed to have had a lot of them. South America too. Actually, almost everywhere. For some places it was just further back in time. They had all sorts of Names, she knew. Shamans, medicine men, sorcerers, prophets – all of them yearning for the Revolution centuries before it actually happened. Only a few managed to propel themselves through time. Or maybe they all did, but only a few modern people could see them.

Jennie didn't care. 'How fabulous,' she said again. 'It's a sign, honey. For our marriage.'

Mike whispered, 'It's some jerk who should have stayed in his own time zone.' He darted a glance at his wife, but she hadn't heard. She hummed softly. He waited a minute, then said, 'Maybe we should go. He could stay down there for hours, days even.' He

169

couldn't tell if she was listening. He said, 'That duty-free shop will close.'

She turned her head, then snapped her eyes back to the swaying figure below. 'Dutyfree? Are you out of your mind? You want to go and buy perfume when there's a precursor down there?' Mike sat down on the ground.

For several minutes they watched the beach, while occasional cars whined behind them. Slowly the sky darkened, and the wind rose. 'It's going to storm,' Mike said. 'We better go back.' His wife ignored him. He stood up, grabbed her arm. 'Will you come on?' he said. 'I don't want you getting sick on our honeymoon.'

Jennie pulled loose so sharply she nearly lost her balance.

'I'm going,' Mike said loudly. 'You do what you want.' He stamped across the road and got on his moped. He wished it was a real motorcycle so he could gun the motor instead of having to pedal downhill to get it started. As soon as he turned the first curve he found the sun shining and the wind gone. He didn't look back.

When Jennie returned, hours later, Mike was lying on the bed, reading a book. She closed the door and sat down on an armchair with her legs out and her arms dangling over the sides. Behind her the sound of the sea came in over the balcony. 'Honey,' Jennie said, 'It was so beautiful. You should have stayed.' He said nothing. 'The waves kept rolling at him, and all these birds, crows or ravens or something, they started circling his head and diving at his face – '

Mike made a noise. 'You find that beautiful?'

'Yes, it was like – like they were cleaning him off – '

'You could use a cleaning off yourself. You're filthy.'

She laughed. 'Dirty but horny.' She began taking off

her clothes. Mike said, 'What do you think you're doing.'

Still in her underwear she sat down next to him and began rubbing her arms and legs and hips against his side. 'Knock it off,' he said as he moved across the bed.

'Come on, hubby,' she cooed, 'it's fucky, fucky time.' She leaned over. Her splayed fingers slalomed down his chest while her lips made kiss noises at his face.

'Like hell it is,' he said, and pushed her away.

'Hey,' Jennie whined. She leaned back to cross her arms over her chest. 'Some honeymoon.'

'I just don't get excited by my wife acting like some cheap whore.'

'Okay. How does an expensive whore act?'

'Very funny.'

'Oh, come on, Mike, we saw a precursor today.'

'And he sure got you worked up, didn't he?'

'Well, what's wrong with that? That's what a vision is supposed to do, isn't it? Do you know how rare it is to see a precursor? And especially at such an important moment. This is the beginning of our life together. It's an omen, Mike. I want to celebrate.'

'Spare me the lecture. All I know is, you never get this horny just for me. Maybe I should dress up in animal skins with feathers through my nose.'

'That sounds great.' She tried to swing onto him but he shoved her away.

'Some honeymoon,' Jennie said. She stood up. 'I'm taking a shower.' When she'd locked the bathroom and started the water Mike shouted, 'Don't you go pouting on our last night.'

Later, after they'd eaten among the palm trees in the dining room, Mike took Jennie to the hotel's Island Ballroom. There he stroked his wife's shoulders and whispered how much he loved her. Later still, while they made love, Jennie tried to remember the way she'd

171

heated up when the birds flew round the precursor's face and the ocean soaked his legs. And still later, a sleeping Mike dreamed that a trio of Malignant Ones, women with thick vaginal lips and breasts like thunder, slapped mud on his face and dressed him in feathers and slivers of bone. A Benign One, in the form of a park commissioner, set him at the edge of a beach. 'There,' he said happily, 'now you can count the waves until the Revolution comes.'

4

For over a year Mike and Jennie lived in Mike's studio apartment on 22nd Street. More and more, Mike began to complain about New York. Life was unnatural there, the city crushed anyone who just wanted a normal life. They began to spend more weekends in Poughkeepsie, more recital and Enactment days. They would stay with Mike's uncle, or with his cousin Carl. Mike would laugh loudly and breathe deeply, as if to demonstrate how the clean air of Dutchess County liberated the body and the soul. For their second Rising of the Light as a married couple, they went to stay with Uncle Jake. On the morning after the solstice, with Uncle Jake sleeping off the post-enactment party, and Aunt Alice in the kitchen stuffing the turkey, Mike told Jennie he had made a decision. They were moving to Poughkeepsie.

Jennie said, 'But I thought you said there were no opportunities in Poughkeepsie.'

'I was wrong, okay? Opportunity is where you make it.'

Jennie dreaded telling her mother about this plan to manufacture opportunity in Poughkeepsie. She went alone, in the afternoon. To Jennie's surprise, Beverley took the news with hardly a pause in her rehearsal (she was practising animal noises on the alto clarinet).

'Mom,' Jennie said, 'I'm moving eighty miles upstate. Don't you care? Doesn't that upset you?' The clarinet barked. 'Stop that,' Jennie said loudly. 'Put that thing down.'

Beverley's eyebrows jumped. She smiled sweetly as she laid the instrument on a plastic table. 'Do you want me to act the possessive mother?'

'I want you to show some interest. I am your only child, remember? And I'm not doing anything you want. Doesn't that bother you?'

Beverley put an arm around her daughter. 'Jen,' she said. 'As long as you stay asleep what difference does it make if you snooze here in my house or in a cabin in Alaska?'

'Sleep?' Jennie pulled away. 'What are you talking about?'

'When you wake up – and I don't know when that will be, but I do know it will happen – it won't matter where you are. You'll find your way. That's the marvel of a sleepwalker.'

Mike and Jennie moved to Poughkeepsie in late January. Jennie tried not to get upset at the chilly pre-fab house Mike had rented north of town, off Pendell Road. It was only to get them settled, he assured her as she stood in the living room with her coat buttoned, and stared at the worn carpet, the greasy-looking flowered wallpaper. They could start looking for their own house right away, he promised, while he and Uncle Jake unloaded the van Mike had hired. Anyway, Mike said, it was better than that tiny overpriced apartment they'd left in New York. At least it was a whole house.

Not quite true to his promise Mike put off looking for a house for several months, insisting his new job as manager of a branch office of a local travel agency took all his time. He did, however, get Jennie her own car, an old Plymouth Duster, its faded gold paint merging into rust on the fenders and doors. Despite violent vacuuming and a whole day with the door open to winter breezes the car always smelled dirty. 'Dusty the Duster,' Jennie called it. She dreamed of riding over the tops of skyscrapers on her bald white-walls. It was Mike who suggested she look for a job. She should meet people, get out of the house. Maybe she could temp. again. But Poughkeepsie only had two temp. agencies, and they expected more skills and experience than Jennie could offer. Halfheartedly she tried lingerie shops, pet stores, and offices, until one afternoon in late Spring she fell asleep in the parking lot of the Breathless Spirit Shopping Mall, with her head on Dusty's steering wheel. She dreamed of running through the great public labyrinth in Washington, down white hallways smelling of the sea, until she emerged into a garden before a huge rock covered with mud. She scraped the mud away to reveal a round face flooded with light. When she woke up she went into a coffee shop and asked for a phone book. She looked up the address of the administrative offices of the Mid-Hudson Energy Board, thanked the cashier in the coffee shop, and drove to the offices on Route 44, where she applied for a job as a guardian Server. On her application, in the space for 'previous experience' she described her dream. She was hired immediately.

While Jennie learned to clean husks, Mike grew more and more passionate about his own work. Each morning he would get up just before dawn and take out a sheet of sanctified paper (made from old cloth collected from the Tellers' residences and sold in packs of twenty five in spiritual supply stores). With his Cross pen (a present from Jennie the last solstice) he would

174

draw a stick picture of himself and label it 'Managing Director of the Journeys of Truth Travel Agency'. Standing naked in the living room he would wait for the sunrise (on cloudy days checking his Bermuda-bought duty-free watch for accuracy), then rub the picture round his chest and face and between his legs before finally burning it with one of the phosphorus matches sold with the paper. He never mentioned these Enactments to Jennie. Lying in bed, pretending to be asleep, she could see him tiptoe about the dark house. Once, she needed to pee so badly she could almost weep, but she made sure to wait a good minute after Mike was back in bed before she allowed herself to get up.

Shortly after Jennie began her job Mike announced that the time had come for them to look for a house. He apologised for putting it off so long, and Jennie had to tell him it didn't matter. She found herself faking what seemed the proper level of enthusiasm. It worried Jennie that she didn't get more excited as they travelled about looking at homes and talking to real estate agents.

After several weeks of houses too small, too old, or too expensive, the agent suggested they look at a hive house. He did it so casually, and Mike responded with such a studied manner of someone pondering a new idea that Jennie was sure they'd arranged the performance ahead of time. 'What do you think?' Mike said. 'It's worth a look, huh? I'll bet you've never even been in a hive.' He seemed to be bracing himself.

'I don't know,' Jennie said. 'I guess we can look at it.' She thought she caught a flicker of disgust pass over Mike's face; she wished she'd realised she should react more forcefully.

Jennie told her mother about the hive over the telephone. She called late, after Mike had fallen asleep watching the *Tonight* show. Beverley laughed with what sounded like genuine delight. She suggested that Jennie paint a slash of red across the door so she could recognise the house. She then suggested Jennie paint a slash of red around Mike's cock, so she could recognise her husband. She added that a permanent marking would be more efficient, and that she knew someone on Christopher Street who was doing the most delicate work in genital scar designs, and she would pay if Michael wanted . . . Jennie said she had to go to the all-night supermarket and said goodbye to her mother.

They drove to Glowwood Hive, where Jennie felt like someone in a play who's forgotten the climax as well as her own lines. She watched Mike discuss the house's construction, she checked for outlets and closet space, they stood together in the bare living room with the estate agent and talked about shopping, taxes, enactment facilities, and walking distance to the local kindergarten.

Only when they'd signed the preliminary papers did Jennie find out they had to visit a 'touchstone.' Mike explained it in a booth in the Italian restaurant down by the river, where they'd gone for a celebration meal. Every six months, all the hive adults gathered, all of them wearing some token of their blocks (this was the first time Jennie had heard of blocks as well, but she thought she shouldn't interrupt). Each person would then cast a labelled stone from his or her front lawn into a wooden drum made from the first tree cut down to clear the land (actually, the agent had confessed to Mike, the drum had been bought in New York). The previous touchstone would then emerge, blindfolded, to spin the drum and open a slot which would allow one stone to fall out. Whoever owned that rock became the new touchstone.

Jennie only half-listened, fascinated by the way Mike

176

wouldn't look at her while he talked, but only stared at his lasagne as if it represented an answer from an oracle. He stopped speaking, but when she didn't say anything he went on to describe the holy office. The 'stone', as they called him, lived in a special house in the centre of the hive, in the hive's sacred grove, a circle of trees on top of a hill. All the hives had sacred groves, Mike said, just as they all had stones. The stone couldn't leave the grove, but he could sit outside among the trees. And it was only for six months. When the lottery had selected the new stone ('Just a kind of bingo' Mike said), a committee chained him – not real chains, just plastic, to symbolise his service to his neighbours. Then they led the stone up the hill, past two rows of people, one of them throwing flowers, the other flailing the stone – gently, Mike emphasized – with leafy branches.

During this speech Mike kept stopping and starting, as if compelled to tell everything. She found his honesty touching, the more so since it appeared unwilling. It took her a moment to realise it when he'd finally finished. She said, 'But what is a touchstone? What does the touchstone do?'

Nothing really, Mike said. 'He's supposed to symbolise the unity of the hive. That's all. He just lives there. The house represents the sacred dimension or something. Access to the Living World. You know more about that stuff than me.'

It suddenly occurred to Jennie that Mike was afraid she would refuse to move because of the touchstone. And why. She asked, 'Will I have to go live in this grove for six months?'

'Only if your stone comes up. Chances are you'll never have to do it at all. Anyway,' he added quickly, 'they exempt you for the first two terms. So you've got over a year before you even have to think about it.'

177

'And we have to go and see this person?'

'It's just a formality. Just a ceremony.'

He poured them each a glass of Beaujolais. Grinning, he leaned forward to kiss her lightly on the lips. 'Let's do an offering,' he said. 'For us and our new home.'

Jennie laughed. 'Right here?'

'Sure. We can do it real quiet. No one'll notice us.' He reached into his pocket and took out a velvet case.

Excited, Jennie said, 'What's that?'

Mike grinned. 'I figured that this special occasion deserved a better offering pin than that crummy steel thing. Come on, open it.'

Gently she clicked open the top. 'Mike,' she said, 'It's beautiful. Oh, honey.' She leaned forward so suddenly her breast knocked over the wine bottle. Mike caught it, though he was laughing so hard he almost knocked it over himself. Inside the case rested a gold needle, three inches long, with a lapis lazuli handle the shape of a bird's head. 'It must have cost a fortune,' Jennie said.

Mike's smile looked like it could break his face. 'It wasn't cheap,' he said. 'But we'll have it for the rest of our lives.'

'Can we really do it right now?' Jennie whispered.

'Why not? We're private enough here. There was even a court ruling about it once. That a table in a restaurant was seen as a spiritual entity – '

'You first,' she said, and handed him the case.

'Are you sure?' he said. She nodded. Mike sterilised the needle in a thin vial of alcohol. He held up his left index finger. With a jab of the pin he pricked the tip, and when a drop of blood oozed out he shook it into his wife's glass. The drop vanished into the wine. 'For our new home,' he said.

Jennie yelped as she jabbed herself, then started giggling in embarrassment. She squeezed her finger to make a drop of blood emerge. 'For our new home,' she said as she shook the drop loose into Mike's wine. They touched glasses, then brought them to their lips. Together they said, 'We Remember the Founders,' and then drank as much of the wine as they could swallow in one gulp.

That night, they made love more slowly and rhythmically than for weeks. In the middle Mike jumped up and came back with the pin. In two quick jabs he'd drawn blood from both her breasts. A moment later his own thighs were bleeding, and then he climbed up to mingle the offerings. As Mike ran a trail of blood down to her groin Jennie moaned and rolled her head. 'Blessed spirit,' she whispered, and wrapped her legs around her husband's back. 'Blessed, blessed spirit.'

The estate agent made an appointment for them on a Saturday afternoon. 'Good luck,' he told them and winked. 'I'll be waiting for you back here with the papers.'

The sacred grove, a ring of five trees, didn't look much like the entrance to another world. A small wooden platform contained a plaster-of-Paris ideal hive family: father and mother arm-in-arm, a boy and a girl and a dog dancing in a circle.

The house itself looked like any of the hive houses except for a mural that ran around the walls. A figure, probably Mirando Glowwood, the hive's patron, raised his arms and shouted as trees and boulders leaped into the air. In another part Devoted Ones (for some reason the artist had depicted them as winged and riding in an aeroplane) dropped gifts on a crowd of residents. The gifts included roast turkeys, refrigerators, and washing machines. They reminded Jennie of a game show on television.

The touchstone that half-year was a retired carpenter

179

named Jack Adlebury. When Jennie and Mike entered the living room they saw Adlebury crouched down with his back to them. He wore nothing but sweat-stained boxer shorts and sneakers without socks. On a stool next to him lay a wooden mask with a 'joy face' painted on it: overwide smile, big eyes, round cheeks.

A small man, about five foot five, with thin arms and legs, Adlebury's shoulders rippled slightly as he sanded a chair with an electric sander. 'Hang on,' he said, 'I just gotta finish this.' Whatever furniture the room originally had had was gone, replaced by Adlebury's tools as well as timber, and all the chairs, tables, and cabinets he'd made since his installation. The place stank of stain and varnish. 'Almost done,' he called. 'Just a bit more. There.' He clicked off the sander and set it down on the sawdust-coated floor.

Adlebury sat back on his heels and wiped his forehead with an arm covered in sawdust. 'Sorry,' he said.

Mike said, 'We're here for the inspection. We're hoping, we're planning to buy a house here.'

'Yeah, I know,' Adlebury said, still with his back to them. 'I got a call. I just – ' He reached out for the mask and held it in his hands. 'I'm not supposed to look at you until I got this thing on. Fact is, I'm supposed to wear the damn thing all the time.' He put it on. When he spoke again his voice sounded slightly muffled. 'That's better, I guess.' The stone grunted as he stood up. He turned around.

Nothing in Jennie's life could have prepared her for that onslaught. Even before the mask faced her she could feel them swarming together. The very act of the stone standing up and turning his head took with it a huge weight, as if a fisherman had attached his net to his face and now swung it up packed with squirming fish. The hive-souls moved in and out of each other, they banged together and slid apart in all the ways of

180

their relationships. Jennie was choking. All those people – all of them staring at her.

She didn't actually see them. She didn't see anything but the doll face imprisoning Adlebury. And yet they were there, sliding in and out of each other, hundreds of voices babbling, arguing, laughing, complaining. Jennie gagged. She stumbled, falling against a half-finished desk. 'Hey,' Adlebury said, 'you okay?'

'What?' Jennie said. As she looked up the touchstone once again became a bored elderly carpenter with his face covered in a painted helmet. She let her breath out and found herself shaking.

'Honey,' Mike said, 'what's the matter?' He put his arms around her.

He didn't see it, Jennie realised. For Mike it was just a formality.

And for the touchstone as well. Embarrassed, and a little annoyed by Jennie's distress, he said, 'Welcome to the hive.'

Hours later, after they'd signed the papers in the bank and then the estate agent's office, after they'd eaten the steaks Jennie had grilled as a celebration, after Mike had run back to 'the place' for some paper-work he'd forgotten, after TV and late night ice cream and coffee, after Jennie had got into her nightgown and Mike into his pyjamas, Jennie asked casually, 'You know that – that thing today? The introduction? I know it's just a formality, but a formality for what?'

'Huh?'

Jennie snuggled up against his chest. He put an arm around her. She said, 'I mean, what's supposed to happen? Theoretically, I mean?'

'I don't know, the hive's supposed to look us over, I guess. See if we fit in.'

'But how?'

181

'Through the touchstone. He represents everybody, so he makes the decision.'

'But that's so symbolic.'

'Sure it is. That's the idea.'

Jennie pressed against him. 'Honey,' she said, 'let's celebrate.' She kissed his ear, then his neck.

'Are you kidding?' Mike said. 'I've got to get to the place early tomorrow. I want to set up some new displays before we open. If we're going to pay for our new house I've got to start putting in some hours.' He turned on his side and closed his eyes.

5

It took Jennie months to admit that something had happened between her and Mike. They were both over-worked, she told herself, or, the house was taking all their attention. It wasn't just that they made love less frequently, or only seemed to talk about their jobs or the lawn or their neighbours. It was as if her husband did everything normally, but only with an effort. As if he had to push himself against some barrier. As if she repelled him and he kept battling to hide it. But why? She could stare in the mirror and tell herself she'd lost her looks, but somehow she knew her appearance, her body, had nothing to do with it.

On the night of Founder's Day, a little over a year after they'd moved into the hive, Jennie and Mike went to a Raccoon block party to watch the fireworks. At home, drunk, Mike began to stroke and kiss her. Jennie removed her clothes so fast she fell on the bed, laughing. Mike joined her and they began to make love half dressed.

Suddenly Jennie jumped up. Mike floated an arm after her. 'Where are you going?' he said. 'Come back.'

'You'll see.' She ran into the den to the altar shelf above the television. She came back with the velvet case containing the offering pin.

'Ta da,' she announced, holding it up. 'Remember that first night we got it? How we used it – ahem – (for other purposes?' She didn't finish her proposal. Mike had stiffened all over, except for his erection.

Jennie stood there, clogged with tears. 'What's wrong?' she said. 'What did I do?'

'Nothing,' he said, then burst out, 'What did you have to bring that thing for?'

'But it's our offering pin.'

'I know the fuck what it is.' Jennie began to cry. 'Oh shit,' Mike said. 'I'm sorry.'

Jennie snapped shut the case and threw it at him. 'I don't want your sorry. I want you. What are you doing to me?'

'I just don't want to make an offering. What's the big deal?'

'But why?' Jennie grabbed the bathrobe off the chair by the bed and threw it over her open blouse and pantihose. 'You gave me that pin. So we could have it forever, you said. You were the one to – you know.'

He shrugged. 'It's just not safe.'

'Not safe?'

'Who knows what the blood will attract.'

'Mike, what are you talking about?'

He wouldn't look at her. 'Didn't you read about that woman in Texas?'

'What woman?' She thought she could start screaming at any moment.

'She did her finger for an offering. At a Recital. At sunset. And it opened a channel. All her blood got sucked out. Boiled off right into the Living World. By the time they got her to the hospital she was dead.'

183

'I can't believe this,' Jennie said. 'You think that's what's going to happen to you?'

He mumbled, 'Not to me.'

'What? What do you mean?' He shook his head. Jennie punched his shoulder. 'What do you mean?'

He shoved her away. 'Will you stop it?'

'Do you mean me? Do you think my blood'll get sucked out if I make an offering?'

'Who knows? Who knows what can happen with you?'

'Great Mother,' she said. 'Mike, I've been drop offerings all my life.' She grabbed the case from the floor, sterilized the needle in the alcohol, and jabbed her finger. Shaking the blood loose she said, 'We remember the Founder. There. See? One drop. That's all.'

'This time.'

'This time? Mike, where did you get this idea?' He looked at the wall. She knew. She remembered exactly when the chill had come. 'The touchstone,' she said. 'It's because of what happened. It was supposed to be a formality and it wasn't. I saw them. The souls of the hive. And you knew. You knew all along and you didn't say anything. That's it, isn't it?'

He got up. 'I've got to go piss.'

She tried to grab his arm but he yanked it loose. She called after him, 'I'm right, aren't I? If that could happen anything could happen, is that it?' She heard the toilet flush, and then Mike came back, only to grab his pillow and the extra blanket. 'I'm going to go sleep in the den,' he said.

'Where it's safe? Where I can't suck all your blood away?' She made a loud slurping noise. Mike said nothing. A moment later, Jennie heard the door to the den slam. Exhausted, she lay down and pulled the quilt over her. She expected to cry, to hit the pillow. Instead,

184

she fell asleep. When she woke up, groggy, a little dizzy, the Sun was up and Mike was gone.

That evening Mike told her he was leaving the following morning on a two week hotel tour of Quebec province, getting firsthand knowledge before the season started. He promised to talk when he got back.

For the first week of Mike's absence Jennie tried to act normally. She chose her clothes carefully and put on make-up every morning. At night she cooked herself complete dinners, trying out new recipes and logging them in a notebook for when Mike returned. Then she would sit on Mike's recliner chair and watch television until she was sure she would sleep.

On the Monday of the second week Jennie went up to Maria after the schedule meeting and told her she was too sick to work that day. Silently she endured Maria's anger and the groans of the other servers who not only would have to work harder but would have to sit through the meeting all over again. When she got outside she found her hands trembling.

Jennie drove south on the Highway of the Nine Wonders until she came to a small store all by itself on the side of the highway, south of Fishkill. Many years ago, before the Revolution, this store had sold fishing equipment, lures, and especially trout flies. Even through the destruction of the Old World fishermen from as far away as Germany and Israel continued to order their colour catalogue. Today the small blonde who ran the shop continued the family business. All day she would sit by a large scarred wood table and glue together bits of plastic, feathers, gauze, holy words written on tiny specks of parchment, and barbed metal.

But now the shop was even more renowned for something else. On the day that the Army of the Saints sailed upriver from New York the current owner's great

185

grandfather had gone fishing. Something snagged his line, and when he reeled it in he found a shirt, as dry as if it had laid in the Sun. The shirt had belonged to Miguel Miracle of the Green Earth, and had been used as a banner to rally the faithful in the Battle of Chicago. The next year the fisherman returned to the same spot at the same time and caught the green and gold box from which Mirando Glowwood had drawn forth the Miracle of the Chocolates.

As Jennie pulled into the small parking lot someone roared onto the highway, spraying the side of her car with gravel. 'Hey!' Jennie shouted as if he could hear her. Some way to act in a sacred shrine, she thought. Not that the place looked very sacred. She'd expected signs, or statues. Instead, the small wooden building might have been the home of a retired fisherman.

Inside, Jennie pretended to look around at the strange equipment until she realised how silly that was. She walked to the back to stand over a fair-haired woman tying coloured feathers to a black metal hook. The woman wore an old grey shirt with mother-of-pearl buttons. 'Excuse me,' Jennie said finally.

The woman set the fly down carefully on the table before looking up at Jennie. 'Can I help you?' she said.

'I'm looking – I'd like – Do you have anything from Ingrid Burning Snake?'

The woman made a noise, then looked at the window. When she turned her gaze back to Jennie she asked. 'Why would I have anything to do with Ingrid Burning Snake?'

'What? Isn't this – '

'Do you really think I would just have something from Burning Snake or anyone else just sitting here? And you could just walk in and order it? Like a piece of cheese?'

'I'm sorry,' Jennie said. 'I'm sorry. She was about to leave when the woman stood up.

'No, wait a minute,' she said. 'I'm sure you're – I shouldn't have snapped at you like that.'

'I don't understand.'

'That's because you don't work here. I just get tired of people making the same stupid mistake over and over. Did you see that guy who was just here?' Jennie nodded. 'He wanted Janet Artwing's shoes. Claimed I was "holding out" on him. As if I had something like that just lying around the shop.'

'I don't understand,' Jennie said. She felt like she was back in Professor Hate-hour's True History class.

'Just think a moment. Once a year, every year, something comes to us from the river. I'll bet you think that's a blessing.' Jennie didn't answer. 'Well, it is, of course it is, but it's also . . . How long do you think those things would last if we sold them in this store? Or anywhere? Even if things came to us every day, how long would they last? How long would this building last if we sold those things here? Do you know what happened when Adrienne Birth-of-Beauty died?'

'They had to guard her body.'

'Right. With machine guns. Even before she was actually dead. Everyone wanted a piece of her clothes. Or a piece of her.'

'But what happens – '

'To the relics? The government takes them. What do you think? We give them over to the SDA which puts them in a vault. They get taken out once a year, for the Founders' Day Parade. And you wouldn't believe that security.'

Jennie said, 'It seems, it seems wrong somehow. Aren't the relics supposed to help people?' The woman didn't answer. 'I guess I must seem pretty dumb to you.'

'The SDA does its best to get the message across. For instance, it's illegal to print any reference to us without saying explicitly that we don't sell relics, the store has nothing to do with them. But people just keep coming.'

'Do you – do you catch them yourself?'

The woman shook her head. 'I knew you'd get to that one. I could just guess. Think a moment. Try to think. If I caught them do you think I could just sit here? Do you know how many people would come and want me to touch them? My uncle does it. He lives on an estate surrounded by an electrical fence. I haven't seen him in ten years, not since he became Fisher King. That's the proper term, by the way. Official SDA title. I'll bet you didn't know that either.'

'No.'

'My grandfather died from some disease caught from a woman who broke into his house and forced him to make love to her. She had a gun. She'd been some kind of agent or something and knew how to get past the security. She thought sex with my grandfather would cure her? Isn't that something? They both died.'

'God,' Jennie said, 'I'm sorry.' A moment later she added, 'I guess that means you can't give me anything.'

The woman laughed so loud Jennie stepped back. The laughter stopped as abruptly as it started. An odd look passed through the woman's face. She stood there, squinting at Jennie, and then she said, 'Stay here.' She went through a white door. When she returned she held her hand out. In the palm rested a small brass box. 'Take this,' she said, 'and don't ever tell anyone where you got it.'

Jennie grabbed the box and opened it. Inside, on a red cushion, lay a blackened strip of skin, about an inch across.

'What is this?' Jennie asked. The woman stood there. Jennie said, 'Oh my God. It's her. It's Li Ku. It's from when she came down off the ferris wheel. It's the piece of skin that stuck to the metal.'

'A little piece of the piece. When my grandfather gave it to the government he cut off a few little bits and hid them.'

Jennie looked at the relic. The box felt cold. 'I don't know,' she said.

'You don't know? You don't know? I'm giving you this and you . . . Don't you understand? This is her *body*. It's not a shirt, or a plastic pen used to sign some announcement. It's a piece of her body.'

Jennie started to cry. 'It's just – you know, it's *her*. Li Ku. I wanted something, I wanted Ingrid Burning Snake. It's – it's for, it's because of my husband. My marriage.'

'Take it,' the woman said. 'Li Ku is the truth.'

Jennie looked at the piece of skin. When she closed the box and put it in her bag the woman let out a breath. Jennie asked how much she owed her.

The woman laughed even louder than before. 'Do you think you could possibly pay me enough for something like that?'

'You're giving it to me?' The woman nodded. 'Why?'

She shook her head. The messy blonde hair swung back and forth. 'I don't know. Maybe I just – Please,' she said, 'just get out of here. Okay? In a little while I'm going to be very angry at myself. So please, go.'

Jennie half ran to her car.

That night, and every night until Mike returned, Jennie stripped naked, put on her reddest lipstick, then used her tweezers to pluck the piece of skin and set it down on the living room floor. With the gold offering pin she pricked her finger, then waved her hand to scatter the drops of blood through the air. 'In the name of Li Ku Unquenchable Fire. In beauty and truth lives

189

her name forever.' And then, 'Please help me. Please let me keep my husband. I just want a normal life.'

Mike came home around eleven at night, with a peck on the lips and an announcement that he'd eaten, and was so tired he just wanted to have a shower and go to bed. Jennie listened to him shower, and when he lay in bed she stood in the doorway, her own arms full of his dirty laundry from his suitcase. She told herself how much she loved him, how they would work it out, how she would do anything to keep him.

THE CONCEALMENT

When a baby enters its mother's womb it first swims through the River of Forgetfulness. Only the Founders escaped this immersion. As they travelled to their mothers they floated above the water, in the silver air of truth.

If the Founders always knew reality, why did they wait to begin the Revolution? The answer to this question is: even the Founders (in beauty and truth live their names forever) must wait for the proper moment. The Revolution could only begin in its correct place, Anaheim, California, and only at the correct time, the Parade of the Animals. Before that *moment* the Founders knew they must not reveal themselves. They lived normal lives, going to school, working, living with their families and friends. And they made sure never to meet each other. For if only two Founders were to stand in the same room, or sit on the same bus, or even work for the same company or shop in the same department store, the light would leap from one to the other, blinding anyone who stood between them.

It happened once that a certain woman received a vision of the Revolution. She learned that the Founders existed, that one day they would join together and create the world. Now, this woman had suffered greatly in her life. Her father had died in a plane crash. Her mother had become an alcoholic and a thief. Her lover had left her for someone else. Two of her best friends had committed suicide, while another had contracted a terrible disease that destroys the body. And every day in the woman's city people were beaten and murdered.

The woman decided the world could not wait for the Revolution. She began to pray, and to chant, and through her desperate devotion she stumbled her way over the boundaries into the deep territories. With clear sight she saw the faces of Maryanna Split Sky, Jonathan Mask of Wisdom, and Li Ku Unquenchable Fire (in beauty and truth live their names forever). And she knew – if she could bring these three to the same place, even to the same city, the Revolution would begin, despite their efforts to postpone it.

She tried one scheme after another: fake phone calls, trick letters, fraudulent invitations. She hired actors and detectives, she bribed policemen. Nothing worked. The three always slipped from her net. Finally she returned to her devotions, for she realised that even the Founders could not overcome the Living World. If she could touch that power she could force them to give up their concealment. She fasted and prayed, and after many months she understood what had to be done. There were several steps, all to be enacted in the right order and the right way. Three things overrode the rest. The operation would take five days. During that time she must not open the door of her house, she must not touch food, she must not fall asleep.

She cleaned herself and prayed once more for help. Then she began the operation. On the first day she heard a knocking at the door. A voice cried, 'Help me!' and then she heard a thumping noise, and an agonised cry, and the voice called again, more faintly, 'Help me!' The woman rose but then she forced herself back to the work. At the end of that day a red light glowed in front of her.

On the second day she heard a knock and then her mother's voice. 'Please let me in,' the voice said. 'I've given up drinking but I feel so weak. I need you. Please.' The woman stood up. She ran to the door. But then she remembered all the mothers and fathers who'd died of drink and all the children left alone. She returned to her concentration. That evening a yellow light filled the room.

191

On the third day her former lover appeared at the window. 'How could I ever have left you?' she said. 'Let me in. I want to stay with you forever.' But the woman thought of all the women and men whose lovers had left them. She continued. That evening a blue light filled the house.

On the fourth day her diseased friend knocked at the door. 'Please let me in,' he begged. 'I want to see you before I die. How can you be so cruel?' All day he banged on the door. She thought of all the sick people and she stayed where she was. That night a great darkness and a great silence penetrated the house and the land around it.

On the morning of the fifth day white light filled the world. It shook the houses and pounded in the Earth. All through the day she heard a roar, like a thousand voices shouting with joy.

In the late afternoon she jumped up and ran to the window. Buildings were shaking and trees ran through the air. About to turn back she heard a soft whimper. She looked down and saw a starving dog lying on the grass. She stood there, looking at the animal while the light surged about the building. She told herself, 'It's already started. Nothing can stop it.' She went outside and lifted the dog. As she carried it into the house, the shouting voices changed to a sigh and then stopped.

But the light remained. She closed the door and set the dog on the rug. She looked at the bones pushing their way through the folded skin. She lifted it again and carried it to the kitchen. She opened the refrigerator but the dog was too weak to take any food. 'Please,' she said. 'I'm not allowed to touch it.' The dog began to cry. She looked around her at the light that looked like it could tear the walls apart. 'Nothing can stop it,' she told herself. She reached in for a piece of hamburger meat and gave it to the dog.

As the animal ate, its body filled out. It became stronger and it grew, taller than the woman. Its jaws hung open as large as a doorway. When it closed them it had swallowed the light. As the dog ran from the house a greyness settled on the walls and the woman and everything around her. 'I haven't lost,' she said. 'I can still continue. I can start over

192

if I have to.' But even as she spoke she fell back against the
sink, exhausted. Her eyelids began to force themselves shut.
'Please,' she wept, 'don't do this to me. I didn't want it for
myself. There's too much pain.' She fell asleep on the floor
in front of the refrigerator.

In the woman's dream she saw Li Ku Unquenchable Fire.
The Founder wore a red dress and silver shoes. 'When we
come,' she said, 'we will not come to end suffering.'

'Then why will you come?' the woman asked.

Li Ku said, 'When we come we will come for something
else.'

When the woman woke up she could no longer remember
the three faces.

The woman's mother stopped drinking. The woman's
lover returned to her. The woman's friend recovered from
his disease and all her other friends became well and pros-
perous. But she herself had weakened her body by her efforts
to end suffering. Though she lived a happy life she died two
years before the Revolution. On the day of her death she
once more saw the Founders, all gathered together in a
vision. She wrote in her diary, 'Now I understand. I am the
saddest woman who has ever lived.'

6

Jennifer's marriage to Mike Gold ended on a piece of
green metal at the exit from Glowwood Hive. A raised
circle about five feet in diameter and set in the ground
beside the Celestial Guardian, the metal plate was
called a 'soul-map.' Its surface bore a diagram of the
streets interspersed with spirit configurations and the
mark of an official blessing from the Mid-Hudson
College of Tellers. Officially, all residents stood there
every time they left the hive. Officially, contact with
the map joined them to the hive's unity. Officially, they
could step on the map and get a jolt that would carry
them through a two-week vacation, so that even swim-

ming in a pool in Honolulu they would feel their neighbours floating beside them with every stroke.

In practice very few people ever bothered to stop their cars to get out and 'mount' the map. The few times Jennie had done it she'd never experienced anything more than a slight tickle in her feet.

On the evening their marriage ended Jennie and Mike were on their way to Shop-Rite for double stamp night. At the exit from the hive they stopped for someone coming up the access road. When Mike stepped on the gas the car stalled. Before he could start it again Jennie said, 'Mike, why don't we go stand on the map?'

'What?' Mike said. 'What for?'

'I don't know, it just seems like – we live here, shouldn't we do it some times? It'll only take a second.'

Mike hesitated, and later Jennie would think how if he'd only started the engine she would have given in and maybe they would have stayed together. But instead Mike said, 'Oh fuck,' and got out of the car.

The two of them stepped onto the map. Jennie tried to take his hand but he jerked it away. Jennie was about to step off when she started to sway. 'What's going on?' she said.

Mike had begun to jerk from side to side. 'Feels like a storm's coming up,' he said. 'Let's get out of here.'

But when they looked back at the hive they seemed to stare down at it from the top of a hill. The streets had stretched out. They rolled on and on, they lifted into the sky, a vast criss-cross of black stripes covering the ground. The houses glowed, they shook and danced, like cartoon houses with windows like huge soft eyes, and doors like smiles. From each house, like a paper thrown into the air, the hive members leaped into the sky. They sang to each other and the voices rose to high-pitched squeals, like bats.

194

Jennie screamed and Mike shouted, 'Stop it! Stop it!' Then the two of them rose with their neighbours, plucked in one motion from the flat Earth to an arched sky burning with light. Jennie looked down, she expected to see her and Mike standing there, entranced, but no, the map was empty, their bodies had risen, they were flying, look, they passed a plane, Jennie waved and all the passengers blew kisses at her, now they rose together in a clump, held tight by a syrupy glue of ecstasy.

Jennie couldn't remember coming down. She found herself stretched out on the grass in front of the guardian, a good four feet from the metal plate. Mike lay next to her, moaning. Jennie sat up and rubbed her eyes. 'Wow,' she said, and grinned. 'Wow. Holy shit.' She giggled. Mike was just starting to get up. 'Honey?' she said, and crawled over to touch his arm.

Mike screamed and rolled away. A moment later he got to his knees and threw up.

'What's wrong?' Jennie asked, or tried to. Her voice sounded so sluggish. A silly smile crept over her face. She bit her lip. This is serious, she told herself. She began giggling again. Mike looked at her, his face squeezed into some emotion, fear, or hate. He got to his feet and pushed himself a few steps to the car, where he leaned against it with his arms across the roof. 'Honey?' Jennie called. 'Where are you going?' She saw him breathe deeply a few times, then slide into the seat where he sat with his head back, gasping. She watched him press his fists against his eyes. Only when he actually ignited the engine and she could smell the exhaust did she realise he was leaving. She jumped up; she fell down again, crying. At the same time, she was laughing, as if she still flew round the world with her neighbours.

Even when Mike's car was gone it took Jennie over

a minute to get up off the ground. She kept thinking she should go and get her own car and follow him. The thought of the two of them skidding round corners, like some cop show on television, set her laughing again. And then she realised she couldn't go after him. She didn't know where he'd gone.

Shakily Jennie stood up. As she walked home she looked nervously at people on the street or in front of their houses. They all looked relaxed and healthy but confused, aware without memory that something had happened. They touched each other, unconsciously, obsessively.

At home Jennie called the travel agency. No answer. She called Mike's uncle, then his cousin. Mike wasn't there.

That whole night Jennie sat in the kitchen, letting cups of coffee grow cold in front of her. Her mood swung from one state to another without any conscious direction. She would cry, and whisper, 'I love you, Mike. Please come home.' A moment later she would close her eyes and remember the hot winds as they flew above the Earth. Or else she would jump up and kick the wall or the refrigerator, enraged that her selfish husband could try to hold her back from a true event.

In the morning Jennie drove to the travel agency before work. There was no one there. Later, when she called the office, Mike's assistant, Lorraine Towers, told Jennie that Mike had called her the night before and asked her to run the place for a few days. He hadn't told her where he was going. Before and after every assignment that day Jennie headed for a phone. She called friends, she called Mike's uncle again, she called her own house over and over.

That evening, at seven o'clock, Uncle Jake called. Mike had gone to New York, he said. He said that Mike wanted him to tell her he just needed time to think things out. He'd get in touch with her in a few days. 'I'm sure he still loves you,' Uncle Jake said. 'He just needs a little time.'

Jennie spent most of the evening on the phone, taking a break only when a fake instinct would tell her Mike was trying to get through. Then she would wait fifteen minutes and start again. She called Sophie, who hadn't seen Mike but asked Jennie to come and stay with her. Jennie refused, thinking Mike wouldn't like it when he came home and she wasn't there. She called all their old friends from the city, she called Mike's former bosses, anyone who might be hiding him. She considered calling the New York police and reporting Mike's car stolen, but she couldn't remember the licence number.

The next day Jennie drove to the Restoration of Joy Plaza, where Montgomery Wards had recently announced a sale in its spiritual aids department. Jennie bought herself a box of candles, two portraits of Ingrid Burning Snake (patron of lost lovers, as well as marriage), and a small set of sanctified chimes. When the cashier had rung it all up Jennie ran back and added on a 'squeaky Founder', a two foot high doll of Burning Snake that sounded a loud bleat when you squeezed its belly.

At home Jennie arranged her aids and her piece of Li Ku's skin, first in the living room, then in the basement when she feared Mike might walk out again if he came home and found it all in front of him. She lit all the candles in their plastic holders, she set up the portraits in their cardboard frames to face each other with the chimes between them. In the centre she placed the relic in its brass box. On one side of it she stood the doll, on the other herself. With the offering pin she opened all her fingers and scattered the blood all around the circle. The candles hissed as drops fell on the flames. She bent down to ping the chimes with their little copper hammer.

Then she closed her eyes. Three times she squeezed the doll, repeating each time, 'Ingrid Burning Snake, in power and truth lives your name forever, please send me my husband back.' She promised various penances, a trip to the Virginia caves, a month's salary to the Poughkeepsie residences, a month of eating nothing but vegetables grown in the sacred greenhouses outside Philadelphia, a journey to the New York College of Tellers, where she would burn her clothes and then slither like a snake under the Arch of Bones. Finally she blew out the candles. She slept for the rest of the afternoon.

Mike was gone for two weeks. The night he returned, Jennie was watching a rerun of *Tragg*, a cop show about an SDA investigator in New Chicago. Tragg had just tracked down a lion cult in the Chicago public labyrinth, when the doorbell rang. Jennie turned, and there, on the other side of the screen door, stood her husband. He wore a light blue T-shirt and blue striped seersucker pants, probably the bottom half of a suit. His hair was shorter and he'd lost weight. He looked tired and annoyed.

'Mike,' she said. 'Mike, oh honey, honey, you're back.' She waited for him to come in. She wanted to cry that he'd rung the bell. 'Aren't you going to come in?' she said. 'You'll get all bitten up out there.'

'Sure,' he said. 'How about opening the fucking screen door?'

'What? Oh!' She ran and unhooked the lock, laughing. As soon as he'd stepped inside she grabbed him, squeezing as hard as she could, then kissing him all over his face. 'You're back. I knew you'd come back. I knew you'd come back. I missed you so much.'

He pushed her away. 'Then how come you locked the door?'

'I'm sorry. Just habit. I'm sorry. I didn't want Gloria or someone barging in on me. It was just habit.'

He sat down on the couch, then got up and moved to the green chair beside the narrow mirror. He bent forward for his elbows to rest on his knees. 'How about some coffee?' he said.

'Coffee coming up,' she sang. 'I'm so happy,' she told him after she'd filled and plugged in the pot. 'I missed you so much. Where were you? I called everyone I could think of – '

'Shit,' Mike said.

'I'm sorry. I didn't make a big thing of it. Really I didn't. I just asked people if they'd seen you.'

'That's not making a big thing? What did you say, that you'd misplaced me?'

'I'm sorry,' she said. She began to cry. 'I'll go see if the coffee is ready.'

'Wait a second.' He stood up. 'Forget it, Jennie. I don't really care what you told anyone.'

'I really didn't make a big thing out of it. Really I didn't.'

'I said forget it. Can we drop it? All right? Anyway, I stayed in a hotel. Down in the city.'

'Are you hungry? Do you want anything with the coffee? I can mix up some tuna fish.'

'No. I don't want anything.'

'Are you sure? It'll only take a minute.'

'I'm not hungry.'

'You want more cake?'

'No. Look, Jennie – ' He made a noise. He said, 'I'm not staying.'

'What? What do you mean?'

'I'm not staying. I just – '

'Why? What do you mean, you're not staying? Why? I missed you so much.'

'I can't stay.'

'You can't – You can't just . . .'

'Please try to be calm.'

'Calm? Calm? You're taking my husband away from me.'

'How about that coffee?'

'You just tell me – you come in, you're gone two weeks – '

'Jennie, please.' The cracks in his voice stopped her from shouting. 'I could have just sent a letter but I wanted to tell you in person.'

'A letter?' Mike sat down again. Jennie said, 'I'll get the coffee.'

In the kitchen she slammed the cups down so hard she almost broke them. She thought, *You bastard. Send me a letter? Goddamn you.* What did he mean? How could he not stay? Where was he going? Didn't he know how much she loved him? That bastard. She wanted to run down to the basement and stamp on the portraits of Burningsnake. *He's got to stay*, she thought. *He can't mean it. Please make him stay. Help me.*

When they were both sitting with their coffee – like a proper hive couple – Mike said, 'I did a lot of thinking while I was away. About everything. Everything that's happened to us.'

'Did you think about how much I loved you?'

'Of course. And how much I love you. I do love you, Jennie. Really I do.'

'Then it's all right. As long as we love each other – '

'It's not all right. I can't take living with you.'

'Living with me? What's wrong?' He didn't answer. 'Tell me what I've done. I'll change.'

'It's just – never being sure – waiting all the time.'

200

'Waiting for what? Please, Mike. If we love each other – '

'It's not enough.'

'Yes it is. Love is always enough.'

'Things happen to you. I can't take it. I can't live waiting for the next goddamn event, or transformation, or whatever they're called. I can't stand it.'

'But – '

'It's like living in the Time of Fanatics.'

'But that was just . . . you mean the map? Is that what you mean? That was nothing. It was an accident. It won't happen again. We don't even have to step on it ever again. No one will know. It won't happen any more. I promise it won't.'

'How can you promise something like that?'

'We won't step on it. We'll drive right past it.'

'What's the difference? If that didn't happen something else would. Something always happens.'

'That's not true. Nothing'll ever happen again.'

'What about the touchstone? Do you think I can stand something like that again?'

'I thought – '

'You thought it didn't happen to me. Just to you. Shit, I was standing right next to you. Things like that are not supposed to happen. Seeing the touchstone's just a formality. Like standing on the map. God. A formality.'

'Maybe it's the hive. We can move. We can sell the house and get an apartment.'

'What about our honeymoon? Do you think everyone who goes to Bermuda sees a precursor? It's not the hive, Jennie. It's you.'

'How do you know that? How do you know that? Maybe it's you?'

'It's not me.'

'How do you know? Maybe you've got a Ferocious

One lodged inside you somewhere. Maybe you should go to the SDA.'

'Come on, Jennie.'

'These things never happened to me until I met you.'

'So maybe I bring it out in you. Maybe sex does. That's what the body path people say, right? But there's still a difference. You enjoy it. You love it. You want them to happen. And I can't stand it. I just can't stand it.'

'I don't want it if it'll take my husband away.'

'Are you sure? Are you really sure about that? Suppose you could make some kind of a deal. You and I stay together in exchange for no more visions, no more events, no more special revelations. Would you want that?'

'Yes. That's all I ever wanted.'

'Bullshit. You'd really settle for a nice normal symbolic life in the suburbs?'

'I moved here with you, didn't I?'

'You're lying, Jennie. To yourself as much as me.'

'I'm not. I just want you.'

'Then why do you keep talking about the Time of Fanatics as a great period? I don't even like hearing about it.'

'I'll stop. I'll never mention it again.'

'It's not the talk that counts.'

'Maybe there's something wrong with me. Maybe I could go and get a scan. Or check in at the hospital for tests.'

Mike laughed. 'How can there be something wrong with you? These things that happen to you, they're supposed to happen. Didn't you tell me that?'

'What do you mean? When did I say that?'

'I don't know. Lots of times. You're always saying you want a real event, not just a symbol.'

'Well, I'm wrong. That's all.'

'No, you're not wrong. You're right. That's something I had to realise the last two weeks. You're probably the only person around here who's really right. The Tellers, and the Pictures, and the Enactments, they're supposed to break things down, open channels, all that stuff. But they only do it when you're around. And I can't live with that. I can't stand it.'

'Well, what good is it then, if it takes my husband away?'

'Maybe you can find someone else. Someone who won't run away from it.'

'I don't want someone else. I want you.'

'Maybe an artist – '

'You bastard!' she shouted.

'I'm sorry, I shouldn't have said that.'

'You're just doing all these things because you hate my mother.'

'I'm doing this because I've got to survive.'

'Why can't you survive with me? I love you.'

'I love you too, Jennie.' Suddenly he was holding her, they were crying, and Jennie thought, *it's okay, he's not going to leave.* But then Mike pulled away. Still crying he said, 'I'm sorry, honey. I'm sorry.'

'Please stay with me. Please. Just tonight.'

'I'm sorry. I can't do that.'

'Why not? Just one night.'

'I can't.' He headed for the door.

'I'll change,' she said. 'It won't happen again. I promise it won't. I promise.' She wrapped her arms around him.

It took several seconds to break her grip. When he did, she fell backwards onto the edge of the couch. By the time she'd got up again, Mike had run out of the door. She ran after him, and when he started to back his car out of the driveway Jennie almost ran behind it. Something, not safety, held her back. She beat the rolled up windows. 'Mike' she shouted through the glass. 'I love you.' He turned the car into the road and gunned the engine. For a moment Jennie stood there, staring after him, until she noticed Gloria and Al Rich peeking out from between their living room curtains. She ran in the house and slammed the door.

Two days later Jennie received a notice from the Dutchess County Court. Her husband, Michael Laurence Gold, had filed for an annulment. The date given was four days earlier, two days before he'd come to see her. Three months later the court granted the annulment, affirming that a true spiritual conjunction had never taken place. Jennie was ordered to resume her maiden name. The court ordered her to break all contact with Mr Gold. Intermediaries would arrange a property settlement. Any property owned jointly, such as the house, would go to one of them, with the other receiving compensation for half the assessed value. (In the event Mike waived all claim on the house and its infant mortgage.) New deeds or official documents would be issued, backdated and showing only the single name. The court allowed two months for these arrangements, with both sides required to cooperate. After that, Jennifer Grace Mazdan must obliterate, in her possessions, in her habits, in her conversation, in her thoughts and memories, all structures, signs, and tokens that she had ever known, or met, or heard of Michael Laurence Gold.

Fragments from THE TALE OF DUSTFATHER AND MOTHERSNAKE, first told by Ingrid Burning Snake at the mass wedding of the Earth and the Sky in New York City.

This tale, recited at all weddings, is never printed in its

entirety. At the same time, it remains the best known of all the prime Pictures. For who, as a child, has not hidden in the huge painted boxes that mark a wedding ceremony, ready to scream and wave noisemakers whenever the Teller mentions the name of the Hooded Man? And who, as an adult, has not joined in the stomping and whistling to drive away the Malignant Ones when the bride raises the black bladed knife to mime the circumcision of her terrified husband?

> My body lies over the ocean
> My body lies under the sea
> My body lies cut in the courtyard
> Please bring back my body to me
> Bring back, bring back,
> Please bring back my body to me
> > Children's song, sung at a wedding.

Dustfather and Mothersnake cleared the city of our enemies. Our parents made the city safe for their children. They climbed to the top of the world, they lay on the twin tower-tops. Dustfather swung his legs over to the side, he banged his thighs with his hands. Across from him Mothersnake flicked her tongue in her mouth. Our ancestors made so much noise that all the fake people, all the straw men and the women made of leaves, all the clock people with their faces drawn by the Hooded Man, all the fakes left their hiding places and ran to throw pieces of concrete at Dustfather and Mothersnake. The Hooded Man saw this, he saw the trap, he flew to warn his children. He was too late. He was too far away. He had followed the false trail, the trail of skin he thought would lead him to Mothersnake hiding in the mud south of the city.

When all the fakes had gathered below the towers, when they stood in their striped pants and checked dresses, throwing concrete stones at Dustfather and Mothersnake, then our parents stood up and clapped their hands. A hot wind lifted the fakes, it blew them backwards, it tumbled

205

them through the streets until they broke apart against the iron wall.

When Dustfather and Mothersnake had hatched all their children, when they had brought our dripping bodies into the world and licked us clean, then they kissed each other and decided to return to the black circle. But when they tore down the wall they found that a layer of ice had frozen over the hole. Dirt had settled on the ice, and trees, and grass and flowers, and in the centre a round carousel with blind horses, their mouths forever open, hungry and silent. Angry, Dustfather wanted to pull out the trees and crush the rocks. But Mothersnake held his arms, she slid her body against him until his rage settled and he could see his children riding the horses, or kicking a ball across the grass, or sitting on plastic chairs and looking around for waiters to serve them ice cream and mineral water. We can never go home, Mothersnake told him, we must find a house and live here with our children.

They returned to the city. Modestly they stood in line by the housing bureau. But as soon as they spoke, as soon as the thunder of their voices splintered the desks and caved in the file cabinets, then their children recognized them. They gave them a domed house on top of the hill at the northern end of the island. There the Bright Beings could visit them and tell them news of the Living World.

There they could look out upon the river and watch the golden ships, with their cargoes of stories, sail to the empty lands. In those places, those empty lands, the Earth would crack open if someone stamped on it, and the trees broke if anyone leaned on them, and the rocks crumbled as soon as someone sat down on them. For the Hooded Man had sucked out all the stories, he sucked them out with a long yellow tube and spat them into the sky. They hung there, in thick clouds, afraid to rain. But after a while the clouds drifted away, and so they finally arrived over the city. Then Dustfather built aeroplanes with loud engines, he showed the people how to fly under the clouds and wake them up; and Mothersnake formed a choir to soothe the clouds and relieve their fears. The clouds broke open. The stories poured down into huge green buckets set along the rooftops. Afterwards, the navy loaded the buckets onto ships. When they came to the empty lands they restored the stories to the Earth, and in that way people could live there again.

Now, all this time Dustfather believed that the Hooded Man had died in a blizzard. The Hooded Man had grown the blizzard himself, he hoped he would freeze our parents when they removed their skins to teach each other how to make love. When he failed his fury released an avalanche that buried the Hooded Man in snow.

But Mothersnake worried because the robot searchers had never found the Hooded Man's body. Sometimes she would wake up at night, certain she could see grey claws about to slice her throat. 'He's alive!' she would shout, and Dustfather would stroke her and kiss her and tell her that the noise and smoke from their children had polluted her dreams.

Though Mothersnake allowed him to calm her, she could hear the laughter hiding in his voice. She never said anything. Later, after Dustfather's death, she wondered why she had never challenged him. She understood then that the Hooded Man had already begun to infect them, from those very first days in their house on the hill. His insects must have flown into their ears while they slept, leaving eggs full of poison ready to hatch when our parents would no longer suspect anything.

The Hooded Man stayed hidden but his servants continued his work. One day, Mothersnake lay asleep in the backyard of their house. Her eyes stayed open so she would not miss any piece of her dreams. Dustfather looked at her and he thought, soon she'll be raving again, 'He's alive, he's alive.' He disguised himself as a dog to go for a walk in the streets below their house. He'd done this many times, but now a trio of cats walked alongside him. Why do you allow her to strut about and flash her breasts and wiggle her bottom as if she, and she alone, made the world? She didn't build the wall, she didn't trap the Hooded Man in the subway tunnel,

207

what did she ever do but squat in the wet sand and wait for you to fill her with life? Now she flings her hair and snaps her teeth and talks about *her* children, *her* creation.

Dustfather began to sweat. He changed into a crow and flew away. The cats became doves and chased him, they cooed, *you* made the world, don't you remember? *You* shook your lightning and broke the seas, don't you remember? You made it with a wave of your hand, you made it with a word, with a breath, remember, remember.

In her house our ancient mother woke up. Mothersnake reared back and turned her head side to side. Where had Dustfather gone? Why couldn't she hear his paws loping through the city? She slithered along the stone floor. Her tongue opened the door. She saw mountains. Instead of the spirally pathway down to the street she saw silvery mountains. Somewhere very far away a bird cried. Mothersnake closed the door and began to weep. She would wait all night for Dustfather to return. Longer than the coil of centuries in the city below she would wait for him. She would sit on their bed of silk and she would wait, Mothersnake would wait for Dustfather through the long night. But she knew he would never return.

The women found Dustfather on the docks. Dustfather wore a long grey coat, torn at the sleeves; he swayed back and forth as he watched the empty boats tremble in the wind. The women were walking together, they wore the black leather dresses given to them by the Hooded Man. Their white masks were tied behind them to hang down their backs to the heels of their silver boots. As they walked they swung their arms, and their fingers touched, and they called to each other in high whistles that punctured the shriek of the storm.

These were the women who belonged to the Hooded Man.

He had come to each of them at three times in her life, on her fifth birthday, on her tenth birthday, and on her fifteenth birthday. To each one he appeared differently each time, as a father playing animals on the floor, or a man selling ice cream from the back of a truck, or an old man waiting for a

208

bus, or a boy friend driving her in a gold and green car over the top of a steep hill. Each time he told her the same thing, that she would meet a man whose song could crack the sun and strip the dead skin off her body.

On her twentieth birthday, each woman woke at dawn and began walking through the streets near her home. Further and further she walked, hour after hour, not knowing why, just filled with an urgency to go somewhere, see someone, hear somebody, hear something said in a casual laugh and a squint at the clouds. They did not know it, but they were hunting for the Hooded Man, they needed to hear him tell about the singer who could break through the twenty layers of crust that covered their bodies. But the Hooded Man will not be hunted, not by women who already belong to him. Many times they passed him, just as they had passed him every day of their lives. He buzzed round them like a fly and they flicked their fingers to get rid of him. He stared at them from a bench, he sat there disguised as a bent woman in a flowered dress full of stains and wrinkles. Their eyes slid over him. How could they trap him? What bait could they offer when he had already eaten them?

The hungry women left their homes, they left their parents and their husbands and their friends, they left as the Sun fled the sky, they found empty boxes along the street and they climbed inside them. The night of her twentieth birthday each of the women heard a voice in her sleep. 'Get up,' it told her. 'Get up. Run. Faster. *Run.*' They ran until the Hooded Man had ripped their clothes with his fingernails, until the strips fluttered away behind them.

The women pushed Dustfather into the warehouse. They sealed the tall metal door with their spittle, they rubbed their bodies against the lock. Dustfather tripped and one of the women kicked him. They kicked him, he fell against the cartons full of rotted milk. The women laughed, they stamped their feet against the stone floor. 'Sing for us,' one of them said, and they all laughed as they kicked him again. 'Sing,' they shouted. 'Crack open the Sun. Sing for us.'

Dustfather opened his mouth. Nothing came out. The

women laughed, their voices bounced off the steel beams.
'Sing!' they ordered. Dustfather opened his mouth. Nothing
came out. 'Sing!' the women screamed. Dustfather opened
his mouth, he shook his tongue. A thin warble sounded, the
breath of a song.

The women stood still, their arms flattened against their
sides. Our ancestor began to sing, and the building shivered.
The women looked around them and instead of the piled
high boxes they saw thin orange lines stretching over buildings and hills. 'Stop it,' they shouted. They closed their eyes.
They hit their eyes with the backs of their hands. Against
the lids the lines extended further and further. The women
began to fly along them, over mountains, over burning cities,
over deserts of lost children. 'Stop it,' they begged.

Dustfather sang louder. Up and down the women's bodies
the skin dried, it cracked open. The part that lived inside
them spilled onto the floor. They slid on the slippery stone
and fell into each other's memories. Unable to stand they
crawled past the boxes, they rolled over the broken glass
until their fingernails could dig into Dustfather's face. They
clawed at him, they tore out his tongue, but he kept singing.
They ripped him in half, they pulled loose the organs that
over the centuries had hardened into black diamonds. Still
the pieces kept on singing.

But the song grew softer. The women discovered that they
could stand. With the pieces in their hands they ran from
the warehouse. Each one clutched a piece of our blessed
ancestor's body, and wherever they could they buried him,
in parks, in the basements of buildings, under roads and
riverbeds.

Only one of the women tried to keep the piece she had
stolen. She had taken the organ that had filled Mothersnake
with seeds, with the voices that had woken up the eggs. She
tried to hide it in her own body, but the Hooded Man sent
his police to arrest her. They locked her in a cell and they
shouted at her until she threw the piece onto the floor. Before
the police could grab it it fled down a hole into the sewer
and from there to the sea.

Mothesnake bellowed her rage at the sky. Buildings fell, rivers swallowed boats of refugees trying to escape her. 'What have you done to my brother?' she shouted.

The committee pressed their grey-suited bodies into the dirt. 'It wasn't us,' they told her. 'We're investigating.'

Mothersnake pulled down the power lines, she gathered the wires into a whip and beat the city until a hurricane of electricity scorched all the buildings. But when the committee dared to look up our ancestor was gone.

Mothersnake disguised herself as an old woman. She rubbed clay all over her body to thicken it and hide its light. She moved into a building in the centre of town, under a huge sign that flashed all night long, 'Mothersnake, forgive your children.' She took a job as a nurse in a hospital and when the doctors attached bottles of food to people's arms Mothersnake spat into the liquid. Her hatred swelled the sick bodies until they burst in their beds, giving off a smell that drenched the sheets. When a woman gave birth Mothersnake scratched a mark on the baby's face so that the mother became sick every time she looked at it.

Still it was not enough. In her dark room under the sign, Mothersnake took bits of wood and stone and glass and feathers. Carefully she constructed dreams which flew across the city and into the mouths of her sleeping children. When morning came, the dreamers gathered together in the park. They announced the Unity Party Church of Ultimate Salvation. They dressed in red shirts and black boots, they marched with gold and red banners to city hall. When they chased away the mayor and the city council, they ordered a camp built outside the city, with high fences and towers filled with guns, and giant ovens to burn the people the Unity Church selected in its weekly lotteries.

Seven years the terror continued. Mothersnake no longer needed to mark the babies, for none of them dared to leave the womb, but closed their hearts inside their mother's bodies. Then one day, in the hospital, Mothersnake heard the other nurses talk about a baby, the first baby they'd seen in twenty-two months.

211

Mothersnake hurried to the nursery. Her fingernail was already sharpened. But when she opened the door she heard singing. It had been a long time since anyone had dared to sing in the city. Mothersnake stood there, her fists clenched, her teeth gleaming with the urge to slice through the infant's neck. The song grew louder, the walls of the nursery shook like a frightened cat.

Mothersnake fell to her knees, her nurse's uniform burst into flames, the clay disguising her body cracked and fell to the floor. It was him, it was his voice, it was him, it was Dustfather, he'd come back for her, *it was him.*

But when she ran to the child she discovered its mouth closed, its throat still, its eyes a bright yellow and coated with images from Dustfather's song. It wasn't the baby singing, but something black and shrivelled that hung around its neck. Mothersnake looked closer, she saw a severed finger all curled and shrunken. She tore the red silk cord binding the finger to the child and held it up. The song grew louder and the walls of the nursery split down the middle. Mothersnake pressed the finger to her forehead and when she took it away the bone had straightened, the old skin had turned to ash that blew away in the wind of Mothersnake's exultation. 'He's alive,' she whispered, and the sound boomed through the streets like an avalanche. 'He's alive!'

Piece after piece they recovered. An old man had found that first finger while digging for clean water in his daughter's backyard. Now the Parks Department tore up all the streets, they sent squads of unemployed students to rip down the walls and tear up the foundations. Slowly they put the puzzle back together. The police cordoned off the middle of the island. The Fire Department burnt down the buildings to make room for the reconstruction. Doctors and art teachers argued over proper placement while teams of engineers directed the crane operators who lowered the pieces into position.

Piece by piece they put him back together. All except one. That precious part of our ancestor, that pump that had filled his sister with the milk of the stars, that single organ was never found by all the searchers.

Only the Hooded Man knew what had happened to it. He had changed to a rat to follow it along the sewer, to a jellyfish to follow it through the sea. A dozen times he had tried to bite or sting it, but whenever he approached it it began to sing and a wave of terror carried the Hooded Man away from it.

The organ washed up on an island in the southern sea. A group of fisherwomen lived there, women who had left their homes years before to avoid the cold men their families had chosen for them. When they found Dustfather's organ some of them had spent so many years away from men they could no longer remember what this strange thing was that changed shape and leaped into the air. Some of them, however, could still recognise it, and they told the others. The women passed it around. Soon they were all pregnant. Eighteen months later those who remembered how such things used to work worried that too much time had passed. But the others didn't care. They happily patted each other's bellies and curled into giant balls to roll down the hill together into the waves. Finally they gave birth to a tribe of girls with dark green skin and golden eyes that could make a rock weep just by looking at it.

Once they'd given birth the women gathered together to decide what to do with Dustfather. Some of them suggested returning it to the sea; the songs it sang every sunrise made them long for a distant city they'd never seen. They might have done it if the Hooded Man had not disguised himself as a butterfly to flutter about from ear to ear, whispering that if they released the life-giver it would generate an army of men with iron hands and stone feet to smash their island and kidnap their daughters. So the women dug a pit, they buried our father in a carved chest filled with flowers and leaves.

Mothersnake howled with rage. She had tried everything, she had gone through every house searching through the cabinets and under the mattresses, she had placed ads in newspapers and magazines: 'Woman seeks precious remnant of husband. Reward for all information.' Nothing. While the Hooded Man danced alone in his cell in the abandoned prison Mothersnake began to look hungrily at all the people lined up behind the police barricades to watch the reconstruction.

The city councillors noticed the way Mothersnake's lips parted as she watched the boys and girls who brought her baskets of flowers. They saw the gleam of her teeth. They called a meeting, they met behind the carousel.

The next morning all the young men gathered in the meadow ringed with brown stones. These were the same stones the Hooded Man had once vomited from his belly while Mothersnake danced around him with her skirts held up. The men lifted their penises, they stretched the foreskins. The women crawled along the grass with volcanic knives held in their teeth. In a great flash of darkness the knives slashed down, the men shouted with joy.

The substitutes cannot last. In the furnace of our mother the assembled foreskins curl and break away from each other. Over and over again our ancient father must restore himself. For without him to calm her, Mothersnake will devour us. And so, all weddings, this wedding, all weddings must end with the black knife, the fall of the blade, the foreskin carried to the roof of the hall at midnight and thrown into the wind. The wind carries it to our ancestors, they will join it to the others surrendered over the years. In love all men become their father, in love they enter the warmth of their mother.

And on the wedding night, when the wife has helped her husband to the bed covered in flowers, he will sing to her, he will sing the wordless melody Dustfather sang to Mothersnake in the nursery. With the song he becomes our father. Wounded, her father enters her.

Again, and again, and again, the broken circle joins together.

9

For several weeks after her failed abortion Jennie managed not to think about the foetus that had barged its way into her womb. The nausea had receded, as if it had made its point and was now content to leave her alone. Either her breasts no longer hurt as much, or she had become used to the tingling pain. If she put on her underwear before looking in the mirror she could avoid seeing the enlarged nipples or the line that was starting to appear between her belly button and her pubic hair. Her stomach stayed flat – well, not entirely, but she was sure any swelling came more from water retention that anything . . . more serious. She seemed to just want to drink all the time. Some days she would get through a whole Thermos of coffee before lunch.

She did make sure to keep herself busy. Movies after work, the annual company picnic, neighbourhood barbecues on the weekends. She avoided Karen. She avoided her mother. She worked hard, checking every alignment twice so that she usually finished the day late, and very tired.

Meanwhile, the world rolled along, like a barrel with Jennie sealed inside it. The government brought out its new economic plan to bring down inflation. The President appeared on television looking her most innocent, her most transported by divine inspiration, under a huge portrait of Rebecca Rainbow. No one paid much attention.

Auto accidents in the mid-Hudson valley declined in the first two weeks of September by seventy-five per cent. The state police could give no explanation for this

215

surge of safe driving. The Dutchess County sheriff's office, however, described it as a sign of heavenly sanction brought on by Sheriff Lauren's programme of compulsory prayer and once-a-week fasting for all deputies.

In Boston, Massachusetts, a men's secret society, the Teeth of the Tiger, performed 'Insulting the Lady', one of the five forbidden Enactments. Dressed in masks and rags they chased women off the streets, battering them with huge rubber phalluses. The action went on for nearly two hours, with the knowledge (and according to some, participation) of the local police. At the end, two teenage girls, sisters, were dragged from their houses and raped. Feminists marched through Boston and other cities along the east coast. *Ms.* magazine described the event as a 'degeneration into the evil shadow of the Old World.' The mayor of Boston declared Teeth of the Tiger an illegal organisation, and promised a full investigation.

Allan Lightstorm made the cover of *Time* once again. He announced his retirement at the height of his career, saying only that he planned a pilgrimage 'to the centre of the voice.' His head Teller, Judith Whitelight, confirmed that Lightstorm had found himself under great spiritual pressure the last months. The mayor of Poughkeepsie wrote to *Time* that Lightstorm planned to settle along the Hudson after his journeys. A columnist with the *New York Times* hinted that Lightstorm had rebelled against the hypocrisy of the modern Tellers. She cited a 'rumour' that Lightstorm had stood on the roof of the Fifth Avenue Hall with his arms out like Adrienne Birth-of-Beauty on her sky-scraper and shouted down the Founder's 3rd Proposition: 'Hypocrisy is the lock that bolts shut the door.' The New York College of Tellers issued an immediate denial of any tensions or dissatisfaction. Privately the College President threatened to 'subsume' the paper's advertisers into his Tellers' Pictures, promising to place them in 'unfortunate' contexts. The paper printed the columnist's apology on the front page.

In Anaheim, California ('Navel of the Revolution') a riot broke out at the Anaheim Rainbow Mall. A group of twenty-two women, some naked, some wearing cloaks made of black feathers, ran into the department stores and dress boutiques, tearing clothes and kicking over the models in the windows. Before the police could arrive another fifty or so women had joined them, stripping naked and battling their husbands or friends who tried to stop them. Arrested and brought before the court the original twenty-two claimed 'diminished responsibility due to ecstasy' induced by two weeks of dancing and chanting in honour of the Chained Mother on a hilltop overlooking the mall. The mall distributor testified he had heard them on his way to work but hadn't petitioned for their removal. Sales had fallen in recent months and he'd hoped the chanting would induce a Devoted One to bless the mall.

Jennie knew about none of these things. She'd stopped reading the paper and only watched the news on television so she would know what people were talking about. Whenever something about the Tellers came on she found herself getting up to wash the dishes or set out her clothes for the following morning.

Shortly after the Day of Isolation, September 21, a low front brought enough rain for the county government and the Tellers's Halls to declare the following Sunday Earth Day. For most of the week Jennie considered staying home. She wasn't sure why. She told herself she just didn't feel like going. On Friday evening Karen D'arcy came tapping at her screen door, suggesting they go together on Sunday. Jennie could

217

hardly look at Karen. She knew Karen hadn't forgotten Jennie's refusal to do the banishment. Now Jennie bent forward on her couch, turning a dish of chocolate cake with both hands. 'Okay,' she said finally. 'You want me to pick you up?'

'I'll come and get you,' Karen said quickly. 'If that's okay.'

Jennie shrugged. There was silence for a moment, then Karen hugged her. When Jennie didn't respond Karen stood up. 'I guess I better go sit home like a good romantic jerk,' she said. 'You know who might call.' Jennie had no idea who but she nodded. 'See you Sunday,' Karen said, and let herself out.

By tradition the Tellers didn't take part in Earth Day. No sweepers would come through the neighbour-hoods, there were no special guests or parades or statues. Earth Day was a 'private' Enactment, one held by the people and not their deliverers.

With the mass facilities of Recital Mount unavail-able, the county designated various sites as 'celebratory centres.' The centre for Glowwood Hive was a hillside in Marion Firetongue County Park overlooking the Hudson. For four days teams of high school students uprooted whatever wild grass had grown at the bottom of the hill, then laid down narrow planks along the hillside as makeshift seats for the adults who would watch the parade of children fling themselves in the mud.

Squeezed in between Karen and Mike Chek Jennie remembered how she used to love this Enactment as a little girl. With no park nearby the neighbourhood would reserve a spot in the Palisades National Park across the river. The journey always took longer than the celebration itself, but Jennie never minded, at least not while her father was alive. She remembered sitting in the car in her tree spirit costume, leaves painted on

218

her face, twigs sticking up from her shoulders, while Jimmy sang to her and Beverley winced under the onslaught of popular music. Finally they would arrive, and Jennie would run from the parking lot to where marshals were organising the children. Then came the parade, the chanting, the roll in the mud. Sometimes, Jennie would get so excited from the costumes and the shouting, she could almost hear the Earth rumble faintly back at her.

Sometimes. Almost. Faintly. In the Days of Awe the Earth, freed by the Founders from the gag tied on her thousands of years ago, used to roar up at the children and the adults watching them. The noise was so powerful it could blast the children right out of their bodies to flutter around the fields until the Devoted Ones could show them the way home again. Jennie had seen old newsreels of boys' and girls' bodies stacked up in bunk beds waiting for their residents to return.

It shocked Jennie when the Shouting of the Names began, shocked her because after all the Earth Days she'd attended she'd completely forgotten this calling on the Mother to bless the community. All around her people had taken out chains of beads, some as elaborate as jade or even pearls, others just wooden lumps, and now they'd begun to finger them as they shouted out the thirty Names of the Earth's attributes. How could she forget this? She didn't even have her beads; she remembered now that she'd thrown them in a drawer the day after her failed abortion attempt.

With her hands together and her fingers moving as if she was manipulating a set of beads too small to notice ('tiny rubies' she could tell people – a family heirloom) Jennie joined her voice to the roar of the hive. And then she stopped. Very deliberately she stuck her hands in her pockets and held up her head with her lips pressed together. Next to her Karen kept glancing sideways. And Carrie Perkins behind her – Jennie could hear the outrage in her voice. Screw 'em, Jennie thought. Screw every one of them.

On the way home, in Karen's car, neither of them said much as they waited to leave the parking lot. Without any children to pick up they were one of the first to go, but there was still a long queue ahead of them. Jennie yawned. She noticed Karen's eyes darting to her, and she wondered what she'd done this time. No hand on the mouth. Pregnant women covered their mouths when they yawned, making sure no Malignant Ones slipped inside to attack the baby. She shook her head. Let them try. If anyone needed protection it wasn't the baby.

She slumped down in the seat and watched the windscreen wipers. Occasionally her body jerked like a marionette as Karen would charge the car forward, then brake to a sharp stop inches from the car in front of her.

The jerking movement reminded her of something. She couldn't place it at first. She focused on the movement, the thought of strings, a puppet – 'This is for you, little puppet.' She had it. Her father. The day he gave her her copy of *The Lives*. She saw him as a thin man, with a narrow moustache and straight blond hair. In her mind he wore blue-striped seersucker pants and a loose matching vest over an open-necked white shirt. Jennie didn't know if he actually had dressed that way the day he gave her the book. She knew those clothes from a photo she used to look at years after his death, when she was a teenager. She would hold the picture and stare at it, sometimes talk to it, tell it what she had done that day, or what was happening in school. In the picture Jimmy Mazdan was running up Mothersnake Hill in Central Park with his daughter mounted on his shoulders and her arms wrapped so tight around her daddy's head she could never figure out how he could see. 'The Jimmy and Jennie show.'

Karen's car jumped like a frog touched by an electric prod. Jennie said, 'Can't you drive a little more smoothly?' She blushed, too embarrassed to apologise. Slightly nauseous, she opened the window but closed it again when the rain leapt at her face.

'Sorry,' Karen said, 'it's the traffic.' Silence again. Karen turned on the radio, then turned it off again. 'Did you like the Enactment?' she asked.

'Sure,' Jennie said. 'It was great.'

'Jennie' Karen said, 'can I ask you something?'

Jennie turned her head towards the window so Karen wouldn't see her grit her teeth. 'Sure,' she said.

'At the Enactment. You didn't say the Names, did you?'

'No.'

'How come?'

'I forgot my beads.'

'Forgot – don't you carry them with you?'

'Well, I was saying them one night when I couldn't sleep. I guess I just left them by the bed. The other day.'

'Jennie, that's terrible. Oh shit. I'm sorry.'

Jennie wasn't sure if this apology covered Karen's outburst or the car's latest attempt to bash the VW Rabbit in front of them.

'It's okay,' Jennie said. 'I mean, I don't mind.'

'It's just – it's not good, it's – You know I like you, Jennie.'

'I like you too, Karen.' What would she do if Karen made a pass at her? She imagined the car veering off onto the side road leading to the Wappinger's Falls Women's World.

'I don't want to see you cut yourself off. It's not good.'

221

'I'm okay.'

Karen made a click noise. 'I don't think you are. Since the – since, you know, what happened at the Recital, on Recital Day I mean, you've got so, so cut off.' She hesitated. 'You never went for the abortion, did you?'

Jennie said, 'No. I didn't – I couldn't decide what I wanted to do.' She realised immediately that that was a mistake.

'That's because you didn't do the banishment. I told you it would be much harder.'

'Please, Karen.'

'If you'd done it you could have made a decision. Instead you're trapped in that awful moment. And now you don't even carry your beads any more.'

'Maybe I just don't think any of it is going to help.'

'But that's the point. That's it. If you start thinking like that – '

'What's it going to do for me? I mean, really. So what if I say a bunch of names?'

'They're not just – '

'Yes, they are.' Jennie twisted round in her seat to face Karen. They had just passed the Sacred Shopper Mall and the traffic was picking up. 'The Earth names, the names of the Founders, they don't *do* anything.'

'Well, maybe we've got to, to bring ourselves to them. We can't just expect them to reach out to us.'

'Karen I don't know what you mean.'

'It's just . . . So what if they didn't protect you? Even if it was the Day of Truth. I know the Tellers aren't what they used to be. So maybe we have to contribute a little more ourselves. Do we have the right to ask them to do everything for us?' When Jennie didn't answer, Karen said, 'And maybe they did – at least, I don't know, notice you.'

'Notice me?'

222

They turned onto Heavenpath Road. Karen said, 'I've thought a lot about what happened to you. And why you wouldn't do the banishment.' She spoke quickly, not looking at Jennie. 'It seems to me that the worst thing, well, not actually the worst, getting – what happened was the worst – '

Jennie thought, *Get me out of this, please.*

Karen continued, ' – but in a way, what's really shocking is the man himself. I mean, that he could do such a thing on the Day of Truth. I don't mean morally. I just mean that he would even want to. That the Recital wouldn't stop him – you know, stop him from desires like that. I'm sorry. I'm not saying this very good.'

'It's okay,' Jennie told her. They were parked in front of Jennie's house now. She wondered if she could make a run for it.

'What I wanted to say,' Karen went on, 'I really thought about this, really a lot, and I suddenly thought, what if there was a connection? Even a horrible one. Wouldn't that be better than no connection at all?' She made a noise. 'This'll sound really weird. And I hope you don't get angry at me.'

'Just tell me.'

'Well, you know the Picture he told. Lightstorm, I mean. He did "The Place Inside." '

'I did hear something about it.'

'Well, doesn't a rape kind of go with that?'

'What?'

'Shit, I knew I'd mess it up.'

'Karen, what are you talking about?'

'Well, suppose this guy sensed it or something. Could feel the Picture coming. Not consciously, you know, inside. And that's what made him do it.'

'You're saying that Allan Lightstorm, and the recital,

223

made someone want to rape me? And I'm supposed to feel good about that?'

Karen held out her hands. 'But it would mean there was some point to everything. That things had an effect. Even a terrible one.'

'Thanks, Karen. I'm sure that makes me feel a lot better.'

'But if that has an effect, so do other things. You can do things against it. Counteract it.'

Jennie said, 'Karen, I know you're trying to help. It's really sweet. But I'm okay. Believe me.'

'You're not okay if you just sit there when everybody's saying the Names.'

'I just forgot my beads. It didn't seem right without my beads. That's all. It's nothing.'

Karen began to cry. She hugged Jennie, who pulled back for a second, then wrapped her arms around her friend. Karen said, 'I'm so worried about you. Please don't stop believing.'

Gently Jennie separated herself. 'Don't worry. Everything's all right. I haven't stopped believing. Really I haven't. Honest.'

Karen reached in her bag for a tissue. 'I'm sorry,' she said. 'I guess you think I'm a real jerk.'

'Of course I don't think that. I'm glad you care so much about me.' Karen nodded. 'Look,' Jennie said, 'I've got to go. My house is a mess and tomorrow's a workday. I'll call you, okay?' With one hand on the doorhandle she kissed Karen on the cheek. She ducked out before Karen could say anything else.

Safely in her house Jennie discovered her excuse was real. She made a face at the smell of dust and damp. The couch was strewn with junk mail and bills, unread copies of the *Poughkeepsie Journal*, and various shirts, jeans, and even underwear that Jennie had thrown off after coming home from work. Between the couch and the stereo (*got to get a new needle*, she reminded herself) squatted the vacuum cleaner on its plastic wheels, like some insect staring up at her. She'd taken it out a week before, planning to clean it before dinner, and instead had gone to sleep. 'I'm sorry,' Jennie said. 'I'll feed you soon. I promise.'

No, she thought, do it now. She stripped off her wet clothes and marched with them to the bathroom where she dumped them on the floor. In the bedroom she dressed in an old jogging suit, red, for action, and tied her short hair in a cotton scarf, yellow, for methodical thoroughness. She went from room to room opening windows, ending in the kitchen where she fished out a filthy green duster (green for new life) and then marched with it back to the living room.

While she rubbed down speckled ash trays and fluted lamp columns Jennie told herself that good cleaning was just what she needed. Do something useful. That's what you did after Earth Day. Clean the house, make plans for the winter, close down the lawn. She'd have to remember the blindfolds for the guardians that dotted the lawn. Buried in the ground with only their heads showing, the Beings would encourage the grass to grow and grow all winter long unless Jennie put them to sleep by covering their eyes. She remembered how Mike used to do that, how the first Earth Day after he'd left she was sure the whole block was staring and laughing at her for having no husband to do the job for her.

She grunted as she bent down to scoop out the old magazines and paperbacks from the rack next to the couch. Exercise, she thought. Make sure this winter to get in shape. Use the time well. She sat down on the couch, half in tears. How the hell could she get in shape with her stomach about to swell up, and her breasts flopping about? It was all so unfair. What did Karen know? All she ever did was wait around for men to dump shit on her. Maybe she *should* exercise. Jog, stand on her head, take up mud wrestling. Maybe that would shake the damn thing loose from clinging to her womb. More likely she'd just break a leg. The Agency would take care of it. What did they care about her, as long as she carried their precious fish?

A fine spray of rain reached her from the dinette. Moaning, she pushed herself up and went to close the window. She waddled slightly as if she already propelled a giant belly before her. In a sing-song voice she said, 'Please don't stop believing, Jennie.'

She sat down on the dinette chair nearest the window, the one Mike used to sit on. How could she stop believing when she carried a genuine, grade A1, certified true event right in her own goddamn body? And yet, how could she forget the Names? How could she just dump her beads somewhere and forget about them? That was weeks ago.

She wondered if the Agency wanted to turn her into a secularist. The thought made her shudder. She remembered the time – she was seven or eight – when she and Mary Geraldo went with Mary's mother to see some clown show on Broadway and she passed, for the first time, one of the secularist bookshops around Times Square. Even as a child she'd cringed at the seediness of the place, the smell of sweat, the two or three men and women with their heads down as they hurried in and out. She still remembered the small hand-painted sign. 'Honesty bookshop – Adults only.' And she remembered Mrs Geraldo yanking her down the street. 'That's not for you.'

The duster dropped from her hand. What was it like being a sec? What was it like in the Old World? How could people ignore the forces that make everything happen? 'God makes the world go round.' That wasn't just a song. It was true. It was just common sense. She quoted, out loud, Adrienne Birth-of-Beauty's 7th Proposition. 'Gravity is a story told by the Sun.' How did they think their lawns grew? By accident? How did they think the atoms in a molecule held together? By written contract?

The funny thing was, they did believe in some kind of God or other. Or at least some of them did. Only, she couldn't figure out what they thought their gods did. How did God pass the time with no work to do? Early retirement. What did they do in their 'church' thingies? They 'prayed.' Jennie didn't know what they meant by that. What would they have done if God had answered them? A message smack in the eyes from the Living World. She laughed. Send them running right out of their churches and under the beds. But suppose God was waiting there too? Maybe lying asleep, like an old dog that everyone's forgotten about. And suddenly growls awake.

And what did they do without stories? God was made out of stories. Everyone knew that. Their children told stories. There were no Tellers and no Recitals but the children told stories to each other. That's why children began the Revolution. And sometimes a few adults would sneak around playgrounds and schoolyards, telling stories to little groups of kids until a teacher chased them away or the police arrested them.

She tried to imagine a world where only children told stories. It must have been a very childish world. And a very empty one. She looked around her, at the dinette table with its single green plastic placemat, at the kitchen and the crumpled tray from a frozen lasagne dinner, at the couch and the vacuum cleaner. Suppose that was all there was? Suppose nothing existed that she couldn't pin down with her eyes?

She went into the bedroom and opened the top

227

drawer of her dresser, the one where she kept her photos of Mike hidden inside a box of old receipts and tax forms. Next to the box lay the case containing the gold offering pin. She held the box up before her so she could see it in the mirror marking a line down the middle of her forehead. Eyes closed, she lowered the box down to her mouth and kissed it. She carried it into the living room.

She stood in the centre of the room and listened to the rain flinging itself at the window. It was already dark outside – no need to draw the curtains. Mike wouldn't have, he never cared who was watching them, like that time in the restaurant.

She shook her head. No distractions. You've got to plant yourself where you're standing for a good offering. Give the Beings a chance to find you. She took a deep breath, letting it out slowly, then another which she blew out with a shout to clear the channels. Now she opened the case and took out the pin. The little light in the room collected around the gold shaft. She dipped it into the porcelain vial of alcohol.

Jennie's breath quickened. She closed her eyes and braced herself. The first time she jabbed she missed and had to open her eyes. She gasped as the point entered her finger. Blood blossomed out around the tip. Though she must have struck deeper than she usually did there was no pain, or queasiness, only a vibrating tension, like a bar of metal struck by a hammer. All around her, in the walls, in the carpet, in the couch and lamps, she could hear a fluttering. Eyes closed, she could almost feel the wings stroking her electrified skin.

She snapped her wrists to fling her blood at the air. The fluttering grew louder without ever making a sound. Jennie's hand moved by itself as if someone was shaking her arm. She blinked her eyes, and she saw – briefly – the room the way someone from the Old

World might have seen it. A desert, with nothing in it but some furniture and a two-legged machine.

Her arm dropped. Her hand was throbbing, and she sucked in her breath at the pain. Blood was dripping on the rug, only a few drops so far. Better bandage it, she thought. She almost grabbed the duster, then remembered how filthy it was, and ran into the bathroom. When she'd wrapped a Band-Aid as tightly as she could around the wound, she raced through an invocation to the household guardians to surround her finger and beat back any Malignant Ones trying to invade the opening. She turned on the shower.

Jennie went through the house closing all the windows, then made the rounds again with a roll of paper towels to mop up the puddles of water on the windowsills and furniture. 'Stupid,' she said out loud as she dumped the used towels in the kitchen garbage. 'Stupid, stupid.' She knew she should try to blot up the blood. The good little hivemaker wouldn't just leave a trail of blood from the living room to the bathroom. What would Gloria say?

She got into the shower, jumping back until she could turn up the cold, then letting her body sag under the spray. Jennie stayed a long time in the shower, turning round and round, tilting up her face and gulping the water. When she finally turned it off she had to bend over to let a surge of dizziness pass before she could wrap herself in one of the thick green towels Sophie had given them for a housewarming. She tugged gently at the Band-Aid. It held. 'The clinic is closed,' she said, and crossed the hall to the bedroom. She dropped the towel on the floor, then lay down on the rumpled bed, thankful she hadn't stripped it. She pulled the blanket up to her chin. Didn't eat supper, she thought. Didn't clean. Later. After a nap. 'Sorry,'

229

she called out to the vacuum cleaner, the duster, whoever might be listening.

Maybe Karen was right. Maybe she should do the banishment. She giggled. Clean herself if not the house. And yet – she didn't know what it was, but something in her folded its arms and said, 'No. Absolutely not.' She fell asleep.

10

Excerpt from THE LIVES OF THE FOUNDERS

Maryanna Split Sky
The silent Teller. She could not speak, for she gave up her tongue as an offering to find her true voice.

At the age of five Split Sky (in beauty and truth lives her name forever) was running along her backyard flying a kite. A large bird slit the kite with its beak. Right then a black dog ran out from behind a tree and growled at her. The dog told her that if she gave the birds a trophy they would teach her to speak to her toys.

Maryanna went into the house and sat on the floor. She moved her dolls and told them stories. But the dolls lay against each other, silent, with blank faces. The next morning Maryanna woke up at dawn and tiptoed into the backyard. There she stood, watching the bird circle overhead. Its wings stretched out as it rose and fell in the sunlight. She watched for an hour and then she went back to bed. For three days Maryanna watched, but on the third she did not return to sleep. She took a knife from the kitchen drawer. As the bird dipped she stuck her tongue out as far as she could. In one stroke the little girl cut the tongue from her mouth. The bird flew down to catch the 'trophy' before it could touch the grass. The wings brushed Maryanna's face as the bird flapped up again.

She went into the house and sat down among her dolls. With her hands she told them a story and the dolls applauded.

When the Revolution began Maryanna Split Sky became Teller to the deaf. She spoke with her hands in the universal language. As she told them her pictures birds flew from her

231

fingers. They perched on the shoulders of the deaf and sang to them soundless melodies of the Living World.

'Mazdan, hang around a second.' Half out of her seat, Jennie sat down heavily. Around her, the other servers glanced curiously from her to Maria before they shifted out of the staff room on their way to their assignments.

'I'll call you this evening,' Jennie said to the back of a black leather jacket. Marilyn Birdan raised her hand and wiggled the fingers without turning around. Jennie moved her attention back to her boss, who sat on the end of her scratched metal desk. Her thick weightlifter's arms were crossed over the bib of her denim overalls. Her head tilted slightly to the left.

She stood up. 'It stinks in here,' she said. She pushed open one of the big swingout windows, letting in a blast of cold late October air. She said, 'Your pal Bill Jackman is out of his soul if he thinks I'm going to let him smoke those fucking cigars in here all winter.'

Jennie stopped herself from saying that Bill Jackman was not her pal. A balding loudmouth who found sexual innuendos in children's educational television, Jackman had only been working at Mid-Hudson a few weeks. During this time he'd twice told Jennie that he only took the job so he could get around the county and 'check out all that available pussy.'

Maria sat down on the desk again. She placed her hands on her knees and breathed deeply a few times as if she was demonstrating how to do it.

'You've cut your hair,' she said. 'Isn't that a little dumb, with winter coming on?'

'It's easier to dry,' Jennie said. 'So I don't go out with wet hair.' She remembered sitting in the chair in the beauty parlour on Raymond Avenue and watching the woman cut too much off and being afraid to say anything. 'Anyway,' she added, 'I've got my hat.'

Maria laughed. 'Right. The crash helmet.' Jennie's furlined leather hat, complete with ear flaps and chin strap, sometimes embarrassed Jennie so much she wouldn't look at anyone in the street. If a murder happened in front of her the police would never believe she hadn't seen anything. The one thing she wouldn't do, however, was take the hat off. The flaps had stopped the terrible ear aches she'd had her first winter on the job.

'Can't I go?' Jennie said. 'I want to stop at the Lamplighter for some toast and coffee. I skipped breakfast this morning.' Maria inclined her head towards the hot drinks machine. Jennie rolled her eyes.

Maria said, 'Are you sure you should drink coffee?'

'Why shouldn't I drink coffee?'

'Bad for the development, isn't it? Brain damage, stuff like that.'

'Coffee's going to damage my brain?'

'Not your brain, Mazdan. A crowbar couldn't damage your brain. I mean the kid's.'

Jennie said 'What kid?' before she remembered. Then her teeth started to chatter.

Maria said, 'No bullshit, okay? You think I can't . . . Let me tell you something. When I was on the wrestling circuit we had this woman, Grace the Masked Giantess they called her, she was kind of tall, with the biggest shoulders you ever saw. Anyway, she got knocked up, and we had this big match in the Divine Plan Auditorium in New Chicago – '

'Does everybody know?'

Maria made a face but dropped her story. 'Uh uh,' she said. 'That crowd never looks at anyone who's not in the mirror.'

Jennie glanced down at her belly. She was wearing a loose green turtle-neck sweater over elastic waist jeans. It did swell out, she could see that, but only a little. Couldn't people just think she'd gotten fat?

'It's the tits,' Maria said. 'Dead giveaway.' Jennie folded shut the flaps of her suede jacket. At Maria's laugh she felt herself blushing. Maria slid down from her desk to come take Jennie's hands. She said, 'I'm not out to get you. It's just the way I talk, okay? I won't ask anything. I won't ask who the father is, if he's still around, what your plans are, any of that stuff. I just want you to know, when the time comes, when you got to take off, I'll make sure everything's okay. I'll make sure fucking Mid-Hudson doesn't try to screw you.'

Jennie whispered, 'Thank you.'

'How far are you gone? Four, five months?' Jennie nodded. 'I thought so. Pretty soon those jerks are going to start noticing. That asshole Jackman's bound to come up with a few remarks. And that Gail Pinter's a regular neo-moralist. She'll probably treat you to some dirty looks. Just tell them to shove it. And if they get too heavy I'll show them something of the divine plan myself.'

Jennie smiled. 'Thanks.' She got up, feeling old. At the door she turned around. 'Maria . . .' she said.

'What?'

'Can I ask you . . .' She wished she hadn't started. She wished she could think of something else to say than what she'd planned, but her mind blocked as she tried to pull it to another track. She saw Maria waiting, arms crossed, head tilted. She said, 'Can I ask – why are you doing this?'

'Because you're my star Server. Haven't I always told you that?'

'No, seriously.'

'Maybe I'm not such a creep as everyone says.'

Jennie looked down. 'I didn't mean that.'

'Anyway, it's not such a big deal. It's just running interference.'

'No, I mean, what I mean is, do you think you're helping me because you really want to, or . . .' She tried to think of how to say it.

'Because I think I should? Forget it, Pinter's the moralist, remember?'

'No, that's not it. I know you wouldn't – what I mean is, do you think something could be making you want to help me? Does it seem like something you would just do? By yourself?'

'Something make me? What kind of something?' Jennie didn't answer. Maria said, 'Do you think I'm charged? Is that what you mean? Do you think some goddamn Devoted One's got to get inside me before I'll help one of my own people?'

'No, that's not – '

'Or maybe it's a Malignant One. Maybe my little attempt to do something decent will send you to your doom.'

Jennie shouted, 'That's not what I meant!' Maria's head jerked back, and Jennie realised she'd never shouted at her before. 'It's not some Being. It's more like an Agency.'

'What kind of agency?'

'I don't know. It's sort of, it's like something, some force or something, that wants me to have this baby. And have it in just the right way. So that everything around me's got to be arranged. And people do things because they think they've got their own reasons, but actually it's just to make sure that things turn out right. The way the Agency wants it.'

Maria was silent for a while. She reached behind her neck to play with her single braid. She looked out the window, then back at Jennie. 'You mean right now it's sunny outside and everyone thinks it's because the guys at the weather bureau and up in the space stations made the right offerings, but really it's because this agency thing figures you and the kid could use some sunshine about now. Is that it?'

'Well, I don't know, I don't think it matters much what the weather is.'

'But if it did, then the weather would have to shape up the way you needed it.'

'The way the Agency thought I needed it. I don't get much say in anything.'

'Fucking hell.' She flipped the braid back again. 'Who's the father of this kid?'

'I thought you weren't going to ask that.'

'The agency made me. Is it some Teller?'

'What?'

'Is it?'

'No, of course not.'

'I thought maybe that's why it seemed so important. Maybe some Teller on the body paths – you sometimes hear how they go out in unmarked cars, picking people off the street.'

'I'm too old, Maria. You think they'd want me?'

'You're not so old. You're not even thirty. Anyway, how do I know what a Teller wants? I'm just an ex-wrestler. I'm not even used to getting sucked up by secret agencies. Hey, maybe it's the government. Maybe the CIA's got their undercover Devoted Ones working on you.'

'Please, Maria,' Jennie said.

'Why not? They're an agency, right? Or maybe it's the FBI. They handle the domestic stuff.'

'Please stop it,' Jennie said. Maria shrugged. Jennie said, 'I better get started on my rounds.'

Maria held on to her arm. 'Mazdan,' she said, 'have you gone for a scan recently?' Jennie shook her head.

236

'Why don't you do that? They can find out what's got hold of you.'

'It wouldn't show up.'

'Yeah? If you're so sure – '

'It's too late. It wouldn't show on a scan.'

'Maybe something else will.'

'You mean, like paranoia?'

'You know what the prince said to Cinderella. If the head fits, wear it.'

'Nothing would show up. Not unless the Agency wanted it.'

Maria barked her sharp laugh. 'Why didn't I think of that?'

'Because you don't have to live with it. Can I please go?'

Maria released her hands. 'Go on. Go and do your rounds.' Jennie was at the door when Maria said, 'I still meant what I said. If anyone bothers you – if the agency sends anyone to bother you, let me know.'

Jennie nodded. Walking down the hallway, past pale green walls and metal doors she wondered if Maria would keep coming at her. Like Karen. It wasn't fair. If they wouldn't let her have an abortion why couldn't she just go through the pregnancy without everyone pestering her? In her mind she mimicked Maria. 'Why it seems so important to you.'

Was Maria acting on her own? Jennie clenched her fists. She didn't know. She'd probably never know. That was the terrible thing about the Agency. Except when it really interfered, like at the abortion clinic, there was just no way to tell.

In the small lobby, by the empty receptionist's desk, the statue of Rebecca Rainbow nodded its plastic and nylon head. 'Bless you in all your travels,' the computerized voice said. 'And have a good day.'

The Smith Street project, the Path-of-Truth

237

building, then down to Wappinger's Falls to the Post Office, and the Shining Body massage parlour. That should take her up to lunch . . .

What was paranoia, anyway? According to her college course (Abnormal Metapsych.) it occurred when somebody came loose from the divine pattern. Floating free, they manifested their own pattern to try and make sense of it all. 'Compensatory meanings,' Professor Kaplan called it. She remembered his half-smile. But she didn't imagine the – the fish swimming inside her. Or the trees at the abortion clinic.

A gust of wind lifted the leaves around her feet. They swirled up in front of her, a clatter of colours suspended in the air. She watched them for a while, as more and more of them joined in the dance. She took a step and the swarm moved with her. She stopped, breathed deeply. She saw the leaves pull the light around them so that the metal building, the trees, the cars faded into a dull backdrop. 'What?' she said.

Some of the leaves pressed against her face, then blew away before she could grab them. A woman in a grey cloth coat and purple high-heeled pumps paused with her hand on the door of her car to look at Jennie. Jennie thought *go away*, and the woman pushed open the door to vanish inside.

The leaves continued to spin and leap. They wanted to tell her something. Okay, she thought, let's get it over with. She braced herself, expecting words to form from the crackling noises of the leaves rubbing together. But not everything speaks in words. The sound, the movement, the spattering of light, they began to do something inside her. A calmness fought against her fears. It's okay, it told her. You're doing the right thing.

'What do you know?' she said out loud. The leaves shifted, formed a figure in front of her – or maybe they just allowed the light to take shape. A child stood in

238

the air. Her arms hung by her side, her head was tilted up. Jennie clenched her fists. A moment later the wind slipped and the leaves settled round Jennie's feet. She kicked them aside and walked to her car.

11

Jennie picked up the phone, and held it in her hand with her forefinger pointed like a formal accusation at the ring of numbers. The dial tone became louder the longer she stood there, biting her lip. She almost thought she could hear the Benign Ones who lived inside the phone lines hissing with impatience. She should slam the phone down, go and wash some underwear or something. 'It's wrong,' she said out loud.

Jennie breathed deeply. She decided to count to three and then decide. At two she stopped, took another breath, then said, 'Shit,' loudly, and began to dial. On the third five her finger slipped and she had to start again. But a moment later the distant ringing began, followed by a woman's dull voice saying, 'Rainbow Telecommunications, directory assistance. May I help you?' Jennie couldn't speak. 'May I help you?' the woman said again.

'I'm sorry,' Jennie said. 'I mean yes. I mean, I'd like a number.'

There was a pause and Jennie imagined the woman with a hand on the mouthpiece, telling her companions, 'I've got a real prize here. Why me? Haven't I purified myself? Haven't I blessed the company guardians?' The woman's voice came back on the line. 'May I help you?'

'Yes,' Jennie said. 'I'd like the number of Michael Gold. I don't know the address.' Dizziness washed through her. So she'd said it. Out loud. She wished she'd used a public phone. Suppose they had her phone tapped. Waiting for her to break the annulment.

The operator said, 'I have eight Michael Golds. Do you wish the numbers?'

'Eight? Oh.' She hadn't thought of that. 'Can you tell me the addresses?' She could just about hear the woman's eyebrows rising. The voice, however, stayed flat as it rolled out the listings like an express train passing through the local stations. '216 Avenue A, 1742 Broadway, 53 . . .' In the end Jennie omitted five of them as too poor or too rich, ending up with an address on Greene Street, one up in Founder Heights, and a third, a long shot because she didn't think Mike could afford it, on West 72nd Street, not too far, she guessed, from the park. 'Have a good day,' the operator said.

'Thank you,' Jennie answered, but the woman had already clicked off. Jennie hung up the phone. No need to call now. She'd got the number. That was the important thing. She could call whenever she wanted.

A week passed. A low front brought the first snow flurries down from Canada. The congressional campaign ended with various accusations. Jennie didn't vote, and when Bill Jackman made some joke about the new senator's tits, Jennie realised she hadn't noticed who'd won. The Poughkeepsie Picture Halls announced a visitors' day. Jennie didn't write down the date. Every morning, and several times during the day, Jennie checked herself in mirrors or shop windows, assuring herself that no one could see, that she didn't stick out that much, Maria was just a fluke. Now and then, in the supermarket or sitting in the movies with Marilyn Birdan, Jennie worried that if she didn't wrench her mind on to another track she'd start broadcasting all her thoughts, and everyone would form a circle around her and begin the sanctifications for someone who's fallen into an access state.

Maria said nothing more about the pregnancy or the Agency. Once, however, when Mary Pinter scowled at

241

her coffee and said, 'I don't know why I drink this stuff. I really don't. I don't like it. I don't need it. You'd think something was making me drink it every morning,' Maria smirked and raised her eyebrows at Jennie who stared down at her purse while she fumbled with the catch.

On the Thursday after her call to directory assistance Jennie called her doctor and made an appointment for the following Tuesday, after work. She didn't want to. For weeks she'd avoided all thoughts of doctors, medicine, babies. She'd even stopped watching *Sacred Hospital* on TV. And she'd switched off *Demon!* one night when the spirit-spy's human contact went to a playground to pick up his grandson. But her body had begun to demand attention. The nausea had faded, but her legs and feet sometimes cramped up in the mornings. Her feet had swollen and she had to wear running shoes all the time. She'd begun to sweat a lot, especially at night, so that she had to change the sheets two or three times a week. One morning, when she took off her nightgown she discovered a yellow liquid around her nipples. 'Go away,' she'd shouted, as she wiped it off with the cotton gown. 'I don't want to know about this. Go away.' The oozing stopped and didn't return.

But it was dizziness that drove Jennie to make the appointment. She would wake up dizzy, unable to get out of bed. Or she would find herself swaying in the late evening, when she stood up from watching television. Finally, just getting out of the car was enough to leave her bent forward, holding on to the door until the wooziness retreated.

Along with a lecture on her carelessness Dr Simmons told Jennie her blood pressure was too low. He gave her a prescription for Vitamin B along with a chant designed to urge her blood to work harder. When the doctor launched his third barrage against her waiting so long before coming to him Jennie switched her silent rage from 'the whitehaired idiot' (as she thought of the doctor) to 'the brownhaired idiot', herself, for not finding someone else. What was she doing here? He was Mike's doctor, Mike's family doctor, he'd treated the little coward since Mike was a brat. She'd only kept Simmons from inertia. She'd only kept her whole life from inertia.

Finally the examination ended. Dr Simmons gave her the name of an obstetrician, and then a card from the Holy Blood Birthing Agency, a fully accredited midwife service. The wives, he said, would do the proper enactments with her. They would also help her communicate with the foetus as the time approached for delivery. *Great*, Jennie thought, *just what I need. What's it like in there, little fish? How's the water?*

On the way out she hesitated before opening the door to the waiting room. Suppose she saw Mike's uncle? Jake must still come here. Unless he was dead. She pushed open the door. There was no one there she knew.

That was Tuesday. On Wednesday morning, taking her pills, she realised a week had passed without her using the list of phone numbers hidden in the zipper compartment of her pocketbook. She grabbed the bag and took out the wrinkled sheet of paper. No sense in calling, she told herself. He'd just be at work. She shoved the paper back.

Jennie hardly ate that day. If she hadn't arranged with Marilyn Birdan to meet for lunch at the Golden Lotus, she probably would have worked right through. Instead she twirled her porcelain spoon in egg drop soup, wondering what the swirls of soup might mean if she could understand their language. Did speakers ever use egg drop soup? 'Good news, madam, this pattern says that God has chosen you for a special mission.' Across from Jennie Mar dumped a spoonful of hot mustard in her chow mein. Outside, people were hurrying in and out of the Shop-Rite – 'Grocers To The Revolution' as they called themselves.

A pregnant woman walked by on her way to the ladies' room. She wore a T-shirt with a large number 1 and an arrow pointing downwards. 'What do you think?' Mar said. 'You think that's safe?'

Jennie said, 'What? What's safe?'

Mar tossed the last quarter of her egg roll into her mouth. 'I don't know. Eating Chinese food. When you're knocked up.'

Jennie stared at her. The other woman wasn't smirking or even looking at Jennie. She'd rolled up the sleeves of her grey corduroy shirt and was trying to keep her chopsticks from crossing over each other. Jennie said, 'Why shouldn't it be safe?'

'I don't know. All that monosodium glutamate.' She grinned. 'Make the baby's eyes slant or something.' She laughed loudly, then lifted a delicately balanced glob of chow mein into her mouth.

Tonight, Jennie thought. She had to call him that night, before it was too late.

At seven o'clock Jennie sat down at the dinette table with the list in front of her, carefully positioned in the centre of the place mat. Maybe she could just write. She could xerox the letter and send it to all three at the same time. She growled and stood up by the phone.

She tried the one on 72nd Street first, the one she considered the least likely. After four rings her heart slowed. Not home. She could try the others tomorrow. In the middle of the seventh ring a man's voice, a light thin voice said, 'Hel-lo.' He sounded excited, like he was expecting somebody.

244

Jennie said, 'I'd like to speak to Michael Gold.' She sounded like a salesman.

'Speaking,' the man said, more subdued.

'Oh. I mean, oh – '

'Oh to you too.' He laughed.

'You're not – you're not the Michael Gold from Poughkeepsie.'

'Sorry. From Denver to Manhattan, that's me. But I once stayed a week in Ellenville, if that'll help.'

'I'm sorry,' Jennie said. 'I've got the wrong number.'

The wrong Michael Gold laughed again as Jennie hung up.

She tried the number in Founder's Heights next. On the third ring a soft voice said, 'Hello.' Jennie wasn't sure if it was a man or a woman. It was old, or maybe the wheeze made it sound older.

Jennie said, 'I'd like to speak to Michael Gold, please.'

There was a pause, and then the woman – Jennie thought it was female – said, 'Who is that?'

'I'm someone . . . I used to know him.'

'What do you want? Who the hell are you?'

'I just want to speak to Mike. Can't I speak to him?'

'Michael Gold is dead.'

'Great mother,' Jennie said. 'How? What happened?'

The woman shouted, 'He died five years ago,' and slammed the phone down.

'Five years?' Jennie repeated. 'You said five years?' She realised she was talking to a dialling tone. She dropped the phone on the hook, then collapsed in her chair, with her head tilted back and her arms hanging loose. *Poor woman*, she thought, and then, sitting up, *Better her than me*.

At least now she knew which one was Mike. Greene Street. Maybe he had a loft. Unless he lived at one of the addresses she'd rejected. She couldn't see Mike at

Sutton Place. Of course, he could have left the city. Or got a place in Queens. Or just an unlisted number. Or changed his name. She stood up again and started dialling. If only she could forget it. Take a shower. 'You forget it,' she said out loud. 'You're not buying me off with a shower. If I wait any longer you'll probably put his phone out of order. I want my husband back.'

The ring sounded tired. It went on for a long time, with Jennie shifting her weight from one side to the other. 'Come on,' she said, not sure if she wanted him to be home or out.

And then he was there. The same flat telephone voice, that slightly suspicious 'Hello?'

Jennie could see, all over again, the judge sitting above her in his silver mask, she could hear the crack of his hammer-shaped sky totem striking the ebony bowl of the Earth.

'Hello?' Mike said again.

'Hi, Mike,' Jennie said. 'It's me.'

Silence. She thought she heard a faint 'Fucking hell,' but he must have put his hand over the mouthpiece, because even the radio in the background – she hadn't noticed it before – dropped away. He was deciding what to do, and she had to stop herself from laughing as she imagined Mike trying to work out the proper, the correct response. He must be furious, she thought. He'd love to hang up but he can't. That would mean he would know who she was. In fact, even thinking about it implied –

'Who is this?' he said.

'Come on, Mike. It's me. Jennie.'

'I don't know any Jennie.'

'Come on Mike. Stop it.'

'Stop it? Are you out –' He caught himself. She heard him tell someone, 'It's nothing, just some crank

246

call or something.' To her he said, 'Look, I don't know who you are – '

'I've got to speak to you, Mike. There's something you've got to know.'

He said again, louder. 'I don't know who you are, but you've got – '

'It's about the annulment.'

'You've got the wrong number.' He hung up.

Jennie almost called him back, but she knew it wouldn't work. He'd feel justified this time in hanging up immediately and then leaving the phone off the hook if she tried again. But God, she'd sure got him going. Laughing, Jennie held out her arms and snapped her fingers, the way you did when you finished a purification.

She sat down, then jumped up to take a bottle of Coke from the shelf. She poured herself a little in a juice glass. Sipping at it she thought how objectively she'd probably made things worse. She'd put him on his guard. But it felt so good to have done something. And at least she'd proved she knew him. Whatever that lawyer had said at the annulment hearing. She knew Mike better than anyone.

Anyone . . . Who was he talking to? Jealousy sliced through her euphoria as she imagined him living with some woman. Someone pretty, she decided, with bouncy blonde hair, even more bouncy tits, and an adoring simper as she listened to Mike build his exploits at some travel agency into a swashbuckling movie. If he still worked at a travel agency. Maybe he'd switched to selling real estate. For all she knew, he worked in an art gallery.

Who was he speaking to? Was he married? He wouldn't just get married again. Maybe he'd met her that time in New York, after he'd run away from Jennie in the parking lot. But how could he just move in with someone? As if their years together meant nothing to him.

She set down the glass. Of course it meant nothing to him. That was the whole idea. Far be it from Good Citizen Michael Gold to disobey a fucking court order. What a shock it must have been for him. He would never think of calling her. She wondered if he'd managed all this time to dislodge from his consciousness, gently but firmly, any images or memories of her. 'No,' he'd tell himself. 'Mustn't think such thoughts. That's not correct.' Bastard. She could bet that Mike didn't keep any secret cache of pictures hidden in an old box somewhere.

A raiding party of tears was gathering in her eyes. Goddamn hormones. But at least she was doing something. She wiped her eyes and grabbed a pencil from the table beneath the phone. On an old envelope half covered with a shopping list (one of a series never filled) she wrote 'NEXT STEP.' After a moment she added, '1. No sense in calling again.' He'd probably just get her arrested. She stared at the paper.

How did people get annulments in the old days? Did a judge do it, like now? That seemed wrong, somehow. Too bureaucratic. Maybe they went to a speaker. Go down to an oracle centre and listen to the word of heaven destroy your marriage. What was she talking about? In the Time of Fanatics they didn't have neat little Oracle Centres with plastic booths and machines blowing mist, and receptionists in cute uniforms like airline hostesses. And you didn't just go and make an appointment, you had to submit yourself for judgement. Humble yourself before the divine voice. And the speakers didn't just analyse a bunch of cards and coins. When they spoke they really said something. In the Days of Awe speakers burst out of the skin of society, howling and spinning down the streets until

248

the healers and the older speakers got hold of them and taught them how to channel the sacred fire.

You just didn't have things like that any more. She smiled, thinking of Gloria, or maybe Al, running through the hive dressed in the other's clothes, waving his/her arms at frightened kids on bicycles. *Why* didn't you have things like that any more? Was it just because people didn't want them? People like Mike? If Michael Gold had had to plead for an annulment by lying face down on a cement floor with mud all over his naked body he and Jennie would probably still be married.

She wasn't getting anywhere. She leaned forward and tapped her pencil on the paper.

Greene Street appeared to be making an effort to live up to its name. Here and there on the sidewalk three foot high concrete boxes displayed clusters of white roses and tiger lilies, the flowers holy to Miguel Miracle-of-the-Green-Earth. At the top of the street, near Houston, stood the smallest sacred grove Jennie had ever seen: three scrawny trees with life signs carved into their trunks and a wire fence to keep away dogs and children.

The few people on the street didn't seem to take much notice of the neighbourhood's attempt at sanctification. They detoured round the trees without even a glance, let alone a step to touch the leaves or earth. Jennie surveyed the block's mixture of income levels. Only in New York, she thought, would you find a jewellery store on the ground floor of a condemned factory.

On the ground floor of Mike's building was a restaurant calling itself 'Green Delights'. The thick metal plating over the door and window made it impossible to see inside, but the thin black letters on the silver sign suggested it attracted the same crowd as the two art galleries, one on each corner by Houston, guarding the street like a pair of lions. Above the restaurant the building rose to six storeys of narrow windows and grimy brick. Jennie could well believe it was once some Old World sweatshop, with immigrant women chained to sewing machines, and electric shock to cauterise their internal spirit centres. What was it now? Luxury apartments, with slate floors and chromium spotlamps? She refused to believe it. Mike could never afford something like that. Unless his new girl friend was giving him money.

It was slightly before nine on Sunday morning. Jennie had spent the night at Hudson Street, showing up without phoning and for once embarrassing her mother. Apparently Beverley had planned some sort of ceremonial sex project with one man and four women from her latest ensemble. They'd moved all the furniture out of the living room and drawn a chalk outline on the floor of a spreadeagled androgyne with double genitals. Various objects lay at the hands and feet and head. Jennie avoided looking at the men and women sitting on the floor. She announced to her mother that she would spend the night in her third floor bedroom, and then marched out. Beverley called to her from the bottom of the stairs. 'I'm sorry, Jen,' she said. 'I didn't know you were coming. You should have called.' Jennie kept going.

She'd slept fitfully, partly from anxiety, and partly from the hours-long tape of chaotic noises booming through the house. Now she had taken up her post across from Mike's building, dressed in a blue suede jacket over a blue sweater streaked with silver, dark jeans with rolled up cuffs, and shiny blue lace-up shoes. A blue wool scarf trimmed with leather protected her from the hard gusts of damp November wind. Not enough, however. She'd forgotten she might have to stand around for hours. She was already chilled. She wished she'd worn her fake fur coat and her hat with the silly flaps. She could have taken the thing off as soon as she'd spotted him. As if Mike would notice or care what she was wearing. She shook her head. As long as he didn't notice her shape. When she'd dressed that morning she was sure the sweater covered her; now she found herself checking constantly in the window of a shop selling kitchen appliances. She tried standing very straight and pulling in her stomach. She couldn't decide if that made it better or worse.

Jennie reached into her jacket to press the lump under her sweater. Her own genuine relic hung there, Li Ku's bit of torn skin in a small gold pouch attached to a strand of silver cord. In the years she'd had it she'd never shown or mentioned it to anyone. 'Li Ku,' she whispered, 'in beauty and truth lives your name forever. Please send me some of your fire. I'm cold and I've got to stay here.'

After fifteen minutes she decided she better not count on Li Ku protecting her from the chill. The sky had grown greyer and the wind had picked up. Hours, she thought. He might not even come out at all. Maybe he and his new pal had screwed all night, like Beverley, and now would sleep the whole day in a kingsize bed in front of an electric log fire. Should she ring the bell? She'd gone over this so many times. If she rang his apartment she'd have to announce herself on the intercom and then he not only wouldn't let her in but he'd know she was there.

She looked around. There was an open pizza parlour, Angelo's, halfway down the block. If she got a window seat she could still watch Mike's door. She walked quickly to Angelo's, hesitated in front of the door, then continued on to a newsstand where she bought a copy of the Sunday *Times* and a *Sacred Digest*.

251

Inside, Jennie's breath added to the steam that already clouded the doors and windows. Worried she might miss Mike she hurried to a red Formica-topped table near the window and rubbed a section of glass before she even put down the paper. She sat down on the armless wooden chair. Warmth. Joy. With her eyes fixed on the window she took off her jacket and scarf, then leafed through the paper for the magazine section. The cover story was called 'What next for the budget?' and showed the President sitting in her oval office while representatives from the Sacred Democrats and the Republican Revolutionaries laid some kind of offerings on either side of her desk. Good old *New York Times*, Jennie thought. Boring, boring, boring. Anyway, she couldn't read. Even just leaving through the pages she kept jerking her head up, afraid he'd slip past her. What did they do on TV? Hold the paper up without reading and peek over the page. She wished she had special powers like the CIA agent on *Demon!* If only she could turn her body into smoke and hover over the doorway. Probably set off a smoke alarm.

When Jennie glanced at the counter she discovered that the owner was staring at her. She should have gone up and ordered. Maybe he'd get angry, tell her to leave. She looked out the window once more then got up and walked over to the counter.

Except for an Hawaiian shirt tucked into his tight jeans the owner looked like a Hollywood Italian – wavy black hair, large eyes and long lashes, straight nose and wide mouth. Jennie thought, *Your mother must have done some powerful beauty offerings when you were born.* Smiling slightly he leaned forward with his forearms on the glass case above the counter. His hands and wrists were white with flour.

Jennie said, 'Uh, do you have breakfast? Eggs or toast or something?' He shook his head. Jennie wanted

252

to run back and check the window but she forced herself to say, 'I'll just have a coffee then. For now. I'll have a slice of pizza later. A little later.' He nodded and Jennie hurried back to her table to rub the fog off the window again.

Her eyes dropped down to the newspaper when she heard him bringing the coffee. He leaned past her to look out the window. 'No parade?' he said. He had a strong New York accent.

She looked up at him. 'Parade?'

'Isn't that what you're waiting for?'

'What? Oh, no, I'm just waiting for someone, a friend of mine.' He nodded. She said, 'Are you Angelo?'

He laughed. 'No, I'm Sam. Angelo's gone. Vanished.'

She checked the window before she repeated, 'Vanished?'

'Yeah. Went on a pilgrimage to one of the rock towers. Down in Texas or some place. Anyway, he transported. Lifted smack into the pattern and never came back. His body's up in one of those state hospitals.'

'And you got this place.'

'Yeah. City auction.'

He had his hand on a chair and Jennie could see he was about to sit down. Quickly she said, 'Look, do you mind if I sit here for awhile? I don't know when – my friend – the one I'm waiting for, he's not expecting me.' She looked out the window.

Sam's shrug was so smooth he might have practised it in front of a mirror. 'Whatever you like,' he said, and strolled back to the counter.

For a while Jennie either looked out the window or pretended to read the paper, afraid to turn her head and discover that Sam was staring at her, leaning forward with his arms on the glass. Finally she got up

253

and announced, 'I'm just going to look outside a second. I'll be right back.'

Sam said, 'I'll guard your stuff.'

Outside, Jennie stood hugging herself against the cold. 'Come soon, Mike,' she whispered. 'Please come soon.' She was about to go in when she spotted something yellow and white at the base of the building next door. Some kind of toy or doll lay between an empty garbage pail and a stack of soggy cartons.

When Jennie picked it up she felt a sudden shock in her 'serpent coil', the spot in the solar plexus just below the navel. The thing was a Revolution Mouse doll, the toy created decades ago to celebrate the Parade of the Animals. Four inches tall, the doll had a human body and a caricature of a mouse's head, with painted eyes and large round ears. Jennie tugged gently at the oversized head. At first it resisted, but then it came off with a soft plop. Underneath was a child's face, gleaming in its original gold paint, with pink lines radiating from around the black eyes.

Jennie held it cradled in her hands, as if the wind might harm it after so many years. The one-piece yellow suit was torn and spattered with grease, the painted on white shoes and gloves were all scratched and discoloured. It must have lain there for a long time, maybe covered in mud or hidden by some construction or something. And now it had found its way to Jennie Mazdan, on her quest to get back the husband stolen from her by the Agency. It was a sign, a gift to tell her she was doing the right thing. She looked around at the street, as if some refraction of light would allow her to see her benefactors. She said, 'Devoted Ones, I thank you for your devotion. I know that nothing I have done deserves your precious intervention.'

A part of a version of the Story of HE WHO RUNS AWAY

At the end of their journey the Army of the Great Liberation
came to a mountainous country thick with clouds. These
people had long known of the Liberator's approach. They
had seen his 'sacred messengers' – children born with oily
grey wings – scouting the peaks. Their speakers had cast
reading after reading with the coloured stones they used for
an oracle. The answer was always the same: 'The unknown
river breaks through the rock. No escape.' Most of all they
had the testimony of the refugees. So many had come to this
dim land, which called itself the Homeland of the Sun, that
the government had ordered them into warehouses, where
they lay in stacks, breathing out memories of their lost
worlds. Outside, the warehouse guards grew dizzy with
images of bright sun or turkey dinners or children playing
games on narrow streets.

At the edge of the Homeland spies dug holes in the ground
to wait for the enemy. When they returned with the news
that the army was carving steps in the lower hills the people
sent committees to the Council of the Wise, a group of women
who'd lived together since childhood. The Council told the
people to take all the weapons and pile them up with a sign
offering them to the liberators. They they must lay themselves down on the more difficult peaks so that the outsiders
would have no trouble climbing over them. In the village
that passed for a capital they must hang all the trees with
ribbons and paint the sides of buildings with the face of the
conqueror.

They must give the conquerors their homes, their bodies,
and their beds. Above all, they must talk with them. With
every drink, with every bite, with every touch, they must tell
the foreigners about the rocks, the sheep, the clouds – and
especially about the mountain called the Father of the World.
For the top of this mountain, the tallest in that garden of
peaks, was covered in clouds, and according to the people of
that country, the clouds protected them from a sight too
terrible to see: God's face.

When the committees had left, the women gave a private

order to a team of builders. Wind machines. Go to the Father of the World and fill the highest ledge with engines the shape of goats' heads and blades the shape of eagles' wings.

He Who Runs Away ran up the stairway of bodies, he crashed open the doors of houses, he tore apart the goats and sheep and people that stumbled into his path. When he had killed enough people to realise that no one would resist him he hid himself in the largest house in the largest village. Slowly the message penetrated his barriers of disgust. Here at the end of the world, where human courage had drained into the rock, there existed a mountain. And above this mountain, the other side of the clouds, rose the face of the enemy. He Who Runs Away left his army at the knees of the World's Father. Breathing ice into his chest he climbed until he came to the ledge where the rows of goats' heads stared up at the mist.

The black blades beat away the clouds. He Who Runs Away shouted over the engines and the wind. He looked up. Nothing. No eyes of fire, no forehead streaked with lightning, no mouth open to swallow the night. Just blank sky. It was all a joke, and his fists opened and closed as he thought of what he would do to these people who thought they could play a trick on the master of life. He looked again. He saw the stars and recognised them as suns so isolated they could no longer speak to each other. He saw swirls of greyish light and knew they were groups of suns so distant from *here* that they'd become less than a swarm of flies around a corpse. And even all these clouds could not obliterate more than a corner of the emptiness. With a hammer torn from the rock wall of the mountain He Who Runs Away smashed the machines.

Below the Father of the World civilisation waited for the leader's return. Laws, agencies, budgets piled up on shelves. In the warehouses the refugees dreamed of games and bedspreads, of cabbages and jewellery. The Council of the Wise played cards for painted pebbles.

Weeks passed. The army's corps of Speakers and Oracles

studied the snow for messages. Their fingers invaded the bodies of birds, searching for clues. One morning a group of soldiers woke to find the Champion of the Great Liberation lying on the ashes of their evening fire. Beside him lay the Head of His Father, as dull as dead wood.

The Council heard a flutter of wind, they smelled the perfumed bodies of sacred messengers flying over their city. One of their nieces went up to the roof with a coil of rope, for the women had learned that the messengers lost their wings at puberty, a tragedy which they mourned in poetry for the rest of their lives. The girl brought down a male and threatened to awake his sexuality if he didn't tell her the leader's orders.

'They're leaving!' she shouted down to her aunt and the others. 'They're going home.' The women threw their cards in the air and began to dance. They were pulling off their skirts so they could kick their legs higher when one of them banged on a pot for silence. It was no good. He needed to take something away with him. Otherwise he would return and kill them all for what God's Face had said to him.

Now, in this country there lived a girl so beautiful that the law ordered her to cover herself in mud, replacing the layers every few weeks when the mud had burned away out of shame from touching her perfect skin. This girl was called Too Pretty For Her Own Good. The army was almost ready to leave when Too Pretty was summoned to the council.

The women invited the liberator to dine with them. He was drinking goat's milk and remembering his Death Squad of lion-men when the girl came in, carrying a pot of tea. Her face, washed clean for the first time in twelve years, floated above the high-necked dress that hid her body. He breathed; her face coated his lungs. The women averted their eyes and sipped their tea.

When the army left the Homeland of the Sun Too Pretty For Her Own Good left with them, walking beside the master of life, talking and waving her arms. Runs Away had promised he would never dress her in mud, but covered her instead with a veil and a long dress embroidered with pictures of the occupied territories. Every time the material tried to settle

257

against her body her beauty pushed it away, like a child puffing on a feather. Too Pretty didn't care. She helped her husband up and down the hills and she listened to his stories and stared at his face and arms. For she had never seen skin that shone, and this man's body glistened with rage.

But when they left the mountains, when Too Pretty For Her Own Good discovered a land so flat she constantly stumbled, like someone expecting an extra step at the bottom of the stairs, when she discovered a cloudless country where the sun shone with the blank determination of an autistic child, then she begged her husband to shelter her. He Who Runs Away built a dark house, with clouds painted on all the windows.

12

She was standing with her hand on the door of Angelo's/Sam's when she saw him. She glanced over her shoulder and there he was, coming out the door. Without thinking she plunged inside, terrified he'd spot her. It was only when she was bending down and peeking at him doublelocking the street door that she realised she had to follow him. It wasn't enough just to stare at his short leather jacket, with its brown fur around the collar (God, it was just like Marilyn Birdan's), his hair slightly longer and much more curly (a perm? Mike?), his red cowboy boots over dark jeans. She had to follow him, speak to him.

She stood up and turned around to see Sam leaning on the counter and smiling at her. 'That the guy?' he said. 'He comes in here sometimes. Anchovies and extra cheese, right?' Jennie nodded. She tried to gather everything together, then dumped the papers as she scrambled in her bag for money. When she'd thrown down a dollar she gave the Revolution Mouse doll a kiss on its greasy ear, then stuffed it in her bag.

'Hey, Nancy Drew,' Sam said. 'Good luck.' Jennie waved, remembering her father reading her *Nancy Drew and the Malignant Ones of the Old Mansion*.

Outside, Mike had reached Houston and was turning west. Jennie hurried to within a few feet of him, then held back. For two blocks they continued, past a gas station and a broken down park littered with smashed bottles. Watching the uneven walk, the faint tilt of the head, his flat behind and sloped shoulders, Jennie tried to work up some desire, some longing to be in his arms

259

again, even the loneliness and fear she'd felt for so long by herself. All that came out of her was anger. 'You weak bastard,' she whispered. 'You deserted me. You let the Agency chase you away.'

At Thompson Street Mike turned the corner and entered a delicatessen, the sort that featured Swedish ice cream and imported beers, gourmet potato chips and twenty kinds of sandwiches on roll or rye or French. In one of its cousins Beverley had suffered her vision of people eating her daughter. Jennie darted in after him.

He was standing by the sandwich counter bouncing up and down slightly and puffing the way people do to chase the damp out of their bodies. 'Mayo and lettuce on both,' she heard him say.

Jennie stood next to him a few seconds before he even noticed her. When he finally saw her he jumped back, almost knocking down a wire rack of pretzels and corn chips. 'Hi, Mike,' Jennie said.

He composed his face into curiosity. 'I don't think I know you,' he said.

She laughed. 'Don't think so, huh?'

To the man behind the counter Mike said, 'I'll just go get a couple of beers.' Jennie followed him to the large glass cooler in the back of the store, then said nothing while Mike pretended to ignore her as he pondered hops and malts from Denmark, Belgium, and Japan.

Jennie said, 'You look good, Mike. What have you done with your hair?'

'Look,' Mike said, 'I don't know who you are, but will you please leave me alone?'

'I can't,' she said. 'I wouldn't have come if it wasn't important. Really important. There's something you don't know.'

He took a breath, like a child about to make a speech

260

in school. 'Ferocious One,' he said, 'I beg you to spare me from your Malignant intervention. Nothing I have done – '

'Don't you dare,' Jennie said. 'Don't you even think it.' He stopped without finishing the formula.

'Will you go away? It's too early to deal with bag ladies or whatever the hell you are.'

'I've got to speak to you,' she said.

'No, you haven't.' He took out a couple of bottles of Dortmunder and closed the cooler door.

Jennie jumped in front of him to block him from marching back to the counter. 'Please,' she said, 'we can pretend we've just met.'

'We have just met.'

'Fine. Fine. Suppose I came in here to buy something.' She looked around, grabbed a box of sacred crackers, little biscuits in the shape of the animals from the story of 'First Teller'. 'Here,' she said, 'I came in here to get this.'

'I don't care what you came in here to get,' he said, but he was no longer as hostile.

'Then will you speak to me? Please?'

'There's – there's someone waiting for me. I've got to go back. We haven't had breakfast.'

'Meet me later. You can tell your friend you want to go for a walk. Tell her you have to check something. At the travel agency.' She smiled. 'I mean, just in case you happen to work at a travel agency.'

He shook his head. 'No. No, she wouldn't – where do you live?'

'Poughkeepsie. Ever hear of it?'

'Poughkeepsie? That's – that's a coincidence. I come from Poughkeepsie.'

'No kidding? Then you can say you ran into someone from your home town. And you want to find out what it's like these days.'

261

'Yes, I could – This is ridiculous. Why should I speak to you? I've got nothing to say to you.'

'I'll haunt you. I'll hang around outside your door and follow you wherever you go. I'll spread rumours in all the stores and restaurants about you. And I'll find out who your girl friend is and tell her all the stuff I'm not supposed to know about you.'

He whispered, 'Why are you doing this? The court told you – '

'Because it's a fake. It's a trick.'

'A trick? What the hell are you talking about?'

'Please Mike, just let me talk to you.'

He was silent a moment. 'There's a place on West Broadway,' he said. 'The Olympia. I'll try to get there by one.' He slid past her to rush down the aisle for his sandwiches and escape.

Jennie's breath came out in a stutter. One damp hand held on to the crackers, the other found the doll and pressed it against her chest where the little leather bag hung with Li Ku's skin. She didn't know whether Mike would show up. She wasn't even sure any more if she wanted him back or if she just wanted to beat the Agency. Nevertheless, she closed her eyes and nodded her head, saying, 'Thanks.'

The Olympia turned out to be a diner with oily coffee, stale cakes in round plastic containers on the counter, fake Tiffany lamps over red booths, and a giant menu with lurid descriptions of Greek pies and roast beef 'dripping from the carving board.' Jennie got there almost an hour early, after an hour pretending to look for clothes, books, and records on Sixth Avenue. The place was crowded, mostly people in their thirties discussing work, relationships, and some scandal at the East Village Teller's Hall on Second Avenue. Jennie found a booth and sat down with her second copy of

The Times. Alongside the salt and pepper shakers stood a guardian, a squat plastic statue with claws and horns and a little button you could push for the eyes to light up and the belly to emit a low growl to frighten away any diseases lurking in the food. Jennie ordered a cup of coffee and a hamburger de luxe. With *The Times* spread in front of her she waited.

Mike came in at two minutes to one. Jennie smiled, remembering his hatred of coming late, or even early. He winced when she held her hand up by her chin and waved her fingers at him. When he'd sat down across from her and the waiter came he said, 'Coffee. Black.'

Jennie said, 'Since when do you drink black coffee?' Right away she knew he'd tricked her.

'How would you know how I drink my coffee?' he said. He was smirking. 'I've never drunk coffee with you in my life.'

Jennie wished she could hit him. Roll up *The Times* real estate section . . .

'Look,' he said, 'I don't know your name – '

'Jennifer. Jennifer Mazdan.'

'Fine. Now listen, Jennifer Mazdan. Whatever you want, can we get this over with quickly? My girl friend's waiting for me at home. We're supposed to go to an opening this afternoon.'

An opening of what? she thought. *A supermarket? Was this another trick or had his new pal lured him into the art world?* She said, 'Maybe you'll meet my mother there. She goes to openings all the time.'

'Will you please tell me what you want?'

'I just want to tell you a story,' she said, wishing she sounded tougher. 'A theoretical story about two people.' He said nothing. 'Suppose two people meet. Here in New York. By the river. By the black freighter.' Still nothing. 'You know what the black freighter is?'

'Yeah, of course.'

263

'Well, how did they come there? I mean, what made them both show up there? At the same time? Especially if one of them, if the man, never used to go there at all.'

'I wouldn't know. Maybe it was just luck.'

'Maybe it was more than luck. Maybe some kind of force manipulated them. Maybe it wanted them to meet and it made them go there at the same time.'

'Force? Is this what you wanted to tell me. Is this why you insisted I meet you? This is nuts.'

'It's not. Think about it. They're both supposed to be working, one of them never goes there – '

'I'm sorry, Jennie – Jennifer, this is ridiculous.'

'Please. Just let me go on. suppose this force, this *Agency*, wanted them to meet.'

'Agency?'

'Yes. An Agency that arranges things, arranges people's lives in order to create certain effects in the world.'

'And you think this agency, whatever it is, made these two people get together.'

'Yes. Yes.'

'Why? Why would this agency, these people, whoever they are – '

'People? No, I don't mean people. People could never arrange something – '

'Then what are you talking about?'

'I told you. A kind of force. A spirit Agency.'

He nodded slightly. 'Malignant or Benign?'

'Not that. Not the Bright Beings. Something – something deeper.'

'I don't understand what you're talking about.'

'You've got to understand.'

'No I don't.'

'Lots of times, things, events have a much greater

meaning than people realise. That's not a crazy idea. It's a known fact.'

'Yeah. Okay. But when people start thinking their lives have such meaning – '

'But maybe they do. If some lives have meaning outside themselves, why not these two people? Why not?'

'What the hell is the point of all this? Suppose there was some kind of special purpose. So what?'

Her eyes avoided him. 'Well, these two people, the man and woman, met because the Agency wanted them together. It didn't care about them. Not as people. It just wanted to use them. But then suppose they fell in love. Really in love. I mean, not just because the Agency, just because God wanted them to. They really loved each other.'

'Not because God wanted them to.'

'The Agency only brought them together. I'm messing this all up. I knew I'd mess it up.'

'Did you really chase me down, and break – just to tell me this crazy story? You do know it's crazy, don't you?'

'Let me go on. Please.' For a moment she thought she saw a certain look he used to give her when she would wrap herself up in some complicated worry that only she could follow. There was sympathy in it, and exasperation, and amusement, and a desire to get loose. And for that moment she felt a real pull between them, and an ache to get him back, to put her head against him while he stroked her and laid his hand on her belly as if he could feel the baby's heart whispering. But then he leaned back and crossed his arms and grimaced. Jennie wanted to hit him.

'Just suppose,' she said, 'suppose they fall in love and finally got married.'

'And go on a honeymoon in Bermuda?'

'Yes. Yes, and then come back and move to a hive.'

'Where they're more in love than ever.'

'Why not? Why can't they really love each other?'

'If they loved each other so much why did they break up? Isn't that part of the story? Didn't they break up?'

'That's the point. That's exactly the point. They broke up because the Agency wanted them to. They didn't stop loving each other. They didn't even stop wanting to be together. It was the Agency.'

'And that's the only reason they broke up.'

'Yes. Yes.'

'How do you know that? How do you know what went on in the man's head?' He leaned forward, lowered his voice. 'How do you know he didn't start hating her? All her nutty ideas.'

'Because that's not what happened. That's not why he left.'

'Just because you made up this story doesn't mean you can make the man into whatever you want.'

'The Agency arranged things. To make him leave. Things happened.'

'What kind of things?'

'Funny things, that scared him and drove him away. Things in driveways and with the hive touchstone. Even on their honeymoon. Suppose they saw a precursor on the road. And it scared him. Wouldn't something like that turn him against her?'

'And it didn't scare her?' Jennie didn't answer. 'That's really the point, isn't it? That's what you don't want to say. That she loved all those things. She loved them more than she loved her husband. This agency – if this agency ever existed, it didn't need to drive her husband away. It didn't need to. All it had to do was seduce *her*. And she was ready. She loved all that true event stuff. She went right along with her new lover.'

'No. That's not true. She was tricked. It tricked her

266

the same way it tricked him. I'm not making this up. It's not a fantasy. Really, Mike. There're things you don't know.'

'And I don't want to know. I got a court order so I wouldn't have to know.'

'Are you sure? Do you really know for sure why you got the order?'

'And now you come up with some paranoid fantasy – '

'It's not paranoid, Mike. We were tricked.' He looked about to get up. Jennie grabbed his arm so hard he stared down at her fingers, then up at her face. 'Listen to me,' she said. 'Will you just listen to me? Just once?'

'I always listened to you. You were the one – '

'Stop that. It doesn't matter. All that old stuff.'

He leaned forward. 'Why does this agency thing, why does it do all these things? Why should it take charge of people like that?'

Tell him about the fish, Jennie thought. He'd have to believe her. She said, 'Because it needs them. First it needs them to get together, then it needs to break them apart.'

'Why? What the hell for? Can't you see how crazy that is? What does it care what happens to these people?'

'It doesn't care. Not about them. It just wants to use them. That's why they have to fight it. Because it doesn't care what *they* want.'

'Use them how? For what?'

Her eyes fell away from his stare and she watched her fingers twist her napkin until Mike pulled it out of her hands. He said, 'Use them for what?'

'Well, maybe it needs, maybe it wants the woman in Poughkeepsie. Maybe it needs to get her there, and the man – the man serves this need.

267

'Why does it want her in Poughkeepsie?'

'I don't know. It just does. Good spiritual configurations. For whatever it wants . . . for her.'

'All right. Fine. It wants her in Poughkeepsie. Then why does he leave? Why not keep him in Poughkeepsie as well?'

'I don't know. The Agency wants him out of the way.'

'Why?'

'*I don't know.* Because it wants her there alone. It can't do what it wants to her if she's got a husband around.'

'What does it want to do to her?'

'How would I know? I'm just a human. "The observer can never learn the purpose of the experiment." Remember Adrienne Birth-of-Beauty. 10th proposition.'

'You're full of shit. You've got some idea in your head. You really believe this nonsense.'

'It's not nonsense.'

'Then what does the agency want to do to her?'

Jennie said, 'People can't know those kind of things. You can't . . . Look at the parents of the Founders. Or their grandparents. Maybe they thought, maybe each of those couples thought they loved each other. Or hated each other. What difference – whatever they thought, they really got together so their children would come together and give birth to the Founders. It didn't matter what they wanted. And they didn't even know. That's the sad part.'

Mike shook his head. 'I've got no time for this, Jennie. I just want to know what's going on. Why this supposed agency wants you – wants this woman.'

'How do I know? It's against the law to know things like that.'

'It's also against the law to break an annulment.'

268

Jennie didn't answer. Mike got up. 'I've got an opening to go to.'

She grabbed his sleeve. 'Please don't go.'

He pulled loose. With a shrug he got out his wallet. He tossed a five dollar bill on the table. 'Here,' he said, 'my treat. Since we both come from Poughkeepsie.'

'Mike,' she said, 'I'm pregnant.'

'What? Holy shit.' He stared at her stomach. 'Holy shit.' Sitting down, he said, 'Is that what this is all about? All this agency bullshit? I don't believe it.'

Jennie sank down in the booth. She didn't want to look at Mike's grin. Inside her, the foetus stirred slightly, not quite a turn or a kick, but definitely a movement. Startled, Jennie looked down at her belly.

Mike said, 'You're not accusing me, are you? You're not claiming I could have – '

'Don't be an idiot. If I haven't seen you for three years how could I say – '

'How would I know? Another one of your goddamn true events.'

'Go to hell.'

He laced his hands behind his head. 'I heard on the news one time about some woman who prayed – her husband was dead, he died suddenly before they could have a child, and she prayed and did a flesh offering – in Sanctified Park in New Chicago – God, I'd hate to work as a garbageman there – anyway, this Benign One came disguised as a milkman or something and knocked her up – '

'You're really enjoying this, aren't you?'

'Personally, I think she made the whole thing up. To get on the news. Or maybe to cover up for screwing the milkman.'

'And that's what you think I did.' He smiled and crossed his arms. 'You think I made it all up. The

Agency, everything else. So I could trick you. Because I'm pregnant.'

He leaned forward. 'That sounds about right.'

'You bastard. You weak – '

'I'm weak? You're the one with the nutty fantasies. You're the one who can't adjust to a simple court order.'

'Simple? If you weren't too frightened to even look at me you wouldn't have – ' She stopped. Accusations, complaints, they were all a trap. She thought, *Tell him about the dream. Tell him how it kept me from the Recital and how it brought Allan Lightstorm, and the car, and Gloria –*
'I tried to get an abortion,' she said. 'I went to this clinic . . . at first I couldn't even remember the name, I had to ask Karen – '

'Karen who? I don't know any Karen.'

'Stop it. I went to a clinic. And I couldn't get in. I couldn't get to the door. Trees grew wherever I tried to walk. They just popped out of the ground. The Agency did that. It wouldn't let me get an abortion. I'm telling the truth, Mike. Doesn't that show its power?'

'Sounds like a good trick. Maybe you could hire out as a gardener.'

She said loudly, 'What's the matter with you?'

A couple of booths away a man sitting alone said, 'Goddamn it,' and got up from his half-finished meal to march to the cash register.

'You're scaring the clients,' Mike said. 'Don't, huh? I've got to come back here. I live around here.'

'Do you think I'm lying?'

'Why not? What else should I think? Lying or crazy. Actually, no. It's possible you're even telling the truth. With you – maybe it did. Maybe the abortion clinic's got a whole new set of shrubbery.'

'Then doesn't that prove – '

270

'Maybe. Maybe everything you say. Maybe this agency got us together and then broke us apart. Maybe it drove me away.'

'But if you believe me – if you believe me – '

'Because I don't care. It doesn't matter how it happened.'

'Of course it matters.'

'Not to me. I don't care what pulled me away from you. I'm gone. Free. That's what matters. I'm free.'

'How can you call that free?'

'Maybe I should do an offering to this agency of yours.'

'How can you call that free? It's the opposite of freedom. Something makes you do things – '

'I'm happy. I like my life now. I don't want anything else.'

'You just think that.'

'Don't you tell me what I think.'

'We had a good life. We loved each other.'

'I thought you told me the agency arranged all that. Pushed us together. So then all it did was let go of me.'

'I don't understand.'

'Why not? It's not very difficult. I've got rid of you. That's all. And I don't care who arranged it.'

'I don't understand. It's not fair.'

'Sounds very fair to me. This agency forces me at you, then it lets me go.'

'Pushes you. Pushes you.'

'Okay, pushes me. A real hard shove. So what? I've still got away from you. That's fair enough for me.'

Jennie thought, *I love you, why are you doing this to me?* She thought, *It's the Agency.* She thought, *You bastard, you coward, you liar.* She thought, *This isn't Mike, this isn't him, they've sent an impersonator to squeeze me and step on me.* She thought –

Mike said, 'If you ask me, we've both got just what

we want. I've got my own life back and you've got your true events.'

'I just want you. I want you.'

'Yeah, I'll bet.' He got up and stood away from the table. 'I'm going, Jennie.'

'This isn't you,' she said. 'It's the Agency. The Agency's making you do this.'

'Yeah? Then I guess that's another one I owe it. Maybe I wouldn't have had the courage without the agency backing me up.'

'You wouldn't need courage. You wouldn't want this. You don't want this. The Agency just makes you think you want it.'

'Forget it, Jennie. If there's one thing I do know, it's what I want.'

'You don't know anything. You don't know anything.'

'Don't follow me, Jennie. Don't ever come back to my house and wait for me again. And don't call me, or write, or anything. I've still got the annulment. If you bother me again I'll come down on you so hard the agency will have to dismantle the whole fucking government just to get you out of jail.'

'Why do you hate me so much?'

'Bullshit. I don't hate you. I just don't want you pushing me around.'

'I'm not pushing you around. It's the Agency.'

He walked away with his shoulders up and his hands in the pockets of his jeans. When Jennie tried to get up the air thickened around her. She tried to push against it only to find herself back in the booth. This wasn't supposed to happen, she thought. They'd promised her. She grabbed her bag and found the Revolution Mouse doll. 'Why did you do this?' she said. 'Why didn't you help me?'

She put it away as the waiter came to clear the table.

He was whistling and Jennie knew he wanted her to leave. He was scared she'd throw a fit, terrify his customers, maybe even bring on a visitation so that the SDA would shut the whole place down as a sacred health hazard.

A high-pitched sound answered the waiter's whistle. It floated on the air, a piercing song narrowed down to a thread sewing the room together in a web of calm. Jennie recognised it. The same song had sent her to sleep the night after she'd gone to the clinic. She knew what it was now. The foetus was singing. To calm her. To protect her, from the waiter, from any hostile customers. Jennie shook her head. 'I don't want your help.' She stared down at her belly. 'Don't help me. Let me keep my own feelings.'

The waiter stood beside her. His cloth hung from his hand and he smiled at her. When she got up she saw all the customers turned towards her. They were smiling and nodding their heads. 'Stop it!' Jennie shouted. The smiles widened. And all the time she could feel joy tugging at her. She just had to give in. Like they were doing. Like Mike had done.

Jennie put on her jacket and buttoned it. She assembled *The Times*, then put the doll back in her bag. She clenched her fists. 'Have a nice day,' she said to the waiter. He nodded at her. She took a couple of steps then turned back and hit the button on the plastic guardian. From table to table she ran, turning on the horned totems until growls filled the diner. No one paid any attention. They smiled and listened to the song of the fish lilting its way through the maze of noise.

273

13

Outside, in the wet wind, the music stopped. Jennie took a deep breath. She was herself again. Angry, confused, frightened. No calm settling over her, no joy grabbing hold of her. She shook her head. As if she *herself* could do any good. The Agency had made it plain where the power was. It had taken her husband from her and plunked him down in this alien land.

She looked around, seeing nothing but the street's unbearable sophistication. Art galleries with faceless concrete walls and metal gates. Clothing stores that sold only one fabric at a time in bizarre constructions. A salad restaurant where the carrots and Japanese turnips were carved in the shape of spirit beings dreamed each night by the chef's paralysed aunt. Mike didn't belong here. Look, there, down by Spring Street, there was that restaurant where Mike once walked out because they served hamburgers on toasted pitta bread and gave you chutney instead of ketchup. Couldn't he see it wasn't him that made him end up here?

She was getting wet, she should get out of the rain, the paper was getting heavier from the rain. She walked a few feet and leaned against a metal grate enclosing a jewellery store. The Agency put him here. To make it easier to reject her.

And everything else. Mike's girl friend, these stores, the kind of coffee in the diner. Were they all arranged? Set up to contribute their bit to keeping her husband away from her? She looked down the street at a middle aged woman slipping and dropping her bag in a puddle. Was *that* arranged? And the little girl up near

Prince walking towards her with something dangling from a string held in her hand. Did the Agency stage her there? Did it bring her parents together and arouse their passion on some particular night, just so she'd be born with the right genes, upbringing, and spiritual configurations to send her out in a cold rain walking slowly at just that moment on just that corner. . . ? And the rain itself. And the people who put up the buildings and opened the shops. And the Beings who pushed the island up out of the sea.

It was too much. To discover something like that, to begin to see the connections, the lines between the pieces . . . She closed her eyes. The paper dropped from her hands. She thought, *I just wanted my husband back.*

When she opened her eyes the girl stood in front of her, the one with the string. She held it a little away from her body, and Jennie watched the doll at the bottom sway back and forth. The doll hung upside down by one foot. The other leg was crossed behind the straight one, and the arms were clasped behind the back. Jennie had seen something like that once, a picture on a card or something. It had to do with precursors, something or other in the Old World that kept the truth from suffocating.

'Miss,' the girl said, 'where do babies come from?'

Jennie stared at her. Sickness washed over her. In her womb she felt that whisper of movement again. She crossed her arms over her belly. 'I don't know,' she said. 'I don't know.'

The girl walked off, swinging her little hanging man in front of her as she headed south toward Spring Street.

Jennie turned north, across Prince and then Houston, past a jazz club and an Italian restaurant. To the right stood the triple towers of the university's lush ghetto. At the edge of Rainbow Square she stopped, looking in on the concrete park. She thought of Rebecca Rainbow camping out there while she threatened to split the Revolution if she wasn't allowed to reopen the factories. Rebecca Rainbow would never have given in. But Rainbow was a Founder. In beauty and truth lives her name forever.

Something tugged at her jacket. She slapped at it without looking. It tugged again, and she turned her head to see a little boy holding on to her with one hand in a torn woollen glove. He wore no hat; water ran down his face. 'Miss,' he said, 'Miss, where do babies come from?'

Jennie backed away, then turned and hurried through the square. She came out heading west towards Sixth Avenue. She'd only taken a few steps when she saw in front of her three dead birds lying together on the sidewalk. Pigeons. White pigeons. 'Shit,' she whispered, then said loudly, 'Leave me alone!' When she looked up she saw three children standing beside her. Dressed identically in jeans and running shoes and plastic jackets they watched her slide away from them. One of them nudged the birds with his foot. 'Hey, lady,' another called out. Jennie hurried towards the avenue before the child could finish what she was going to say.

On Sixth Jennie stood for a while, not sure which way she wanted to go. She found herself looking at the line of cars waiting for a green light. Steam rose from their hoods like the anger of neglected spirits.

A groan turned Jennie towards the West Fourth Street subway entrance. She saw a woman huddled on her side in the alcove by the stairs. The woman wore a long purple coat, running shoes with holes and broken laces, and green stockings that had fallen down around her ankles. Strands of grey hair stuck out from under a green nylon wig. Blood trickled down her neck from a shallow cut on her left cheek. Behind Jennie people walked past, looking and then hurrying away. One of them bumped into Jennie, saying, 'What're you, a statue?' A man and woman in the blue jackets of registered penitents bent down to touch the woman's cheek and then anoint their own foreheads and throats with her blood. Jennie wondered if she should help the woman to a shelter. Probably the shelters weren't open yet.

The woman lifted her head and fixed her eyes on Jennie. Without thinking, Jennie stepped sideways, out of sight, then hurried across the street. As she stepped off the kerb she heard a man say, 'You can't stay here. Do you understand? You've got to move.'

On West Fourth Street Jennie passed some German tourists trying to decide between a Cuban or an Italian restaurant. She walked on, past a card store and a second hand clothing boutique. She told herself she should be thinking about Mike, thinking about what she should do. She stopped in front of the basement display window of the Pounding Heart sacred sex shop. Along with the usual sanctified whips (made from bulls sacrificed in the Parade of the Blind in Dallas on the winter solstice), and gold and silver chains, the shop was featuring a special display: blessed enema bags, their gleaming black rubber adorned with gold insignias, stories of purification through flood, and even the face of Irina Speakeagle, who first told the Picture of Dark Mother chained at the bottom of the sea.

Jennie moved away when she noticed some man watching her while pretending to look in the window. Again she headed west, towards Sheridan Square. At the next corner a man was going through a garbage pail. He wore only a corduroy jacket over a T-shirt and torn pants. He was wearing sandals and no socks. When he found something in the garbage he would stuff it in a plastic bag or else slip it into a jacket pocket. Jennie took a step closer. There was something wrong with his back, she saw, for he couldn't stand upright even when he paused from searching. Now she saw bumps on his neck and on his hands, hard bonelike things, that made it impossible for him to lift his head completely or straighten his fingers.

Jennie thought, *He doesn't deserve this. No one could possibly deserve this.*

The man looked up. Before he could speak to her Jennie turned left onto Jones Street. Known mostly for an African restaurant and a bookstore that sponsored the kind of readings where Beverley was likely to accompany the poet, Jones Street was crowded today with a group of well-dressed people holding umbrellas.

When she came closer she realised it was a funeral. The men and women in the centre of the loose circle held their umbrellas over the corpse of a child lying in its varnished box. The coloured ribbons tied about the boy's body and draped over the sides of the coffin reminded Jennie of her father's funeral, with her grandmother explaining how the Benign Ones would catch hold of the ribbons and carry 'Daddy' safely to the land of the dead. As the crowd on Jones Street bent forward to begin their 'lamentations of departure' Jennie walked around them to reach Bleecker.

The Agency. The Agency wanted her to learn about real suffering. As if her pain didn't mean anything. As if she was being uppity to complain about losing her husband. But it wasn't just Mike. It was her whole life. They'd taken her over. And what about those people? Did they lose their son just so Jennie Mazdan could be put in her place? Couldn't the Agency see how wrong that was?

She knew she should head north, that was the quickest way to her mother's house where she could dry out. Instead she walked south, back towards Sixth Avenue. She stopped for a moment to look through the window of The Benevolent Tongue, the famous restaurant where Jan Willem Singing Rock performed the ceremony known as 'eating the ancestor.' Inside, a group of people sat on velvet cushions around an open space in the blue carpeted floor. Soon the staff would bring out the body, various foods formed into a sculpture of a human being, each finger a different spiced meat, the mouth and eyes dripping with sauces. Jennie made a noise. The original ancestor was made of minced meat, vegetables, and bread sticks. The people who took part sang afterwards for three days and nights in a stream of languages. These people here, with their silverware designed by Tiffany's, and their souvenir bibs with Singing Rock's picture on them, they looked excited enough, but with the kind of excitement that came from doing something their tourist book had labelled 'an absolute must during your stay in the Eternal Apple.' Inside, a couple noticed Jennie looking at them and laughed. Jennie walked away.

She passed Leroy Street. At Carmine Street she realised she'd better turn left or she'd end up back at Houston. She noticed she was limping slightly, trying to walk on her heels and spare her toes, swollen from the damp. She wished she could sit somewhere and take off her shoes. At the intersection with Bedford Street she stopped, uncertain whether to turn, or continue past Seventh Avenue to Hudson. She liked Carmine Street. With its hardware stores and cheap Indian restaurants it was shabbier but more interesting than the residential streets surrounding it. Across Bedford Street, on the other side of Carmine Street, she could see some tourists looking at the pictures and mandalas in front of The Ancient Drum, the nightclub

279

that pretended to guide its visitors on a journey through the Deep Worlds.

Jennie turned right onto Bedford Street and found herself before the ground floor window of a small apartment building, the kind that survived because the landlord couldn't think of how to get rid of his rent-stabilised tenants and remodel the building. She looked through the window at a group of people who took no notice of her. In the centre of the room, in an old manually cranked hospital bed, lay an elderly woman. Near total paralysis and emaciation made it difficult to guess her age, but a second woman, who called the first 'Mamma,' looked about fifty-five. The old woman had been sick a long time, Jennie thought. The room looked arranged for an invalid, with trays on either side of the bed and chairs set around it for visitors. Facing the bed, photos of adults and children surrounded a small television. Only one photo resembled the woman herself, and that one, a picture with a man in front of a suburban house, also showed a car in a model from over twenty years ago. The television was on – a game show – but no one was watching.

Apparently the woman could move only her head and her right hand, but neither of those would stay under her control. The head turned from side to side, like somebody saying 'No,' over and over, while the hand grabbed weakly at the air. Occasionally, the daughter, who sat beside the bed, would hold the hand down, but she always released it a few seconds later.

A third woman in the room appeared to be the mother's nurse, though she wore ordinary clothes, including large hoop earrings and a gold necklace. In her right hand she held a bottle of red and green capsules, while the left ('the healing hand') kept trying to insert a capsule into her patient's mouth. Each time

280

the capsule passed the lips the woman spat it out again. 'We've got to take our pills,' the nurse said. (Jennie wondered, for just a moment, how she could hear them through the closed window.) 'Be a good girl. Will you be a good girl?' She tried again and again but the old woman kept spitting the pill onto her chest.

'Please, Mamma,' the daughter said. 'You know what happens if you don't take your pills. Don't you remember how swollen you got? Remember how you had to go to the hospital?'

The woman's mouth opened and closed several times, as if she was gulping for air, but she apparently was saying something, for her daughter leaned closer. A moment later the daughter sat back, then turned her head and wiped her eyes. She turned back to say, 'That's not true, Mamma. You know you don't want that.' Looking up at the nurse she said, as if her mother couldn't hear her when she spoke to someone else, 'Every time she says that I just – I can't stand it.'

The nurse said, 'Take your pill like a good girl, and I'll give you your dinner.' She put down the bottle and held up a spoonful of some mashed vegetable. 'It's still hot,' she said. 'If you're a good girl you can have it while it's still hot.'

Jennie couldn't breathe. *I've got to get out of here*, she thought. But before she could leave, the doorbell in the apartment rang and Jennie stood and waited while the nurse went to answer it. She returned with another woman, middle aged and still wearing a dripping raincoat.

'I've been robbed,' the woman said. 'Thank God you're here. Oh damn, damn, I've been robbed. Everything's gone. Everything. They tore all my clothes, they just cut everything, everything they couldn't take. The whole collection, it's all ruined, the whole . . . What am I going to do? Janet, what am I going to do?' The

281

nurse took her in her arms, while behind them the old woman's head continued to turn from side to side.

Jennie looked down at her belly. 'Sing for them,' she pleaded. Her womb stayed silent. 'Why won't you sing for them?' Nothing. She walked away, half staggering. 'It's too much,' she said. 'We don't deserve this. None of us could possibly deserve this. It's all wrong.'

Just before Seventh Avenue a group of about fifteen children gathered about her. Around each of their eyes Jennie could see gold lines, like the radiance surrounding the eyes of the doll she carried stuffed in her bag. Their teeth shone with light as they said all together. 'Excuse me Miss, where do babies come from?' Jennie ran around them to Seventh Avenue.

And there she was standing when a large metal object came rolling down the road and knocked her to the ground.

Jennie never actually saw the ferris wheel. Nor did she see the woman lashed spreadeagled to the hub, turning cartwheels above the street as the wheel rolled down Seventh Avenue. She did glimpse an instant of fire. Later, when the witnesses and the cops and the man from the SDA told her what had happened, she realised that the fire must have come from the hair and the hands and the feet, for according to her teachers in college, those were the parts that perpetually gave themselves, 'burning but not consumed', sacrificing their integrity to maintain the flames of Li Ku Unquenchable Fire, whose name and spirit, as the Book tells us, live in truth and beauty forever.

At the time the wheel hit her – a glancing blow – Jennie knew only an instant of pain, and at the same time a flash of wild delight that somehow mingled with all the sorrow of the world. Then she fell into a deep sleep, disturbed only by a dream of climbing a stone stairway on her hands and knees.

She awoke to see a black cloud just above her body. She laughed, recognising it as an umbrella, held by a tall woman in a brown leather jacket. The jacket reminded her of Marilyn Birdan and then of Mike. 'Don't get up,' the woman said, and Jennie realised she was lying in the street, with a blanket over her and a plastic cloth under her to protect her from the wet. She stared at the woman until she spotted the police badge, and then she looked around. Quite a crowd had gathered, thirty or forty people most of them standing about eight feet away from her, behind a line of wooden horses.

'What happened?' Jennie asked, and several people laughed.

'An Occurrence,' the lady cop said. She must have been over six feet tall, with thick blonde curls that made it impossible for her to wear a cop hat.

'An Occurrence,' Jennie repeated. 'Which one?'

For a moment no one said anything, and then another cop, a man, told her, 'The Ferris Wheel.'

'Naturally,' Jennie said, 'what else?'

Lady cop told her, 'It's still a genuine Occurrence. One of the five official ones. You know, just as good as holes in the hand or any of the others. You'll go down in the records.'

Jennie said, 'I want to get up.'

'Hang on,' the man cop told her, 'We've got to keep you here for the SDA people.'

'The SDA can go to hell,' Jennie said, and the people around her tried to hide their shock. Jennie started to get up but the cops held her down. She closed her eyes and waited. People called out to her, asking her to bless them.

Finally, a man from the West Village Spiritual

283

Development Agency arrived. He passed various instruments over Jennie's body, wrote down bits of information, took depositions from witnesses, and gave Jennie several forms to fill out and return within seven days. Then the lady cop helped her to her feet, while the crowds applauded until the male cop chased them away.

The cops offered to escort Jennie home, but she sent them off. They left her leaning against a drugstore window on Seventh Avenue. Tired, she wanted to close her eyes, but every time she did she just saw that old woman spitting out her pills.

Hunger opened inside her. The SDA man had asked if she was hungry; he'd looked a little surprised when she'd said no. Jennie walked until she spotted someone standing in the rain with one of those pushcarts selling chocolate chip cookies and ice cream wafers. An odd thing to sell, she thought, so late in the year. She crossed the road. Horns sounded behind her.

'What would you like?' the vendor said. A young man, he wore a white denim jacket over an open-necked shirt and tight jeans. Neither the cold nor the rain seemed to bother him. His sodden clothes and the water dripping down his head didn't stop him from smiling at Jennie as if he'd waited for her all day.

About to ask for a half-pound of choclate chip cookies Jennie looked up from the cart to his face. Something about it – she squinted. If she looked quickly his face appeared bland, like the eager faces on those awful revelationist realism paintings, but when she tried to look more closely she couldn't seem to focus on it. The features kept slipping away from her. As if she was chasing it. Smiling, it floated in front of her, as if she only needed to look from the right angle to see it as it really was.

'What would you like?' he repeated.

'Help me,' Jennie said. He nodded but said nothing. 'I wanted my husband back. I just wanted my husband. And they're punishing me for it. Showing me things. Telling me my pain doesn't count. It's not – not big enough. But it does count. My suffering is as real as anyone else's. But all those people – I never wanted . . . I didn't want . . .' Her hands began to wave in the air.

He caught the wrists. 'No one is punishing you,' he said.

'Yes they are – I didn't want to see those people.'

'There are some things you can only know by knowing.'

'But what if I don't want to? And what about them? What about that woman? She just wanted to die. And instead it was that little boy. They don't deserve that.'

'Suffering is not a punishment.'

'Then why is it there? We don't deserve it.'

'Suffering exists for its own sake.'

'No.' She tried to pull loose her hands. 'It's not right.'

Still holding her wrists he said, 'Listen to me, Jennifer.' Jennie fell silent. 'There are only two things in the world. Suffering and ecstasy. Do you understand?'

Jennie began to shake. Her chest tightened and she couldn't seem to get any air past her mouth. She knew what she should do. Nod, and accept the information. Try to understand the message. All she had to do was say 'yes'. But if she did that she was saying 'yes' to all their manipulation, to everything they'd done to her and to all the others.

'No.' She shook her head. 'No. Oh God, I'm sorry, but you're wrong. That's not right.' The shaking stopped. She could breathe again. 'There's pleasure,' she said. 'And hope.' He said nothing. 'And love. What about love?'

'Love is a form of suffering.'

'Suffering. Not ecstasy?'

'Love belongs to the tomb world. Without death love is meaningless. But ecstasy has no purpose. It obliterates love.'

Jennie thought of her father lying in his coffin, streaming with ribbons. She thought of her mother practising hour after hour as if Jennie no longer existed. And she thought of the annulment demanding that she cut Mike loose from even her memories. 'You're wrong,' she said, then blushed. 'Please forgive me, but you're wrong. Love – love is what won't let go. What remains when everything else is taken away. The part that won't give in. Love is the answer to suffering.'

'And if I tell you there is no answer?'

'What do you mean? I thought you said ecstasy is the answer.'

'No.'

'But you said – you called them the two poles – '

'I said that only those two things exist.'

'I don't understand. You're not letting me understand.'

'You don't let yourself understand. Listen to me, Jennifer. There are no answers, no solutions. Love – and pleasure and hope and fear and desire – they all belong to suffering. But ecstasy exists apart from suffering. They exist apart and at the same time. They exist together in the same place.'

'They don't connect?'

'They connect totally. The life of one becomes the road to the other.'

'Then they do answer each other. Ecstasy justifies suffering.'

'No. The opposite. By its own reality, ecstasy makes

people see that suffering is real. And without purpose. Ecstasy is a light that illuminates pain.'

Jennie was silent a moment. She looked down at the wet street. When she looked up again she said, 'Those people. That dead boy. And the old woman. Were they put there because of me?' He said nothing. 'Did that woman lie there all those years because of me? So I could see and learn about suffering?' Silence. 'So I'd be ready for all your explanations? Answer me!'

'You believe the tumour crushed her brain for your sake. And the thought is crushing you. Be relieved, Jennifer Mazdan. Her suffering exists only for itself.'

'Are you sure?' He said nothing. 'I don't know. There's an Agency – ' She paused, expecting him to interrupt her, but he just waited. 'There's an Agency that uses people. It just uses people for what it wants to do. And it doesn't care, it doesn't understand the cost. Do you know what I mean?' Again he said nothing. 'It can use that woman. It doesn't care what happens to her. If it thinks I need to see something like that, it *can* crush her life, it can keep squeezing her for twenty years just to make her ready for when I come stupidly walking down Bedford Street. That's what's wrong with it. It doesn't understand the cost.' She pulled loose her hands. 'You said she didn't suffer because of me. But are you sure? Are you sure?'

'Do you think the Agency needs to create suffering? Do you think it cannot find enough examples on any street you might choose to travel?'

'I don't know. Maybe that's true. But maybe it doesn't care. Maybe it knew, twenty years ago, I would come here today. And so it set that woman up. Because it was easier than looking for something else. Is that what happened?'

'Do you really want to know? Suppose I said "no". Suppose her suffering had nothing to do with you.

287

Would that lessen her pain? Would it release you from caring about her? And suppose I said "yes". Would that convict you of some crime?' Jennie said nothing. 'Do you see, Jennifer? It doesn't matter. What I told you before remains. Whatever its origins her suffering exists only for itself. As does yours. No one was belittling your suffering. All human pain is the same.'

'You act like that woman doesn't matter. Like I only care about her because I feel guilty. But the fact that I care at all means that love exists.'

'You love her because you can share her misery. Didn't I tell you that love belongs to suffering?'

'Excuse me,' came a woman's voice, annoyed. 'Can I get some cookies?'

'Sure,' the vendor said, and Jennie waited while the woman bought a mixed pound of chocolate chip and walnut chunk.

As soon as the woman had gone Jennie said, 'Why does the Agency have to use people?'

'What else can it use?'

'But what does it want?'

'It wants to help.'

'Why can't it leave us alone?'

'You mean, why can't it leave *you* alone? You would sacrifice everyone else just so you would not have to discover things you would rather not know.'

'Sacrifice what? I don't understand.'

'Listen to me, Jennifer. People will accept suffering because they must, but they will do everything they can to avoid ecstasy.'

'Because it obliterates love?'

'Because it is real. And because it demonstrates to them that suffering is real and cannot be answered or justified. They will battle that with everything they've got. However much we open the road they build new barriers. They cover themselves in mud and wrap

288

themselves in steel to weigh themselves down. But we will not allow them to do that.'

'Why? Because you love them?'

'We serve reality.'

She shook her head. 'Your reality. A reality that doesn't understand people. A reality that thinks – thinks I don't matter. That what I want doesn't count. That love doesn't count. Just because it belongs to the tomb world. But that's where we live. How can you understand us if you don't understand love? You think you can push people together and then cut them apart just to create an effect. That it doesn't matter as long as you get the effect you want. That I'm just selfish or something because I don't want to be pushed around. But if I don't count, and Mike, and my father, and that old woman, then who does? I'm sorry.' She was crying. 'I'm sorry. I know I shouldn't talk to you like this. I wanted help, and you came, but you can't help me. I should have realized. I'm so stupid.'

The vendor opened the lid of his pushcart and stuck his arm down to the bottom. He came up with a large yellow cookie dotted with chocolate. 'Take this,' he said. Jennie took the cookie in both hands and held it close to her chest. She could feel nothing from it. The vendor said, 'When you can't climb any higher eat a piece of this.'

'Climb?' She looked at the cookie and noticed that each piece of chocolate was shaped like a face. She put the cookie in her bag beside the Revolution Mouse doll. 'Thank you,' she said.

'I'm sorry I couldn't help you,' he said.

'Are you?' She was about to leave when a thought occurred to her. She said, 'Where do babies come from?'

'I'm sorry,' he said, 'I'm not allowed to tell you that.'

289

Jennie shrugged. Sick of Seventh Avenue she headed northwest up Bedford Street. At the corner of Morton Street she looked back. The vendor still stood there, selling cookies to a group of children.

Morton Street turned to the right after one block to intersect Barrow Street. On one side Jennie passed a pair of old houses with a garden between them. The garden was small and closed off by a low concrete wall. Inside, a white metal chair lay on its side against a tree. The head of some metal deity stared out from the garden's centre. Though Jennie didn't recognise it from any of the ones she'd seen in shops or catalogues, she looked with longing at the way it seemed to protect the houses around it.

On the other side of the street she passed a theatre with a red awning, and then a tavern. On a ledge above the tavern's doorway a small windmill, no more than a foot high, spun its blades.

Jennie walked up Barrow to Hudson, where she turned right, past an antique store and the children's bookshop where her father used to drop her off, and the owner would formally serve her milk and spirit crackers on a silver tray while she sat in the corner and pondered which book Jimmy should buy for her.

Just past Christopher Street she passed an open doorway leading into a bare room where a group of people sat around a naked woman who stood speaking and gesturing to them. Jennie stepped through the doorway into a vestibule off the main room. Dripping water and mud onto a pile of shoes she watched the woman move her arms about. Long needles pierced the skin above the elbows and the knees, but the woman didn't seem to notice them. She crouched or spun around, cupping her hands in front of her or lifting them up above her head.

She's a storyteller, Jennie realized. She was telling them a story. It didn't sound like any of the official ones. It didn't sound like anything Jennie had ever heard before.

'In those days,' the woman said, 'all the people were slowly turning into dust. The world was emptying itself out. Each day the buildings became more and more transparent and the janitors had to close off the top floors to prevent people being lifted through the holes in the roof and carried away by metal birds. The Tellers had all shrunk to the size of dogs. When they had to face the people they hid behind cardboard pictures of themselves. They used wires to pull the arms and to open and shut the mouths. They wore microphones, and when they could no longer even speak they switched to voice simulators. They cut holes in the cardboards, otherwise the wind would have grabbed the pictures and smashed them against the sides of buildings.

'In those days all the people were slowly turning into dust. The Tellers had become afraid of their stories and ordered the faceless workers to bury the stories in boxes under the ground. All night the Tellers played loud music, otherwise they would hear the stories weeping and begging their former lovers to release them.

'Now, in that time there lived a musician, a woman born with a stone whistle between her lips. As she became older and had played in every land she lost all desire but one – that her daughter follow her in carrying the "traces of God" to the people. But the daughter refused, and whenever her mother bought her a new instrument she spat on it.'

Wait a second, Jennie thought. *That's me. She's talking about me and Beverley.*

The woman said, 'So the musician fasted and rubbed herself with sap from the sacred forests, and she slept

291

in a room full of steam to open herself for a message. In her dream a Benign One came to her. He came disguised as the brother of her dead husband.'

Idiot, Jennie thought, *Jimmy didn't have a brother.*

' "Be at peace," the Benign One told her. "Your daughter will give the world something more precious than music." '

'Years passed and the daughter became a woman. One day she went to a Day of Truth Recital where a group of cats knocked over the cardboard puppet to reveal the shrunken body of the Teller. All around her people wept, but the woman walked into a field full of yellow flowers. She plucked the flowers from the ground until nothing was left but mud. "This is what they've done to us" she shouted. "They've left us nothing but our bodies. I will give you my body." '

Jennie said, 'That's wrong. I never offered myself.'

'The woman prayed all night,' the storyteller said. 'She collected all her tears in a white bowl made of fish bones and in the morning she mixed them with blood and spit and even her urine and then she went up on the roof and threw the liquid towards the rising sun. A great wind came up and clouds covered the sky. For three days the sun didn't appear while the wind smashed open the gold doors of the Tellers' residences.

'On the last day a huge swan flew down and knocked the woman to the ground. Just as the swan penetrated the woman's hymen, a shout shook the city. The stories shouted with joy that the deliverer would release them.'

'No,' Jennie said loudly. 'That's all wrong. I didn't ask. I just fell asleep. That's all. And I wasn't a virgin. I was married. I mean – '

People turned and shushed her. The storyteller went on, 'On the night the woman gave birth the moon laughed out loud. The sound shattered mountains. It split the sky so that all the people gathered round the

292

woman's house could see the lines of souls waiting patiently on the other side.

'The shrunken Tellers realized their danger. They sent out armoured cars to kill the deliverer. But the road cracked and broke the cars' axles. The enemy marched on foot. But the wild dogs of the city bit their legs and forced them to retreat. Then some of them turned into birds and flew towards the house, hoping to peck out the baby's eyes and tongue. But helicopters flew up and the blades blew the birds across the river into the Broken City. And then the shrunken Tellers knew they had lost.'

Jennie said, 'It won't happen that way. It's not going to be like that.' She shouted, 'You've got it all wrong. What about me? Why don't you think about me?'

Two men with amulets around their necks came and stood before Jennie. They looked like they might be father and son. 'Please leave,' the older one told her.

Jennie crossed her arms. 'Go to hell,' she said.

The younger one said, 'You're disturbing our story.'

'You're damn right I'm disturbing your story.'

With astonishing quickness they lifted her by the elbows and set her outside the door. She was still demanding 'Let go of me,' when the door slammed, and she was standing alone in the street. She rattled the door handle. 'Liars,' she shouted. She kicked the door. 'Liars!'

14

Jennie groaned, shut the door behind her. She leaned against it, letting her bag drop on her muddy feet. With an effort she reached up to touch the belly of the threshold guardian mounted to the left of the door. 'Blessed One,' she murmured, 'protect me and restore me to the perfect enclosure of this house.' Her hand fell with a slap against her side.

Jennie stood a few seconds listening before she bent to wrench off her shoes. Quiet. Wonderful, peaceful quiet. No practice squawks from the studio, no tapes on the speakers. Maybe Beverley and the gang had gone to work out their enactments at someone else's house. She wondered if she should take off all her clothes before heading upstairs, to avoid getting cursed by the cleaning woman. She yanked up her bag for the trudge to her room all the way up to the third floor.

Halfway up the first flight she saw the door of her mother's bedroom swing open. Beverley stepped out onto the landing. She wore her blue silk dressing gown tied at the waist with a copper sash, a present from one of her lovers, who had the material left over from a piece she did in which she wrapped a replica of Manhattan Island in wire mesh. With her hair pulled back and her face giving off a scrubbed glow Beverley looked very young. Jennie felt childlike and clumsy. 'Hi,' she said. 'I'm going up to take a bath. Please don't make dinner or anything for me.' As if her mother was the type to bring her milk and cookies.

'Well, no wonder,' Beverley said. 'You never did remember to feed them properly.'

294

'Feed them properly?'

'Now they'll just keep coming back. They'll just keep breaking the windows.'

'What are you talking about?' She tried to step round but her mother seemed to flutter about the landing without looking at her.

'That's the trouble with dead people,' Beverley said. 'They always think you owe them something.' She giggled. 'You remember that time they stole Annie's dress. Ripped it right off her back that day she went to visit the refugee camp.'

'Refugee camp?'

'I don't want you drinking any of that stuff. You'll just vomit up again like the last time.'

What have they done to her?, Jennie thought. She backed away around her mother. Beverley followed her, saying, 'You've got to watch out they don't get at your liver. That's the way they work. That's what they're really after. It's not the eyes. It's the liver.'

'Stop it,' Jennie pleaded. Was she always like this? Talking nonsense, words reeling off a tape somewhere, real conversation simulated only by accident. 'Is that what you're doing?' she said. 'Are you speaking from a tape? Are you making a tape of this now? Is this one of your goddamn experiments?'

'First they disguise themselves. They pretend to be someone you know. They're really very clever. Then once they get inside you they start tearing at everything.'

Jennie shoved her mother away and hurried down the landing. Behind her Beverley thumped to the ground, still talking, still waving her hands.

Jennie ran up the stairs to her bedroom. When she reached it the door was closed. She was sure she'd left it open. Jennie held the doorknob without turning it. She wanted so much to go inside and fall on the bed, lock the door against her mother, against all dreams and revelations. But what if there was something there? She was sure she'd left it open. *Please,* Jennie thought, *please let go of me. I can't take any more.*

She turned the knob and pushed delicately at the door. It swung about a foot, just enough for her to see the end of the bed, the crumpled quilt, the floor . . . There was something wrong with the floor. She could see into it, it kept pulling away from her, further and further the more she tried to fix her eyes on it. She'd seen something like that – The cookie vendor. His face, the way his face –

Jennie knew. They were going to answer the question. They were going to let her know where babies come from.

There were faces in the floor, a crowd of dead faces, slowly turning into dust. *It's the land of the dead,* Jennie realised. *It's not where babies* – But it was.

She could hear voices, endless voices talking over and around each other. Voices, stories. *It's all the same place,* she thought. *It's where stories come from. Babies and stories. They're the same thing. And it's the land of the dead. It's all the same place.* She whispered, 'I don't want to know this.'

Jennie turned round the end of the corridor. There stood a narrow red door, the stairway leading to the roof. She pulled the door. It was stuck, maybe even locked. She yanked as hard as she could. Nothing. The cookie. The vendor said she should eat the cookie when she couldn't climb any higher. Jennie searched in the bag she still held pressed against her body. When her fingers found the cookie it broke in pieces; the damp had weakened it. Trying not to notice the chocolate faces Jennie stuffed the biggest piece in her mouth and chewed as fast as she could. She waited. If anything, she felt weaker, too worn out to keep struggling any more.

She heard a scratching noise on the other side of the door, and then a loud creak as the hinges turned. The door opened a couple of inches, wide enough for a large rat to run through and down the landing. Jennie laughed. A rat. *A rat.* What would her professors have made of an intercessor in the form of a rat? She pulled the door open and stepped into the stairwell. The door closed behind her. She leaned against it, catching her breath.

Dust lay on everything, the red walls, the narrow stairs, the metal banister. At the top, a window in the roof door let in enough light to show her the way. She began to climb, each step a battle against the weight of her feet. In a few moments she'd forgotten everything except how tired she was, how much her back hurt, how the dust made it hard to breathe. Should she go down? If she went back now, could she rest? She looked up at the window. The light pulled her onwards.

A couple of steps and she'd gone halfway, and then it no longer seemed so hard. Her feet didn't weigh her down, even the dust had left her lungs and she straightened her back as she took a deep breath. The window glowed, casting a golden tint on the banister, which now felt warm and smooth. At the top the door opened the moment she touched it. She stepped out into a fresh breeze.

The rain had stopped, and though the late sun hid behind the buildings, it still lit the sky with a pattern of gold and red, like some story woven on a loom. The moon had risen as well, full and pensive, with a faint smile. Jennie waved at it. She noticed her clothes had dried, and all the mud had fallen off. Her pants even looked pressed. She wondered if that was what paradise would be, a place where your clothes were always ironed. When she rubbed the backs of her hands and touched her cheeks the skin felt soft, warm.

She heard laughter behind her and turned to see small groups of people sitting around tables at the other end of the roof. They laughed and gestured and Jennie could breathe their joy all through her body. She walked up and found herself inside a Chinese restaurant. She saw a large Chinese family at a round table in the back, near the kitchen. The smell of dumplings and wind dried duck and odd-flavoured chicken danced through an atmosphere like a young forest. Jennie looked around; at every table the food and the people shone in the sun and moonlight, and all their clothes looked ironed. Beside her a Chinese woman stroked her daughter's hair. The little girl's cheeks filled with love.

In the middle of the restaurant Jennie saw a naked man with ribbons tied to his arms and legs. 'Jimmy?' she whispered. He turned around, and yes, it was Jimmy Mazdan, still bedecked for his funeral. He gestured with his head and Jennie ran up to hug him. 'Jimmy!' she cried, 'Jimmy, I love you.' When she let go she saw Mike standing on the other side of her. With a grin he said, 'I told the judge to fuck his annulment. I love, you Jennie. I want to be with you forever.'

And then a woman stood up, and it was Beverley, and at her feet Jennie saw a pile of smashed instruments. 'I love you, Jennie,' her mother said. 'I've always loved you. I love you more than anything in the world.' Then they all came and stood together, hugging and laughing and crying, while behind them the waiters came, bringing all Jennie's favourite dishes.

A part of the Story of TOO PRETTY FOR HER OWN
GOOD

The Liberator set about his task of creating the world. He
tore down the shacks and built houses with black and white
taps pouring out perfumed water. He banged together street-
cars which broke down on the freshly laid roads, and when
the trolleys split open automobiles drove out from their
bellies. His scientists invented soap powders, and posters,
and dried cereals, and flags, and lamps that moulded themselves into the faces of vanished lovers. The leader gave his
empire a name: the Celestial Republic. He called his capital
the Democratic City of God and his home the Bleached
House. He named himself Sacred President, and his wife
Blessed First Lady.

The President put on the Head of His Father and ordered
his aides and secretaries to ask him questions. They asked,
'What do we do when two farmers want the same land?'
'What happens when no one wants to work?' 'How can I
make my son visit me?' Whatever the President answered,
his aides wrote it down, and then his messengers flew across
the Republic, announcing the 'divine code of law and moral
correctness.'

In every territory the Sacred President had left someone
in charge. Now he began a yearly pilgrimage of surprise
visits to check that the finger of heaven still stroked his
surrogates with wisdom and mercy. He arranged tests for
them. He ordered them to split rocks with the brilliance of
their judgements. He ordered the women to reason with the
animals and speak with the birds.

All this time the Blessed First Lady waited in her dark
rooms. At first she tried to push herself into the sun. Her
husband demanded it. The people wanted to see her. Too
Pretty For Her Own Good begged for more time. She tried
to pray but gave up, convinced that the Sun burned her
prayers before they could escape the sky. Months passed,
until the President told her she could have all the time she
liked. He left her house and did not return.

At times Too Pretty became sick with cramps for her

mountain home. But then she would remind herself how her husband had rescued her from servitude in a mud dress. And she'd draw another picture of her longing for him and beg her blind servants to pass the drawing to the President. Late one night she disguised herself as a speaker and escaped from her house, pretending to search for divine messages in the litter that filled the streets of the City of God. Instead, she was searching for her husband. She did not find him that night.

Too Pretty limped through the city, unused to the flat streets (her rooms were built with sloping floors), listening to the competition of languages, watching thieves glide through crowds, seeing homeless women die in front of restaurants. She returned home at dawn, only to set out again the next night and the night after that. After a week of this she saw a sacred messenger asleep on a window ledge and climbed up to grab his ankles before he could fly away. She exposed one breast, just long enough for him to understand that the sight of both together would catapult him into puberty and lose him his wings. He directed her to where the Sacred President stood on a platform higher than the Palace of Justice.

Machines crowded the platform. Shaped like lions' heads, their mouths spewed what looked like black smoke into the sky. Too Pretty's husband ordered her to leave. Instead, she threatened to strip naked, knowing that even machines broke apart at the sight of her body. 'Tell me what you're doing.'

'I'm expanding the sky,' he said. Every night his lions pumped out blackness and dust, opening the sky wider and wider until the mountain, the Father of the World, would become lost, isolated by oceans of emptiness. *His* emptiness. The Lady begged her husband to stop. He ordered his assistants to bind her hands and feet so she couldn't undress, and then they carried her home and sealed the doors of her house.

The Blessed First Lady began a spell against her husband. At first she tried to guess what the old women would have done. She drew diagrams and recited poems. She stopped, knowing her own hate would serve her better. Each day,

300

behind her shrouded windows, she added to the curse: drawings, strips cut from her dresses, scrapings from the walls,
words and dances and stillness, toenails and spittle, urine
and blood. She opened it up as fast as her husband opened
the night. And even when the curse started to eat him, when
his legs collapsed and his stomach caught fire, even when he
shut down his machines, his wife continued, recognizing
before her husband that the work had grown beyond its
target. She would always find something more to add; no
solemn phrase or line of thread could ever mark an end to
her life's creation.

He came and lay at her feet and begged her to release
him. For disease had begun to gnaw at his face and genitals,
and the buildings round the edge of the city had begun to
decay back into shacks. Name something, he told her, name
something he could give her that would buy his freedom.

She said, 'Build me a mountain.' A true mountain, stone
and trees and ice, with clouds to force away the Sun. The
President stood up. A mountain.

A kind of wind blew away his sickness. He went to the
window and rubbed away the painted clouds. He looked out
at his flat streets. A mountain. *His* mountain.

That same day he ordered a new tax across his territories
– a tax of trees and rocks, of water, pebbles, and snow. And
children. For he knew that no adults would believe such a
thing possible, and whatever they would build would collapse
around them.

Every day the mountain grew, and every night Too Pretty
For Her Own Good came to inspect it. She examined angles
and textures, she laughed at the mistakes of a builder who'd
never seen a hill until after he'd filled his hands with bodies.
Then one night she found the locks back on the doors. A
servant told her the Sacred President had heard of threats
against her life and was worried for her safety. She knew
that he wanted the mountain for himself. But what could she
do? She'd stopped her curse too soon, she'd given up her
work for his. And now it was too late.

The President too had given up everything but the mountain. He no longer sat on the Seat of Heaven. He no longer

301

visited the outer territories or marched in parades. He gave up reciting his 'Song of the Modern World' by which all the inventions maintained their existence. Outside his Democratic City of God the highways had begun to crack, the cars and buses caught fire, the taps and toilets filled with flies. The television stations broadcast nothing but memories.

The work continued. When the children grew old enough to doubt, the President piled them in warehouses and sent for replacements. But the warehouse walls split open and the children escaped. As they told their stories the citizens of the Celestial Republic realized that their President had deserted them. On the day that the Liberator announced his mountain complete an army attacked the City of God.

The President's soldiers went armed with tanks and rocket launchers. These worked no better than the cars and televisions. The rebels yanked the soldiers out of their metal shells and crushed them with wooden clubs. In the Bleached House He Who Runs Away searched for the Head of his Father. He found it behind cartons of dance music ordered to celebrate the mountain. The Sacred President led his beloved followers into battle.

For days the fight rolled on, with He Who Runs Away growing stronger with every slaughter. His own excitement defeated him. As a fresh wave surged towards him he shouted with joy and charged ahead of his troops. He swung about so violently in his search for victims that he shook the mask off his shoulders into the torn belly of an old man. The President found himself surrounded by women dressed in lion skins with iron penises strapped to their groins. 'You're all dead,' he told them. 'I killed you all.' And then they got their hands on him, and that was the last anyone ever saw of He Who Runs Away.

15

Jennifer Mazdan lay in the old four-legged bathtub on the second floor of her mother's house. When she'd come down from the roof the cold had finally caught up with her and she'd started shivering uncontrollably until she could dunk her body in steaming water. Across from her, above the brass taps, a guardian carved of African blackwood stuck its tongue out at her. Of all the rooms in the house only this and Jennie's bedroom escaped Beverley's periodic renovations. No moulded toilet seats, no expressionist bathtub. Aside from the gilt edging round the mirror above the sink the room's only decoration was a large dieffenbachia plant beside the window. A rope held the plant's two trunks together.

Jennie closed her eyes and slid further down in the tub, not bothering to try and lift her hair above the water line. She wiped the sweat off her face. When she opened her eyes Beverley was standing in the doorway. She wore her blue dressing gown and her ridiculous mule slippers with their pink pompoms. 'Can I come in?' she said. Jennie nodded, and Beverley came and sat down on the edge of the tub, pulling her gown closed over her thighs. A surge of love almost propelled Jennie out of the bathtub and into her mother's arms.

Beverley said, 'Where have you been all day?'

'Just walking around.'

'In this weather?' She laughed. 'Are you doing a penitence?'

'Not intentionally.'

'What?'

303

'Nothing. I was just – just walking around.' She couldn't think of anything plausible. She wanted to tell her mother everything.

Beverley trailed her hand in the water, then rubbed it on her face. 'Nice,' she said. 'Nice and warm.' Jennie noticed faint smudges of colour on the cheeks and neck, remnants of paint from the ceremony the night before. 'Darling,' Beverley said, 'what were you doing on the roof?'

'How did you know I was on the roof?'

'I heard something moving. And then I saw the door was open. What were you doing there?'

'I wanted to see the Moon rise.'

Beverley nodded. 'Has the Moon become important to you?'

Jennie became aware that her mother was looking at her belly. If only there was some way she could suck it in. 'I just wanted a look.'

Beverley looked away a moment, pressing her lips. 'Jen,' she said, 'if you ever need anything, any help, will you come to me?'

Jennie nodded, then said 'Yes.'

'Do you promise?'

'I promise.'

Jennie could see a pink glow of light around her mother's face. Beverley said, 'I love you, Jennifer.'

Do you? Jennie thought. *Do you really? Or is this just some kind of reward?*

Her mother stood up. 'There's nothing in the house, but would you like to go out to eat somewhere?'

'No. Thank you. I'm too tired.'

'I could call for something. Shall I do that? How about Chinese? You always like that.'

'No. No Chinese. You just get what you want. I'm not really hungry at all.'

Beverley shrugged and Jennie realised how much her

304

mother wanted the two of them to eat together. She wished the thought didn't make her ill. 'All right,' Beverley said. 'But if you want anything . . .' At the door she added, 'Or if you want to talk about anything . . .'

'Thank you,' Jennie said. Before her mother could close the door Jennie called after her, 'Mom?'

Beverley turned around. 'What is it? Do you want to tell me something?'

'When I came in before – '

'Yes?'

'Were you – were you standing on the stairs?'

'On the stairs? No, of course not. I was lying down. I would have seen you if I was on the stairs.' Jennie said nothing. Looking at her daughter, Beverley shook her head slightly.

Jennie said, 'I love you, Mommy.'

Beverley walked back to kneel beside the tub. 'I love you too, Jen,' she said. Jennie wrapped her wet arms around the blue silk. For a long time she hugged her mother. When Beverley left the room Jennie lay back, weeping into the water.

16

The official residence of the Poughkeepsie Committee
of Tellers occupied a four storey wooden building
beside Vassar lake. The property lay outside the city
limits, at the end of Raymond Avenue, across from the
stone wall separating Vassar College from the world of
profane ignorance. The Residence was an old-fashioned
building, with black and white panels of wood broken
by bay windows, and a large glass-enclosed porch at
the back. Set close to the road the house stood guard
before a sloping back lawn that led to a small patch of
dense woods, like a sacred grove gone wild. To the left
of the house another stretch of lawn led to the water,
more a pond than a lake. Despite the night-time frosts,
high weeds surrounded the water's edge.

Five chimneys broke the line of the roof. Jennie
imagined rustic stone hearths, with fires casting glows
over fourposter beds, and furniture carved by country
craftsmen. Only a very few of the county's hundred or
so Tellers could actually live in the house. They were
the ones closest to the True Voice, the ones who
officiated at major recitals. Jennie had parked her car
up the road from the house. She could see the back
lawn and the edge of the trees. She kept the motor
running and the heater on. The December sun had
done no more than show up the dirt on the windscreen.

Jennie was wearing her first official maternity dress,
bought the week before, at the Sacred Heartbeat Mall,
in a shop with pink and blue walls. The shop was run
by a middle aged woman with fine scars all over her
face – from an initiation, she had told Jennie. She

wouldn't say which one, but she had invited Jennie to touch the scars. 'As an omen,' she'd said, 'for the baby.'

Jennie hated the dress. Grey, with a small collar, it just hung there, pushed out by her swollen breasts and belly. She wished she could have stuck to the sweatshirts and elastic waist jeans she'd been wearing every day to work. But what would the Tellers have said to someone who came begging for help without even the courtesy to make herself presentable?

She opened her bag to take out her mirror and inspect her make-up. Instead, she made a face at the jumble and snapped the bag shut again. Being dressed up hadn't helped her at the Fifth Avenue Hall three days before. Jennie stared out of the window and thought about the Palace, the Tellers' residence on Madison Avenue, across the street from the back of the Hall. She remembered the red marble staircase, the arched ceiling, the fireplace flanked by stone dolphins spouting water into gold sunbursts. And she remembered the woman smiling at her from behind her long wooden bench.

The woman's grey overalls, traditional uniform of the faceless Workers, had been made of thick velvet, with gold trim at the wrists and neck. Above the left breast the woman had worn a silver pin in the form of a spiral. A black chain circled her right wrist. Her make-up looked like she had had it done in Saks before going on duty – arched eyebrows, glowing cheeks, a slight pout to the lips. She'd asked, 'Do you have an appointment?'

'I want to see Allan Lightstorm.'

The woman's smile had flickered on and off, like a wind-blown candle. She'd said 'Master Lightstorm no longer graces this Hall.'

'What? What do you mean?'

307

The smile solidified. 'The Master has chosen to retire.'

'Why?'

'The whys of a Living Master do not concern you or me.'

'Well, where can I find him? I have to speak to him.' The receptionist hadn't answered. 'Where has he gone?'

'No doubt,' the woman had said, 'into the depths of the Voice. Or across the boundaries. Or into the Black Feast. No doubt the SDA will give you his flight plan.'

'Well, can I see his head Teller then?'

'Master Lightstorm has no head.'

'What? Oh, I mean the head Teller for the Hall. I don't know the name.'

'Her name is Judith Whitelight, and she does not see petitioners without appointments. If you wish an appointment you may apply in writing, three typed copies, no xeroxes, stating the purpose of your petition and the offerings you propose in return for the Teller's benevolence.'

'And if I do all that,' Jennie had said, 'will I get to see her?'

The woman's shoulders had twitched. 'That is not for me to say.'

'Look,' Jennie'd said, 'this is an emergency. I wouldn't have come here all the way from Poughkeepsie if I – '

'Poughkeepsie? You're not a resident of this district?'

'No.' *Shit*, Jennie had thought. *Stupid*.

'I see. Well, I'm afraid you'll have to petition your own district committee.'

'Come on. You know that a place like Poughkeepsie doesn't have the same power as – '

'All districts have ultimate power.'

'Oh, for God's sake.'

'We are all one body,' the woman had said, misquoting the Guadeloupe Proclamation.

'This is ridiculous,' Jennie had said, and headed for the stairs. Two men in grey uniforms with guns had appeared in front of her. They wore badges on their left pockets, silver spirals on brass discs. Black chains, heavier than the receptionists's, circled their right wrists. Jennie had looked at the woman smiling from behind her desk. 'You goddamn stooge,' Jennie had said. The woman had laughed as Jennie left the building.

And now here she was, ready to try again. She leaned back in the car seat. Why couldn't she just give in? That was what you did when the Spirit took hold of you. Let everything go and rolled around on the floor with it. Shrieked away in foreign languages. You didn't whine about Agencies. You took off from work with a holy exemption and ran through the streets in mismatched clothes, waving your arms or carrying placards.

If only they'd asked her. If only . . . They just took over her life, invaded her body, planted their damned fish inside her . . .

She laid her palms gently against her belly. 'I'm sorry,' she said. 'It's not you. Really it's not.' The baby turned, a settling into position. Jennie began to cry. 'I'm sorry. Please don't hate me. I just don't like something taking hold of me.' If only she could separate the baby from the Agency. She just wanted – she wanted to fight.

She turned off the car and stepped outside. It was late afternoon; the sun was already dipping behind the buildings. She walked onto the long side lawn, towards the visitors' entrance at the back of the house.

At first she thought the crowd of some dozen people included both men and women. When she came closer she recognised the women as men in oversized dresses

309

padded into exaggerated female shapes. They weren't transvestites or drag queens, she saw. They made no attempt to look like actual women. Some of them wore huge bras on the outside of their dresses, and on these they'd drawn faces in lipstick. Others had drawn mouths with sharp fangs over their groins. Jennie shuddered at the sight of those lipsticked teeth.

When she looked at the ordinary men she saw that they'd also disguised themselves – as men. Rubber or homemade codpieces, some in the shape of knives, others looking like rockets, dangled from their groins. Some wore football padding on their shoulders. Others had decorated their sweatshirts with animal hair. All of them, 'men' and 'women' both, carried plastic shopping bags, or sacks slung over their shoulders. And all of them wore translucent masks, the kind where your own skin colour shone through to give solidity to the film star or politician's face painted on them. Jennie squinted at the masks, surprised. They were outlawed. After that scandal in Brooklyn where all those people found their personalities eaten away by the expressions on the masks. Outlawed or not, there they were.

And there the men were, talking, laughing, drinking beer through straws stuck through holes in the masks. Jennie couldn't think of what they were doing there until one of them noticed her and pointed her out to the others. Immediately they all began to whistle and clap their hands. 'A volunteer,' someone said loudly. 'You coming to volunteer?' They laughed, and someone else called, 'You want to help us with our enactment? You'll love it.' One of the pseudo-men threw something at her. A tomato, she saw, as it hit a tree behind her. Apparently that was going too far, for one of the pseudo-women shoved him, and another said, 'Arsehole. What are you going to throw when the real thing starts?'

310

'Insulting the Lady,' Jennie realised. They were getting ready for 'Insulting the Lady.' Fascinated as well as a little afraid, she edged closer. Jennie had studied accounts of the enactment in college, but she never had thought she would see it. Like the masks, 'Insulting the Lady' was illegal. But like the masks, there it was.

It didn't occur to Jennie to turn back. She only wondered what they were doing here, why the Tellers didn't chase them away. She wondered too what it meant that she'd shown up the same day as this most irregular of enactments. She knew it formed an omen, but which way, good or bad? After her misreading of the Revolution Mouse doll, she didn't dare to try her own interpretation.

The wind cut through her coat, and Jennie wished she could go home. Drop the whole thing, let the Agency do what it wanted with her. Go home in front of the television. Let Karen do the goddamn banishment for her. She quoted out loud, ' "The only way to do it is to do it." 9th Proposition,' and walked forward.

The men began whistling and clapping, some dancing in front of her or pushing their masked faces at her. A few of the cartoon-women bumped their padded hips at her, a couple of the 'men' waved their codpieces. Furious, Jennie walked faster. Did she know any of them? She couldn't distinguish the faces under the masks, but she could well imagine Bill Jackman or Al Rich joining a secret men's group.

When she reached the porch the noise stopped. Jennie glanced back at them, all clustered together, standing and watching. She raised her hands towards the bell, then made a fist and knocked on the door. The wood hurt her knuckles. A faceless Worker opened the door. Tall, mostly bald, with a large nose and thick shoulders, he wore grey demin overalls and short red boots. A black chain bound his wrist.

Jennie said, 'I want to see the Tellers.'

He looked her up and down. 'What are you doing here?'

'I want to see the Tellers.'

'How did you get through the barrier?'

'Barrier?'

'The street's closed off.'

Jennie looked back at Raymond Avenue, empty of traffic. She said, 'I don't know.'

'Well, you'll have to leave.'

'No. Let me inside.' She tried to slide past him. Automatically he stepped in front of her.

He said, 'You're lucky they didn't get carried away and decide to start early. What are you doing here?'

'I told you.'

'There's not supposed to be any women here. Can't you see that? Don't you know what's going to happen?'

'I don't care about that. I've got to see them.'

'We'd better get you out of here.'

'Please let me in.'

'Let you in? Are you crazy?'

'I need help.'

'Mark,' came a man's voice, 'what's going on here?' Jennie leaned around the Worker. She knew that voice, the resonance and faint lilt, the way it lifted slightly at the end, like a glider caught by a breeze. Dennis Lily, Poughkeepsie's most notable Teller. He wasn't much, Jennie knew. Past his prime, everyone said. Voice sometimes dropped into a monotone, sometimes got a little shrill as he dashed through the Picture itself to get to the Inner Meaning. A moralist, people said. Nothing like the Living Masters in the Fifth Avenue Hall. But Jennie had gone to hear him. She'd sat on the hill and watched him dancing in his skin. And here she was, standing only a few feet away from him.

Still blocking Jennie, the Worker said, 'It's nothing, sir. Just some woman who got through the barrier.'

'Let me see.' The Worker stood aside and Jennie got a clear view of Dennis Lily-of-the-Valley. Instead of his recital skin he wore a warm-up jacket and faded pink jogging pants. He looked about to work out in a gym – except that he'd stained his face, his hands, wherever she could see, a deep red, and on his temples he'd glued two plastic horns, black, curving out and then forwards, like the horns of a bull. *He's going to lead them*, Jennie realised. *He's getting ready for his role.* That was why they'd gathered on the lawn, why no one had chased them away. They were waiting for Dennis Lily. And he belonged with them. He looked like them, just another middle aged businessman going out to get drunk and run through the streets attacking and humiliating any woman unlucky enough to get in their way. As the Teller came close to her Jennie could smell beer on his breath. She backed away.

'Who are you?' he said. 'What do you want?'

'I wanted help.'

'What kind of help?' Jennie said nothing. 'What kind of help? Why did you come here instead of the Halls?'

'I needed to see you.' Why did she ever think they could do anything?

'Do you need a special penance?' He smirked as he looked her up and down. The horns bent forward, then up, like an actor taking a bow. 'Do you want to make a special offering?' Jennie saw the Worker, Mark, stare at the floor.

A woman came down the staircase behind Lily. 'Dennis?' she said, 'Who are you talking to? Who's there?' She stood to the side of the doorway. Short, with curly red hair, a delicate face and pale hands that she wiped on an overlong dressing gown, Alice Windfall looked even frailer than she did when she would stand on the top of Recital Mount in her Denise Ravendaughter recital skin. Her voice wavered as she spoke, and Jennie remembered hearing that she used a hidden mike when she told the Pictures. The thought reminded her of the storyteller on Hudson Street, with her shrunken Tellers manipulating cardboard puppets. *They can't help*, she thought. *They've given it all up.*

Lily said, 'It's nothing, Alice. Why don't you go back to your rooms? You know the men mustn't see you tonight.'

'I don't want to go back to my room. I want to know who this woman is. Anyway, they can't see me from here.'

Lily said, 'She says she needs our help. Our personal help.'

Windfall examined Jennie. She said, 'What do you want? What do you want us to do?' In that short speech Jennie heard a faint trace of the True Voice, the living being that once commandeered the Founders' vocal cords to crack open the world.

Her own voice came out in a whisper. 'I wanted you to fight God.'

For a moment there was silence, and then Dennis Lily snickered, and Alice Windfall giggled. 'We are God,' Windfall said. 'How can we fight ourselves?'

'Or at least God's voice,' Lily added, and the two of them laughed.

Jennie turned around. She took a step to the end of the porch, then stopped. The men had come closer, silently waiting only a few yards from the house. She thought, *I've got to get out of this. I've got to get through this.* And then the singing began.

High and thin like the times before, like a line scratched through the twilight, it pierced through cloth and

314

padding, through dangling weapons and balloon breasts, it cleaned the hearts of hate and envy. It penetrated the trees and the porch, while above Jennie the first stars of the evening pulsed brighter. The men grinned, then smiled, and some of them hugged or kissed each other, while others sat on the grass with their heads resting on their knees.

Jennie stood as straight as she could. *This was my fight*, she thought. *Don't rescue me.* She clenched her fists and screwed up her face, and as soon as she did so her hands opened and her face fell loose, and it was all she could do to remember to tighten up again. 'No,' she said. 'Let go of me.' The music spun out of her womb into the air and rolled back to soak her body.

She looked behind her. Lily and Windfall were on the floor, hugging each other and laughing. Mark stood in the doorway, staring at Jennie with amazement and love. 'Bastards,' Jennie said. 'Why won't you help me?' But she didn't dare to waste her strength on them. She put her hands over her ears, only to find them so filled with music they acted like headphones. She pulled them away and hit them on the porch railing. The pain fell away from her into the air. She shouted, a sound like a siren, but her voice changed into accompaniment. She stopped just in time before she would have melted into the joy of singing.

She took a step, another, and another, she reached the lawn and forced herself to jerk forward, to stamp her feet against the urge to sit down, to sing, forget, give in. In the trees, the branches bent forward, filled with birds and squirrels. She wanted to wave her arms, chase them off, but she could feel her body sliding away from her. It became harder and harder to tense the muscles, harder to clench her fists, harder to keep walking, not to give in. She leaned against a tree, all

315

the men turning to look at her. 'No,' she said, and shook her head. 'No.'

And still shaking, still saying, 'No,' she laughed, and slid down against the tree, with all its bark and meat and sap sodden with song. And laughing and weeping, and still shaking her head, never giving in, never, Jennie could no longer hold on, but was swept away in a roller coaster of bliss.

Excerpt from THE LIVES OF THE FOUNDERS

The Founders created the Bright Beings. They created the Malignant Ones and they created the Benign Ones. The Beings do not know this, or pretend not to know it, but it is true. The Founders, focusing the limitless power of the Voice through Alessandro Clean Rain, created the Ferocious and the Devoted. It happened this way.

After the Revolution many people clung to their Old World belief that life ran like an electric current between poles of good and evil. These people formed themselves into camps called 'saints' and 'sinners', and they pestered all their neighbours with their endless preaching, their tedious temptations, their good and bad deeds. A delegation of people who had suffered from these moralists came to the Founders and begged help in banishing them. 'Send them to their own country,' the delegation pleaded. 'Give them an island or a piece of Antarctica.' But when Clean Rain (in beauty and truth lives his name forever) looked under the skin of the moralists he saw them clogged with a sludge preventing their hearts from pumping revelation through their bodies.

Clean Rain sang a single note in a frequency so high that of all living creatures only certain insects could hear it. But the sludge found it unbearable. The illusions lifted from the hearts of their victims and fled out their mouths. The redeemed spread themselves flat on the ground to give thanks to the Founders.

The illusions fled into the Living World. There they tricked the source of all creation into giving them life and form and

316

even history. They called themselves the Bright Beings, the Malignant Ones and the Benign Ones. Many returned to muddy the Revolution with their private battle of good and evil. Others retreated through time into the Old World, helping or hindering the coming of the Revolution itself. In this way the Beings convinced themselves that even the Founders depended on their never-ending competition.

Some true historians have presented an alternative view. According to these accounts (the Founders' Institute has accepted both versions as true) the people themselves refused to live in a world not shaped by the dance of good and evil. The delegation that came to Alessandro Clean Rain came not to abolish moralism but to establish it. The Founder took pity on them and himself reached into the Living World for spirits willing to join the opposing teams.

When first hired, the Devoted Ones, and the Ferocious Ones took up their tasks with great dedication. They harangued people constantly, attacking or saving them until their targets lost all track of what was happening. The Beings waited on street corners and bus stops, they appeared as faces in mirrors and soda bubbles. Each year they chose some unfortunate man or woman for their championship. One man, who later swore he had done nothing to antagonise either side, found his business ruined, his wife and children dead, his body a playground of disease and all his friends replaced by Malignant Ones who told him he was only getting what he deserved. Then the Benign Ones came to drive away the false friends, heal his body, arrange a loan for him to start a new business, set him up with a wife who promised him seven sons and three daughters, and finally appear to him in a whirlwind to assure him the whole exercise was of great value and would instruct future generations.

After several years of such scandals the Founders summoned the Beings and laid down the limits and rules under which they compete today. Despite these restrictions the Bright Beings still consider their battles the basic pattern of the world. When an adolescent receives a 'summons to the Voice', that is, an inner call to become a Teller, the Malignant Ones consider it their duty to block the soul from

317

realizing its glory. They intercept the girl or boy, chop her or him into small pieces and bury each piece deep in the Earth or under the foundations of large buildings and public monuments. Then the Benign Ones come and dig up the fragments. They reconstruct the future Teller (often with slight errors, requiring corrective plastic surgery) and deliver her or him to the nearest Picture Hall or College of Tellers.

The Beings retreat to their camps, convinced they have performed a vital service. The Ferocious Ones, however, never notice that the chopped up pieces do not suffer but bring a blessing to wherever the enemy buries them. Nor do the Devoted Ones recognise the pain they cause by wrenching the scattered child loose from its union with its Mother. Still, the Benign Ones' action does produce a benefit. The sudden withdrawal from the Earth gives the Tellers their most notable characteristic: their overwhelming desire to help their listeners.

WE REMEMBER THE FOUNDERS.

318

17

Jennie stood in front of the oven, feeling the heat leak out through the glass door. Outside the kitchen window the snow continued to parade past the small blur of light cast by the lamp over the door. Jennie glanced at the snow, then back at the oven. In her arms she held a large open book, its glossy pages pressed against her chest. How long would it take a book to burn? Did it make a difference that the oven was electric and not an open gas flame? And how long would it take to clean it up?

Wondering if she should tear the pages up first, maybe crumple them up in a casserole, Jennie lowered her arms to where she could see the faded picture: Miguel Miracle of the Green Earth passing out cakes in green-striped wrappers. She shook her head, filled suddenly with the memory of her father's finger pointing at the cake, and his voice telling her you could still buy the same cake today if you went to Vera Cruz. Had Jimmy known the stuff for sale was fake? Presumably. She shrugged and flipped the pages. Denise Ravendaughter glided above the San Francisco spotlights. And there stood Jonathan Mask Of Wisdom surrounded by blind children on the edge of the canyon. And there came the Army of the Saints, marching through the three day darkness to surround New Orleans and do nothing but breathe softly on the city until all the enemy destroyed their own weapons. And there – there stood the ferris wheel, with Li Ku Unquenchable Fire bound to its hub, shouting for days on end to chase away the Malignant Ones.

Jennie looked around the kitchen as if she'd find something there to save her from what she had to do. She walked over to the table, and sat down with the book in her lap and her legs stuck out in front of her. There was a purple stain on the page, just below the fiery feet. Jelly. Grape jelly, from when she was ten years old and reading the book one summer afternoon while eating, and looking out the window at some kids fighting on Hudson Street. Quite a few of the pages were stained – coffee, wine, here and there, blood offerings – and some were torn and taped. Jennie knew she could recite the circumstances of every mark. And then there were all those pages where she'd underlined passages, or even written notes or drawn pictures along the margins. She remembered her shock at seeing the clean pages in Betsy Rodriguez's copy of *The Lives*. When Jennie was nine she'd written her own little story about Danielle Book of the People, above the text on – she closed her eyes a moment – page ninety two. She'd erased it immediately and then the next day asked her teacher if she'd committed some terrible crime. Ms. Cohen had told her the Founders expected us to write in the book. It was one of the things that would bind us to the Tellers. Maybe Betsy Rodriguez didn't care about binding herself to the Tellers.

Cowards. Useless goddamn cowards. She grabbed the page with Li Ku's picture on it, held the paper away from the book. She should tear it out. Tear them out one by one, every useless page, crack the spine, break the cover. She dropped the book on the table. She pushed herself up, and with one hand on the small of her back she walked over to the stove and turned off the oven.

Excerpt from A TALE FOUND ON A FERRIS WHEEL

Too Pretty walked out into the country of the dead. While the advisers and congresses and speakers and ambassadors and generals and press agents all argued how to divide the Celestial Republic, the Blessed First Lady slid and crawled over arms and legs, over emptied out stomachs and lakes of blood. It had to be there, she told herself. No one could have lifted it. It belonged to her and it wouldn't move for anyone else.

For in the short time since the President's death the Blessed First Lady had convinced herself that she and He Who Runs Away had loved each other, that her years long spell had protected him from his enemies. And now that the spell had failed (she blamed herself for his defeat), now that their enemies had destroyed him, she believed that her husband wanted her to finish his work.

There wasn't much time. Right now they were planning the funeral. The undertakers had gone out with their bright scarves over their faces and their red gloves that reached to the elbows, and they'd collected enough parts to put together a body. Right now they were sculpting the face, using putty and paint, working from coins and postage stamps. Soon they'd mount him on display, and while all the delegations shuffled past, the negotiations would solidify. And when they'd worked out some scheme and ordered the speakers to claim they had read it as a diagram in heaven, then someone would remember the First Lady. They would lock her back in her house, they would dismantle her mountain and flatten the Earth. But if she found it, the thing that belonged to her . . .

On the seventh day of the woman's search the birds and the rats watched her pick up what looked like a misshapen head with a disfigured face. The Blessed First Lady raised the Head of His Father above her body. The sun recoiled in the sky.

Jennie arrived at Karen D'arcy's house on a snowy Thursday evening. In the driveways along the street men in scarves and tree stump boots were shovelling away the first inches of snow. Inside the houses the children had retreated to their bedrooms, where they stripped naked, drew symbols on their chests and legs with non-toxic paint and then kneeled before their guardians to promise some penance or offering if only the Beings would keep it snowing long enough to cancel school. Walking through the untouched snow of Karen's driveway, Jennie thought how she used to hate all these little family events. She hated getting out with a shovel when all the wives could send their husbands. It was one of the things that had drawn her and Karen together after Mike had left.

Karen took a long time to answer the bell. When she did, her 'God, Jennie, what are you doing out on a night like this?' sounded so rehearsed Jennie was sure Karen must have peeked through a window and debated whether or not she could safely pretend she wasn't at home. Jennie said, 'Can I come in?'

'Yes. Yes, of course. Come on. Just leave your boots by the door here.' Jennie stepped into the small entrance area where she bent down to undo the laces holding her boots tight around her padded jeans. Karen said, 'Those look great on you. I wish I could wear snug boots like that.' When Jennie didn't answer Karen reached for the plastic totebag Jennie had leaned against the door. 'Here,' she said, 'let me put that somewhere for you.' She laughed. 'I hope you didn't bring any cake. Or chocolate. I'm on my latest diet.' Karen was wearing a loose purple jumpsuit gathered at the wrists and ankles. Jennie felt shapeless and slovenly in her jeans and overlarge sweatshirt.

'No, give me that,' Jennie said, and took the bag out of Karen's hand.

'Sure. Whatever you want.' There was silence briefly, and then Karen said, 'Sometimes I think there's a special squad of Malignant Ones assigned to throw chocolate at me whenever I try to diet.' Jennie took her coat off and shook the excess snow onto the plastic mat. At the sight of Jennie's bulging middle Karen said, 'Shit, there I go slamming my hoof in my mouth again. Just what you need to hear, huh? Diets? Putting on weight? Sorry, Jennie.'

'It's okay,' Jennie said. 'I don't mind.'

'Well, I still could show a little tact.'

'I said I don't mind.' She sat down on the couch, still holding the totebag in front of her. Calmly, she watched Karen look quickly from Jennie to the small stone guardian on its wooden platform by the entrance to the living room. When it was clear that Jennie didn't intend to go back and touch it, Karen slid her own hand over the grey face. She did it quickly, as if she hoped Jennie wouldn't notice, but she still closed her eyes and mouthed some formula – maybe protection against the accursed.

Karen sat down in a chair opposite the couch. A moment later she stood up again. 'I don't know what's wrong with me tonight. You want some coffee?'

'If you're having some.'

'Great.' She hurried into the kitchen. 'Sorry I can't offer you anything,' she called. 'Only way I can diet. Empty out the whole house.'

Jennie didn't answer. She leaned her head back against the cushion and closed her eyes.

Karen stayed in the kitchen the whole time the coffee was brewing. When she came back she set the cup down on the small square table at the end of the couch and touched a finger to Jennie's knee. 'Jennie?' When Jennie opened her eyes, Karen jumped back. 'I thought you'd fallen asleep,' she said.

'No, just resting.'

'It's tiring, huh? What is it now, almost the sixth month?' Jennie nodded. There was silence a moment, then Karen said, 'Hey, are you sure you should be

323

drinking coffee? Great, huh? Now that I've gone and made it, I ask whether you really want it. But you know what I mean.'

Jennie smiled. 'Don't worry, Karen. Nothing could harm the baby.'

'Oh. Well, there's so many reports. I saw in the *Holy Digest* – not my usual magazine, but you know waiting rooms. Anyway, it said the soul needs "digestive serenity" when it's forming the body around it. I love that phrase. "Digestive serenity." ' She laughed. 'I could use some of that myself.'

'Believe me,' Jennie said, 'nothing could possibly confuse this soul from secreting whatever body it wants.'

'I guess so,' Karen said. The two of them sipped their coffee. 'Remember that guy? The one I was hoping would call?' She laughed and gave a little shrug. 'I even checked with the phone company to make sure no Ferocious Ones were blocking my line. I don't know what's wrong with me. One of these days I'm going to get smart and give up men instead of chocolate.'

'Karen . . .' Jennie said. She stopped, made a face.

Karen leaned forward. She crossed her arms and held on to her elbows. 'What is it?' she said.

'Karen, I want to give you something.'

'Give me something? I don't understand.'

Jennie said, 'Several things, actually.' With the totebag in her hands she hesitated, filled with a sadness that angered and confused her. This should be easy, she told herself. She didn't want these things any more. They didn't mean anything to her. She took out the Name beads first, holding them by the string so that the blue and gold stones dangled in front of her. 'Here,' she said, but Karen didn't move. 'Come on,' Jennie said, 'put out your hand.'

Karen obeyed. When Jennie dropped the beads in

her hand she looked from them to Jennie and then laid them down on the table, careful not to twist them or let any overlap. 'Why are you giving these to me? Have you gotten a new set? I thought you got these from your father.'

Jennie didn't answer, but as she reached into the bag for the Squeaky Founder doll, she thought, *It's true, Jimmy gave me most of these things. That's probably why I didn't just burn them.* She gave Karen the doll.

'What are you doing?' Karen said.

'I don't need these any more. I want you to have them.'

'Jennie, why don't you need them any more? Have you got new ones?' When Jennie reached into the bag again Karen grabbed hold of her arm. 'Please stop. I want you to tell me what you're doing.'

'Karen, I'm not a child. I just don't want these any more. And I know you'll appreciate them so I want you to have them. That's all.'

'That's all.' Karen sat back and watched as Jennie took out sanctified salve, a miniature Founder's shirt, and several other small ceremonial objects. Karen said, 'It looks like you've emptied out your whole house.'

'I guess so,' Jennie said, but she knew it wasn't true. She'd kept the Revolution Mouse doll, the offering pin Mike had given her, and one thing more, the piece of Li Ku's skin, which still hung around her neck.

After she'd emptied the totebag of all the smaller objects Jennie lifted out her copy of *The Lives*. 'I'm not taking that,' Karen said. She leaned back in her chair.

'Please,' Jennie said. 'I don't want – I can't just get rid of it. I want you to have it.'

'Why should you get rid of it?'

'I can't explain. It's too difficult.'

'I think you can't explain because you don't know. You need help, Jennie. Don't you realise that?'

325

'The only help I need is for you to take these things from me.' She laid the book down with the rest.

'This is what comes from not doing that banishment. That's what started all this.'

'It's got nothing to do with it.'

'Of course it has. You don't really think you're making any sense, do you?'

'I don't care if I'm making any sense. I didn't come here to make sense. I just wanted to give you these things.'

'Just wanted – What kind of an act is that, Jennie? Can't you see there's something deeply wrong with you? Oh God, I feel so responsible.'

Jennie laughed. 'Where do you get that idea?'

'I didn't make sure you did the enactment. I knew I should have kept after you. I just knew it. And now look at this. It's like you're throwing away your – your soul.'

Only the decorations, Jennie thought. But then, *No. No, these things are real.* That was why she couldn't burn them. Not just because Jimmy had given them to her . . . Because they were real and she loved them. But refusing them was real as well. An act all her own, as genuine as the interventions of the Agency. Out loud she said, 'Believe me, Karen, doing that banishment couldn't possibly have affected what I'm doing at all. You've just got to take my word for that.'

'Your word? If only you could hear yourself. Really hear yourself. What exactly do you think your word is worth? When you're trying to cut yourself loose from all the points that connect you – '

'I'm just giving away a bunch of old – ' She stopped herself. This was no time for lies.

'You know very well what you're doing. This isn't some sort of spring cleaning.'

'All right, all right. I want to break my connections.'

326

'And that's sick.'

'Maybe I want to make my own connections. Can you understand that?'

'That's ridiculous.'

'Well, ridiculous or not, it's my decision.'

'The very fact that you can say something like that – '

'What? That I want to make my own decision?'

'Yes! How can you make any decisions at all if you cut yourself off like that?'

'I never thought you'd – you'd get so excited.'

'Of course I'm excited. I care about you, Jennie. You're my friend. We share the same pattern. If you rip yourself loose like this, don't you think that does something to me?'

'I'm sorry, Karen. I don't want to hurt you, or upset you. Believe me, I don't.'

'Then get help. Go down to the Hospital of the Inner Spirit. Or go to a private healer. They can restore you. You've just got to give yourself to them.'

Jennie smiled. 'I've given too much of myself already.'

'Don't think you can put me off with some stupid blasphemy. I just won't listen. I want you to go see someone.' Jennie said nothing. 'Do you want me to find a name for you? My cousin went to somebody – '

'Please, Karen. I just won't go. You know I won't.'

'I'm going to get you help, Jennie. Trust me. I won't let you destroy yourself.'

'And there's no way I could make you see I'm not doing that?'

Karen slowly shook her head. 'No. Absolutely not.'

Jennie couldn't think what to say. She finally managed, 'I've got to go.'

Karen gathered the things from the table, 'Here,' she said. 'Take these back with you.'

327

Jennie walked past her to the entrance mat. 'You keep them. Please. I'll just throw them away.' She began lacing up her boots.

'I'll keep them,' Karen told her. 'For you.'

'Fine.' Jennie pulled her coat from the closet. With her hand on the door she said, 'Oh, hell. Karen, I'm sorry. I didn't want to upset you.'

'You don't have to apologise. You're not responsible for what you do.'

'The funny thing is,' Jennie said, 'that's all I want.'

'What? What do you mean?'

'I just want to be responsible for what I do. I just want things to be my own decision.'

'Then get help.'

'I'm my own help.'

'No, Jennie, you mustn't talk like that. You're never alone.'

Jennie kissed Karen on the cheek. 'Thank you,' she said. 'I'm glad you care so much about me.'

'You're my friend.'

Jennie remembered a poster her third grade teacher kept at the end of the blackboard. 'God is your friend.' *Not true*, she thought, *not true. Karen D'arcy is my friend.* She hugged Karen, then slid loose to open the door. The cold leaped in at them.

As Jennie stepped into the snow Karen said, 'I'll get help for you, Jennie. I promise.'

Jennie nodded. She put up her hood. When she stepped into the path leading to the driveway she noticed that most of the shovellers had given up and gone back inside. Behind her the door closed. Alone with the snow she set off for home.

The Meaning of a Story: *A moment in the life of Valerie Mazdan*

After the New York riots Courageous Wisdom

vanished from public knowledge for several years. She left her College, she refused to speak at Recitals, and after the magazines and television networks stopped surrounding her she travelled under another name to some anonymous city where no one suspected their neighbour of fame.

Several years passed, and then on a certain Day of Truth a group of people gathered in the Fifth Avenue Picture Hall in New York City. They sat between the stained glass windows and listened to a Living Master tell the Picture of Chained Mother. They sat with eyes closed, and now and then a wavelike sensation would roll over their bodies. But these feelings always passed before they could take hold, leaving the listeners with a sense of something not quite awakened.

After she'd told the end of the Picture the Teller announced the formula, 'And this is the Picture's meaning.' At that moment a wind blew open the high doors at the back of the hall. Everyone turned and there stood Valerie Mazdan in her famous coat of transparent pockets. She called out, '*I* will show you the meaning of a story.'

Everyone waited, frightened some raving horde of tattooed maniacs would sweep in and knock them to the ground. Nothing happened. They all turned to each other and laughed. When they looked again to the back Mazdan had gone. The embarrassed laughter blew into a gale as each one imagined she or he had survived some great danger. At such a moment no one wanted simply to go home. They wrote all their names and addresses on a list and swore to meet again the following year.

The year passed and the people forgot their plan. The next year a small group sent out letters to organize a reunion, but when only a few people responded, the committee dropped the idea. Ten years passed and finally they all decided to meet. Now, some still lived in New York, but others had moved away so they decided to book space in a hotel and hire one of the hotel's convention rooms. When they'd all assembled it looked at first as if half the group had stayed home. As they began talking, however, and each told about the ones he or she knew, they discovered that a large number had died in the past decade, some from disease, some from accidents or crime, some from suicide.

They enacted a brief memorial, in which one of the younger women, a diamond assayer from Sixth Avenue, acted the part of Courageous Wisdom. But when the assayer stood in the room's doorway and shouted, 'I will show you the meaning of a story,' a bucket of cement, stored on a shelf above the door, fell down and killed her. The horrified witnesses decided to go on a pilgrimage. Otherwise the woman's angry spirit might escape from the land of the dead and return to torment them.

They chose a certain holy pool of water in the dunes outside Amsterdam. According to accounts on television, immersing your face in the water restored lost memories and raised you up so refreshed that any beings stalking you would fail to recognize you. They filed their plans with the SDA and then they stood in a circle in Rainbow Square, with their hands on each other's shoulders and pledged to help each other fulfil the pilgrimage.

Now, one of the group worked as a Speaker, and he gathered a coin from each of them, then tossed them all at the statue's feet. By the pattern the coins formed he determined that they mustn't travel by air. They chartered a boat, a small steamship specially fitted for pilgrimages, with penitence rooms and sanctified saunas. Once they reached the open seas, however, it turned out that the captain and crew planned to rob them and abandon ship. A fight broke out; several of the prilgrims died before the rest realised they had better surrender.

The crew left in a small boat which had pulled alongside. For days the steamship drifted, while the food and water ran out, and the Speaker studied the wave patterns for clues to their escape, or at least an explanation for the disastrous reading achieved in New York. Each dawn and twilight they cast more and more of their possessions as offerings into the sea. But instead of deliverance a storm rose up at them. By the time it had ended, twelve of them had died; some fell overboard, some died of exposure, and one man ruptured his stomach.

At last a submarine spotted them when it surfaced for a solar ceremony. After some discussion with his crew the captain radioed for permission to bring the group to Amsterdam. There the mayor met them and a hotel offered to put them up for free. On their third day in Amsterdam the Heineken brewery took them on a tour ending with a party. Unfortunately, a terrorist organisation had infiltrated the catering agency. Half the group died from eating poisoned herring.

The remainder of the pilgrims stayed in Amsterdam for two weeks, visiting the shrine in the dunes every day. The water always produced the same effect, a sense of something almost remembered, then lost again when they lifted their faces. Meanwhile, their numbers continued to dwindle. One met a boy walking along a canal and went to live with him in the boy's commune. One night the commune members all transported together. When they returned to their bodies the pilgrim and the boy entered each other's bodies by mistake. In the confusion the two of them fell through an open window. Another two pilgrims joined a balloon club, only to have the balloon punctured by a stray laser beam from an American-owned laboratory.

The remaining five pilgrims met in their hotel lobby to talk about everything that had happened to them. It seemed, they all said, as if they could never rest, but must always run from some enchantment. They wept and hugged each other and promised to stay together for the rest of their lives. When they stepped outside them found themselves carried off in a mob running from the police. A group of students had tried to seize an office building. The police chased them with tear gas and clubs, only to fall back themselves before an onslaught of motorcycle gangs who had come in from Rotterdam and Groningen for the excitement. Only one of the five pilgrims survived.

Isolated from the rest of humanity, this last member of her tribe flew back to New York. For weeks she did nothing but walk up and down the streets. One day she was passing the Fifth Avenue Picture Hall when she heard voices inside. Only as she walked up the steps did she remember that the day was June 21, the Day of Truth. She walked in and sat down in the same seat she'd occupied all those years ago, when Valerie Mazdan had interrupted the Teller.

And there at the back stood Courageous Wisdom, and there at the front sat the Living Master, and there she saw all the others, all in their places, each one believing that she or he alone had survived the rolling death. They looked at themselves and they saw the same clothes and smelt the same air, and just as they realized that no time had passed, that they'd never left their seats, that all the years had evaporated like a dream in sunlight, Valerie Mazdan's voice thundered from the back of the Hall.

'And *that* is the meaning of a story.'

18

The next time Jennie saw Karen was two weeks later, on a bright Saturday morning. Jennie was half-heartedly attempting to clear the refrigerator when the doorbell rang. Wishing she could ignore it she shoved the vegetable bin back in place and stood up. She groaned at the pain in her back and legs as she turned the corner from the dinette into the living room. She stopped.

An SDA van stood parked in the road in front of the house. Around it, like a clump of dark bushes in the sunlit snow, stood a crowd of Jennie's neighbours. None of them had come onto the property, but they stood two and three deep in the street. The moment Jennie appeared before the picture window they all began talking. Some made hand signs at her. Feeling slovenly, with her hair greasy and her face streaked, Jennie wanted to run out to the back. The bell rang again. Wishing she could at least wash her face Jennie went and yanked open the door.

A whole group stood round the door. Karen, Gloria and Al Rich, Marcy Carpenter, Jim Browning, Jackie Schoenmaker, and two people Jennie had never seen. One was a woman in an open grey overcoat, a man's double-breasted suit, and wingtip shoes, with her hair cut short and parted on the side. Her aviator sunglasses and her gold tieclip both bore the winged insignia of the SDA Special Branch. The flying squad. Behind her, looking around with great curiosity, stood a young man wearing rubber boots, red gloves, a shapeless green coat, and a thick woollen dress hung with small bones and feathers, screws and nails, and broken bits of tools and kitchen utensils. A black silk rope tied the dress around the waist. At first Jennie thought him a Speaker on loan from some oracle centre, and she assumed they'd come to do a reading. But then she saw the drum he carried in his left hand. It was made from a two gallon oil can with the ends cut out and some kind of skin stretched tight over one of the holes. In his right hand he dangled a bone about seven inches long. Jennie wondered if it came from a dead teacher. As she looked at him his face opened in a huge smile. He was a healer, one of those they called 'pure' from his lack of a system, or medicine, or props other than his 'boat', the drum. For a moment Jennie thought of the precursor she and Mike had seen in Bermuda.

'What is this?' Jennie said, 'a vigilance committee?'

Jim Browning said, 'Yeah, you can call us that. Those old committees did a lot of good.' Despite the cold he wore an open corduroy jacket over a flannel shirt, with no gloves or scarf. Like the others he wore his raccoon hat.

Jennie turned her head to look directly at Karen. She said, 'So you brought me some help. I should have known I could count on you.' Karen looked at the ground.

The SDA woman spoke in a soft voice that jarred with her outfit. 'Are you Jennifer Mazdan?' she asked.

'Sure,' Jennie said.

'I order you to invite us in.'

'And if I don't?' She didn't wait for an answer, but added, 'Oh, come on. Come on in.' When they'd all marched inside Jennie said, 'You can put your coats on the chair over there. I'm sure you won't mind if I don't offer you coffee. Shall I close the curtains?'

'We prefer them open,' the woman said.

'Fine.' She turned and saw Marcy Carpenter

squinting at her. 'Spot something, Marcy?' she said. 'My fangs showing?'

'Look,' Marcy said. 'She's marked her forehead. She's made a mark there.'

Jennie leaned over to look in the narrow mirror facing the couch. She laughed. 'That's a smudge,' she said. 'From cleaning the sink. Do you ever clean your sink, Marcy?'

'Let's get started,' the cop said. 'Everybody sit down.' The healer squatted on the rug.

Jennie said, 'You'll have to bring chairs from the dinette.' She thought of sitting on the couch to see if anyone would join her. But then she would have to get up again if anyone did. She sat in the green chair beside the mirror.

In the centre of the room the SDA woman, still standing, took a miniature cassette recorder from her jacket pocket. Her thumb clicked it on and she recited the date, the addresss, and 'Investigation of Jennifer Mazdan on charges of possession and/or conspiracy with Malignant Ones and/or beings unknown.'

Marcy testified first. Her pregnant sister had come to visit her, she said. Before she came she went for a check-up and the doctor pronounced the foetus in perfect health. On the third day of her visit she'd gone for a walk and had passed Jennifer Mazdan's house. That night she'd doubled over in pain while watching television. By the time they'd got her to the hospital she'd lost the baby.

'Has she ever miscarried before?' Jennie asked.

Looking at the cop Marcy said, 'What difference does that make?'

Jennie laughed. 'None at all. Just curious.'

Gloria leaned forward on the couch. 'You can make all the jokes you like,' she said. Al tried to pull her back but she pushed him away. 'You're going to get what you deserve.'

Softly, Karen said, 'Shit.'

'What's the matter,' Jennie said to her. 'Aren't you happy? You're getting me help.'

Jackie Schoenmaker came next, testifying that Jennie had caused her and her girlfriend to break up. 'She's gone to live in the women's world. That one by Wappinger's,' she said, twisting the end of a yellow silk scarf and hunching up her right shoulder. 'She'd never do something like that. I was the one who wanted to go there, not her. She never wanted to go there. She wanted to come here.'

It was like her and Mike, Jennie thought. He'd been the one to insist on moving into the hive, and now he was in some loft on Greene Street. To Jackie she said, 'Have you tried going after her?'

With a vehemence that startled Jennie, Jackie said, 'Why? So you can curse us again?'

Jennie said, 'I didn't curse you.'

'We loved each other. She never would have left me. Never.'

Jim Browning then charged that Jennie had prevented Allan Lightstorm from moving to Pough-keepsie. It was simple, he said, when the SDA woman asked him to explain. Lightstorm had volunteered to speak in Poughkeepsie. No one had asked him. Obviously he planned to move there as long as he got the right reception. Well, the whole town had turned out. It was a reception good enough for a Founder. All but Jennifer Mazdan. She'd gone to sleep. She said. And the next thing they knew they'd never heard from Lightstorm again.

The cop looked at Jennie. 'No questions,' she said. She hoped she sounded like that lawyer on television, the one who was always solving murders. And possessions.

Gloria came next. 'This woman,' she said, and pointed at Jennie, 'cursed her whole block on the Day of Truth. Because of her – because of her *helpers*,' – she looked around the room as if she could spot the Ferocious Ones floating in the air – 'none of us could truly merge with the Picture. We all came longing for our Master's voice, but *she* blocked us.'

'How'd I do that?' Jennie asked. 'Just by staying away?'

'Do you really think we believe your little story about falling asleep?'

'Believe whatever you want. But I've got a question. Have you ever "truly merged with the Picture"?'

'You're not going to trick us,' Gloria said.

'You're just tricking yourself. After you get rid of me what's your next excuse going to be? The Tellers have deserted you, can't you see that?' Silence. Karen began to cry, while the cop squinted at Jennie.

Gloria held out her hand towards Al. 'The box, please,' she said, and Jennie thought how Gloria must watch the same lawyer show on television. Al handed her a wooden box about four inches wide and two inches deep. It looked like something you'd buy to keep paper clips in and rubber bands. She opened it up and passed it to the cop, who glanced inside, then handed it back. Half standing, Jennie could see a small pile of ashes. When she'd closed the box Gloria said, 'My children found these ashes buried in Jennifer Mazdan's back yard.'

Jennie laughed. 'Do your children usually go digging in my back yard?'

'Don't you dare interrupt me,' Gloria told her. To the cop she said, 'These ashes are all that's left of an effigy she made. A raccoon effigy, burned on the Day

337

of Truth to prevent us from merging with Allan Lightstorm.'

Jennie said, 'Even if your little brats had found the ashes how do you know they came from an effigy?'

'Because of this,' Gloria said loudly, and reached in her purse for a raccoon hat with one side charred, as if someone had held it over a candle. 'This lay beside the ashes,' she said, just like the great lawyer springing a trap. 'It wouldn't burn because it represents the immortal part of us.'

'Oh, for God's sake,' Jennie said. 'Where did you get that, Gloria? It looks like a children's size. Did you steal it from one of your own kids?' Gloria smiled at her. No doubt she considered it a smile of triumph. Jennie thought it looked sickly.

Al got up from the couch to stand beside the SDA cop. When he took the pipe out of his mouth his smile looked anything but sickly. He said, 'I think the record should show the look of contempt filling this woman's face. She thinks she can just go ahead and curse her neighbours, and the SDA, and now even the Tellers. And I think we can see why, too.' He puffed once on his pipe and then turned the stem to point to Jennie's stomach. 'She thinks her Malignant friend will protect her. The one who gave her that *thing* she's carrying around inside her.'

'Al,' Karen said, 'I told you – you promised – you know how that happened. And why we've got to help her. You promised me, Al. I told you – '

'You told us what she told you. I would think, Karen, that even you would realise – '

'What do you mean, even me?'

'All right,' the cop said. 'That's enough. You can all fight it out later in your block meeting.'

Gloria said, 'Don't you see what she's doing? We

never used to fight. Karen, Al and I love you, don't you know that? We love all the raccoons.'

Karen said, 'Oh, Gloria, will you just shut up?'

'This is your fault,' Gloria said to Jennie. 'You and that monster you're hiding inside you.'

'That's enough,' the SDA woman said loudly. 'Sit down.' When Al and Gloria had retreated to the couch she said, 'Any more charges?' No one said anything, but first Al, then Gloria, and then the others looked at Karen, who stared at the floor. 'Any more charges?' the woman repeated. The healer pounded once on his drum. Briefly the woman squatted down beside him to stroke his cheek. The sun through the window lit the two of them like some vision during a mountain pilgrimage. The cop smiled and stood up again.

Karen said, 'I've got a charge.' She lifted her eyes to look at Jennie. 'I've got a charge.' For several seconds she said nothing more, then 'Two weeks ago she came to my house. And she gave me her Name beads, and some sacred aids . . .' She paused. 'And the book. The Book of All Wisdom,' she said, giving *The Lives Of The Founders* its official epithet. 'She wouldn't explain why, and when I begged her to keep them she laughed at me and said she'd just throw them away.'

'Did I laugh?' Jennie asked. 'I don't remember laughing.'

Karen went on, 'I put them all in an honoured place. And then – ' She stopped, and Al told her, 'Go on, Karen. Tell us what happened.'

'Yeah,' Jennie said. 'I can't wait to hear it.'

'You be quiet,' Gloria ordered. A warning look from the SDA woman pushed her back in her seat.

Karen said, 'Well, for a couple of nights I kept hearing crying. I'd hear it while I was sleeping and then I'd wake up and it would go away.'

The cop said, 'Did you get the dream analysed?'

339

'No. It wasn't a dream. It had nothing to do with my dreams. It was someone crying in the house. I just kept hearing it. Then, one night, it happened again, and when I woke up I could still hear it. And when I went and looked, it was the Book. It was the Founders. They were crying because she'd tortured them.' Her eyes, which she'd kept on Jennie the whole time, fell away.

'What?' Jennie said. 'I tortured them? Are you out of your soul?'

Half crying, Karen said, 'They told me – '

The SDA woman cut her short. 'When did they tell you? Right then? In the room?'

Karen said, 'No. No, it – when I went back to sleep. They talked to me in my sleep.'

'And they said she had tortured them? Jennifer Mazdan?'

'Yes.' She nodded. 'They thanked me. For rescuing them.'

Jennie said, 'Rescuing them? I brought them to you. I asked you to take them because I didn't want to destroy them.'

Gloria shouted, 'She's admitting it. She's admitting it.'

To Karen Jennie said, 'If I was having such a great time torturing them why would I give them up?'

Gloria said, 'Because you couldn't control them. You knew they'd contact us. You knew our loyalty was too strong for you. You and your helpers.'

'So I went and gave the book to Karen D'arcy. Isn't she one of the loyal ones?'

No one answered. A moment later the cop asked Jennie, 'Do you deny these charges?'

'I don't deny that I gave away my copy of *The Lives*. And some other things. But that's all. The rest of it, it's just garbage.'

'Why did you give away your copy of *The Lives*?'

Jennie's thoughts jammed with answers, excuses, declarations. Finally she sat back and said nothing.

'Why did you give away *The Lives*?' the cop repeated.

'I wanted to.'

'Why did you want to?'

Jennie stood up. 'All this is supposed to lead up to a scan, right? Otherwise they're just verbal accusations. And you can't charge me with anything until the scan shows up positive, right? So let's go.' She looked at Al and laughed. 'Let the record show the accused consented to have her configurations scanned.' She laughed again.

The healer laughed as well. He untied the black rope from around his waist, then looked around the room. He slid over to the couch. With a crooked finger and a tilt of his head he gestured at Jackie Schoenmaker to come join him on the floor.

Jennie ignored them. 'Where do we do it?' she said.

The cop looked at her curiously. 'Outside,' she said. 'The equipment's in the van.'

'Can I get my coat? And my shoes?'

'Yes, of course.'

Rolled along by fury, Jennie marched into the bedroom and kicked off her slippers. She was pulling on her boots when the rage broke in her like the water surrounding a baby. A scan, she thought, and realised she'd resisted doing one for months. The doctor had suggested it, Karen (good old Karen), the clerk at the Oneiric Agency, even Maria at work. Each time, Jennie had pushed the idea from her mind. She realized now how scared she'd been. Scared not that they'd find something, but that they wouldn't. Like the clerk who couldn't find the elements of Jennie's dream in the catalogue. Scared she'd fallen so far out of the pattern that nothing at all would show. A blanked out spirit.

341

When she came back to the living room she found Jackie tying the healer to the leg of the couch, with the healer whispering to her to pull the rope tighter or else his soul would run away when he forced it to go to work. Looking very uncomfortable Jackie yanked on the rope.

Outside, silence settled on the crowd. Jennie looked up and down the block. The crowd was bigger than she'd thought, with people from other blocks joining the raccoons. It made sense, she told herself. It wasn't every day people got accused of collaboration with Ferocious Ones and/or beings unknown.

'Come on,' Jennie said, 'this way's quicker.' She marched across the lawn smiling at the thought of the cop getting snow in her wingtip shoes.

Except for the cab and a couple of frosted panels in the rear door the van was windowless. No letters or insignias marred the high gloss paint job. None were necessary. Everyone recognized the dark purple with the gold stripe running around it. While she waited for the woman to unlock the back door Jennie recalled the competition a few years ago when the SDA vehicle contract had come up for renewal. Every night the news had shown top executives from the auto companies outdoing each other in penances and offerings. One of them – the head of General Motors, she thought – had fasted for five weeks, then stood naked outside his Detroit headquarters while his vice-presidents threw buckets of petroleum waste at him. Jennie couldn't remember if he'd got the contract.

'Enter of your own free will,' the Special Branch woman said. She held the door open.

'And if I don't?' Jennie asked as she climbed into the back. The cop didn't answer. The inside of the van was light and warm, with fluorescent lamps set into the ceiling and a small heater at the front end, both powered by a generator nestled in the corner. The van was built high to prevent any need to stoop. Jennie stood on the yellow carpet and looked around. It really did look like a scanner's office, everything miniaturized and crowded together. There was the same white table in the centre, the same rows of dials and needles and computer screens. *It's been years*, Jennie realized. She hadn't gone for a scan since the one required for applying to college. She'd been scared for years.

The cop set some instruments, then turned towards Jennie. 'According to Celestial Court decision Kambru vs. the United States, you do not have to submit to a scan at this time. If you refuse I have the power to formally charge you and bring you before a judge. And then he'll order a scan. So you might as well do it.'

Jennie shrugged. She bent down and unlaced her boots. When she'd taken off all her clothes she said, 'What happens when the scan shows I'm clean?'

'If the scan clears you it'll weigh heavily in your favour.'

'Despite all that powerful testimony?'

The cop grinned, showing a dimple in her left cheek. 'Please lie down,' she said.

Jennie lowered herself onto the contoured surface of the table, pleased to discover it warm, probably from coils under the surface. 'I hope you don't mind my lying on my back,' she said.

'Not at all. Umm, the scan won't affect the baby, you know.'

'Not even if it's a monster?'

The woman didn't answer. From the sides of the table she pulled out retractable wires. Fixing the ends with some kind of sticky conductive material she attached them to Jennie's forehead, throat, chest, solar plexus, wrists, thighs, and soles of her feet. Jennie's breathing tightened. When the woman had placed all the wires she made a hand sign over her own forehead and muttered some quick incantation. Jennie knew the cop expected her to say something in return; call on the Benign Ones and the Founders to protect her and insure a good result. She said nothing.

'Drink this,' the woman said, and held a small paper cup to Jennie's lips. Lifting her head slightly Jennie gulped down the chalky liquid. She made a face and tried to lick clean her lips with her tongue.

The cop sat down on a round stool before one of the computer screens. 'The first part you won't feel anything,' she said, as she flicked her fingers at the keys. She waited a moment, made a sound, then tapped the keys again. She looked over her shoulder at Jennie, but all she said was 'Prelims look good.'

Eyes closed, Jennie thought, *Please don't start singing again. I want to get through this by myself.* Without any further warnings she felt the real thing coming on. It began with dizziness and an awful hint of something crawling over her. The blank wall behind her eyelids wheeled around, perpetually falling to the left. She fought against the impulse to open her eyes, knowing that would only make it worse.

Calm returned. And then, like a slap, the memories came: Mike in his leather jacket looking like Mar Birdan, Sam leaning on the counter of his pizza parlour, the bleeding woman by the subway, the cookie vendor taking her hands in the rain, a Chinese restaurant filled with people eating their ancestors. There was more, images and tastes and sounds all jammed together, until she couldn't distinguish them. At the end, one scene stood out in her mind, and that one Jennie hadn't actually witnessed, but only heard described: a burning ferris wheel rolling down Seventh Avenue with a woman attached to the hub.

The images passed, leaving Jennie nauseous on the

table. Behind her she heard the rattle of a printer. When she turned her head to the side she saw the SDA cop looking at her with her mouth slightly open, and the sunglasses dangling in her hand. The woman grabbed the printout off the machine and stared at it, then up at Jennie. 'You had an occurrence,' she said.

'That's right.' The nausea was subsiding, more a memory than a provocation.

'Why didn't you say so?'

'You didn't ask me.'

'Which one?'

'The ferris wheel.'

'Oh. I think I read about that. In the bulletin.'

'Can I get up?'

The woman laughed. 'Sure. Sorry.' She plucked loose the wires, then helped Jennie sit up.

Jennie grunted. 'That's worse than morning sickness,' she said, and took her bra from the cop, who seemed determined to metamorphose into Jennie's maid.

'Listen,' she told Jennie, 'don't worry about your neighbours.'

'I wasn't planning to. I've got enough work worrying about myself.' She winced at the cop's loud laughter.

Back in the house everyone was turned to look at them. While Jennie hung her coat up the SDA woman squatted beside the healer, who was hitting his drum in a slow ponderous rhythm. She placed her hands against her cheeks and whispered something to him. He shook his head and kept drumming.

Gloria got up and stood behind the Special Branch woman. 'What'd it say?' she asked. When the woman ignored her Gloria said louder. 'What were the readings?'

The woman turned her head. 'Sit down,' she ordered.

'We just want to know.'

'Sit down.'

'I think we've got a right,' Gloria said, but she returned to the couch, where Al put his arm around her.

Once again the cop whispered to the healer, and this time the drumming stopped and he stared at her as if she belonged to some new species he'd never heard of. When she'd untied him he closed his eyes and leaned against her for her to stroke his hair and his back.

'Why did you stop him?' Gloria said when the cop stood up again, 'What did the scan say?'

'It says you better hope this woman doesn't decide to sue you.'

Slumped in the green chair Jennie watched them all look at each other, then back at the cop. Karen said, 'What do you mean? Do you mean she's okay?'

'She's more than okay. She's a community resource.'

Jennie thought, *someone shut her up*.

Karen said, 'Then why did she give away those things? Why wouldn't she do the enactment? I don't understand.' When the investigator didn't answer Karen turned to Jennie. 'Why? Is there some reason we don't know about?'

Jennie squinted up at her. 'Do you really think I'd tell you?' she said. She felt no pleasure, only a slight disgust, when Karen shrank back from her.

Like a speaker filled with the message from her oracle Gloria announced, 'She's got to go to the touchstone.' And like a Speaker she looked as surprised by this revelation as anyone else.

The SDA woman said, 'The scan cleared her of all charges. More than cleared her.'

'I don't care what the scan says. I mean – she's – she's poisoning our totems.'

The cop smiled. 'More charges? Do you know how close you are to a slander suit?'

346

Al stood up. As if to announce his entry into the conversation he blew a puff of smoke at the ceiling. 'Charges aren't really the point here,' he said, deepening his voice like a high school actor playing a judge. 'Jennifer belongs to the hive. To our block. It's up to us to decide whether or not she goes to the stone. That's our right.'

Karen said, 'What's the point, Al? What's that got to do with anything?'

Gloria said, 'She doesn't belong here. She doesn't fit in. She hates us.'

The cop looked at Jennie. 'Do you hate these people?' Jennie didn't answer. To Gloria and Al the cop said, 'Maybe it is a block decision. But you're not the whole block. What makes you –'

'We represent the block,' Gloria said. 'They chose us to represent them.'

Jackie Schoenmaker said, 'I don't understand. What good will the touchstone do?'

Gloria said, 'The touchstone speaks for the whole hive. It can tell her to get out.' Karen took off her raccoon hat and threw it at the door. Gloria turned on her. 'Is that what you think of us? Maybe we should send you to the stone too.'

'Maybe you should. This doesn't solve anything. We shouldn't be trying to get rid of her. We should try to bring her back.'

Jennie said, 'Will all of you shut up? God. You want me to go to the stone, Gloria? Great. Terrific. Anything to shut you all up.' With a grunt she got to her feet.

The cop said, 'Are you sure you want to do this? You can force them to get a court order.'

'Please,' Jennie said, 'I just want to get rid of them.'

'You want me to chase them away?' Jennie shook her head. 'You'd probably win any case they could bring against you. You could even bring a countersuit. I'd be happy to testify for you.'

'Thank you. But it's not necessary. There's nothing they can make me do that I don't want to do. Believe me.'

The cop smiled. 'Yes. Yes, I believe you.'

When Jennie stepped outside again, with the cop behind her and the raccoon delegation piling out after them, the crowd up and down the street began making noises and hand signs, calling things out, chanting prayers to the Devoted Ones who had exposed the menace. A few snowballs lobbed against the house. Jennie knew that they thought she was being taken away, that the healer couldn't discharge her. The SDA woman flashed the light from her sunglasses up and down the street, and then shook Jennie's hand in both of hers. A moment later she decided that that wasn't good enough, and gave Jennie a hug followed by a kiss on both cheeks. While astonishment rolled through the spectators the cop shook Jennie's hand once more before she took the healer's arm and led him back towards the van.

Unable to wait until the competition was safely away, Gloria stepped in front of the group to frame her hands around her mouth, the way people did in mystery plays when they announced the birth of the great stories. The pose reminded Jennie of something, but she couldn't remember what. 'We're going to the touchstone,' Gloria informed the community. 'The touchstone will decide whether or not this woman belongs with us.' Al patted her on the shoulder.

That's a lesson for all of us, Jennie thought. Lose a battle? No problem, just pretend it never took place. Afraid Gloria would jump into the lead she marched across the lawn to the road, where the line of onlookers broke apart for her to pass through. Soon they'd all regrouped to follow the posse as they made their way along Blessed Spirit Drive to turn right up Heavenpath Road.

In the front Jennie walked with her hands in her pockets and her head tilted down to shield her eyes from the sun. The cold hurt her ears and she wished she'd brought her scarf.

Karen came up beside her. 'What happened with the scan?'

'That's none of your business.'

'But she said you were all right.'

'Surprise, huh?'

'I'm sorry, Jennie. I'm really sorry.'

'Leave me alone.'

'It wasn't supposed to – this isn't what I wanted.'

'Great. What did you want, Karen? To drive the evil one out of me?'

'Yes. Yes.' She was crying. 'I don't understand. I still don't understand.'

'Maybe I'm the evil one.' Karen jumped away. 'Oh, for God's sake,' Jennie said. 'Go back to Gloria. Leave me alone.'

As the parade climbed the hill to the sacred grove more and more people came out of their houses to fall in line. A few even brought along toy drums and processional trumpets, left over from the Skull Parades at the end of November. Jennie glanced over her shoulder at them all, then up at the grove. She remembered that time with Mike when they all rose into the air together, and even though it drove him away from her, even though the Agency might have arranged it as part of its campaign to get rid of her husband, she still smiled when she thought about it. For one moment, they were all together. For one moment, everything had worked the way it was supposed to work. The way the Revolution had promised.

She glanced down at her belly. *I know you're needed,* she thought. *I know that. I'm not stupid. It's just – I've got to make my own choices. Can you understand that?*

A part of THE TALE OF THE PLACE INSIDE

The Blessed First Lady stepped onto the balcony. She stepped out from the President's bedroom, onto the balcony above the funeral where the secretaries and generals pulled the coffin with gold chains attached to leather halters worn over their shoulders. She stood there watching while lines of girls and boys whipped the mourners who hauled the coffin past rows and rows of benches filled with citizens chosen for their loyalty by the secret police. She stood above these people and she knew that, like herself, they loved her husband and hated themselves for destroying him. She shouted at them the thing they most wanted to hear. 'I am your Sacred President.'

The mask amplified her voice until it pounded in their heads. 'You are my people and I could not bear to leave you. I have come back from the dead and entered the body of my First Lady because I love you, and I could not bear to leave you.'

She shouted, 'Take that useless body. Take its pieces and throw it to the rats. This is my body now. In this body I will rule you and love you.' The spectators nearly trampled the official mourners in their rush to pull apart the rigged up corpse. When they tore at the pasted skin they discovered nothing underneath but a hollow wooden frame. 'Do you see?' the new President called to them. 'They tried to take my heart. They tried to shred it and cook it and eat it to give themselves the courage to betray me. But the birds rescued it. They lifted my heart from the hands of my enemies. And they brought it *here.*' As she pounded on her chest the secretaries and generals and police chiefs ran from the cheers and shrieks of the mob.

19

The touchstone that year was a woman named Doris Baxter, from the Sparrow block at the far end of the hive. Jennie knew her very slightly and remembered her as one of those people who look perpetually exhausted, always shrinking back from some expected burden. But that was before the stone lottery had chosen her to leave the profane world. Now she wore a dress of soft green silk, with dark red pumps crossed by green and gold side panels. Grey tights concealed Doris's legs, but her arms and the cleavage exposed by her dress glowed golden from a pair of sunlamps that stood in the back of the living room beside a narrow velvet couch. Above all this the child's eyes and round cheeks of the mask looked as incongruous as a lump of wood balanced on a champagne glass.

She loved it, Jennie realised. She'd probably never got away from her husband before. On a round table with delicate bowed legs lay one of those blank books, the kind with thick pages and a cover decorated in gold swirls. When Doris turned aside for a moment Jennie opened the book to see lines of poetry in lavender ink.

The room itself had changed. Gone were Jack Adlebury's graceless tables and cabinets. Gone was the smell of sawdust and varnish. Instead, a thick perfume hung in the air above the couch and a single chair beside a round table. There were no dishes in the sink, but Jennie did notice a box from 'La Maison du Vallée', a delicatessen on Market Street which described its food as 'nouvelle cuisine Américaine'.

Doris shifted her weight from one foot to the other,

embarrassed in her beautiful clothes. She said, 'I'm not sure what I'm supposed to do with you.'

'As I understand it, you're supposed to say whether or not I belong here. Whether I'm a fit neighbour.'

'Oh. All right.'

Jennie looked at the mask. She could see nothing of the squirming souls that had rushed her the other time. She said, 'I think you're supposed to examine me. Touch me or something. Channel the hive through your fingers.'

Doris looked at her hands, then wiped them on the sides of her dress. 'All right,' she said. 'Umm – please stand still.' She took a couple of steps towards Jennie, then closed her eyes as she lifted her hands. For a moment the hands patted the air in front of her. She opened her eyes to take better aim.

The fingers leaped back from Jennie's skin like the magnets used to demonstrate spiritual repulsion in grade school meta-science classes. Doris stared down at her red hands, then up at Jennie. 'You burned me,' 'You burned my hands.'

'I'm sorry,' Jennie said. 'I didn't know this would happen. Please believe me.'

'Get out,' the touchstone told her. 'Get out of my house!'

When Jennie stepped outside there was Gloria, at the head of the crowd. 'Get out,' Gloria told her. 'Get out of our hive.' At first Jennie thought she had heard Doris. Or maybe they had all felt the touchstone's pain in their own hands. She soon realized that none of them knew what had happened. Gloria would have said the same thing if Jennie and Doris had jumped on the velvet couch and made love.

'Get out of our hive,' Gloria said again, and this time Jim Browning and a few others joined in, like actors who've waited too long for their cue. 'Get out,' they said. 'You don't belong here.' Soon the children were chanting it and clapping their hands. 'Get out, get out, get out of our hive.'

To Gloria, Jennie said, 'I suppose the hive will buy my house?'

Al nodded. 'That's the usual procedure.'

'Researched it, have you?' She looked at the crowd. They were laughing, shouting, so excited. 'All of you,' she called out, 'listen to me.' An amazed silence rolled through the mob. 'Where is this going to get you? You think it'll make you happy? You think it'll take away your pain? Or replace what you've lost? Can it replace what the Tellers have taken away from you?'

Someone shouted, 'Liar! The Tellers give us everything,' and someone else added, 'They gave us the Revolution.'

'They've thrown away the Revolution,' Jennie said. 'You all know that. You just don't want to admit it. They got scared and threw the Revolution away as soon as they could.'

Someone started a droning chant of protection and soon most of the crowd had taken it up. A few people yelled, 'Get out, get out, get out of our hive.'

Jennie called, 'You've got to start doing things for yourselves. That's the real lesson. That's what you've got to learn. The Tellers have abandoned you.'

'Liar,' a couple of people shouted, and a few others yelled, 'Evil One!' It was hopeless. The chant boomed in her whole body, people were stamping and clapping to drown her out. Next to Jennie Gloria smiled sweetly at her. *You fucking bitch*, Jennie thought. Gloria, perhaps achieving a moment of telepathy' laughed.

Jennie took a step down the hill, then stopped. Turning her head side to side she looked at the wild faces. She said, 'Once, the mother of all the people lived among her children.'

Near Jennie the adults and the children stopped chanting. They sat down in a semi-circle in front of her, listening. 'The Mother lived in a stone building in the centre of the city.' Now more people were sitting down. Jennie spoke no louder than when she used to stand in the kitchen and talk with Karen; but the drones were dying, and the whistles, the clapping. 'All day she sat outside on a bench and the people could come and touch her.'

'What are you doing?' Gloria said, but she was whispering, and no one paid her any attention. And then she too listened, as Jennifer Mazdan told her a story.

THE QUEEN OF THE PROM: A version of Jennifer Mazdan's story, as remembered and written down years later by Susan Rich (five years old on the day of the Telling):

Once, the mother of all the people lived among her children. She lived in a stone building in the centre of the city. All day she sat outside on a wooden bench, and the people could come and touch her.

At first everyone gave her offerings and came to sit beside her, telling her all the news. But after a while people forgot. At night they would play loud music so she couldn't sleep. In winter, children threw snowballs at her to see them melt. If it rained, people would wipe their hands on her as they passed. In the old days, which people came to think of as a dream, they would paint their cars with the Mother's favourite colours, then dress themselves in the skins of her favourite animals to drive past in a slow procession from dark until midnight on the Rising of the Light. As the bells rang for midnight they would switch on the lights and honk their horns. But now that dreamtime had ended, and people dressed in black leather raced their cars throughout the year along the 'old straight track' as people called the highway that ran in front of the Mother's house. The air filled with smoke, while every morning the road stank of rubber.

On the Day of Truth one year a woman wanted to spice

354

up her pot of Founder's Stew. She sneaked up behind the Mother, who sat sleeping on her bench. With a small knife the woman cut a little piece of skin and ran back to chop it up into the stew. Everyone liked it so much she went back the following week and soon every day, and then she told her friends, and all the women of the neighbourhood began to sneak out at night with scarves or stockings over their faces and black knives in their hands. It doesn't hurt her, they told themselves. It'll just grow back. She's so big she'll never even notice.

And then one morning the Mother was gone. She had changed herself into a river to flow around the city and down to the sea. A storm came. The river began to flood the town, and everyone stood on their rooftops to beg the Mother to let them live. Water roared through the streets. Finally a young woman painted her body with spirals inscribed with pleas for forgiveness. Then she leapt into the flood. She vanished, but soon after that the storm ended and the river settled into a normal path.

The city council kept the girl's death a secret, announcing only that the tears of all the people had melted their Mother's rage. For several years the river remained placid. The town decided that the Mother had given them a blessing. They built sewage plants and factories and let the pipes drain into the water. Then one year the water began to rise again and the sky darkened with clouds. The mayor and the city manager and the Chief of Police met secretly to plan what to do. The river needed a sacrifice, they decided, another woman who would give herself so that the town might live. They came up with a plan. The high school had just chosen its Queen of the Prom. They would go to the Queen's house, tell her she had won a special award and lead her out of town. Then they would give her a chocolate filled with drugs to make her sleep. They would tie her up, dress her in a white gown, and throw her in the water. The Chief of Police, who had just trained a pack of ferocious dogs, suggested they should kill her first. Leave her overnight, he said, let the dogs loose at her, and then in the morning they would give her to the river.

Now, the city manager tried to say that that was not what had happened before. Then, the woman herself had dived into the water. In fact, he said, no one really knew that she had drowned. Children playing by the river sometimes claimed they saw a beautiful woman dancing on the water. Maybe, he said, they should ask for a volunteer. Or maybe one of them should give himself. The others told him he was being ridiculous. There was no time, they said. They needed to act.

When they came to the Prom Queen's house her younger sister opened the door. The girl thought the mayor looked suspicious. Instead of calling her sister the girl said that she was the Queen. 'Come with us,' they told her, 'you've just won an award.' The girl went to get her things and on the way she went into the kitchen and gathered a knife and several biscuits which she had just baked as a present for her sister.

The mayor led her to the river and gave her the chocolate. The girl sniffed it, and realizing it was drugged, she didn't swallow it. Instead, she pretended to fall down asleep, and when the mayor and his gang weren't looking she spat it out into her hand. They dressed her in the gown and tied her up to leave her by the water.

As soon as they were gone the girl cut her ropes with the knife, and climbed up a tree. When the dogs came she threw them the biscuits and they ran off, never to bother anyone again. At dawn the mayor returned to throw the body into the river. He saw the girl lying on the ground, the ropes gone, her dress and body untouched. Surprised, he bent down to look closer. The girl leaped up and jammed the chocolate into his mouth. Before he could think, the mayor had swallowed the drug and a moment later he lay asleep on the ground.

The girl ran home. She sent her family away and locked all the doors, drawing seals of protection on them so the police couldn't break in. The telephone rang. The girl pulled it out of the wall.

Soon the mayor arrived, leading a team of council men, teachers, and police. Please come out, they begged her, they

356

just wanted to speak to her. The girl didn't answer. Then the mayor shouted that it was true they wanted to offer her to the river. But she had to think of the rest of them. Already it had started to rain and the water was rising. The girl's teachers joined in, reminding her how they had tried to instil a sense of civic duty in her.

Finally the girl became so sick of all this that she told them she would go and speak to the Mother. By now a TV crew had come up and the girl knew the mayor wouldn't dare attack her. So she marched to the river, with the whole crowd behind her. When they got there they saw that the water ran black and thick and the sky hung grey with clouds. The frightened people all ran away, leaving the girl alone by the water.

'Please,' she said, 'why are you attacking us? No one ever meant any harm.' But the water only splashed over the girl, and the sky thundered. She went home and once again barricaded herself in her house. When she looked in the mirror she discovered that she had aged and was no longer a girl.

Once again the crowds surrounded the house. Now all her friends from school joined them, begging her to save them. Again she left the house and again everyone fled when they came to the river. Clouds sat upon the Earth, and the wind blew. The woman said, 'They're frightened. They know how weak they are, and the world scares them. That's why they behave so badly. Can't you forgive them?' A wave of oily water crashed down on her. When she got home and looked in the mirror she discovered she had become an old woman.

Now her own family had joined the crowd. 'Why should everyone die,' they told her, 'just so you can live? Do you think that's right?' Disgusted, she left the house. When they saw how she'd aged they wanted to run, but she insisted she would only go to the river if they all followed her.

As they came closer they saw great rocks fly through the air. Beyond the river the mountains trembled, while all about them the clouds smashed against each other. The old woman called to the river, 'I understand. They're no good. But can't you let go of them anyway?' The rain swept over her in a

357

great roar of wind. The people fell down and covered their eyes, but the old woman shouted at them to watch.

She stepped into the river. The rain ended, and the ground stopped shaking. She took a step further. The water rose over her waist, but above her the clouds began to clear. Finally the waves of foam covered her head. The sun came out and the water ran smooth again.

For a long time no one could see anything of the old woman. Some of the people went back to town, but others waited for the body to float to the surface. All night they sat there, silently staring at the water and holding hands, while back in town the others got drunk and ran through the streets.

Morning came. The people who'd celebrated woke up sick and no one wanted to look at anyone else. All day they argued, and at night they lay awake, afraid to sleep. By the river, however, the smooth silver of the water began to ripple. The girl stepped out, as young as when the mayor had first come knocking on her door. She led the people upstream to a place where the air was sweet and the water as pure as the sun. There they created a new city. In the centre of it they built a stone house, with a wooden bench. When the girl became an old woman she would sit there, and the people would sit beside her and tell her their stories.

When Jennie finished speaking she stood there, staring in amazement at the amazed faces of the crowd. She was dizzy and she had to grab hold of someone not to fall down. For a moment she thought they'd flown again, lifted together into the sky, only this time she too had forgotten. She began to walk down the hill. Someone – Karen? Gloria? – reached out to touch her. She kept going. At the bottom she turned to lean against someone's car. She looked up at them. They all just stood there, unmoving, their faces as clean as the snow.

20

That night Jennie slept over at Marilyn Birdan's house, and the next day she moved into a motel on Route 44, in Pleasant Valley. Three days later she brought her two suitcases to a dreary apartment on Cannon Street, east of Market Street and the county offices building. The following week she went back to the hive with Mar and a van full of cartons to pack whatever she didn't want to leave behind. The whole day, as Jennie and Mar worked, people seemed to hover round the house: children on bicycles, adults walking or driving, they would come close, slowing down or stopping in the road, stay for a moment or two, and then hurry on. Jennie even thought she caught a glimpse of Gloria Rich at the line dividing the two lawns.

After a while Mar began to notice the parade of neighbours. 'Hey,' she said to Jennie, 'maybe you should go speak to these people.'

'Why?' Jennie asked.

'Maybe they're sorry, you know?'

'Then let them come and say so. Let them come knock on the door, ask to come in, and tell me they're sorry.'

'Hey, they're probably scared.'

'That's no excuse.'

'Wow. You're really tough, you know that? I never knew you were so tough.'

'Tough,' Jennie repeated. 'Blessed Spirits. Tough.' She turned and began packing towels, afraid she'd start to cry and ruin her new image. If only Karen would come. Karen was the only one she really cared about.

359

If she just came, just up the walk, she wouldn't have to say anything, or even knock, Jennie would run out to get her. But Karen had to make that effort. It wasn't pride; Jennie didn't care about that. It all had to do with choice. Karen had to choose to come to her.

Three weeks after Jennie moved her belongings the estate agent closed the deal selling the house and furniture at an assessed price to the committee representing Glowwood Hive. With the money from the sale Jennie could have moved to a more modern apartment on a street with trees instead of offices. She thought about it. She looked at the rent ads in the *Poughkeepsie Journal*, and even circled a couple. She never got around to calling them.

On the night that Jennie's house was sold, in homes up and down the hive, people found themselves fighting with each other or bursting into tears or tripping and banging their shins against the bathtub. On Cannon Street, meanwhile, the residents all broke into laughter at the exact moment that the Sun set, while shortly after nine o'clock many people claimed they saw a large bird circling above the street. The next day people who had been driving on Cannon Street the night before claimed that a formation of either flying saucers or winged women had hovered above the buildings and then returned to their secret bases far from human knowledge.

More from *That Story*

On the seventy-eighth day of the rule of 'Mr President' it happened that in a certain suburb of the Democratic City of God a lion attacked a young woman who had gone out in the street thinking she heard someone weeping and calling her name. The next night the lion came again and killed a waiter who had stepped behind his restaurant to retrieve a bottle of wine. After two more deaths the community sent a delegation to ask the risen President to destroy the evil.

The President and the remains of the administration marched through the city, accompanied by child drummers, rows of police carrying banners, and sacred messengers circling overhead. They arrived at the village square and they stood among the flowers and the cracked concrete while the exhausted sun lowered itself beyond the edge of the world.

It came. Slowly walking, its back and shoulders rippling, its gold skin flecked with black, its mane like a curled halo about its face, it stopped six feet away from her. The movement of its muscles flicked light into the air. For an instant words formed and then the bits of light broke apart in the sun. With its head tilted slightly to the left the lion stared at her, while her hands hung open and her ceremonial gun fell beside her feet. One of the police lifted his rifle; she knocked it out of his hands.

It's him, she thought. He *has* come back. Not for them, but for me. He couldn't bear to leave me.

The lion strolled away.

Jennie's apartment occupied one-half of the top floor of a four storey building across the street from the Cannon Street parking lot. A small legal firm kept the ground floor bright and clean, a contrast with the rest of the building. Two doors down stood a large building with high rounded windows in between white stone columns. Letters chiselled in the stone blocks above the door pronounced it a 'Masonic Temple.' Jennie had no idea what that might mean. On the other side of this curious building stood a modest bank with the immodest name, Empire of America.

The other apartment on Jennie's floor housed a divorced hotel manager. Below Jennie lived a hair-dresser whose front door displayed a medallion of the Hidden Sisters, from Cleveland – his home town, he explained to Jennie. The hotel manager was an

361

alcoholic; Jennie could smell it on his body, and she suspected he wouldn't be holding on to his hotel much longer than he'd held on to his wife. The hairdresser now and then played his stereo late at night, but he always stopped when Jennie banged on the floor, and the next day he would bow his head, as if posing for a government poster urging penitence. If he saw Jennie on the stairs he would ask how the baby was doing, how much time she had, whether or not he could do any errands for her, if she'd decided on names, and did she want him to call the hospital or the midwives when the moment came.

The apartment – three small rooms, kitchen, and bath – looked like the last occupants had belonged to one of those groups who vow never to clean themselves or their homes, as a penance for some crime committed in a past life. 'Dirt-lovers' people called them, or just 'dirties.' As Jennie scraped at the grease coating the cooker, or carried away the shower curtain at arm's length, she thought how the dirties could have held their national convention right there in her apartment.

When Jennie had lived there for a week it came time for the 'Rising of the Light', the most important of the Winter Enactments. All over town, people were crowding the department stores for last minute presents, queueing at the supermarket for turkeys, baking cakes in the shape of sunbursts, and ironing white dresses or polishing white boots. Jennie made sure to stay in all that day. As evening approached she thought of everyone squeezing into their neighbourhood Picture Halls, all of them wearing long black coats or even opera capes to conceal their white clothes. At nine o'clock the heat died in the radiators; Jennie banged on the pipes and when that failed she went down to the second floor where the superintendent lived. No one was home. *He's gone to the Enactment,*

362

Jennie realized. *He's turned off the goddamn heat because he's figured everyone's gone to the Enactment.* She climbed the stairs back to her apartment. When she got there she lay down on the bed she'd bought the week before (the apartment had come furnished but Jennie had thrown out the bed after one night) and covered herself with the quilt Betsy Rodriguez's mother had given her in college. There she lay, imagining the Tellers intoning the Pictures, seeing everyone lighting their gold candles, hearing the shouts as the spotlights came on in the Hall and everyone threw off their black coverings to hug and kiss each other in their whites.

Late that night whoops of laughter from the hairdresser's apartment jerked Jennie awake. 'Damn it,' she said, and sat up, all set to bang her shoe on the floor. Then she remembered what night it was. For nearly a minute she sat there on the edge of the bed, itching in the reborn heat. At last she got up and went to run a bath. In the street people were honking their horns and singing. Jennie sat on the toilet and waited for the water to fill up the bathtub.

She should have accepted her mother's invitation to come 'home' for the holiday. She shrugged. Too late now. She stared at the water as the beat of an electric bass pounded in the walls.

21

Maria sent Jennie home on a Thursday, the sixth work day in a row Jennie had arrived late for the morning prayers and assignments. 'Take off,' she told Jennie, 'I'm putting you on maternity leave.'

'What are you talking about?' Jennie asked. 'The baby's not due for two months yet.'

Maria shrugged. 'What the hell, I can always make it sick leave.'

'I don't want to be sick.'

'Doesn't matter what you want.'

'Maria, I can do the work. I just have trouble getting going in the morning.'

'And getting back at night. You think I don't know how late you come in? I see your goddamn time card. And I give you the easiest routes.'

'But I want to work. I can do it.'

'Come on, you look like shit.' Maria rubbed her braid between her fingers. 'Look, I had this dream a couple of nights ago. Weird stuff, all about collecting urine samples in old milk cartons, and then the President coming down in a helicopter and telling me I did it all wrong. Anyway, I went and got the dream done, down at the OA, and you know what NORA said? She said I'm ignoring a responsibility. So I looked around and you're it. You're the only ignored responsibility I could find.'

'It's the Agency,' Jennie said. 'It must want me out of here for some reason.'

'Do me a favour, don't start that agency stuff, okay?

Look, I'm not going to change my mind. So go home and relax.'

'Relax.' With a grunt Jennie picked up her bag from the front row of wooden chairs. 'What should I do, go home and paint the nursery?'

'You could try praying for a good delivery.'

'Sure. That's just what I'll do.'

Back in her car Jennie made a face as she squeezed her stomach under the wheel. She wished she could move the seat back further, but she already had trouble reaching the pedals. On the way home she stopped at the mall for some groceries. All up and down the aisles people were looking at her, working out how much time she had. By the time Jennie reached the checkout counter she was so angry she nearly broke a bottle of juice slamming it down on the counter.

Back in her apartment Jennie told herself, *It's almost over. Less than two months. And then it's done. Finished.* She was crouching down with a paper towel to scoop some rotten radishes from the vegetable bin when it suddenly struck her – nothing would finish but the pregnancy. She would have a baby in two months time, and unless the Agency somehow arranged to take care of it, she would end up stuck with it. The idea, and the fact that it had never occurred to her before, struck Jennie so forcibly that the air glittered in front of her. Grabbing the edge of the refrigerator she kept herself from falling backward until she could go sit down on one of the wooden chairs.

'I'll be stuck with it,' she said. And then another thought came to her. 'It's my baby. It's going to be my child.' She laughed at her own astonishment. Whatever the Agency had done to put it there, the baby was growing in her body. It belonged to her. Her baby.

That night Jennie found herself unable to fall asleep.

No position seemed comfortable; on her stomach impossible, on her back too weighed down, on either side too unbalanced. She alternately crunched and fluffed the pillows, she tried reading, she tried more blankets, then less, nothing worked. The two or three times she thought she might drop off she kept thinking she had to pee and by the time she got back in bed she was awake again. Just as she thought she should give up and go watch television, the baby began to sing to her.

A flash of anger gave way almost instantly to eager relaxation. Her arms and legs lay loose as doughy lumps lying on the bed. She smiled. This was her child singing to her. There was no reason to fight it. Not any more. It was her child. And then even her smile drained out of her face, and she eased into deep sleep.

Outside, in the street and in the neighbouring houses, people saw a light flare up in a window on the fourth floor of 221 Cannon Street. It started in one room but soon spread to the other windows, and then the whole building. Calls came in to the Fire Department. Though the firemen connected their hoses they somehow couldn't bring themselves to start pumping the water. Meanwhile, those firemen who most recently had received a blessing against smoke inhalation ran through the building with their axes riding on their shoulders. They found all the doors unlocked and all the inhabitants asleep. In the fire room itself, there were no flames and the air was so cool it massaged their windpipes and lungs. None of them, however, could bear to look at the sleeping woman. The light around her body shone as brightly as that burst that once struck down a certain federal judge named Li Ku on the road to Cincinatti.

When the light subsided, the firemen left, and after them the crowd. All of them encountered a great reluc-

366

tance in themselves to tell anyone what they had seen. A television crew had come, as well as reporters from the *Poughkeepsie Journal*, but when they developed their films and ran their tapes they found them ruined, the same as with similar crews at the town abortion clinic some five months before. Somehow, the lack of any pictures induced the journalists to report the event as a minor incident, giving no details, either as to the woman's name or the street where she lived.

A report did go to the Dutchess County SDA, where it swam through the bureaucracy to reach a certain Flying Squad investigator. Sitting in her office with her chair back and her wingtip shoes on the desk, she glanced at the one page account and threw it on a pile. She picked it up again to look through the jargon for the name of the woman. 'Sonofabitch,' she said, and wrote a long note at the bottom of the page.

The report never entered the files. For no reason she could name she folded it very carefully and placed it in her wallet. That evening, on the way home, she stopped at a spiritual supply shop, where she bought a small relic case made of sanctified steel, with a silver neck-chain. In her apartment she took out the offering pin her parents had given her when she'd finished her training. With a single drop of blood she bonded herself to the report, and then she placed it in the case and the case around her neck. There it remained for the rest of her life. When she died and the curious undertakers opened the case they found only ashes that blew into the air as soon as a curious finger tried to touch them.

A piece of the Story of SHE WHO RUNS AWAY

Mr President left the Bleached House in the same disguise she had worn the night she found her husband pumping dust into the sky. She wore the same clothes, but she no longer

367

had to battle her beauty. The sun had evaporated the layers of her splendour. No longer did she need a coating of kitchen grease to persuade the clothes to stay against her body. No longer did the sight of her exposed face cause stone to sweat with anxiety.

As quickly as her mismatched legs would move her she made her way through the city towards the suburb where she had seen the lion. Along the way she passed a sleeping lizard, a huge beast over six feet long. The creature had lain there since before the Sacred President had built his city. The first construction teams had tried to move it, but when all their cranes and pulleys broke they'd raised the city around it, so that in some places the Democratic City of God was known as the City of the Lizard.

That night, the creature raised its thick eyelids and hissed at the passing woman. She heard a voice hidden in the sound and knew that she had received her new name, to wear until the day of her death, when all earthly names are blown away in the storms that forever border the circles of the dead. She Who Runs Away. It's not true, she thought. She was running to her husband. Together they would return and crush their enemies. Together they would build a world better in all ways than this decaying monstrosity.

When She Who Runs Away reached the suburb she found the lion waiting for her. She limped towards him, but before she could touch him, he ran. He stopped several hundred feet away from her. Crouched down, he waited until she came within a few feet and then he once again loped out of reach. In this way he led her away from the city and into the flatlands she had dreaded for so many years. Each night, when she could no longer stand but must fall asleep on the ground, the lion would lie down just beyond the length of her arm. When she woke up she would find food beside her, a freshly killed animal or bird. And beyond that, the lion, waiting.

Then one day they came to a hilly country, filled with stunted trees, half completed government offices, and abandoned machines decaying into stone. Here, on slanted ground, she could stand upright again for the first time since

368

she had left her house. Though she could move more quickly she kept to her earlier pace, and though she no longer felt tired she mimed exhaustion at the usual time of day. When she lay down, the lion came to join her.

She leaped on him. She flung her arms around his neck and rolled across his body. When she slid under him he pinned her shoulders and legs to the ground. They locked together for three days until the heat of their bodies split the Earth under the woman's back and she fell into a damp crevice. When she climbed out again the lion was gone.

22

Enactment For 'Consecrating a Baby to Serve the Blessed Spirit'

If the mother, during or before pregnancy, receives a true message that she must surrender her child to the powers, and if the message is confirmed by a speaker, she must tell this to the midwives during the pre-natal consultations. When the mother's time comes the team of three midwives brings with them a fourth, who wears a faceless mask and does not take part in the birth, but waits at the foot of the bed.

After the birth, when the three active midwives have cleaned the baby and properly disposed of the after-birth, they take positions around the head and the sides of the mother's bed, and then all four wait for the first feeding. This feeding establishes the baby in the world, for it is dangerous to attempt a consecration while the child still remains partly in the land of origins. After the feeding, the midwives take the baby from the mother and lay it on a blanket, on the consecration table if the birth takes place in a hospital or, if at home, on a clean tabletop, preferably wood, and preferably with squared corners. With a compass they arrange the table so that the baby's head points north.

The fourth midwife takes from its case a wooden wand carved from the heart of a tree in one of the national forests. Each of the four presses the wand to her forehead and her lips. When the wand has returned to the faceless midwife she uses it to draw a double spiral in the air above the child. The midwife on the right holds up her hands, palms up. She says, 'I give this child to the sun,' and flings up her arms. The midwife on the left repeats the action, saying, 'I give this child to the moon.' The midwife at the head says, 'I give this child to the wind,' and finally the midwife at the feet, the faceless midwife, raises her arms and cries, 'I give this child to the sea of dreams.'

In this way they open the vertical axis, from the great above to the great below, for the child to discover the gift, forever offered yet forever rejected by those who live only in the flat world of hunger and appeasement.

Jennie was in Sears buying some electrical tape to repair a lamp when something hardened inside her. It started in her lower abdomen and spread throughout her groin, like a body builder flexing his back. Carefully, in more fear than pain, she made her way out of the store to the Bagel Nosh restaurant. By the time she eased herself into a chair her uterus – she knew it was the uterus, she knew that much – had loosened up again. It couldn't be labour, she thought. She wasn't ready yet. It was weeks too soon. When the waitress came Jennie ordered a Founder's Delight, the cream cheese and anchovy bagel that Irina Speakeagle supposedly ate whenever she visited New York.

The contractions didn't return until the next day, and by that time Jennie had searched through the books on pregnancy she'd bought weeks before and stacked on the floor beside her bed. She recognised the pains now as preliminary contractions, the uterus getting itself in shape. Nothing to worry about. They hardly even hurt. According to all the books, the real thing would hurt much more than any of these feeble exercises.

And suddenly it occurred to her, after so many

months, that without midwives or doctors, without friends, she'd have to deliver the baby herself.

She tried to remember the name of the midwife agency the doctor had recommended. Something Blood or something. Maybe she still had the card somewhere. Maybe she could find it in the phone book. What would they say if she called them so late? She could always just go to the hospital. But she didn't even have a doctor.

And then she sat up, as straight as she could. No, she thought. This wasn't like other pregnancies. This baby wasn't like other babies. With a glance at her belly, she said, 'You'll take care of us, won't you? We don't need any outsiders.'

The foetus didn't answer.

On the evening of March 20, the day before the vernal equinox, a sudden storm struck the mid-Hudson valley, knocking down telephone lines and TV antennas. At Recital Mount north of town, and at the local Picture Halls around Poughkeepsie, the wooden huts built to celebrate Spring collapsed under the weight of snow and ice. At some of the Halls the doors blew open, drenching the Tellers rehearsing their processions from the entranceway to the altar.

At Cannon Street Jennifer Mazdan, wearing only a bathrobe, fell asleep a little after ten. For more than two days she'd felt occasional twinges of pain, not enough to commandeer her attention. At a quarter past midnight on March 21, she woke up to discover a contraction shaking her body. When she looked between her legs she saw that a small amount of mucous had leaked out to stain her robe and the chair. Her labour had begun. She had no idea what to do.

The midwives broke into Jennie's house sometime in

the early morning. It wasn't difficult. Jennie had not bothered to put the chain bolt on, and one of the wives had spent twenty years as a burglar before a Devoted One, in the form of a parole officer, had laid a hand on her shoulder and suggested she put herself in the service of moving babies from the darkness to the light. They broke in and they took a look at Jennie's feeble preparations, her plastic washbasins, her stack of towels, her pile of books beside the bed, and one of them, a heavy woman with curly red hair and a slight limp, began clearing the area around the bed, while the other two, the burglar and a skinny man whose long hands and feet stuck out from his yellow overalls, began carrying in and setting up equipment.

Jennie's reactions bounced between outrage, relief, betrayal. For hours she'd lain on her bed, getting up only to go to the toilet, reading all her books, trying out different postures and movements, practising breathing techniques she knew she should have practised for weeks, and fighting off panic each time another contraction swept away all her belated study. She knew that she couldn't do it all herself. Once – early – she'd grabbed the phone to call her mother. But the phone was dead, knocked out by the storm.

The thing was, Jennie still didn't expect she would have to do it all herself. The baby would take care of it. She just had to wait, just hang on through the pain and terror, just until the singing started. But the hours had gone by and her womb had stayed silent.

And so, when the scratching at the lock heralded not thieves ('Go away!' she'd shouted, 'I'll call the police. Go away or you'll be struck down. This house is protected by God') but midwives, Jennie's outrage could hardly hold its own against her relief. Someone had come for her. Help had come. And yet, they were

373

outsiders. They belonged to – the other side, the Tellers.

The midwives set up machines, laid out instruments, washed her and dressed her in a hospital gown, turned up the heat and the lights, all the time chanting Jaleen Heart of the World's birth story (the model for all births) in a sing-song call and response that made them sound like one person raising and lowering her voice.

Jennie looked from one to the other. The big one, with the limp and the red hair, wore the mask of the beautiful woman. The man represented the hag while the burglar, a small woman with a lined neck and whitish blotches on the back of her hands, was the young girl. They all wore overalls over pink sweatshirts. On each overall's left front pocket, embroidered over a picture of Heart of the World, appeared the words, 'Holy Blood Birthing.'

'How'd you find me?' Jennie asked. 'Who told you?'

She thought at first that their hesitation signalled a reluctance to betray their informant, but a moment later the redhead leaned forward and said, 'You'd better thank the Devoted Ones for their devotion, because it's certain that nothing you've done deserves their precious intervention.' Jennie looked from her to the small one, the girl, who explained that the three of them, each in her or his apartment, had received an impulse to go to the hospital, despite the storm, despite the early hour, and visit a child they'd delivered the day before. When they'd arrived in the nursery the child had begun to speak to them, telling them that a woman needed their help, and they must go, without doctors or healers or anyone else, to a certain apartment on Cannon Street, where the supervisor would let them into the building.

'You'd better give thanks,' the woman said again.

374

'There's someone looking out for you even if you won't look out for yourself.'

Whatever Jennie might have answered vanished as a contraction took hold of her body. While the man timed her and the redhead examined her the burglar massaged her abdomen, beginning above the groin and spreading out towards the hip bones. 'Try to relax,' she told Jennie. 'Breathe deeply. Have you ever done any meditation classes?'

'In college,' Jennie said. 'Club med.'

'Then do some pre-trance breathing. Low and deep.'

'I don't want any meditation.'

'No, no. Just the breathing. Just try to relax.'

The man, the hag, said, 'That's the wrong rhythm. She's already starting to dilate.'

'I know,' the girl said, 'but there's no time to teach her anything fancy. We've just got to get her to relax.'

Jennie paid no attention to either of them. The pain kept rising until she thought it could float her right off the bed. And in fact the hag and the girl were holding her down, one on her hips, the other hanging on to her legs. It was only when the pain subsided that Jennie realised they were just keeping her still while the woman shaved her groin.

Jennie didn't want her groin shaved. She remembered lunar enactments in her dorm at college where a few of the girls had shaved each other. It had given her a queasy feeling just to look at them. Her attempts to twist away only made them press harder. The redhead said, 'Don't move. Don't make this any more of a mess than it already is,' and the burglar added, 'It's all right. This doesn't hurt. Just relax. We're not going to hurt you.'

By the time they'd finished, another contraction had started. While Jennie grabbed the sides of the mattress, and the burglar urged her again to relax, the other two

375

stood on the side and argued over something. The burglar joined them, and when she came back to Jennie she said, 'My Mother –' (Jennie looked from one to the other until she realised the term was an official one; the woman would refer to the man as her 'Grandmother') ' – thinks we should take you to the hospital. I agree. Will you go to the hospital? There's still time.'

'I want to stay here.'

Gently she said, 'You can't stay here. There's no preparation. You don't know what you're doing.'

'No hospital.'

The Mother said, 'We can't force you. We've got our wonderful courts to thank for that. Not unless there's an outright emergency. And by then it'll probably be too late.'

'No hospital.'

The daughter asked, 'Who's your doctor?'

'No doctor.'

'We've got to at least call him so we'll know whether you need anything special.'

Jennie was about to say she didn't have a doctor when she remembered the phone was out. She gave the name of the doctor at the clinic on Smith Street.

'A clinic,' the Mother said. 'Great. It'll be closed today. Let's hope he's at home and not doing some private penance ahead of the enactment. Where's the phone?'

'In there,' Jennie said and pointed back to the living room. She lay down and closed her eyes until the redhead came in again.

'Not working,' the midwife said. 'We better not take any chances.' She turned to the Grandmother. 'Maybe you better drive down to the hospital and have them send back an ambulance.'

'No hospital,' Jennie said again.

'Damn it,' the woman said, 'what's the matter with you?'

'The Devoted One,' Jennie said. 'It told you no one else. Remember?'

There was a pause and then the Mother said, 'All right, all right. We'll stay here. But at the first sign of real trouble you're going. Do you understand?'

Jennie said, 'Why are you treating me like this? I thought midwives were friendly.'

The woman laughed. The 'Daughter' took Jennie's hand. 'Don't mind her,' she said. 'She just gets excited.' The Grandmother, the man, picked up an aluminium case from among the neat pile of instruments. He placed it on the floor and the three of them bent down to lay their hands on it. When they'd pronounced a sanctification he unlatched it and they took out several small jars of paint, three brushes, and a velvet box with ribbons, costume jewellery, and small objects attached to strings. Just as Jennie's body began to harden for another contraction they began to paint signs and stick figures on her breasts and abdomen. 'Stop that,' Jennie said, and tried to push or kick them away. 'I don't want any of that.'

Smoothly they switched to one of them painting while the others held her down. The redhead told her, 'Now you listen to me. We're not in the mood for any more of your sec nonsense.'

'Sec?' Jennie repeated. 'You think I'm a secular? Is that why you're treating me like this?'

'What the hell are we supposed to think? No guardians by the bed, none over the door – '

'I'm not a sec.'

'I don't care what you call yourself. We came because the Benign One sent us and because it's our duty. And because the baby can't help your perverted ideas. But we're not giving you the chance to sue us

377

later for malpractice. If you try to rub off the paint, or take off any of these adornments, or break the enactment in any other way, we'll strap down your arms and legs. That's a promise. Do you understand?' Jennie didn't answer. 'Say yes.'

'Yes.'

When they'd finished the painting they decorated Jennie with bracelets and ribbons, stones and feathers. Afterwards they unrolled a ball of red yarn and laid it clockwise around the border of the room. The daughter announced, 'This room has now entered the Living World.' While the Grandmother sprinkled rock salt in a circle around Jennie's bed, the Mother taped a stuffed rag doll above the door and the Daughter covered the door itself with a chalk drawing of Mothersnake giving birth to her children. Through all of this they intoned a health and safety chant, invoking Jaleen Heart Of The World, Mothersnake, the living spirit of the Earth and the Sky, and the Chained Mother underneath the sea. After the first few verses they paused for Jennie to answer them or join in. When Jennie said nothing, the Mother shook her head in disgust, while the Grandmother sang louder and the Daughter wiped Jennie's forehead.

The foetus fed on the last remnants of her beauty. Wherever she went people turned away from her. They threw stones, they stoned her the way they'd stoned the President when he was a boy and called himself Son Of A God. Wherever she tried to rest they drove her away, frightened her tongue would poison the water, her toes would infect the soil. Posters warned people of 'the hideous woman' whose sweat could spoil the food in the supermarkets, whose stare could make men beat their wives, make women stab their husbands. She hid during the day and at night disguised her ugliness the way she once had disguised her beauty.

She planned her revenge. When the baby came, when their

378

child came, when it grew and could wear the Head of His Father, then all those who had humiliated her would receive their punishment. She longed for their confusion as well as their agony, their wonder at why they were suffering, and she pictured the exquisite moment in which she would step from the shadows to confront her dying enemies. 'Look at my face and remember.'

There was no Sun that day. Though the wind stopped by nine a.m. a squadron of clouds stood guard against the light. In the midst of her pain Jennie remembered the storyteller on Hudson Street, with her prophecy of a three day darkness. She thought *I can't last three days, it's too much.*

Shortly after ten the doors opened and a man in jeans and a short white jacket strolled into the room. He carried a canvas bag slung over his right shoulder. To the midwives' questions he said only, 'You three look awfully hungry. I'll bet you haven't had any breakfast.' He reached into the sack and with his left hand held out three chocolate chip cookies. They each took a bite, and another, and slowly the exhaustion and the anger and the confusion all drained out of their bodies, replaced by peace and a kind of surprise that was almost recognition.

'What have you got for me?' Jennie said. 'I hope it's strong.'

'I'm sorry,' he said, sitting down in the chair the Grandmother had placed beside the bed. 'I'm afraid you'll have to go on a little more.' He picked up a compress and wiped the sweat from her face. The touch of his fingers, even through the gauze, sent a warm shudder through her body. 'Too much suffering,' she said.

'Suffering's not something you can measure. There's no quota or upper limit. It's just there.'

'No lectures,' Jennie said, and gasped in pain. 'No goddamn lectures.'

He became her nurse, massaging her, directing her breathing, reassuring her she would get through it. 'Take me to a hospital,' Jennie demanded, and he told her it was too late. 'Am I being punished?' she asked him, and he explained again how things were just the way they were. She paid no attention, only screamed with the pain, and wondered afterwards why the neighbours didn't bang on the walls or call the police.

Again and again, looking at the dream-soaked faces of the midwives, she asked him for one of his cookies. Each time he told her it wouldn't work on her the way it worked on them. Finally, in the late afternoon, he held one out to her. 'What flavour is it?' she asked.

'Chocolate-chocolate chunk.'

'Is that the one you gave them?' He didn't answer. As the next contraction began she grabbed the cookie and jammed it in her mouth.

She was spinning round, slowly turning, with her naked body strapped to something. A ferris wheel, she was tied to a ferris wheel, she'd got one of the faceless Workers to do it, that was days ago, for days she'd turned round and round, her feet and head exchanging the sky between them. Flickers of red and orange light tinted the air. She remembered now, she was on fire, the story had appeared and set fire to her, she could feel that blessed heat surge through her body, 'a sweetness beyond description', as Adrienne had called it. Below her she could see the glow on the faces of the people standing watch at the base of the wheel. And beyond them she saw the city and the burning buildings of the Revolution.

Soon the Workers would take her down. She could

lie in a bed again, rest. But not yet. First she had to wait for the story to finish. The 'Picture' as Danielle would say. She could almost feel the end now. The last pieces had begun to climb out from the crack that had opened in the world.

'You bastard,' Jennie said. 'You gave me the wrong cookie.' Her nurse paid no attention.

'Listen carefully,' he said. 'You're fully dilated now. The cervix is open. That means the contractions are going to change. Do you understand?' Jennie didn't answer. 'They won't be as regular, and they may hurt a little more.' Jennie shrank away from him. 'But this whole period won't last as long. Only about half an hour. But you mustn't push. Do you understand? It's too soon.'

Jennie shook her head. Flickers of fire scorched the pillow on either side. 'I don't understand anything,' she said.

'I'm going to show you how to breathe,' he said. 'Pay attention.'

'Pay attention,' she repeated. 'That's from Birth of Beauty. Proposition number – ' She gasped in pain.

It was only a small hill, overlaid with ragged flowers like all the others, but as soon as she began to climb she realised she had found it. The centre. The place where she could rest and wait for her baby. At the top she came to an indentation pressed into the rock by the weight of heaven. She Who Runs Away squatted down with her back braced against the curve of stone.

It was time for her children to emerge. More than one. She could feel them rolling around each other.

Jennie did her best to follow the complicated breathing shown her by the cookie vendor. She was supposed to suck in air in small gulps and then blow it out all at once. The trouble was, she could practise it in the in-between times, but as soon as the contractions began everything became confused.

She could feel the baby sliding around in her, as if it had finally woken up and decided it was time to move into position. She wanted to get rid of it, push it out, but he wouldn't allow her. 'You'll rupture the perineum,' he said, whatever the hell that was. Why couldn't he leave her alone?

She smelled something foul, and felt the midwives lifting her, cleaning her off. They were stuffing the sheet in a plastic bag, sliding another sheet under her. The smell followed them as they carried the bag into the bathroom.

Just then a man entered the room. Tall, with white hair, he wore a filthy coat, but when he took it off, his shirt shone so white Jennie winced from the glare. He stood in the doorway, staring round like a sleepwalker waking up in someone else's house.

One of the midwives, the daughter, came up to him and tilted back her head to get a better view through the mask. 'You're Allan Lightstorm,' she said. 'I saw you last Summer. You're Allan Lightstorm.'

Magruder pushed her aside to come and kneel at the foot of the bed. 'Bless me,' he said to Jennie. 'Release me.'

'You're too soon,' Jennie told him. 'I'm not the one.'

When the storm ended, at six o'clock, the owner of a riverside restaurant drove down to check for damage. Before he could even take a look at the building, he heard a loud whistling noise coming off the river. When he went to investigate he saw something, some kind of swarm, rising out of the water just before the mid-Hudson bridge. They looked like insects made of coloured aluminium foil. They hovered in the air in front of the suspension cables, fluttering about like tiny

382

excited birds, all the time whistling. Then they blew away in a gust of wind to vanish over the cliffs on the other side of the river.

The restaurant owner returned to his car. For a while he sat there, staring at the water, trying to remember. He was sure he knew what it was, he just had to remember.

Of course. The children. The souls of the children who had served the Army of the Saints in the Battle of the Waters. For decades they'd clogged the river, scaring the fish, jamming boat rudders, forcing him to close his restaurant every night at ten to avoid the weeping that always began at a quarter past eleven. No one could live there because of the weeping. Most of the land along the riverfront was near worthless because of it. He'd opened his restaurant there because he could get the property so cheap, but he'd always had to fight against people's reluctance to come there during the day.

And now they were gone. Something had released them. He should tell the SDA, he thought. And the papers, and the TV. But first – He laughed and hit the dashboard with excitement. First he would contact an estate agent.

The cookie vendor said, 'It's time to push, Jennifer. Do you understand?' She shook her head. He lifted her shoulders and tilted up her chin. His touch made her smile. For a moment the pain rose off her body to hang in the air in front of her. Then he passed her to the redhaired midwife and the pain sank into her again. 'Come back,' she said, 'don't go away.' The midwife held her gently, with love she stroked Jennie's shoulder.

The cookie vendor hadn't left. Instead, one hand gently tilted back her chin while the other pressed slightly on her lower abdomen. As the next contraction started she found herself pushing, as if she was expelling a deep breath through the vagina. With his hand on her it seemed so effortless. She had no idea how long it lasted. When the contraction ended, and he stood up, she said, 'Is it over now?'

He smiled at her. 'Not yet. Just a few more times.'

'It's not born yet?'

'Almost.'

Someone was holding her hand. Kneeling by the bed. It wasn't the cookie vendor, or the midwives, they were all doing something, supporting her back, her legs. She twisted sideways to see. It was that man with the white shirt – Allan Lightstorm, that's right, the midwife had claimed it was Allan Lightstorm. She laughed, remembering how she'd tried to find him, how that bitch at the Fifth Avenue Hall had refused to tell her anything. She laughed again and closed her eyes.

Jennie never knew how long this final period actually lasted. It carried no sense of time, neither extended nor short, only the endless pushing, which somehow never strained her, but only made her think of a ribbon pulled along in the air. In between, the midwife would let her down on the pillow and her nurse would take his hands away, leaving her alone for the fear and pain to grab hold of her again. But then the pushing would start again and he'd return and it would be all right.

She never saw the baby emerge. The other two midwives had rigged up some mirror at the foot of the bed, and as the pushing came closer to the end, they shouted at her to watch (at least she thought they shouted) but she kept turning her head away, not knowing what it was she was afraid to see, only certain that she couldn't bear to look.

'It's coming,' she heard the Daughter say, 'there's the crown.' The cookie vendor was telling her something, the Grandmother was urging her to look in the mirror . . .

But when she opened her eyes and looked down it wasn't the baby's head she saw, or her own blood and ooze, but people's faces – the face of her mother, of Karen, Mike, even Gloria and Al, all of them smiling as if they'd let go of some burden they'd carried all their lives.

Jennie closed her eyes. The faces vanished. In their place Jennie saw waves, the sea, the water parting. A woman was rising from the sea, her head back, the arms out like a dancer. Her feet touched the bottom of the world, her face rose above the sky, while all about her body pieces of broken chains fell off in the cascading water.

Jennie's eyes snapped open. She stared at the cookie vendor. 'Just a little more,' he told her. 'It's almost done.'

He doesn't know, Jennie thought. *He didn't see*. She laughed loudly.

There were two of them, a male and a female, and they clawed their way free of their mother like athletes in a competition. She Who Runs Away saw only a glimpse before the blood carried her out of her body. She took that glimpse with her, and when the guides took her to her room in the Mansions of the Dead, she saw the image of her children floating on the walls. Lions' heads; thick hands with claws for fingers; human bodies with muscles like stone.

Jennie felt a weight placed on her and she knew the midwives had laid the baby on her belly to give it a chance to adjust to the outside before they cut it loose from the cord connecting it to its home. She'd have to look, she knew, she couldn't keep her head turned away any longer.

For an instant Jennie wasn't sure what she was

seeing. It looked so dark. Then she smiled and reached out a hand to take it. She realised now what she'd expected: a perfectly formed miniature adult, with a light shining round it and a hand raised in sanctification to all those who had assisted in its birth. Instead she saw a wrinkled baby, head like a soggy melon, useless arms, all of it covered in blood and mucous. *It's normal,* she thought to herself. *Oh God, it's normal. It's a normal baby and it's mine. It's my child.*

The midwives were telling her something, some phrase they wanted her to say. She paid no attention, only reached for her baby. 'You've got to welcome it,' the redhead told her. 'Just repeat after me.'

'It's all right,' the cookie vendor assured the midwives. 'She'll be fine. I promise you.' The midwives backed away from the bed, one of them almost tripping over Allan Lightstorm who was still kneeling on the floor. With a confused stare he looked from the baby to the mother, as if he'd been expecting something that hadn't happened.

Jennie turned the baby over and saw it was a girl. A daughter. Her daughter. When she held it to her chest, the bag with Li Ku's skin pressed between them. 'Li Ku is the truth,' that woman had told her. But Jennie Mazdan was also the truth. Love was the truth.

One of the midwives, the Daughter, tugged gently at the baby. Jennie held on. 'We'll give it right back,' the burglar said. 'I promise. We've just got to cut the cord and chase away the Malignant Ones.'

Chase away? Jennie allowed them to lift her daughter. She thought back to her books and remembered that the midwives hit the baby's bottom to jar loose any Ferocious Ones attracted by the smell of a helpless human. To herself she thought, *They're going to hurt you, my darling, but don't worry. I'll make you feel all better.* The man, the Grandmother, held the child up by the ankle. The Daughter slapped her.

Instead of a cry the baby laughed. It opened its eyes and looked at Jennie, and its laughter bounced off the walls and out of the windows to the street where people stopped their cars to listen to it. In the house the midwives tilted back their heads like people greeting the sun after a month of rain.

The buttons on Allan Lightstorm's shirt fell to the floor. He looked down at the shirt, then up at the cookie vendor. 'What do I do?' he said. There was no answer. He tightened his face up, concentrating. Then he took off the shirt and clumsily draped it over the baby. The Daughter adjusted the shirt, wrapping the child in it before handing her back to Jennie.

Jennie paid no attention to any of them. For in the sound of that laughter, she knew her daughter would never be hers. The child might live with her, accept her love, her milk, and later on her advice and teaching. But the child would never belong to her. The cookie vendor said, 'Does any child belong to its mother?' but Jennie wasn't listening. She was thinking of her daughter, how one day the girl would kiss Jennie's forehead, or smile, or *something*, and say, 'It's time for me to leave. I have my work to do.'

The blood spread out over miles, a thin slick covering the earth. Wherever it touched, the plants withered, the people and animals fell dead, the rivers dried up, the stones crumbled into dust. Only the man-lions could live there, sometimes raiding the outside world for victims, at other times devouring each other or their own children.

The people built walls around the emptiness. They told each other that some day a redeemer would come, one who with power and courage would go behind the wall to lay hands on the ground and draw the curse from it. The rivers would flow again, and the man-lions would shed their claws

387

and teeth. But no redeemer ever came. In time they gave the desert a name, and except when the enemy attacked some village or farm they did their best never to think about it. The name they called it was 'The Place Inside'.

It made no difference. As soon as she held her daughter again, Jennie knew that. However long they had together, she would love her child and take care of her. For as long as possible she would protect her daughter against the knowledge of who she was and why she had come into the world. 'I love you,' she said, and kissed the face and the shoulders, and the soft belly before she hugged the child to her breasts. 'You're my daughter and I love you.'

Everything that needs to be known is known.
scientist speaking on the BBC

Nihilism is not the last word. The last word is imagination.
Peter Bien

THE LIVES OF THE FOUNDERS

Allan Magruder lived for a time at the Young Men's Truth Association on South Avenue in Poughkeepsie. Eventually the residence committee kicked him out for refusing to attend any enactments. For several years he travelled from place to place, working in factories, on farms, and now and then as a faceless Worker in some of the smaller Picture Halls. He did not enter public knowledge again until some fifteen years later, when he turned up in New Chicago, dressed in silver clothes with a rainbow coloured band round his forehead, to start the movement later known as Neo-Fanaticism.

*

The three midwives resigned from the Holy Blood Birthing Agency and registered with the government as collective pilgrims, eligible for a monthly aid allowance. Instead of travelling anywhere, they moved into an apartment down the street from Jennie Mazdan and her daughter Valerie. From there they watched and followed Jennie, taking pictures of her with a telephoto lens, and sometimes sorting through her garbage for what they called 'relics.' At first Jennie tried to stop them, but after a while she decided to ignore them.

Jennie's mother Beverley surprised Jennie by not marking her granddaughter's birth with so much as an anthem. Instead she took the train to Poughkeepsie (the first time she'd ever done so) to take care of Jennie and the new baby. On Valerie's fifth birthday Grandma gave her a toy saxophone, with real keys and a plastic reed. When Jennie and Beverley began shouting at each other, Valerie played a short melody of such perfect yearning that Beverley became frightened and tried to shake it out of her head. Valerie handed the saxophone to her. 'You take it, Grandma,' she said. 'Mommy doesn't like it.'

Valerie Mazdan lived with her mother for seventeen years. She attended Heart of the World Primary School on Noxon Street and Singing Rock High School, where she played hockey and basketball. One day during her senior year she cut her afternoon classes, and on the corner of Grubb Street and Worrall Avenue, she met a man selling chocolate chip cookies. Several weeks later she applied for entrance to the College of Tellers in New York City.

Jennifer Mazdan lived on Cannon Street until the mock-funeral held on the day her daughter 'went up' as the expression has it, to College. That same night she moved to her mother's house on Hudson Street in New York. On the day of Valerie's first major appearance, the day Valerie told Li Ku's Picture 'The Woman Who Ran Away', Jennie stood in the back of the crowd. That night she opened an old cardboard box she'd kept for years. It contained a white silk shirt and a small metal box with a piece of dried skin inside. She took them down to the river where the black freighter waited for the Founders to return and sail away from the world. Jennie threw her treasures into the water. She said, 'I won't say thank you, because it's not what I feel. But I know she's needed and you did give us longer than I expected. So I guess it's a fair deal.'

Back in the house Beverley was listening to an excited reporter describe the Telling at the College. 'Jen,' she shouted, 'Jen, come here. Come here. You've got to hear this.'

Jennie went upstairs and lay down on her bed. From the night table she took a photo of Valerie and held it to her chest. She smiled, and a moment later she fell asleep.

We remember the Founders.